Forgive Me Father

Forgive Me Father

MARY SWEERE

authorHOUSE®

AuthorHouse™
1663 Liberty Drive
Bloomington, IN 47403
www.authorhouse.com
Phone: 1-800-839-8640

First published by AuthorHouse   07/20/2011

ISBN: 978-1-4634-3822-7 (sc)
ISBN: 978-1-4634-3824-1 (hc)
ISBN: 978-1-4634-3823-4 (ebk)

Library of Congress Control Number: 2011911978

Printed in the United States of America

This book is dedicated to my wonderful husband Joe, who has always supported me and allowed me to 'complete myself'.

Our creative children and their families, who have taught us far more than we ever taught them, and finally, to all the other dreamers in this world.

. . . And lo, as I opened my eyes, before me stood the great archangel Michael in all his glory. He stood in judgment and in his hands he grasped the mighty sword of spirituality. The sword was double edged and the point was imbedded firmly into the earth. The right side of the blade was bathed in a glorious light and the left side was drenched in blood. The light on the right side formed a golden stream and I knew it was the light of justice and common sense. The blood on the left side also formed a stream and I knew it was the wages of deceit and selfishness. Both streams flowed into the pool of natural consequences and the pool covered the earth.

Prologue

September, 1949
Glenwood, Minnesota

The church was cool and dark in contrast to the brilliance outside. The heavy door opened only a small crack at first and then slowly the shadow of a small boy crept in. After he had satisfied himself that there was no one else in the church, he awkwardly made his way to the side altar. He had come to see the beautiful lady. The child was unusually thin and frail looking, not like the other children who played in the schoolyard on the hill above the church. His white blond hair was so fine it resembled a summer dandelion that had gone to seed. At times the wispy fluff gave the appearance of being almost pink where his scalp showed through the part in his hair.

The boy had a noticeable limp, but it didn't appear to hinder his mission. He carefully stepped around the communion railing and got down on his knees, reverently making the sign of the cross. He prayed softly to the lady, telling her how she was his mother, just as she had been Jesus's mother. He whispered of his love for her and how he knew she watched over him because he had no other mother to protect him. He told her how hard he had been trying to be good so that he would especially please her and her son. With deepest sincerity he looked up into the beautiful lady's placid face and told her of the story he had been reading about her. The story said that sometimes when certain people had shown special love for her, marvelous things happened to them.

He swallowed hard, and took a deep breath. With cautious boldness he continued by saying that sometimes if they loved her completely, with all their might, she was known to heal them.

There! He had said it. The reason for his visit to the beautiful lady had been spoken. In his heart he knew no one could love her more then he did. He searched her inscrutable face looking for a sign. Maybe a tear trickling down her cheek, or a nod or a gesture, but there was nothing he could see to acknowledge her awareness of him.

He knew then he must show her even greater love. Totally unselfish love with nothing held back. Carefully he reached into his pocket and brought out his most treasured possession, which he gingerly held up for the lady to see. It was the first real gift his grandpa had given him, a small pearl handled Jackknife that had been accompanied by a stern warning not to lose it. The child had solemnly promised to keep it safe, but now at this moment, he somehow felt this was different. When the beautiful lady answered his prayer his grandpa would understand why it had been necessary. He would see what it had been exchanged for, and be proud to see his grandson running and jumping like all the other children.

Hesitantly the child rose to his feet and leaned closer to the statue. As he reached up to slip it into her waiting hand next to the plaster rose she already held, the silence was shattered by a loud crash. A bolt of panic struck the child and he clumsily spun around to see who might be watching. He trembled with the fear of being discovered but there was no one there. With relief he realized he had accidentally knocked a book off the communion rail as he reached up to place his gift in the lady's beckoning hand.

His body felt rubbery and his armpits itched. With a pounding heart he turned back to the statue and slowly reached out with a sweaty, trembling hand and carefully placed the treasured gift into hers. He stepped back, then impulsively leaned down and kissed the white and gold slippers that peaked out from under her blue gown. The ultimate sacrifice, the greatest love he was capable of showing had been bestowed on the beautiful enigma in the church.

Later that day, a very tired Father Gerald Schaffer returned to the church to retrieve the book of meditations he had left on the communion railing after morning mass. As he rose from picking it up off the floor he noticed something unusual in the palm of the Virgin Mary's statue. On closer inspection he observed with some irritation a small pearl handled knife. As he walked away examining the object he shook his head in disbelief wondering why someone would put something so inappropriate in Our Lady's hand. He grumbled to himself about what the world was coming to as he tossed it into a drawer in the sacristy.

In the following weeks the child's earnest prayers were repeated less often as he struggled to understand why the beautiful lady had not answered his plea. After awhile he tried not to think of it. Nothing had been gained but something more precious than his knife had been lost. Something deep inside, in a place he could not quite identify disappeared that day.

Chapter 1

June, 1983
Minneapolis, Minnesota

The rain pattered comfortably on the skylight above the bed. Harry Scarley was unaware of the steady drip, drip that was forming a puddle on the bare floor to the right of his bed. He lay quietly in the dark, refusing to leave the refuge of his dreams. The dilatory ascent from the deep sleep he had been in was reflective of his abject condition. He paused on the bridge of consciousness, and like Lot's wife could not resist looking back. Slowly he became aware of the drumming rhythm on the roof above him, but in his dream the sound was on the tin roof of a different house. He was a child again, maybe seven or eight, sleeping in the playroom in the upstairs of his aunt Dora and uncle Stan's home in Lowry, Minnesota. The rain was striking the tin roof over the eves above his bed. He could feel the warmth of the goose down quilt as it was pulled up around his chin, and he felt safe and loved. His aunt and uncle's voices filtered up through the iron heat vent in the old wooden floor and slowly the muffled voices blended with the smells of an early breakfast. The aroma of coffee mixed with the tantalizing sweetness of aunt Dora's cinnamon rolls. In his sleep Harry inhaled deeply, savoring the moment. His uncle Stan would soon be leaving for his job at the highway department and Dora would be calling up the stairway to wake Harry and his cousins.

Harry moved his legs slowly, as if unwilling to disturb the spell of the moment. As he stretched his cramped legs, a crashing sound wrenched him from his childhood dream and hurled him back into present day reality. He awoke to full consciousness with a jolt. "Jee-zus!" His eyes flew open and his heart pounded wildly. In his confusion he struggled to sit up, sending Ms. Sasha, his calico cat, flying from the bed to the safety of the half opened closet. The crash, he realized, was an almost empty bottle of Merlot falling from his bed. Harry immediately became aware of the fact that his head was pounding and his armpits were itching. The former was a result of the wine he had consumed, and the latter was something that always happened when he became nervous or frightened. He groaned and lay back on his pillow closing his eyes wishing he could make the day go away. Rolling onto his side he tried to ease the aching in his back and leg. The pain continued to dominate his body and he could feel himself breaking into a cold sweat. His body shuddered involuntarily and he felt he was going to be sick. Clumsily, he crawled from the bed and made his way into the tiny bathroom. A low moan escaped from him as he hung his head over the toilet. Even though his stomach was churning he was unable to bring up anything except some bitter tasting yellow phlegm. Slowly his nausea subsided and he stood up and leaned heavily on the sink. He turned on the faucet and splashed cold water on his face but avoided looking in the mirror. After using the toilet he headed back to bed but failed to notice the cold puddle of rain that had formed on the floor. "God Damn it," he cursed under his breath as he momentarily studied his wet sock. Lying back down on the sagging mattress he stared at the inky blue light that was beginning to filter through the cracked skylight above him. The rain was subsiding from the night before and the clock on his bedside table said 6:10. He found himself wondering why he always awoke so early.

"Oh God!" The thought hit him like a thunderbolt. Today was the day he was to go for a job interview. Just thinking about it last night had made him very edgy and he had only planned to take one small drink to steady his nerves. One small drink had ended up almost emptying the bottle. He felt a great sinking feeling inside as he rolled to his side and searched the nightstand for the small plastic container that contained his pain medication. Finding it he took out the last small pink and gray capsule. The sinking feeling intensified when he realized this was his last Darvon and he would need another in four hours. He also realized he had almost no money and would not be getting his disability check for another week. Shame engulfed him as he still could not accept that his life had sunk so low. He knew it happened to other people but it should not have happened to him. What in the hell had gone wrong? As he lay staring up at the bleak morning light as it filtered into the dingy room his mind drifted back to a time when his life had been much kinder. A time, he realized, he had taken for granted, oblivious to the fact that circumstances could change so quickly.

After graduating from Glenwood High School in 1961, he used part of the money he inherited from grandpa Scarley and enrolled at the University of Minnesota to study accounting. Aunt Dora helped him find a place to stay through a friend of a friend, with an elderly lady named Bessie Crimshaw. Bessie owned a large, older home, and Harry helped her with odd jobs. In return Bessie kept him well fed and provided him with friendship. Later, as Harry progressed through college, he returned her kindness by helping with her bookkeeping and taxes, or whatever else she needed. Shortly after Harry graduated from college, Bessie fell and broke her hip. Her youngest son, Bart, his wife, and their three children moved into the house to care for Bessie and within days Harry realized they needed the extra space. Since he had already found a job with a local manufacturing company, Sindler and Sindler, he felt this was the perfect time for him to find an apartment of his own. He found a comfortable one bedroom on the second floor of an old brownstone just a few blocks from his work. He was grateful it had a working elevator, which eliminated the need for him to climb steps. Next, he bought an almost new car, a white 1960 Studebaker Hawk. It was the first car he ever owned and he was extremely proud of it.

Life was good. He loved his work, as numbers made sense to him. Black and white, constant, the columns either added up or they didn't and were much easier to understand than people. Harry had a knack for being able to spot discrepancies or errors and soon became known throughout the company as the man who could solve any bookkeeping problem.

Reaching back into his bedside table Harry pulled out a pack of Camels and lighting one made a mental note for the hundredth time that he must quit smoking. As he inhaled, he felt the pseudo calm settle on him as the nicotine invaded his lungs. He had been lonely sometimes during those years he worked at Sindler's, but truthfully he never had a lot of friends. Of course, as a child he felt he really didn't need them as his cousin Molly had always been his all time special friend. She had been the sister he never had, his confidant, his defender, his advisor and his nemesis. Harry smiled to himself, thinking that Molly had been the only best friend he could have wanted, or survived. Together they had trudged through childhood, laughing, crying, fighting, providing alibis for each other when trouble loomed, which happened quite often, and now, he thought ruefully, he didn't even know where she was.

It was about in nineteen-seventy-eight that his life started to change. Inhaling deeply Harry reflected on how subtle it had been. He had become friends with a man at work named Gil Meyers. Gil was an engineer and self-proclaimed genius who had started working for Sindler's about two years earlier. He remembered the day Gil invited him to have dinner with him. At first, Harry had been surprised and flattered that such an intelligent man found his company entertaining enough to invite him to his home. Later, he was not surprised to realize that Gil only wanted help with his income tax. In spite of that, they became friends, and although Harry admired Gil's intelligence, he also felt he was a bit of an arrogant dreamer. Gil was always bragging to his co-workers that he was on the verge of discovering something so important that it would ultimately change the world and give him the wealth and recognition he deserved.

About a year later, Gil convinced Harry to become partners with him in a business venture. Gil had already obtained several patents and assured Harry this was an excellent opportunity, not only to make some serious money but also to help humanity. Harry agreed to supply the start up money, which he had carefully saved through the years, and keep the books. Gil would supervise the work and provide the creativity, which included several new revolutionary ideas he was convinced would change the way energy was produced. At first things seemed to go well and they even made a small profit. About the same time, Harry began a friendship with a young woman who was a waitress at the small cafe where he often ate his dinner when he worked late. Her name was Teresa, but many of the regulars at the café called her Trixie. As he grew to know her better he learned she was an aspiring actress who often found herself without acting jobs and struggling to support herself on her salary as a waitress. Occasionally he loaned her money to pay her rent, or get new headshots, and she always paid him back. As time went on, Harry found himself looking forward to seeing Teresa even though he knew she had a steady boyfriend. He didn't mind listening to her as she told him about her boyfriend Rocky, even after he came to realize what a selfish jerk the guy was.

During this time, Harry pretended to be only a good friend, but he honestly knew he was infatuated with her. Deep down in the depths of his lonely heart he hoped Teresa would finally wise up and see Rocky for the loser he was. Maybe then she would turn to him with love in her eyes, and be able to overlook his handicap and accept him for what he was, a good, kind, honest man who would do anything to make her happy. His wish never came true. For several more years they remained only friends and slowly Harry came to accept the fact that theirs would never be anything more than a platonic connection. Her relationship with Rocky continued but was anything but an ideal romance. Harry knew Rocky had been a football star back in high school, and had gotten a scholarship to play for the University of Minnesota but at the end of the first season, was injured and dropped from the team. In Harry's assessment, Rocky was dumber then a box of lint, and one of those rare perpetual high school jocks, who was never able to move beyond his juvenile mentality and success.

Harry had to laugh the day he actually heard Rocky, who's real name was Rodney, refer to himself as rocket man. Not only did rocket man have a failure to launch, he went up in self-defeating flames when he punched the coach who had the misfortune to inform him he had been dropped from the team. It was also no surprise when he flunked out of college, and from then on, Rocky's life became a series of temporary jobs including construction worker, bouncer, bartender, and truck driver. None of the jobs lasted very long because of his drinking and foul temper. On at least two occasions Teresa showed up with bruises on her arms and face but both times denied her boyfriend was responsible. Her acting career was at this point almost non-existent, and again it was no surprise when she informed Harry she had moved into Rocky's apartment, so they could both cut down on expenses. Who was kidding who?

In June of nineteen-eighty, Teresa got a small part in a coffee house theater play. She asked Harry if he would come to see her act because this could be an important break for her. Harry accepted her invitation and though he did not care much for the sarcastic humor, he had to admit Teresa was rather good in her part. During the performance, Rocky showed up and started causing a disturbance. It was obvious he had too much to drink, and it took two sturdy men to evict him. After the performance the director told Teresa that if her boyfriend showed up again she would be replaced in the play. Teresa left in tears and moved to the bar next door to the theater where she started drinking. She refused to leave when Harry tried to convince her to go home. He left her there against his better judgment because he felt he had no choice.

About two A.M., Harry awoke to knocking on his door and found an inebriated, disheveled Teresa leaning against the hallway wall. She threw her arms around his neck and between sobs told him she had a terrible fight with Rocky and he had tried to beat her up. Harry helped her inside and over to the couch. He gave her a cold washcloth for her puffy, discolored eye, and listened sympathetically while he made coffee. She continued sobbing as she explained what happened after Harry left the bar. She had confronted Rocky and told him she needed to end her relationship with him. That was when he tried to use her as a punching bag and someone she didn't know had pulled him off her. He stormed off shaking his fist in her face but not before he punched her in the eye. He also made it very clear he was not finished with her, and now she was afraid to go home. Harry assured her he would assist in any way he could, including helping her find an apartment of her own. Teresa put her arms around him and kissed him and for one fleeting, foolish moment he felt as if his dreams might be coming true. Loud pounding on the door accompanied with yelling and obscene language shattered his short-lived reverie. Both Harry and Teresa knew Rocky had come looking for her and there would be no reasoning with him. Harry motioned to her to follow him into the kitchen and opened the door that led down a steep staircase and out into a back alley. He watched her disappear down the steps and vanish into the darkness.

As he turned back, he found himself staring into the red face of a very angry rocket man, who had kicked in his front door and barged into his apartment. Harry vaguely remembered some of the obscenities Rocky directed at him but to this day honestly didn't know if several of them could have been humanly possible. He also remembered a huge fist making extremely painful contact with his face, the metallic taste of blood, and the bizarre feeling of finding himself reeling backwards down the long flight of stairs and onto the asphalt below. The next thing he remembered was coming to in the University Hospital Intensive Care Unit. He would never forget the excruciating pain and weeks of heavy medication that left him in a nightmarish limbo. Later they would tell him he had a broken nose, a concussion, a fractured pelvis, broken ribs, and a severely fractured right leg and ankle. In other words, he was lucky to be alive. So much for unrequited love, and his hopes of living happily ever after. Harry lit another cigarette and inhaled deeply.

Months later when he was released from the hospital, he realized his business partnership with Gil Meyer had also ended. Gil was gone, along with the money in the business checking account. He had run up huge bills, using the money that was intended for the lease on their business property and rent money for Harry's apartment for his personal use and to pay off his gambling debts. To add insult to injury, he had taken Harry's beloved Studebaker. After Harry paid most of the bills, overdue rents and someone to help him close down the business he was left penniless. All the money he had carefully saved was gone as well as his inheritance from grandpa Scarley. Harry was devastated. In exchange for giving his landlady most of his belongings and furniture she agreed to let him spend three more months in his apartment rent-free to help him recover from his injuries.

Rocky was arrested for assault and spent a month in jail, but was let out on good behavior plus community service when he somehow convinced the bleeding heart judge he had undergone a remarkable life changing epiphany. In the end the whole episode was viewed as an unfortunate accident. Because Rocky didn't have a pot to pee in, there was no possibility of Harry collecting any kind of restitution. The lawyer the court appointed to represent him said he was sorry, but the bottom line was that because Harry was broke, he was simply s.o.l. Fortunately, his employer's group insurance plan had taken care of most of his hospital bills and physical therapy but when that ran out he had no choice but to apply for assistance. He had to leave his comfortable old brownstone and most of his belongings and felt he fortunate to have found this small studio apartment with the cracked skylight.

As the months passed Harry sank deeper into depression and the medication the doctors prescribed for his unrelenting pain made him sleepy, which he found himself doing most of the time. George Sindler sent a note expressing his regards but explained they needed to hire a permanent accountant to replace him. Visits from his coworkers and friends became less frequent and finally stopped altogether.

Harry spoke to Teresa only once after he left the hospital. At first she tried to avoid looking at him when they passed on the street, but was finally forced to acknowledge him when he greeted her. There were dark circles under her eyes and she appeared to have aged considerably from how he remembered her. Nervously, she showed him her wedding ring and told him how happy she was. She didn't look directly at him as she assured him that Rocky was good to her, and that he hardly ever drank anymore because he was a severe diabetic and often not able to work. When Harry inquired about her acting career she tried unsuccessfully to smile as she assured him she had given up on that silliness. She was now a mother to a little girl with another baby on the way, and with her full time job at the cafe there wasn't time. She added that Rocky had been right all along, it was just a stupid dream and she had been wasting her time. Hurriedly she excused herself saying she was late for work, then hesitated and added how sorry she was for everything that had happened. There was no sparkle of life left in her and he felt no anger towards her, only a deep sadness.

Ms. Sasha peeked out from the closet and when she was quite convinced the coast was finally clear, jumped back on the bed and nuzzled affectionately under Harry's chin. At the same time she meowed softly to let Harry know she had no food in her dish. Harry took one last draw from his cigarette and putting it out scratched the small cat behind her ears.

"Well little girl, I guess it's just you and me against the world. If I don't get that job today we'll both be eating out of the garbage cans just like you were when I found you." The small cat paced back and forth across Harry's lap in an effort to show him she was getting very impatient with her empty dish. Reluctantly, Harry got up and poured the last of the dry cat food into her dish as he continued his conversation with her. "That's it little one, we've reached the bottom of the bag."

Harry washed up and since he had no decent clean clothes decided to forego his shower and shave until later. He checked his small refrigerator and viewing the dismal contents decided instead to stop at the small cafe down the street. The Busy Day Cafe was owned by Virgil Nelson, a pleasant, short, balding man and his skinny, bad tempered wife, Myrtle. Harry wasn't really hungry but realized if he didn't get something into his queasy stomach he might be sick. After breakfast he planned to walk the five blocks to Our Lady of Hope Catholic Church and if he was lucky, Father Sean Flarhety would loan him a few dollars.

Painfully, he made his way down the long, dark staircase and once out on the street was relieved to know the day was warm and clear. He squinted as the brightness of the morning hurt his bloodshot eyes and once again became aware of his headache. As he walked towards the cafe he noticed his reflection in the store windows and was a little surprised how shabby and discouraged he appeared. His clothes were wrinkled and looked as if he had slept in them, which of course he had. Even though his beard was light and rather sparse, he could see how it added to his street person appearance. He reached up and tried to pat down his uncooperative bed hair and wondered why anyone would be interested in hiring him.

Following his accident he hadn't been able to fight the black depression that engulfed him and the medication the doctors prescribed only seemed to complicate things. After his insurance ran out and he could no longer afford the drugs, he simply quit taking most of them. Suicide had crossed his mind several times. That was when he started using alcohol to relieve his physical and mental pain. The alcohol wasn't helping his recovery but it did give him short periods of reprieve.

As he entered the cafe he was relieved to see Virgil pouring coffee at the front counter. Harry sat down on one of the stools near the door as the older man placed a cup of coffee in front of him. "Tough night, huh?" Virgil grinned and winked at Harry.

"Uh, yeah." Harry had a sheepish look on his face. "I'll have a small glass of orange juice and a piece of white toast."

"You got it." Virgil's laid back manner put them both at ease.

Harry noticed Myrtle peering out from the kitchen like a curious predator rodent looking for prey and then scowl at him and her husband. Virgil laughed, "Look out for Mert this morning, she's on the warpath again. She had it out with the fry cook first thing after we came in and he told her to take her lousy job and shove it where the sun don't shine. There's going to be holy hell to pay around here today!"

Harry decided not to tell Virgil about the job interview in case he didn't get it. He also wanted to leave before Myrtle had a chance to come over and spew out more of her nasty meanness. Virgil brought the orange juice and toast and set it down by Harry's half empty coffee cup. Harry gulped down the juice and picking up the toast left the last of his money on the counter. Making a quick exit without saying goodbye he ate most of the toast and then decided to forego the rest as his stomach did a flip-flop. Tossing what remained to a nearby flock of pigeons he headed in the direction of the church.

By the time he reached the rectory his leg was throbbing and he found himself regretting he had lost his corrective shoe somewhere during the past year. He knocked on the rectory door and held his breath. After a few minutes the door opened and he was greatly relieved to see Father Flarhety.

The old Irish priest greeted Harry warmly and then added, "Saints preserve us you look as if you have a banshee riding on your shirt tails. I think I've got something to help you."

Harry protested weakly as the old priest ushered him into his office. At this point the thought of coffee sounded positively revolting. The contents of his queasy stomach were sloshing back and forth, and the coffee and juice were at war and threatening to retreat up the same path they had taken down. Father Flarhety was not a man to be put off and he left the room and quickly returned with a steaming mug in his hand. Gesturing towards it, he encouraged Harry, "Go ahead lad, as God is my witness you'll feel better." Harry swallowed hard to be sure the toast and juice would not come roaring out to greet the coffee he was about to choke down. With shaking hands he picked up the mug and took a small sip. To his surprise the coffee had a strong lacing of fine brandy. It burned his throat on the way down but he gratefully took another swallow.

Father Flarhety, in his best Irish brogue commented, "Tis a wee bit of the hair of the dog that bit you. God, help me but that treacherous rascal has sunk his teeth into me a few times."

Harry took another swallow of the brew and could feel the warming sensation enter his body. In a matter of minutes the nausea subsided and he could feel his stomach relax. He smiled weakly at the priest on the opposite side of the desk. He was peering intently into Harry's face and his gaze caught Harry off guard and embarrassed him. He was not used to people looking at him that intently because throughout most of the last year people simply passed him by as if he wasn't there and he had learned first hand what it meant to be one of the invisible street people.

"Life has not been so good to you the last few years, has it Harry/"

"No, actually, it's been a . . . bitch." He felt like he should apologize for swearing in front of the priest but he didn't. Old habits did not die easily but pain and poverty could change even the most devout man. He continued, "Father I need to ask a major favor of you. As you know, I lost everything after my accident. I get a small amount of money for my disability but I've been using part of it to pay off some of the bills I still owe. Today, I have a chance to interview for a job, but I'm in a bind because I don't have any money. I overextended myself and now I'm broke. I need to get some decent clothes and a few groceries. Not much really. I can get the clothes at the Salvation Army. I . . . I need your help." The last sentence was barely audible.

The old priest jumped up so quickly it startled Harry and he almost dropped the mug he had been nervously clutching.

"Then why didn't you come right out and say that in the first place instead of sitting there looking like a pile of last week's dirty laundry?"

Father Flarhety left the room and Harry was still marveling that the old priest could move so quickly when he became aware of raised voices in the hall. He overheard Father Sean sternly addressing someone. "If we can't trust in the Lord to provide for us, it's a very sad day."

Father Flarhety burst back into the room with cash in hand and gave Harry two twenties and a ten. A young priest, who appeared to be about thirty-five, followed him into the room. He was tall and thin and his blond hair was trimmed neatly in a crew cut. His red face and scowl reflected the fact that he was very upset.

"Harry, my man, I'd like you to meet Father Aston." The older priest stood his ground. "He comes to Our Lady of Hope to help me with the growing responsibilities." Father Flarhety stopped and pulled himself up, staring intently at Father Aston as he continued, "But he has to be on his way now to attend to his many important duties."

The young priest glared at Harry and the older cleric, but held his tongue. He left the room muttering under his breath and Harry was sure he caught the words freeloader and financial ruin. Father Flarhety grinned mischievously, "I'm not sure what is troubling the lad today but he seems to be a bit out of sorts now doesn't he? Maybe he's got his head somewhere it shouldn't be." He winked at Harry and as they were walking to the door he added, "I'll be praying for you."

Harry thanked the priest and said, "I'll pay you back Father. I promise you'll get your money back."

"I know you will lad, I have no worry about that."

Harry felt much better after he left the rectory. He wasn't sure if it was the brandy or the fifty dollars in his pocket. The hair of the dog had settled his stomach and for now the toast and the juice appeared to have made friends. His next stop was the Salvation Army store to see if he could find some decent clothes to wear to the interview. He could already feel the heavy weariness settling into his body by the time he reached his destination. He waved to Betty Bartusek, the lady who ran the store for 'Major somebody-or-other' as Betty liked to refer to her boss. Harry was never aware who the Major was but he was quite sure there were a few unresolved issues between her and her employer. Betty's incessant smoking being the most perplexing problem.

"Hey Buddy, how've you been?"

"Fine."

"You could've fooled me. You look like shit." Betty laughed loudly as she leaned her ample body against the counter and lit another cigarette.

"Thanks Betty." He felt the urge to add, like I really need to be reminded. Tell me something I don't already know, but he didn't. Sometimes the truth hurts.

Betty inhaled deeply, and then said, "Just kidding, you know I adore you."

Harry could see she must have been a rather pretty lady at one time. Almost elegant, in a kind of unpolished way, but the years had taken their toll. She spoke with the low raspy voice of a heavy smoker but you could still hear a trace of a southern accent.

"What can I do for you today?"

Briefly Harry told her about the job interview and his need for some better clothes.

"Good for you Buddy. Jesus, how I wish my ex-husband would get a job. He's not even looking. God knows, it's not good for anyone to sit on their ass all day long."

At this point Harry was feeling a little defensive about his unemployment, but chose not to respond and instead started to sort through the racks of men's pants. He was relieved to see Betty was waiting on a customer, which meant he could pick out the items he wanted without her input. Carefully, he selected two pair of dark pants that were in fairly good shape, a white shirt that still had the original store tags on, and a lightweight dark windbreaker jacket. As he started back towards the cubical that served as a dressing room Betty headed him off and handed him a pale blue, polyester knit leisure suit.

"Try this Buddy. I spotted this the other day and think you might look real spiffy in it."

Against his better judgment, Harry took the suit, for he knew from previous experience she wouldn't give in until she saw him in the 'spiffy' leisure suit. He tried it on first to get it out of the way, and groaned out loud as he looked in the mirror. He knew he didn't want anyone to see him in this awful outfit. Even on his thin torso the pants and jacket were too tight and the pant legs and sleeves of the jacket were about two inches too long. "Crap!" he groaned again and muttered under his breath. "This sucker must have belonged to Ichabod Crane." Just then Betty jerked the curtain open and blowing smoke directly into his face, started to laugh in a most undignified manner.

"Holy shit! It fits you like a cheap hotel!"

Harry knew better than to ask exactly what that meant but Betty punched him playfully on the shoulder and continued. A cheap hotel . . . no ballroom, get it?" She broke into laughter again which ended with her coughing so hard she had to go back to her counter and sit down. Discarding the leisure suit Harry selected one pair of dark pants, the white shirt and jacket. On his way to the check out counter he grabbed two pair of boxer shorts and three pair of dark socks. He was relieved that Betty didn't bring up the spiffy suit again as he paid for his purchases. Tucking the bag under his arm he assured her he would let her know how he made out at the interview. As he left the store he knew he had two more errands to attend to before he would be able to head home and clean up.

The next item on his agenda was to stop and check on his friend Peter. Peter Milton Brentwood IV lived a few blocks away in an old Queen Anne style Victorian house. Harry had met him over a year ago in a bar where Peter was doing an impromptu performance from Shakespeare's *King Lear*. His drunken soliloquy promptly got him ejected from the bar, and Harry helped him find his way home. Peter was English and spoke with a distinguished accent even when he was very, very drunk. Which Harry quickly came to realize, was very, very often. Peter claimed his ancestors had been in England from day one, and his lineage included kings, queens and other notable royalty. The youngest son of a wealthy family, he was academically highly intelligent and had attended and been sent home from many carefully selected private schools. His major claim to fame appeared to be that he had never held any kind of honest employment in his entire thirty-four years of life. Against his doting mother's protests his father had shipped him off to the United States when Peter's older brother became a member of the English Parliament. Peter was viewed by his family as an unexplainable embarrassment. He was provided with a generous monthly check issued by the family solicitor, which enabled him to live comfortably and maintain a constant state of inebriation. On those rare occasions when he was relatively sober Harry found him to be extremely entertaining with his exotic tales of the rich and famous and his gambling days at Monte Carlo with this Prince or that movie star.

He also liked to allude to his many questionable liaisons with a variety of colorful and scandalous individuals of both sexes. Harry never really knew how much of it was true or fabricated, the product of a mind constantly deluded by alcohol.

As he approached the old Queen Anne he could see that even though it was showing signs of neglect, it must have been a grand sight when it was first built. Instead of housing one family as originally intended it was now split into three separate apartments, one of which was occupied by the caretaker and his wife, and another by his friend Peter. According to the sign in the front window the third apartment was now vacant.

Climbing the front stairs Harry knocked on Peter's door, but no one answered. Finding the door unlocked, he entered the foyer with its beveled glass windows and large winding oak staircase that now went nowhere since it had been blocked off when the house was split into apartments. As he continued into the living room he couldn't help but admire the crystal chandelier and the huge carved fireplace that now served as a receptacle for Peter's empty vodka bottles. His apartment consisted of most of the original first floor and was by far the nicest of the three. The library now served as Peter's bedroom.

Harry paused, standing outside the half opened door. He called out to Peter but wasn't surprised he didn't receive an answer. He could hear the mumbled, drunken rambling of his friend who seemed to be having a conversation with a nonexistent audience his theatrical bent ego craved so much.

As he entered the bedroom Harry found Peter sprawled across the bed with the remains of the bottle of vodka he had been drinking spilled onto the floor. His usual dapper look was gone and Harry noticed with disgust that Peter had wet himself. The room smelled of urine and vomit and at that moment Harry felt a shock of reality run through his soul as he realized this could be himself in a few years if he didn't begin to straighten out his life.

The thought seared itself into Harry's brain and he stepped back from the disturbing piece of humanity in front of him. Regaining a hold on his consciousness he took twenty dollars from the pristine Bible on Peter's bureau and left the apartment. Finding the caretaker's wife Emma at home, he gave her the money and in return she promised to clean Peter up. Harry thanked her and set out to finish his last errand.

The pain in his leg and lower back was becoming unbearable as he headed toward the small grocery store that was around the corner. The store was one of those mom and pop grocery/pharmacy stores that somehow had survived in spite of the modern strip malls and chain stores. It was owned and staffed by an older couple, Ruth and Jacob Freedman. Ruth operated the grocery section and Jacob, who had been a pharmacist in Poland before they had immigrated to the United States, took charge of the pharmacy.

Both, he learned, survived World War II, first by being forced to live in a ghetto in Warsaw and later the concentration camp they had been sent to. He would never forget Ruth's face when she confided they had witnessed things no human eyes should ever see. The color had drained from her cheeks and her voice had taken on a tight, high pitched timbre, as if it took great effort to speak the painful words.

As he entered the store he didn't see Ruth and finding Jacob, greeted him and gave him the small plastic container to be refilled while he shopped. Harry took one of the wicker shopping baskets and carefully selected the items he needed. Jacob brought the Darvon and a small glass of water to Harry. As Harry set the basket on the counter, Ruth appeared from the back room with an arm full of towels and greeted him breathlessly. Even though she was well into her seventies she appeared to have unlimited energy and personified the stereotypical Jewish mother. Their only child, a boy named Levi, died of pneumonia while they had been detained in Warsaw. With no other family Ruth took it upon herself to mother Harry and other less fortunate customers by slipping extra food or pharmacy items into the grocery bags when it was obvious that their finances were strained. This was one of the few stores where credit was available and a promise to pay was still honored. As she rang up the items on the old brass National cash register she quizzed Harry.

"Have you been over to see your friend Peter today?"

Harry nodded affirmatively. Ruth continued, "Such a shame. He's a bright young man that Peter and wastes his life by being drunk all the time. He's rotting his brain you know." Pausing, she looked directly into Harry's eyes, and added, "Too many people are drinking these days. They don't know how good they really have it. Maybe it's something in the air, a kind of spiritual pollution, don't you agree?"

Harry shifted uncomfortably as he caught her not too subtle remark but didn't answer. Ruth continued as she rang up the Old Spice, "Looks like you're getting all spruced up. You got a special lady in your life?"

Again Harry felt a gentle twinge of irritation at the way his friends seemed to feel the need to comment on his personal life, but he managed a weak smile and answered, "No, I have a job interview this afternoon."

Ruth's manner softened and she smiled, "Good for you. I know you will do well." Then ringing up the pack of Camels added, "When you get rid of these dirty things your life will be much better." Turning to the shelf behind her, she took down a bottle of Murine eye drops and placed it into the grocery bag. Before Harry could protest she cut him off with the wave of her hand. "Trust me, you'll want them, our gift to you, from me and my Jacob. You're a good man and you want to look your best. Everyone needs some good honest work in their life to keep them happy. Should I write the groceries up for you? Until you get back on your feet?"

"No, thanks Ruth, I have money. I can pay today. You and Jacob are good friends. Thank you."

The Darvon had kicked in and Harry left the store feeling better. The spring air was warm and fragrant and he could smell the lilac bushes that were in full bloom. As he climbed the stairs to his tiny apartment he knew he wanted this job more than anything in his whole life. The disturbing scene of Peter had shaken him to the core of his being. He fixed a bowl of tomato soup and a cheese sandwich. As he ate lunch Ms. Sasha lay on the small table purring contentedly while teasing him with her tail. When he finished he washed the few dishes, polished his shoes and laid his new clothes out on the bed. He carefully shaved and showered and upon stepping out of his small bathroom found Ms. Sasha lounging on his dark pants. Pushing her off he admonished her for getting fur on his new clothes. Realizing he did not have a clothes brush he spit on his fingers and attempted to brush the unwanted cat hair off his trousers.

After he was dressed he stood on a chair to get a better look at himself in the mirror on the medicine cabinet above the bathroom sink. Satisfied with his appearance he reluctantly decided he really wasn't a bad looking person when he was cleaned up. At forty years old, his hair was thinning more than he would have liked, and though he stood five foot seven, well, maybe even five-eight on a good day, he had to admit he was probably a little thinner than he should be.

His short right leg caused his pelvis and spine to tilt notably to the right and now that he no longer wore his special corrective shoe his limp was quite obvious. Studying his posture he consciously straightened his shoulders and recalled how after his accident he had developed a tendency to slump. He made a mental note he would stand straighter and hold his head up, as he remembered how his cousin Molly had often admonished him, "It's not how you look, dip shit, it's how you project yourself to others. It's all about attitude! Dazzle them with confidence, and if that doesn't work throw in a little bullshit to boot. What ever works, to make people believe you're special. We are special you know, and don't you forget it" It always seemed to work for Molly but lately he hadn't been feeling very special.

Harry inspected his image one more time before he climbed down from his perch. He re-combed his hair and critically noticed how dull and limp it was, concluding it was probably the result of his poor nutrition during the last few years. Somehow he had lost the initiative to prepare himself proper meals and often ended up eating whatever seemed easiest at the time. Noticing his eyes were bloodshot, he carefully put a drop of Murine into each eye, and after a few moments had to agree with Ruth that it did help his overall appearance. Showing up for a job interview with a hangover was not the brightest thing to do.

At two o'clock he was ready and even though he didn't have to be at the interview until four, he was becoming so anxious he could no longer wait. He paced back and forth as he rehearsed his qualifications. He had no written resume but the woman he spoke to assured him it was not necessary. Once again, he took the letter he received in the mail the previous week, and reread it even though he knew it by heart.

Dear Mr. Scarley,
Sullivan Glass currently has an opening for an assistant accountant. You were recommended to us by your previous employer, George Sindler. If you are interested please call our downtown office for an interview appointment.

Thank you,
Ann Bennett.

Harry showed the letter to Ms. Sasha and she reciprocated by affectionately rubbing her body against his dark pant legs leaving grey and tan cat hair on them but Harry didn't notice. He could feel the anxiety rising up inside and constricting his chest. Saying a quick prayer, something he had given up after his accident, he started down the long stairway and in the direction of the bus stop. The bus was on schedule and he clocked the time the ride would take for future reference. It took slightly under a half hour and he was relieved at this time of day there were not many people sharing the bus with him. As he got off, he was again relieved to see the large brown granite building in front of him bore the same address imprinted on the letterhead.

Finding an unoccupied bench in the lobby he waited until ten minutes before four and entered the office with the name Sullivan Glass Company printed in bold letters. Remembering to stand erect with his head up he nervously reached for the doorknob while trying to ignore the fact that his hand was shaking.

The office was cool and beautifully decorated and he remembered later how fragrant and inviting it smelled. Not like a commercial office but rather a well kept home. The slightly plump woman at the desk looked up and smiled warmly at him. "Mr. Scarley?"

It was at that moment he realized how really scared he was. His mouth was dry and he had to lick his lips before he could answer. He took a deep breath and silently thought to himself how it was all in the attitude and he needed to get a grip on himself. "Yes. I'm Harry Scarley and I'm here to apply for an accounting position." He was relieved to hear his voice sounded fairly normal and he managed a half smile.

"Please take a seat. I'll get Annie Bennett. She's on the phone now but should be off soon and will be right with you."

Harry was grateful for the opportunity to sit down and upon doing so felt a little more relaxed. As he looked around the office he marveled at how beautiful and bright it was. A marble table held a lovely bouquet of spring flowers and without thinking he leaned over to smell them.

The woman at the desk had been watching him intently and she commented, "Aren't they great flowers? After one of our cold Minnesota winters I think we appreciate beautiful flowers more than most people."

Harry nodded his agreement as the door to the office behind the receptionist's desk opened and a petite, dark haired woman stepped out. She placed a stack of papers on the desk and commented, "I didn't think I'd ever get off the phone. It's been one call after another. What can I do for you Janet?"

The receptionist motioned in Harry's direction and answered, "Mr. Scarley is here to see you about the accounting position." The young woman looked in Harry's direction and smiled a warm, friendly smile. She walked toward Harry and extended her hand.

"Hello, Mr. Scarley, I'm Annie Bennett. I've been looking forward to meeting you."

Harry stood up and as they shook hands he could see behind her thick glasses that she appeared to have scarring around her eyes and part of her face and neck. When he realized he was staring at her scars he became embarrassed and dropped his eyes. Annie responded gently, "Don't be concerned. The first time most people see me up close it does give them a bit of a start. I had a car accident when I was younger and it almost took my sight away. I can still see, just not the same as before."

Harry felt more at ease until he realized he was still holding her hand. Awkwardly he quickly let go and silently cursed his clumsiness but she appeared not to have minded. She stepped back one step as if to give him additional comfort space and said, "Come into my office, we'll visit a bit and then I'll introduce you to David Sullivan, the owner of the company."

As Harry followed her he couldn't help but think how Annie Bennett looked like Snow White. He knew it sounded bizarre to be thinking that at this particular time and on such an important job interview but somehow the thought tickled him and helped him feel a little more at ease. As she explained about the company and how it would be if he were to consider working for them he found himself also thinking in spite of her scars how beautiful she was. Annie was delicate, with long black hair and thin arched eyebrows. Her skin was creamy, smooth and pale, which only enhanced her beautiful blue eyes. He flushed as he realized how attracted to her he was and tried to refocus on her words, only to find himself thinking that the scarring on her face only made her appear more vulnerable and desirable to him. He had never felt this way about any woman in his entire life. When he became aware that she had asked him a question and he had no idea what she said, he felt his neck redden as if he were back in junior high school and one of the cheerleaders had asked to copy his math paper.

Appearing slightly amused Annie patiently repeated her question and Harry made a renewed effort to focus on the conversation instead of her. She continued, "You come very highly recommended. Your previous employer, George Sindler, was a friend of the founder of our company, Grant Sullivan. Grant has since passed away but his son David, who now runs Sullivan Glass still relies on George's wisdom, experience and business knowledge."

Harry was aware of how Annie appeared to be studying him but for some reason it didn't seem to bother him and he enjoyed looking into her beautiful blue eyes. She interviewed him with such ease he did not mind telling her about his accident and how his life had changed so unexpectedly. Somehow he knew she understood and didn't judge him the way many people did.

After about twenty minutes she escorted Harry to a larger office at the end of the hall. As they entered, Annie introduced Harry to David Sullivan. Harry had expected to see an older man in a business suit but was pleasantly surprised to realize the owner of the company may be only in his late thirties.

David Sullivan was dressed casually in Levi's, a white shirt open at the neck with the sleeves rolled up and tennis shoes. He too, greeted his guest warmly and immediately Harry found himself wondering if this handsome, athletic man found Annie Bennett as beautiful as he did. Harry felt himself falling back into the old mode of self-doubt as he wondered how she could work for such an attractive, successful man and not be in love with him. He chided himself for even thinking about this as he was here to secure employment, nothing else.

David spoke with the same laid back ease that Annie had as he explained what the job entailed.

Harry acknowledged that he was familiar with the sample ledgers David showed him, and even though he knew about computers he had only limited experience with them but was sure this would not be a problem. He had been a good student and a fast learner. Yes, he would be willing to take any training they deemed necessary to be sure he would be able to fit in at Sullivan Glass, but no, he had no idea what he expected his salary should be. His mind stalled but he finally stated that what he had been paid previously at Sindler's would be acceptable, then quickly added he would work for less if he had to because he really needed the job.

At that point, David quoted him a generous beginning salary with full benefits. Upon hearing the numbers, Harry thought he would fall out of his chair. David also stated that after one month they would provide him with a company car as he would need to attend meetings at their various plant locations where the raw glass was stored, fabricated, coated and shipped. As he explained about the stock options and opportunities to invest his money that were available Harry felt his brain swimming with disbelief. His future employer concluded with the comment that if Harry should decide to move to a different apartment or house that would be closer to Sullivan Glass, they would be happy to help him with that as well.

By the time the interview was over Harry was speechless. He had the job! No waiting for a call back. Not just any old minimum wage job, but a really fantastic, unbelievable, dream job!

Before leaving the office both Annie and Janet congratulated him and told him they looked forward to seeing him the following Monday. When Annie added that his family would be very happy for him and he replied that his family included only Ms. Sasha, his calico cat, he failed to notice the interested smile on Annie's face. As he boarded the bus back to his apartment he felt the urge to shout to the other riders that he had a job, a really great job, but he didn't. He was afraid that if he bragged too much, if he got too cocky, it might disappear like the dream he had this morning of being a child home safe in his own little bed. It also crossed his mind that he really should give prayer another chance.

Chapter 2

Annie paused at the door to David's office and studied her boss who appeared to be lost in deep thought. Over the past few years she had grown to understand his moods but actually knew very little about his relationship with his father. In spite of this she was almost positive where his thoughts had taken him. "Thinking about your father and how he would have liked our newest employee?"

Her words appeared to pull him out of his deep reflections and he looked up and smiled. "I think you know me too well. Probably better than I know myself."

"Grant would have liked Harry. He's an honest man. I know we made a good decision by hiring him."

"I think so too, and yes, I was thinking about my father. How much I miss him and my regrets for all the years we lost."

"Would you like to talk about it?"

He looked troubled but finally answered, "I've tried to keep that part of my personal life separate from my work but I've come to realize it's unrealistic not to expect one from influencing the other. You have been so honest about sharing your past with me and have probably wondered why I have been so reluctant to share my private thoughts concerning him with you. Maybe I owe that to you. Do you have time?"

Annie nodded and slid into the chair across from the desk.

"I was thinking about how certain memories never leave you. Years can slip away fading into oblivion but certain memories are imprinted so indelibly into your psyche that you are destined to carry them to your grave. Growing up I felt my father was emotionally unavailable to me. Other fathers played catch and took their sons fishing but my father seemed to be only interested in building this company. Even family vacations were planned around his work. He was good to me but nurturing was left to my mother. I wanted and expected much more but he never seemed to have time for me. By graduation from college the rift between us had grown so deep that I was not the least interested in mending our differences. That was back in 1968 when racial riots were tearing cities apart and antiwar demonstrators were protesting the Vietnam War on college campuses. Every week hundreds of soldiers were being sent home in body bags and I felt the moral obligation to express my opposition to the war. My father didn't really support the war efforts but he had no patience or compassion for those who opposed it. It was the last thing my father and I quarreled about. It was his final damning words that have never left me. He accused me of being unpatriotic and a coward. How does the saying go? Someone can tell you a hundred times they love you and you still need to hear it repeated again and again, but if someone tells you once they hate you, you never forget it. I never forgot or forgave his words. My father was highly respected but he was also extremely stubborn when it came to his beliefs. I now realize in some ways we were very much alike even though back then I never wanted to be like him. I left Minneapolis for Vermont with an older man I had met on campus on the previous Thanksgiving Day. His name was Warren Barrows and he was the grandfather of my future wife, Angela. He told me his son owned a holistic healing center in the beautiful hills of Vermont and he described it like living in a little piece of heaven. A place away from all the confusion and stress our society thrusts on us. An earthly haven to plant the seeds of hope for a better world and to me it sounded perfect.

For almost ten years I never looked back. I became the proverbial prodigal son but was able to justify my actions because I felt I was living the more spiritual life. I met Warren's granddaughter, Angela and we fell deeply in love. My mother came to our wedding but my father didn't. I took this very personally and used it to sustain my anger. What I didn't know was that he was already sick but was too proud and stubborn to admit his health was failing. In my youthful naiveties I felt my life was perfect and I was foolish enough not to care about what the future might hold for any of us. As you know, Angela died of a brain aneurysm a few days before she was due to deliver our son. My wife and the son whose futures I vowed would never include the mistakes I felt my father had made with me, had vanished from my life. That fateful day I lost the two most important people in my life. I think about finding her lifeless body sitting so peacefully in that rocking chair looking as if she had dozed off for a nap. The memory is so painful and so surreal I still have trouble wrapping my mind around it. For some unexplainable reason the universe, or God, or whoever is in charge of our destiny, had chosen to teach me a devastating lesson on loss I did not want to learn.

My father didn't attend the funeral because of his failing health but I was too distraught and angry to care. By the time my mother called and told me I had to come home it was too late. He had suffered a major stroke and was on the verge of death. I remember touching his skin and thinking how cold it was, almost as if death had already claimed his body but somehow he had the inner strength to stay alive until I could be with him. My only consolation was that the frail shell of a man who had been so commanding and vital, somehow found the will to hold on long enough to acknowledge my presence with a feeble squeeze of my hand."

Then David sat silently, again lost in deep thoughts that even Annie couldn't penetrate.

"Have you finally been able to forgive him?"

"Yes, I believe that I have, but I will never forget our misunderstandings. I know now it's me I have trouble forgiving. The thought of all those wasted years and what might have been still haunts me. For this prodigal son there was no happy homecoming, no celebration, but only a funeral for a stubborn old man and the regrets of his foolish son."

Annie stood up and circling the desk, kissed her boss on the top of his head. She patted his shoulder and whispered in a reassuring manner, "There will come a time when you realize all of this happened for a reason. Important lessons were learned by both you and your father, and when you fully accept that truth, you will be able to let go and move on."

"I hope so, and thank you for listening." He reached up and patted her hand," I've held this pain inside and not allowed myself to share it. Today seemed like the day to let it out. Maybe this is the first step to healing."

Chapter 3

Harry worked at Sullivan Glass almost six months before he was able to really know and appreciate the senior accountant Cecil Baxter. Previously his relationship with Baxter, as he liked to be called, was casual and usually only concerned the financial aspects of the business. As Harry became familiar with the workings of the company he also gained tremendous respect for the dedication and intelligence Baxter continuously exhibited. Cecil Baxter was an impressive figure to say the least. At first Harry would smile to himself when he heard the other employees refer to Baxter as the gentle giant. On their first meeting Harry was completely caught off guard as Baxter stood an imposing six-foot-nine inches tall. He had to weigh close to three hundred pounds and was also one of the darkest African American men Harry had ever met. Standing next to him he felt like one of the munchkins from The Wizard of Oz.

The morning of his six-month employment review Harry was nervous but felt his evaluation would go well. After all, he assured himself, he caught on quickly and was willing to learn anything new Baxter suggested might be useful. Technically computers were not a problem and to Harry they made perfect sense. He would work with a new program for hours until he mastered it and felt a great sense of pride and satisfaction when he could help someone else figure out something he himself had just learned.

That morning Harry waited patiently expecting Baxter to call him into his office to do a formal review but the door remained closed. About eleven-fifteen Harry stepped out of his office and was tempted to knock on Baxter's door but sensing his anxiety, Janet assured him his supervisor was in his office but asked not to be disturbed.

At exactly twelve o'clock Baxter appeared at Harry's door and said quietly, "Get your jacket, we're going out for lunch." It was a cool, crisp day in early October, but the sun was bright and gave the false impression that it was warmer than it really was. Harry had to almost run to keep up with Baxter's long strides as they made their way to the restaurant. As they entered the maitre d' waved to Baxter and even though the place was very crowded, immediately led them to a spacious booth.

Baxter nodded his approval and said only, "Frederick, this is Harry."

Frederick returned the nod and replied, "It's a pleasure to meet you Harry. Please be seated and enjoy your lunch. Your waitress will be here to take your order shortly."

As Harry sat across from Baxter he found himself becoming very uncomfortable. The thought of a final meal being given to a condemned man popped into his head and he wished he were in a more private place if he was going to be fired. Finally Harry broke the silence by clearing his throat and saying, "About my review, I believe it was supposed to be this morning, wasn't it?" Baxter looked directly at Harry but didn't immediately reply. In those few seconds Harry felt a sinking feeling as he prematurely started to prepare himself for the worst. His thoughts were interrupted by Baxter's calm voice. "Oh yeah, the review. I completely forgot about it until a few minutes ago. That's why I figured I owed you a lunch or something to make up for my bad memory. No, you're doing just fine. One of the most conscientious, best workers we ever had. Hell, I'd give you an A plus."

Harry took a deep breath, "You mean I get to keep the job?"

Baxter grinned, his smile lighting up his face. "Yes, and a company car for your personal use. You've done excellent work and we all agree you're the right man for the job."

Harry breathed a sigh of relief and for a moment he felt his throat and chest tighten but he quickly regained his composure. "Thank you so much for this opportunity. You'll never know how much this job means to me." He added quietly, "You may have saved my life."

Baxter sat silently looking at Harry as if he were weighing his own thoughts. "Actually, I think I know exactly how you feel. Sometimes it's hard to believe in yourself when you've been knocked down a few times. You get up but after a while you keep waiting for someone to come along and knock you down again. When you've been kicked around enough you either get real mad and try to fight back, or you give up. This old world can be a cruel place if no one is willing to lend you a helping hand. I'm not sure if you're aware of this but several of the people employed by Sullivan Glass have backgrounds and circumstances similar to yours. Most of us have experienced first hand what it means to be down on our luck. I won't go into anyone else's life but I will tell you about mine. If you're interested?" Harry nodded affirmatively.

Baxter began, "Ten years ago I would have hidden my past but now I know it's an integral part of me and the path that brought me to where I am now." The waitress poured their coffee and took their orders. Baxter sat back in his chair as he continued. "I was born in Georgia, near Atlanta. My parents were poor, and I mean dirt poor. My daddy worked himself to death trying to put food on the table for us six kids. When he dropped dead my mama cleaned houses for wealthy folks during the day and at night she brought their laundry home with her to earn a little extra. Trust me, there was never any extra at our house no matter how hard all of us worked. When I was eighteen I got my girlfriend Rosie pregnant and married her and by twenty realized I couldn't earn enough money to feed her and our little boy, Joey.

One night after I had a couple of drinks I guess I got a little crazy and I tried to rob a liquor store. Of course I got caught because everyone in town knew who I was because of my size. Since I used a gun, even though it was old and couldn't fire, they still considered it armed robbery. I got sent to prison for six years but because of good behavior I was out in four. You might say in prison I was lucky, because nobody dared to mess with big Cecil Baxter so I used to spend all the time I could in the library educating myself in business and accounting. I was also lucky because my Rosie stuck by me even if I was a fool.

As soon as I got out of prison we headed to Minneapolis to start over. At first I couldn't find work and Rosie had to support us by cooking in a restaurant and I ended up taking care of Joey. One day I saw an ad in the newspaper for a night janitor at Sullivan Glass. Even though they knew I was an ex-con David's father hired me anyway. God bless his soul. I worked here for a year vacuuming floors and cleaning bathrooms. All this time I kept going to the public library and studying. One day as I was emptying wastebaskets I found some records that one of the accountants had thrown out and during my breaks I would learn everything I could about Sullivan Glass. After doing that for a while I think I knew more about the business and financial part of the company than most of the people who worked in the main office. With a little creative investigating I started to see ways the accounting department could help the company save money and slowly I developed a financial plan that I felt was economically very attractive.

All the time I was working on my ideas I was very careful not to step out of my role as Baxter the janitor, just in case someone would catch on to what I was doing. I didn't want anyone accusing me of snooping around or calling me an uppity nigger. Back then people still felt justified to think and say things like that.

One day my little boy Joey came home from school crying because some older kid teased him that his daddy cleaned toilets for a living. I thought my heart would break seeing how ashamed he was of me. The very next day I went to Grant Sullivan and after I reintroduced myself I leveled with him and explained what I had been doing. I briefly outlined the plan I had been working on and explained how I felt there were a number of ways Sullivan Glass could be saving large amounts of money. I remember how he sat there looking at me, not saying a word, so like you, I figured the worst. Finally he said, "Cecil, I want you to turn in your mop."

At that point I figured it was all over, and that I had made a major mistake. As I turned to leave, he continued, "I want you to report to the accounting office. I admire a man with initiative and who is honest. I'll give you a chance to see how your ideas work out. If what you believe proves to be true, I think you'll have earned yourself a full-time position in the accounting department."

That was a long time ago, and I will always be grateful for the chance Grant Sullivan gave me. His trust enabled my family to start a whole new life we could have only dreamed about before. Grant was one of the finest men I have ever met and if you could get behind that reserved exterior you would find a heart of pure gold. He could be tough as nails and stubborn as the day was long, but as long as you tended to business and did not cross him he was more than fair. He changed our lives and we will always be indebted to him for that. Any little thing I can do to help this company to grow and prosper, I will do. I consider it an honor to be helping Grant's son David. He's a fine, honorable man, and I know he is doing the same thing for you his father did for me. I hope you will appreciate it the same way I did, and keep on working for the good of the company. In many ways we are all family."

Harry cleared his throat, which was still feeling tight. "I was worried this morning when you didn't call me into your office for my formal interview. I thought maybe I had screwed up and that was your way of letting me know I wasn't working out."

Baxter set his glass of water down, and peered intently at Harry. "Damn, I'm sorry. I didn't mean to put you through that. I guess I've been so wrapped up in my own little world I forgot about you. A few days ago my Rosie had a breast biopsy done. Her doctor told her the results looked normal but he was a little concerned about something or other and wouldn't know for sure until the final lab report came back. She was pretty shook up because breast cancer runs in her family and is what her mother and older sister died of. I guess this morning I shut myself away from everything until I heard from her. About eleven o'clock she called to tell me everything was fine. I have to admit I spent the next ten minutes on my knees thanking God for saving Rosie.

After that, I called a travel agent and booked tickets to England and France. We've never done much in the line of travel except maybe a small family vacation every few years. The past few days showed me it's time to lighten up a bit while we both still have our health. We're not spring chickens anymore." He grinned his big easy smile. "I plan to take a whole lot more time off if it's okay with you."

"It's totally fine with me. You've taught me well. What made you choose England and France?"

"Rosie was born in New Orleans. She lived there the first ten years of her life. She loved the French Quarter, and spoke some French herself. About a month ago she started to study French in one of these night classes and has caught on very quickly. I figured this would give her a chance to use it first hand. The kids are all grown up and we don't have any grandchildren so it seems like this is the perfect time."

Harry couldn't help but notice the excitement in Baxter's face and knew that even though he didn't often express his emotions, this was a man who loved his wife and children very deeply. The waitress brought their food and for a while they ate in silence. As they strolled back to the office Harry genuinely felt he belonged somewhere and Baxter had summed it correctly when he said the people at Sullivan Glass were like family. He no longer felt as though life had shut him out and resolved he would never let go of this feeling ever again.

Chapter 4

A few days after his meeting with Baxter, Harry took the afternoon off. It was the first time he had taken personal time since he began working at Sullivan Glass. He was surrounded by people he admired and cared about and they in turn seemed to truly appreciate him. After his review and conversation with Baxter he started to notice a subtle positive shift in his attitude. The despair of the past few years was slowly being replaced with hope and he had now come to believe that everything that was happening was very real and the bubble was not going to burst.

He arrived at the office a little earlier than usual and completed his most pressing work by noon. Before leaving he stopped at Janet's desk and assured her that everything she might need was done and he would be taking the afternoon off. Annie was standing nearby and casually inquired what his plans for the afternoon included. Harry was secretly pleased that she had been interested enough to ask but he only smiled and said he had some old debts to repay.

He grabbed a quick lunch and then stopped at the nearest florist and selected two large bouquets of long stemmed roses. While standing at the counter waiting to pay he impulsively picked out a large box of Swiss Chocolates. As he placed his purchases in the company car he felt an overwhelming sense of gratitude and knew he would never take the use of a car for granted.

His first stop was the Busy Day Cafe where he was able to find a parking space in full view of the front window. He selected one of the bouquets of roses and an expensive box of cigars he bought the day before. As he entered the cafe he held the roses behind his back. The lunch crowd had thinned and he could see Virgil sitting alone at the counter reading a newspaper. Virgil casually glanced up and after saying a friendly obligatory hello continued reading the paper. Harry paused to see if Virgil would look up again and then replied, "Hey Virgil, what's new in the old neighborhood?" At the sound of the familiar voice his friend looked up and did a double take.

"Holy shit, look at you. I didn't even recognize you. You look great! Kind of like Mrs. Astor's plush horse."

Harry looked at Virgil's bloodshot eyes and grinned, "Tough night, Virgil?"

Virgil returned a sheepish grin, "I look like shit, right?"

"I've seen a corpse or two that looked more lively than you. Here, these are for you. I know you enjoy a good cigar. The guy at the tobacco shop said these are your favorite. It's just my way of saying thank you for all the times you were good to me."

Virgil laid the newspaper on the counter and stared at Harry, "I don't know what to say. You didn't have to do that. Thanks a lot."

Harry saw Myrtle's pinched face peering inquisitively out from the kitchen. He was quite sure she didn't recognize him because she wasn't scowling. Her full attention seemed to be riveted on the box Harry handed to her husband. "I have something for Myrtle too."

Virgil looked over at Myrtle and then back at Harry, "You're kidding, right?" There was an amused but incredulous ring to his question.

"No, I'm serious."

Virgil shook his head in disbelief and motioned to Myrtle, who in response made a 'who me?' gesture. Virgil, now grinning from ear to ear, nodded affirmatively.

Myrtle cautiously crept forward to the counter and it was obvious to Harry she still did not recognize him. He brought the bouquet of American Beauty roses out from behind his back and presented them to her.

"These are for you Myrtle, for all the good meals I enjoyed here when I lived in the neighborhood."

Myrtle stared at the roses with her mouth hanging open and a rather idiotic look on her face. She peered directly into Harry's face and all of a sudden it must have clicked in her mind who he was. Her jaw dropped even farther and her eyes widened as she surveyed his neat appearance. At the same time Harry noticed a telltale redness creeping up her scrawny neck and into her cheeks. She stammered out the words, "Thank you . . . ah Mr . . . ." She looked over helplessly at Virgil. After all the meals Harry had eaten in their restaurant it was painfully evident she had never bothered to find out anything about him. Not even his name.

Virgil stared at his wife for a brief period as if he was secretly enjoying how uncomfortable she was. Then he added in a matter of fact manner, "Harry."

"Yes! Mr. Harry!" She looked as if she was either going to puke or faint.

Harry had all he could do to keep from laughing but he soberly added, "Well, I must be off now, I have another stop to make." He left the cafe knowing every eye in the restaurant was on him, and chuckled to himself on the way to the car. His true intention had not been to show off. Virgil had been a good friend and for that he would always be grateful, but deep inside he felt a sense of empowerment and hoped the acid tongued Myrtle would learn a much needed lesson about treating people with a little more kindness. He was quite sure by the look on her face she was not used to having her customers bring her flowers, especially those who she deemed as undesirable, which now included almost everyone in the economically depressed neighborhood.

He pulled into the parking lot of the Salvation Army and was pleased to see Betty was working. She was in her usual position leaning heavily on the counter lighting a cigarette from the one she had just finished. When she spotted Harry she called out in her raspy voice, "Well, look what the cat drug in. I thought maybe you died and went to heaven."

Harry placed the candy on the counter and presented the bouquet of pale pink roses to her. He leaned over and gave her a light peck on the cheek and said, "Elizabeth Dufoe Bartusek these gifts are for you to show my appreciation for being such a good friend to me when I was down on my luck and needed someone to talk to."

Betty took the roses and carefully pressed her nose into the blooms. After a few seconds she looked up at him and said quietly, "Buddy, you don't know how many years it's been since anyone brought me flowers. Pink roses, how did you ever remember pink is my favorite color? You are one special person."

Now it was Harry's turn to blush, and to cover his embarrassment he added in a joking voice, "The candy probably isn't the best for your girlish figure but you can always share them with your family."

Betty threw back her head and laughed loudly, "Not in this lifetime. These are for me and me alone. I plan to savor each and every one of these precious little hummers myself."

Harry was pleased to see how much Betty seemed to be enjoying the gifts. He looked around the store and commented, "It's very quiet here today, where is everyone?"

Betty laid the roses on the counter and finished lighting the cigarette she had been working on earlier. "The Major," she said with obvious disdain in her voice, "saw fit to jack up the prices a bit. Seems we weren't making quite enough money. It'll cut down on the traffic for a while. It takes older people a little while to get used to the price increase. The younger ones seem to have more money than they know what to do with. They only shop here because they think we're trendy."

A little old man came into the store and inquired about a pot that would be suitable to cook oatmeal in. Betty ushered him into the back room where all the kitchen utensils were displayed. As she walked away Harry studied his friend carefully. Betty was shorter than Harry by six inches easily but outweighed him considerably. Her long gray hair was piled loosely onto the top of her head and often looked as if she had not quite finished fixing it in the morning. In the warmer months she wore loose floral cotton shifts she referred to as wash dresses. Most of her outfits were in various shades of pink, her favorite color. Resting beneath the single layer of soft fabric, her large unfettered breasts slumbered prominently giving her a slightly off balance list. In cooler weather she added a men's flannel shirt not necessarily coordinated with the dress she was wearing. Her nylons were rolled down below her fat little knees accompanied by colored cotton socks also not necessarily in a matching color scheme. Her shoes always seemed to be in the sad state of being run over at the heels and were referred to as her happy hikers. She had the habit of sliding her feet out of her shoes as often as possible to ease the pain and then only halfway back on when she needed to wait on someone.

Harry had to admit her eyes were by far her most attractive feature. She had soft brown doe eyes that could fill with tears when talking about a small child or an older person she knew wasn't getting enough food. She considered the poorest of the poor to be her people and Harry knew she often charged them little or nothing for the items they needed. This all too frequent practice, which was tolerated in the beginning, now represented another bone of contention with her boss, but somehow she managed to keep her job. Her justification was that charity was charity, and she merely eliminated the middleman. Following a night of drinking it was Betty who helped Harry find new shoes after he had lost the corrective one he needed to keep his pelvis in balance. He still couldn't remember how that could have happened. After that unfortunate incident he became more careful about the amount of alcohol he consumed. Usually.

Betty put a medium size cooking pot into a bag for the old man but Harry didn't see any money change hands. She returned to the back room and emerged with a large glass vase. Adding water from the sink in the bathroom, she carefully arranged the roses one by one and then placed them on the counter where she proudly admired them. The store was empty and Betty sat down on the stool behind the counter, kicked off her shoes and motioned to Harry to sit in the nearby chair.

It had been some time since they visited so Harry inquired about her family. He remembered she had an ex-husband named Dominick and a son Robert whom she referred to as Bubba.

Betty lit another cigarette, "Oh, fine I guess. Not much changes at our house. Same old. Same old. Neither one has a job. Bubba has a hard time with life. He's special you know. Maybe he'll never be able to hold a job. Dom, now that dumb shit, he's never been one to hold a job very long. Sometimes when I start thinking about him and how he changed my life it makes me very sad. I wasn't always like this."

Her voice was softer now, and she let her gaze drift off into space. "I was so pretty when I was younger and a whole lot smaller. I was only a slip of a girl when I met Dom, a real southern belle. We were not blueblood wealthy like some folks back then, but my mama and daddy were pretty well off. My parents were Tyler and Elvira Dufoe. My daddy owned a big mill down in Mississippi and my mama stayed home and raised me and my older brother Tyler Junior who was eight years older than me so I guess I was a bit of an after thought, but I was a wanted surprise and our mama loved to spoil us. There was nothing she wouldn't give us. We even had a colored nursemaid to help with our care. Her name was Amanda but we called her Mandy. My childhood was wonderful. Damn near perfect."

She smiled at Harry, "My daddy used to call me his little princess and he and mama always made sure I had plenty of new frocks to wear to all the parties. I was only seventeen the first time I saw Dom. Sometimes I'm tempted to curse that day, but then he reminds me I was a more than willing participant and he did give me Bubba. He was the one gift Dom gave me that changed my life for the good and didn't need penicillin to cure. My two best friends, Melody Blake and Hannah Dietrich and I had seen him when a carnival came to town. Back then he was so handsome with his large dark eyes that made you want to drown in them. He had black wavy hair and looked like a gypsy prince. We all fell in love with him, but for some godforsaken reason he took a shine to me. Even though he was five years older than me, I didn't care. Before I knew it I was head over heels crazy in love with him. Of course it didn't hurt that he had a little sports car and lots of money. He would bring me flowers and tell me how beautiful I was. I thought he was my one and only true love. He was my Prince Charming. That man had a body to die for and before I knew it he was in my underpants. Even though I was just a little virgin child when I met him I learned very quickly what passion was all about."

Harry looked away for he felt now he was learning more about Betty than he really wanted to know.

Betty laughed and said, "Now don't you go getting all tight-assed embarrassed on me buddy. I'm sure you've had your hands down some girl's drawers more than once or twice."

Harry looked down at his shoes and Betty peered intently at him and said, "Well, I'll be damned. No matter. You're probably the smart one. God knows I sure as hell wasn't."

She continued to puff on her cigarette and her voice took on a dreamy sound. "Those three months he courted me were the best, most exciting, most foolishly awful times in my life. No girl had ever been pursued more romantically. He brought me flowers, candy and champagne. That's how he got into my drawers the first time. I guess I was a little drunk. After about four months I figured I was PG because I had missed two of my monthlies. I didn't tell my folks or him, or anybody else because I wasn't completely sure I was pregnant and didn't want to scare Dom off. Finally, right after I graduated from high school, I decided to run away with him. I could tell he was getting itchy feet by the restless way he was acting. I chose not to tell my family or friends but when I was leaving Mandy caught me packing my suitcase. She sat me down and looked at my palm and all the time she was looking at it she kept tisk, tisking and shaking her head. Finally, she said, Ms. 'Lizabeth don't you do it. Don't you be fooled by Mr. Dom. That sorry excuse of a man won't bring you nothin' but a life of sadness and pain. He ain't nothin' but a gol damn snake oil salesman. He comes from a long line of bad blood and spawns of the devil.

Sometimes I can still hear her words like she is standing right next to me, but sweet Jesus, I didn't listen because I was in love and knocked up to boot. Lord knows, I've cried a river and a half of tears because of it."

At that point, a large tear ran down Betty's cheek and she made no effort to wipe it away. "We got married by a Justice of the Peace. I wanted a priest because I was raised Catholic, but Dom insisted it was a J P or nothing. I gave in and we drove until we made it clear to Des Moines. We looked in the phone book and got the poor guy out of bed. Dom gave him a little extra money to record my age as eighteen. Since it was already so late we found a cheap motel and Dom dropped me off at the door saying he wanted to buy me a wedding surprise. I thought, what the hell, in the middle of the night? To make a long story short, that mealy mouthed little son of a bitch didn't come back for two days. I near cried my eyes out thinking he had been killed or hurt. It turned out he found a poker game and forgot all about his new little bride. He won over five hundred dollars and couldn't understand why I was so upset. In the end he convinced me he had done it for us and we kissed and made up. Even though deep down I was hurting so bad I could hardly stand it I pretended everything was fine. I think by then I already knew Mandy's prediction of my disastrous life with Dom was coming true but I foolishly felt I was in too deep and there was no turning back."

A few people wandered into the store but no one asked for help so Betty continued her story. "I was already going into my fifth month when Dom finally figured out I was pregnant. We had been moving from town to town staying in cheap, cockroach infested motels. Dom barely managed to keep us in food and gas money by playing poker. I've never seen anyone get so mad about anything. When he confronted me about my pregnancy he screamed like he was some kind of crazy lunatic and stormed out of the motel. I didn't see him again for a full week. Luckily, I still had the two hundred dollars I had gotten from my high school graduation tucked away and was able to eat and pay the rent on the room. When he returned a week later he was flat broke, one eye was swollen shut and he had a chipped front tooth. Someone had beaten the living crap out of him because he couldn't pay a gambling debt. My romantic gypsy prince looked like hell warmed over twice. What a gol damned loser!

By this time I knew for sure I had made a huge mistake but he begged me to take him back, promising he would find a job. He did find work, lots of times, but I soon learned that every job he took was beneath him and lasted about a month or until someone waved a deck of cards under his nose."

Betty stopped and rang up a shirt and two ceramic pots for a young hippie woman. Turning back to him she asked if he would like some iced tea and without waiting for a reply poured them both a generous glass from the small refrigerator by the counter. Sitting down she lit another cigarette, inhaled deeply and inquired if Harry really wanted to hear the rest of the story. Harry nodded and urged her to go on.

"It's just like some gol damn ol' soap opera isn't it?"

He smiled sadly at her.

"We were living outside Montgomery, Alabama in another rat trap motel when I had Bubba. Dom had been gone for two days when my water broke and a kind neighbor lady took me to the hospital in her beat up old car. We barely made it before he popped out. I only stayed one day in the hospital because I didn't have any way of paying the bill. A few years later I was able to pay every last cent of that bill. Even though hospital costs were a lot less back then it was still hard to get it paid. Bubba was two weeks old before Dom ever laid eyes on him. I found out later at the time I was having our baby he was shackin' up with another woman. That's when I threw the no good bastard out. Bubba was six years old before he ever saw his daddy again."

The door opened and a small, stocky man with a lot of obviously dyed black hair poked his head in and looked around. Whatever he did or did not see must have pleased him because he entered the store. As he swished past the check out counter he said, "Hi there, Betty" in a coy little voice.

"Hey, Eldon, what's new with you?"

Eldon giggled a high pitched laugh and dramatically posed himself by thrusting his pelvis forward and placing his hand on his hip as he replied, "Not much." He appeared to pout, then slowly licked his lips with the tip of his tongue before he continued. "Did you get any new little treasures in, love?"

Betty winked at Harry and at the same time answered Eldon in a tone that almost conveyed they were girlfriends about to share some extra juicy tidbit of gossip. "You really need to check out the first row of shoes in the women's section and the table next to it with the sale sign. I think there may be a few spiffy items that might interest you."

Eldon disappeared into the racks of shoes and Harry looked at Betty with a quizzical expression and asked, "He likes women's shoes?"

"You got that right. We call him the shoe sniffer."

"I don't think I like the sound of that. You don't mean . . . ?"

"Each and every pair. Sometimes it takes the better part of an hour."

"What is his problem?"

"Different strokes for different folks." Betty shrugged and continued. "Let's see, where were we? Oh yeah, then we didn't see Dom again until Bubba was about six. We were living in Iowa at the time and somehow he found us. He showed up long enough to borrow a hundred dollars and left again. I figured it was worth a hundred bucks just to get rid of the dumb ass for a few more years. Instead he showed up the following month and claimed he had a job interview and asked if he could stay a couple nights until he found a place of his own. Against my better judgment I told him he could sleep on the sofa for two nights but Bubba and I were going to see my folks in a few days and he would have to be gone by the time we left. He agreed. My folks had only seen pictures of Bubba because I never had money to go visit them. I lied and told them I had an important job as a supervisor and it was hard for me to get time off. Since neither of them were in very good health they couldn't come to see me and the kid either. They didn't know how bad my marriage was and I was too damn proud to tell them the truth. I scrimped and finally saved enough for Bubba and me to take the Greyhound to Atlanta where they were living.

On my way to work the next morning I dropped Bubba off as usual at my friends who had been watching him during the summer months. Dom was still asleep because his job interview wasn't until later that day so I never gave him another thought. When I got home from work that night my little house had been ransacked. The bus tickets and all the money I had saved were gone along with that sneaky rat of a man. I was so furious I made up my mind if he ever showed up again I would make him suffer. I cried and cried and even seriously considered finding someone to put a curse on him even if he was still my husband and the father of my child. Of course it's a lot harder to find a qualified witch doctor in Iowa than it would have been in the Bayou." She winked at Harry.

"About two nights later I heard someone come into the house during the middle of the night. I knew it was him drunk out of his mind so I pretended to be asleep until he passed out on the sofa. I got up and grabbed Bubba's baseball bat and went into the living room and I know in my heart of hearts my intention was to put an end to all the suffering that dirty skunk caused me. My whole body was shaking and I don't know how long I stood there looking at him because there was an uncontrollable raging storm of hate exploding inside my head. All of a sudden I became aware of a gentle tugging on my sleeve and I heard Bubba asking me what I was doing. His sweet face was all white and pinched in the moonlight and he looked so little and scared. Just seeing that look on my son's face brought me to my senses and I knew I was the one who needed to be there for him. That if he and I were going to survive, Dom would have to be out of our lives. I couldn't risk doing anything that might land me in jail.

I picked up the phone and called the police and had Dom arrested for burglarizing my house. They took his sorry ass to jail and I filed for divorce. Then I called my folks and told them the whole sad story. They were so kind and understanding and sent money so Bubba and I could fly home. We stayed ten days and it was wonderful. My folks forgave me for running away and they adored Bubba. He still talks about that vacation. That is, what he can remember about it. About a year later my daddy helped us move to Minneapolis. I know my parents would've liked it if we had moved closer to them but finally agreed a clean start in a new place was probably better. My daddy gave us money to buy the little house we live in and made sure we had enough money to live on until I found this job."

Betty stood up and asked Harry if he would keep an eye on the register while she visited the little girl's room. She had no sooner left when Eldon poked his head around the corner and chirped, "Peek a boo!"

Harry smiled weakly and said, "Betty went to the bathroom. She'll be back in a minute."

Eldon piled several items on the counter including a pair of lavender satin slippers with marbou feathers, a platinum blonde wig, and a pair of red glittery heels, which he held up to Harry's face. Aren't these just divine?" he inquired in a rather intimate voice.

"Yeah, they really are . . . special." Even though Harry's voice contained an element of doubt it did not appear to dampen Eldon's obvious pleasure. Harry grinned and then added, "Looks like they may have been left over from Dorothy's estate sale after she found her way back to Kansas."

Eldon cocked his head to one side as if he was seriously contemplating what Harry said and finally asked, "Dorothy?" All of a sudden he pointed at Harry and started to giggle. "Oh, I get it! You mean The Wizard of Oz Dorothy! That is just soooo precious."

Harry continued to study Eldon as he watched him fondle a sheer red lace trimmed nightgown before he cautiously asked, "Exactly what kind of work do you do, Eldon?"

"I'm a mortician's assistant. Someday, I hope to own my own funeral parlor but for now I only help out."

Betty came out of the bathroom drying her hands on a paper towel. "I see you found some shoes. Those are pretty classy heels."

"Aren't they just too adorable?" Eldon's voice had taken on a gushing tone and he reached up and coyly played with a lock of his greasy black hair. He smiled at Harry exposing large yellow stained teeth.

Betty bagged the purchases and Eldon paid her and started to leave. He stopped at the door, turned and gushed "Bye-bye for now love, and tootles to you too, big guy,"

After he left the store Betty and Harry looked at each other and she started to laugh.

"I think he likes you."

"Unbelievable and totally bizarre. I'm still in awe of his hair. Didn't they call a doo like that a pompadour back in the twenties?"

Betty managed to keep a straight face, "Did he tell you what he does for a living?"

"Oh my God, yes. Kind of makes you want to consider instant cremation, doesn't it? That is one strange puppy. Aren't you a little afraid of him?"

"Hell no. I'm pretty sure he's harmless." Then she added dryly, "At least to the living."

"Don't say any more, I don't even want to think about it."

Betty sat down on the stool and lit another cigarette. "You really have lived kind of a sheltered life haven't you?"

"In that kind of a world, yes, maybe. I guess I'm a relatively simple, straight forward guy." He wanted to change the subject so he added, "Tell me the rest of your story before it gets busy again."

Betty inhaled deeply on her cigarette and said softly, "Nothing beats a nice leisurely smoke. Well, let's see, we lived here in Minneapolis almost two years before Bubba got hit by a drunk driver while he was riding his bicycle. My neighbor was a retired judge by the name of Floyd Nelson. He and his wife Libbie lived in the house with the hedge around it east of us. They were kind, honest people and we were good friends. The accident happened directly in front of our house just as Bubba was coming home from school. Floyd saw the accident and notified the police even though the person took off without stopping to see if Bubba was hurt. His reporting the accident helped us get a settlement for Bubba. I never did find out who hit him because for some reason the whole incident was hushed up and all the records were sealed. All I ever learned was the woman responsible for the accident was someone important and very rich. The accident never made the news even though it was a hit and run. It was like the whole thing was swept under the rug.

Unfortunately, Bubba suffered a serious head injury and now is mentally handicapped. In the end all his hospital and doctor bills were paid and a trust was set up for him. He will be taken care of for the rest of his life, even after I die. I made the lawyers promise that when I'm gone Dom will never get his greedy gambling hands on any of the money and Bubba will go into some kind of a group home until he dies."

Her eyes clouded with sadness. "I saw my sweet little boy who was so quick and smart before the accident completely change overnight. Bubba's never been the same and he didn't really finish high school. They just passed him along and gave him a blank diploma so he could feel good about himself. He's a nice boy and wouldn't hurt a flea. Floyd and his wife were real kind to him, teaching him how to plant a garden and tend roses. When Floyd's wife died of cancer, he and I got to know each other better. He had two grown daughters but they didn't seem to mind that we kept company. Over time we learned to care for each other but because he was considerably older than me we never married. He felt it wouldn't be fair for me to be tied down with him if he became feeble. We had some wonderful years together and I guess if you were to ask me if I had ever known true love I could say yes without hesitation. It kind of made up for all the pain and sadness I had with Dom.

Six years ago Floyd went into a nursing home and I would visit him at least three times a week. One day he closed his eyes for a nap and didn't wake up. After the funeral, one of his daughters came through the opening in the hedge to tell me they had sold the house. She commented on how worn the little path through the hedge was. Then she smiled and handed me a thick manila envelope. I told her I didn't want anything but she insisted saying if I didn't take it I would dishonor Floyd's memory. When I opened it I found a note telling me how much he had grown to love me and Bubba. It also contained ten thousand dollars in cash. I cried for a whole day after that. I still think of him as my one true love. Besides my daddy, he was the finest man I have ever known."

A few more people trickled in and Harry checked his watch, "Betty, I enjoyed our visit, but I'd better be going. I don't want you to get in trouble with the Major, whatever his name is."

Betty touched Harry's arm, and said "Thank you. Not many people ever bother to find out about each other nowadays. It seems they just don't care. You're one in a million. Why can't there be more people like you in the world?"

Chapter 5

Harry sat in the living room of his comfortable new apartment and brooded. He knew he was feeling sorry for himself but he didn't care. He was having his own pity party. That was what his cousin Molly called it when they were back in high school. He couldn't shake the effect of the conversation he had earlier with his psychologist, Dr. Charles Preston. Even though the quality of his life had improved dramatically in the last year there were still times he could feel the depression that plagued him over the years creeping back into his life. He confided this to Annie and she recommended Dr. Preston, saying he had been very helpful when she was going through a difficult time.

Usually he enjoyed his sessions with him, and found himself looking forward to them. Harry would do most of the talking, frequently about his childhood, other times about his accident, and now about his new life and plans for the future. Both men considered it a major breakthrough when Harry finally admitted how angry he was at his chimerical biological father. A father he had never met or known. He wept openly when he told Dr. Preston how as a child he fantasized that one day he would be leaving school and a big black car would be waiting outside the door and a handsome man would step out and introduce himself to Harry as his father. The other children would gather around and his father would pick him up in his arms to take him away to live with him in some wonderful place. Back then he still believed in fairy tales with happy endings.

Sometimes his tears turned to anger as he confided that as he got older he imagined his father as being old and worthless and of his angry desire to kick the crap out of him for what he did to him and his mother. It was during these times he hated himself, for what kind of person could feel that way about the man responsible for giving him the gift of life.

Today the usually sensitive doctor appeared rushed and a little less attentive. As the session was about to end, he took off his glasses and looked directly at Harry. For a while he remained silent and finally said, "Harry, I believe we've made some excellent progress in the past few months. After careful consideration I think now might be the time for us to leave the past and its sadness for a while and concentrate on the present. As important as it is to examine the past and deal with your family issues honestly, there is also a time to let go and move on. Now is now, and you are no longer a sad little boy but a grown man with great potential. Have you ever tried to find your father?"

The sudden change of direction and unexpected question threw Harry off guard. Finding his father was something Harry had considered on many occasions but the thought of being rejected a second time had always prevented him from acting on it. "I don't think that is something I will ever do." Harry tried to keep his reply firm but a tell tale quiver in his voice betrayed his emotional state.

Dr. Preston continued to study him and in a quiet voice said, "Are you afraid he won't want to see you? That he may reject you again?"

"No, not really . . . I don't know. He's had a lot of years to find me. Maybe he's already dead, I'm not sure I really give a shit at this point."

"I think you do care, or you wouldn't be here. You are a very sensitive person. Give it some thought. It could be a very important step in your healing. Find out what really happened, not just what you imagined happened."

Harry got up to leave feeling rebuffed, silently thinking he may not continue therapy. As he reached the door Dr. Preston made one last comment, "Judging from your reaction, my opinion is this is a very painful area that needs to be examined with total honesty. A major part of becoming a happy, healthy person is the ability to act on life's situations, not just react. Give the idea some careful thought. You'll know when the time is right. Sometimes you need to put it out to the universe and see what happens. I'll see you next week."

As Harry sat alone in the dark, he thought of something else he and Dr. Preston talked about. They discussed stepping back from the anger, sadness and embarrassment of his life and start looking at it as if it were someone else's, objectively, without the nagging childhood emotions that still whirled around and tortured him inside his head. He thought about all the times he cried alone where Molly or aunt Dora couldn't see him. There had always been the underlying pain and humiliation he felt for being ashamed of who he was, in spite of how often aunt Dora had tried to convince him none of it was his fault.

As he lay back in the recliner and shut his eyes he could picture himself at about ten or eleven years of age. His aunt and uncle had moved their family to the neighboring town of Glenwood and he was living with them on a permanent basis. He and Molly had been thrilled at the prospect of leaving little Lowry school for the much bigger Glenwood school system. That particular day there was a lyceum program scheduled in the auditorium. Everyone was looking forward to it because there were to be live animals brought in and the program would last all afternoon. The man presenting the program went by the name of Captain Bob and one by one he brought out his wonderful creatures. Two talking parrots, several large snakes, three dogs, a large cat, a pot-bellied pig and finally, a full grown baboon.

Harry put his hands over his eyes as if unconsciously attempting to block out the image of the baboon. Inside he felt a sick feeling rising up in his chest and stomach as he reacted to the dreaded memory of that goddamn, moth-eaten baboon. Before Captain Bob brought out the baboon he asked for a volunteer to help with the next trick. Many of Harry's classmates jumped up waving their hands, anxious to be picked to assist on the stage. Captain Bob stood with his hand on his chin studying the excited children and finally asked "Let's see . . . is there an Axel in the audience?" There were loud giggles. "No Axel, how about a Napoleon?" More loud giggles. "No Napoleon? We're not doing very well are we?" Then he spoke those dreaded words. "How about a Harry?"

Harry was horrified to hear his name and remembered how he tried to slouch down into his chair. The last thing in the world he wanted was to go up on the stage in front of everyone and risk making a fool of himself. Of course, all the children around him were whooping and hollering and he felt himself almost being pulled out of his chair. He recalled the strange sense of relief that flooded over him as he heard Captain Bob announce over the microphone, "Here we are. We have our volunteer. Come right up Harry. Step right up onto the stage."

An explosion of laughter caused Harry to sit up in his chair and he once again experienced the awful embarrassment that engulfed him as an ugly brown baboon wearing a red and yellow clown suit sauntered across the stage toward Captain Bob. There were hoots of laughter and jeers as the children acknowledged the motley looking volunteer. Harry's face burned red with embarrassment as an all too familiar voice called out loud enough for the entire auditorium to hear, "Hey, Scarley, his name is Harry too! Maybe that's your old man!"

In his mind he could see himself bolt from his chair and not stop running until he was several blocks from the school. By this time stinging tears of humiliation were streaming down his face and he knew he couldn't go back. He made his way down onto North Lake Shore Drive where he and Molly had built their clubhouse behind uncle Stan and aunt Dora's house. Flinging himself down he lay sobbing in the soft grass until there were no more tears left to cry. Later he remained staring up into the sky through wild cucumber vines that draped over a small maple tree and formed the roof and walls of the clubhouse. Seething with anger, Harry plotted his revenge on Curtis Dahms as, despite the crowd of shouting children, he had recognized his archenemy's voice. He would hunt Curtis down and beat him with his fists until he cried out in pain and begged for mercy. Then he would smile the same evil smile Curtis did when he was hurting someone, as he, Harry the avenger, gleefully pushed his fingers into Curtis the cowardly's eyes, and made him apologize. He would apologize not once, but over and over again.

Several hours later he awoke to the sound of someone running up to the clubhouse. There was a soft familiar whistle and Molly came crawling in through the vine covered entrance. She was out of breath and looked as if she had been crying. Harry sat up rubbing his eyes and desperately hoped he didn't look as bad as she did. He studied her and cautiously asked, "What happened to you?" Molly looked intently at him and then answered in her usual inappropriate casualness, "Oh, not a hell of a lot. I kinda' got into a little trouble." She tossed her bright red hair as if to emphasize how unconcerned she was.

Harry was relieved to be talking about Molly rather than his own devastating situation, so he asked, "Oh yeah? What kinda' little trouble?" Molly nonchalantly reached up and pulled a wild cucumber from one of the vines and popped it between her fingers. "I beat the shit out of that asshole Curtis Dahms."

Harry felt a sinking feeling as he realized they were indeed talking about what had happened in the auditorium. "God dang it, what did you do that for?" His face burned with shame. He was trying to sound tough, but he knew exactly why she had done it.

"Don't be a dumb jerk, you dumb jerk. You know perfectly well why I did it! Because of the stupid ass thing he said about your dad. Someone had to do it and anyway, he's been getting on my nerves big time lately. I've been planning on doing it for quite sometime and this just provoked me over the edge. I think I could have gotten away with it but that old bat Mrs. Alexander heard me call him a dirty name and she blew the whistle on me. I had to go to the principal's office."

Harry thought he detected a definite hint of pride in her voice. "Oh yeah?" Harry was curious now, "So what did you call him? An asshole like you call everyone you don't like?"

Molly looked thoughtful and paused a moment as if she was giving the conversation serious consideration and then she said confidently, "No, it was definitely worse than that." She grinned mischievously as she pretended to examine her short, dirty fingernails."

"Much worse?"

Molly shook her head up and down and her grin took on an almost diabolic twist and Harry got the clear message she was getting a lot of enjoyment out of the conversation even though earlier she had almost looked a little remorseful.

"Bastard?" Harry cringed slightly as he hated that particular word. Molly ran her tongue around her lips and made a terrible face as if she had tasted something immensely unpleasant.

"Soap." She rubbed the back of her hand over her lips and spit on the ground.

"Soap! No way! You got your mouth washed out with soap?"

"Yep. Dora, did it after we got home from the principal's office." There was a new casual tone to Molly's voice as if boasting it wasn't that big of a deal.

"This is serious shit! What did you call him?" Harry could hardly believe what he was hearing. His distress had lessened as it moved on to forbidden excitement.

Molly moved in closer to Harry positioning her face right next to his, her eyes in little slits, and said in a hushed voice, "Do you remember what we heard my brother and his friends say the night we sneaked up on them in the tent? The word they heard at the Forada Tavern?"

Harry thought hard but finally said "No." Then a great look of disbelief came over him as he whispered, "You didn't!"

"I did."

"Jesus!"

"No, not Jesus, you dip shit. Think harder!"

"I know what word, but how could you?" His voice was barely audible. "You called him a cocksucker?"

Molly clapped her hands together as she screwed up her face in a triumphant grin. "You better believe I did!" She paused and bit her lip, "But it was even much worse!" She hesitated and her voice quivered ever so slightly. "Cocksucker turd!"

"Holy shit!" Harry flopped back on the ground and started to laugh. "You're crazy! Do you even know what that means?"

Molly looked defiantly at Harry as if not only her sanity but also her integrity was being questioned. "Yes of course I do!" Then she added, "Well no . . . sorta' . . . Well, okay, I don't know. I just know it's really bad. I didn't mean for it to come out, it just kinda' slipped out. Anyway, whatever it means, I'm sure if Curtis isn't one already he is well on his way to becoming one." She crossed her arms over her chest, vindicated and confident the subject was closed for discussion.

Harry still had a look of disbelief on his face as he propped himself up on one elbow, "What did your mom say?"

Molly's posture softened and she shrugged, "Not much, you know how quiet Dora gets when she's really, really upset. Except on the way home she was mumbling something about sewing my lips shut permanently and that maybe I really was incorrigible." She grinned and added, "She also muttered something like raising children was a lot like getting stoned to death with little pieces of chickenshit, what ever that means. Like that was a nice thing for her to say. We both know she never swears so my guess is she was pretty pissed."

They both started to laugh but it was a bittersweet laugh for they were still hurting. Molly got up to leave and as she smoothed her dress Harry noticed one of her sleeves was hanging at a strange angle and there was only one tie in the back. She smiled innocently at him, "I gotta go. I'm really supposed to be sitting in my room thinking over my life so I can amend my wicked ways." She rolled her eyes back like she always did when she had no intentions of listening to anything she considered unbelievably stupid. "You know, mea-a-culpa and all that other shit. I better sneak back in before anyone notices I'm gone and sounds the alarm. You coming home for supper?"

"Yeah, I'll be home, I gotta' wash my face first."

"Good idea. You look like crap." She hesitated and peered at him with little slits of eyes. "I hope it was okay to beat up dirt bag Curtis. You're not mad at me are you?" Molly had an unusually genuine look of concern on her face. "I think you would have done the same thing for me, wouldn't you? You know we gotta' stick together."

Harry lied, "I guess so." He crossed and uncrossed his fingers twice to take away the lie. She was always the strong one.

Molly peered at the tear stains mixed with dirt on Harry's face. As she was leaving she turned back, crossed her eyes and said, "In-cor-ig-a-bull!" She emphasized the bull. Mr. Carlson said if I'm not careful I'll end up in some ree-form school." Then she lowered the pitch of her voice, "You better mend your evil ways missy! Blah, blah, blah! Mr. big friggin' law!" She let out a loud battle cry and took off running and Harry remembered at that moment just how much he really, really liked her.

That was then and this was now. Harry uncovered his face and stared up at the ceiling. Maybe he did brood too much and it was time to let go and face up to his life as it is now, not back then. Shut old doors and open new windows of opportunity. Try Dr. Preston's suggestion of turning the past over to the universe and seeing what happens. It could work and he had nothing to lose. He smiled as he recalled his cousin's parting words, blah, blah, blah! Mr. big friggin' law! She never appeared to let past mistakes derail her for very long. Onward and upward. The incredible, incorrigible, precocious, unsinkable Molly Brown.

Chapter 6

Harry remembered exactly the day he knew he wanted to marry Annie Bennett and spend the rest of his life with her. He had worked at Sullivan Glass for a little over a year and slowly as he grew to know her better so did his love and admiration. That particular day Annie had set up an interview with a temporary receptionist to take over Janet's duties until she recovered from an elective surgery scheduled for the following week. All Harry knew was the surgery had something to do with Janet's uterus, and upon learning that, had chosen not to know any more of the particulars. Annie had already interviewed three other applicants but it was the last one that really stuck in Harry's mind. The young woman was about thirty years old and very beautiful. She had long blond hair and that perfect California girl look right down to the deep sun tan and sparkling white teeth. Both Harry and Janet had to agree she was exquisite. He remembered standing in the reception area by Janet's desk talking with Janet and Annie when Laura Lane, 'Just call me Lonnie' swept into the room. She immediately asked to see David Sullivan about the receptionist position being offered and even though she was thirty minutes late gave no explanation for her tardiness. Annie stepped forward and after introducing herself explained she would start the interview in her office and later they would meet with David Sullivan.

As Annie reached out to shake hands Lonnie brushed by her ignoring the welcoming gesture and breezed into Annie's office as if she owned the place. Annie followed her but not before she turned back and rolled her eyes and grinned at Harry and Janet. Janet muttered under her breath, "Aren't we special," and went back to working on the forms she and Harry had been preparing.

In less then ten minutes the two women emerged from Annie's office and Janet informed them David was finishing with a conference call and it would be only a few minutes before he would meet with them. As they stood in the reception area Harry watched carefully as Annie took Lonnie's well manicured hand into hers and admired her many expensive looking rings. As Lonnie began explaining about the rings Harry noticed Annie was not looking at them but was peering intently at Lonnie. First she studied her face and then appeared to be concentrating on the area around Lonnie's head.

This was not the first time Harry had seen Annie do this with a prospective employee and he had grown increasingly curious about her interviewing techniques.

The intercom buzzed on Janet's desk informing them David was ready for Lonnie's interview. As Annie went to open the door, the prospective employee stepped in front of her and casually said "Thank you, dear," as if she was dismissing her. Annie stopped and made a slight gesture with her hand indicating Lonnie should enter and then shut the door behind her. She smiled at Janet and Harry, and said "Well, let's see what Mr. David Sullivan thinks about Ms. Laura, just call me Lonnie Lane."

Lonnie was in David's office for over thirty minutes when the door opened and they both emerged laughing as if they were old friends. Harry was more then a little surprised and couldn't help noticing the flirtatious way Lonnie moved in closely to David and touched his arm. He also noticed the soft, intimate way she cooed that she was looking forward to hearing from him. Lonnie then exited the office with a breathless, "Bye dears." For about ten seconds no one said a word then all four of them started to laugh.

Annie was the first to interrupt the laughter by saying in a full, breathy voice, "Well now Mr. Sullivan, how did you like Ms. Lonnie?" David grinned mischievously and said, "It was kind of like a repeat of my last week with Greta." Everyone started laughing again as they recalled during the previous week how Greta, David's purebred Collie had been in heat and raised havoc with two of his neighbor's male dogs. David continued, "I'm not sure I could deal with her on a daily basis. I guess my vote goes with Barbara, the second lady we interviewed."

About a week later Annie asked Harry if he would like to join her for dinner at her home. He was delighted to accept the invitation. As she finished preparing the spaghetti their conversation drifted back to Lonnie's interview. Harry commented to Annie how he'd noticed that at some point she always briefly held the hand of the person she was interviewing and at the same time appeared to be studying them intently.

Annie seemed a little surprised at his comment, and in a joking voice said, "Why sir, how very astute of you to notice that. Up to this point I thought I was being extremely subtle about what I was doing."

Harry added, "I remember how you held onto my hand when we first shook hands and how you looked directly into my face, almost as if you were looking straight through me."

Annie giggled and said, "Yes, and I remember you turned beet red and got all embarrassed and nervous." Then she added casually, "Actually I just enjoyed holding your hand." She seemed to be studying him intently and when becoming aware of his uneasiness dropped her gaze. It was apparent her last comment had made him self-conscious.

Harry looked directly into Annie's eyes and said in a voice so soft she could hardly hear his words. "I thought you were the most beautiful woman I had ever met." He paused nervously and Annie could see the red creeping into his cheeks as he shyly added, "And I remember at that moment I thought you looked like Snow White." Annie couldn't help herself as she broke into laughter but quickly recovered when she realized how serious Harry's comment had been.

"Oh, Harry I'm sorry, I didn't mean to laugh. In fact, I think that is the nicest and sweetest thing anyone has ever said to me. It caught me off guard. You see, I don't often think of myself as being beautiful. Not any more, since the accident." She paused and then added in a joking tone, "Relatively good looking, but definitely not beautiful."

For an instant Annie looked down and when she finally looked up Harry could see the little tears that were forming in her eyes. She smiled, "Well, let's eat, everything is ready."

They sat down at the small round glass topped table Annie had set with flowered placemats, and delicate white bone china. The small bouquet of pale yellow roses matched the placemats, and the soft glow of candles reflected on Annie's face in a beautiful romantic way.

For a while they ate in silence, neither of them feeling the need to say anything that would break the intimacy of the moment. Both seemed to savor the feeling that love was becoming a reality. Harry gently broke the silence as he commented, "This is wonderful . . . the food I mean." He stammered a little as if searching for words, then took a painful deep breath, as if what he was about to say was taking a great effort, "Not just the food. Everything. Being here with you. It's like the most wonderful thing in the whole world. Something I never thought could happen to me."

Annie reached over and gently touched his hand, "Harry, you have no idea how long I have waited to hear you say that. I really care about you. I hope you can believe that. I have from the first day we met, but I was afraid to say anything."

"I felt that way too. My whole life I have believed that somehow, for some reason I was unlovable. I simply accepted the fact that I would always be alone and would have to make do with whatever little bits of love I could find and learn to accept it. Now I know that isn't enough, and I want more. I want you to share my life with me." He had impulsively spoken the words he had never expected to say, and there was no turning back. "Annie, I love you, will you . . . . marry me?"

As he studied her face she appeared to be shaken, the color draining from her already pale complexion. There was a sinking feeling deep inside him and instantly he felt he had misinterpreted what she had been telling him. He wanted to run, just as he had the day Harry the baboon had entered his life. Only now he was an adult and would have to stay and endure his humiliation.

Annie seemed to sense his pain and leaning forward softly kissed his lips saying in a quiet but determined voice. "Harry, I love you too. There is nothing more in this world I would rather do than to become your wife. However . . ." Annie appeared to be struggling with her words. "Before I can accept, there is something I need to tell you about me. About my life before I met you. Then if you still want to marry me I will be proud and happy to be your wife." Her voice had taken on an emotional quality and for a moment it appeared she might start to cry.

Harry could feel his heart pounding. Her words had rekindled his hope but he couldn't fully comprehend what she was trying to tell him. "I don't understand."

"You will, and it will also answer some of the questions you posed earlier." As they finished their meal, Annie's story began to unfold. "My parents, who as you know, I never talk about, live in Saint Paul. We have no contact with each other. My father is Steven H. Bennett, a prominent attorney to the rich and famous. You probably have seen his name in the newspaper. My mother is Klara Stattler Bennett, an equally prominent child psychologist. You may have seen her on local television. I was to be their dream child, the perfect culmination of the union of two brilliant minds that would dazzle and astound the world. For a while when I was younger I almost seemed to fulfill their expectations. My parents had a great need to portray themselves to the outside world as the perfect couple and the perfect parents of a perfect offspring. For them it appeared to work. It was me who couldn't fit into their illusion. I remember as a small child how I slowly became aware of this reality. It was subtle at first but as I became older I began to experience the feeling of withdrawal of the unconditional love parents are supposed to have for their children. It seemed I could never quite be the perfect child they expected me to be. Punishments were never physical but rather more emotional and usually consisted of banishing me to my room for long periods of time. Maybe it was never longer than a day at a time, but to a small child it seemed like an eternity. I've never forgotten that and for years I walked on eggshells fearing I would disappoint them. Unfortunately it seemed to become a self-fulfilling prophecy.

Annie stood up, cleared the plates and poured them each a cup of tea. She sipped slowly trying to decide how to go on with her story. Harry couldn't help but notice the troubled sadness in her eyes.

"About puberty I started to experience what I called special feelings. Not just the hormonal changes that all adolescents go through, although I was having that going on at the same time. It was difficult for me to identify exactly what was going on inside my head. At times I felt like I could feel what other people were experiencing on the inside. Not only what their voices were saying but rather what they were really feeling inside their hearts. I would hear my parents and teachers telling me one thing but deep down I knew it wasn't true. They would tell me something was for my own good, but I knew it was more for their own good, so I would fit better into their perfect little worlds. Over time I think I started to develop a paranoia and the few times I did try to discuss my feelings with anyone, including my parents, I was told I was being silly, overly imaginative, childish, or just plain difficult. As the feelings intensified, I became afraid I was going crazy, and I threw myself into anything that would keep me distracted from having these thoughts. I forced myself to excel in everything, schoolwork, cheerleading, orchestra, dance, choir, you name it I was in it and was very good at it.

My parents were elated when I started dating a football player whose father was a surgeon and belonged to the same country club they did, and I'm sure at that point they felt their dream child was finally well on her way to becoming a reality. Sadly, however, beneath my poised self-assured exterior, my soul was screaming inside and I was slowly falling apart."

Annie placed her teacup on the table. She paused, took a deep breath and closed her eyes. As she opened them she continued, "Skipping all the gory details, I made several serious mistakes the last part of my senior year. The most serious one was I got pregnant. I'm not sure why I did such a stupid thing, but I think I wanted someone to love me for who I really was and not for the way I could perform." Annie raised her hand slightly as if she wanted to touch Harry's arm but changed her mind and instead picked up her napkin from her lap.

"This is very painful for both of us, I know, but I feel I have to go on before our relationship goes any farther. The tears were trickling down her cheeks and she used her napkin to wipe them away.

"Of course when I told my parents they were horrified and they made me promise not to tell anyone, not even the boy who had gotten me pregnant. It was my mother who surprised me the most. I thought she would become very angry and start crying but instead she told me not to worry and very calmly informed me the next day she and I would take a trip to a private clinic and rectify this temporary little glitch in my life. She and my father assured me they loved me and this little error of judgment on my part didn't change the way they felt about me.

While this is what they said, I remember my inner voice telling me that they would never be able to forgive the reprehensible thing I had done. I also remember before my appointment at the clinic, my mother and I picked out the perfect white prom dress as if nothing was wrong in their not so perfect daughter's life. As I lay on that cold table, before the doctor performed the little procedure on me, as my mother so tactfully referred to it, I prayed that God would forgive me and then let me die. I also prayed that all the doctors who performed abortions would burn in hell. Obviously neither of my prayers was answered.

After that, as I had expected, I again experienced the withdrawal of my parent's unconditional love. The difference was that this time it was permanent. Even though we continued to go through all the motions of being the perfect family, our lives and relationship had changed forever. It was as though their love had become a great void. We never spoke of my indiscretion again as if it had never happened, at least externally. Inside, however, we were all broken.

I finished high school at the top of my class and after a summer of playing in Europe with friends of the family, I attended the College of St. Catherine in St. Paul. Once again, I excelled in everything and my parents seemed contented with my performance. What they didn't know was that their perfect daughter had a not so perfect life outside of college. The day I graduated I left the party my parents had given in my honor to be with the man I had secretly been dating during the last two years. An important part of our relationship had been the use of drugs and alcohol. He more than me, because of my perceived need to still appear perfect. That night we celebrated big time and we ended up in a terrible car accident. He was killed instantly and I barely survived. I was thrown through the windshield. That's how I got these scars on my face." She touched her cheek. "The doctors were able to save part of my sight but, as you know, I am legally blind as I have limited peripheral and frontal vision.

I'm grateful for the sight I do have and for the fact my life was spared. My parents and insurance paid for all my medical bills, including the reconstructive surgery, but the doctors could only do so much, and as you see I am no longer perfect. Slowly my parents withdrew not only their support but also their claim to ever having a daughter. I remember the numb feeling I experienced when I saw my mother being interviewed on one of the local television talk shows and when they asked her if she had any children she replied with a emotional quiver in her voice that their beautiful daughter was no longer with them. The last I heard they have a Jack Russell Terrier that is very obedient and does all sorts of amusing tricks."

Annie quickly stood up and awkwardly asked Harry if he would like more tea. Sensing her grief, he reached out and gently took her hand in his. He could see the conversation had drained her and he wanted her to know that nothing she had shared with him changed his love for her in any way. She hesitated briefly but then pulled her hand away and said quietly, "Wait, there's more." Annie sat down again and sipped the warm tea she had poured into her cup. "It was at this time I met Sister Mary Rose. She was the head nurse on the floor I was on during my rehabilitation at St. Mary's Hospital. It was her that got me back on my feet emotionally and eventually introduced me to David.

Slowly David helped me understand and accept the part of myself that had caused so much mental anguish. Through his kindness and instruction I learned to accept my special abilities. Earlier this evening you asked why

I hold people's hands at some time when I am interviewing them. It's really quite simple. I'm a reader or what some refer to as a sensitive. I read people's auras and can actually see their energy and tell what kind of people they really are. That's why David has me interview all the employee candidates before we hire them.

Harry looked at Annie to see if she was teasing him and when he saw the serious look on her face couldn't help but show his confusion. "I'm not sure I have the faintest idea what you are talking about. Maybe you'd better go on."

"Hey, it just gets more weird. Remember when I told you about my strange feelings back in high school? After my accident those sensations started to intensify. When I lay in the hospital with my head and eyes heavily bandaged there were times when it almost seemed like I could see. I would hear people's voices and colors would come into my mind. I soon learned I could tell if the people were kind, honest, angry or sad. Not so much by what they said or didn't say but rather by the colors I saw in my mind's eye. It became like a game to me and was something to pass the hours as I lay in the hospital bed. After the bandages came off I saw the world very differently. There were colors and lights, a heightened sense of smell, the feeling of warmth, and sometimes around certain people, the dark, heavy feeling of coldness. It was as if I could feel other people's energy. Later I experienced pictures almost as if a film was being played in my brain. It was as if I was dreaming but I was fully awake. There were deep, unmistakable sensations I had never known before and it was David who helped me understand and accept these feelings."

She looked into Harry's eyes and seeing the puzzled look said helplessly, "And you have no idea what I am talking about, do you?"

Harry grinned and said, "No, but don't stop now, I think you're on a roll. Tell me about just call me Lonnie."

"Don't laugh at me, I'll try to explain it in an easier way. First I read her aura, the colors and energy around her head and body, and in her reading the colors showed her to be very self-serving. I think that was evident to you and Janet just by talking to her. The colors also showed greed, self-absorption and deceit, and an inner frightened little girl. A child who had been hurt so severely she hides her pain deep inside where she doesn't have to deal with it. When I touched her hand it was as though a picture flashed in my mind of someone mining for gold, or as people would say a 'gold digger'. There were other things to but they were more private and I'm not really sure it would be appropriate to mention them."

"You're being serious with me, right? So, what did you see when you held my hand?"

"You weren't difficult to read. I would refer to you as an open book. You are what you portray. At times, much inner sadness, but you have a pure heart. Honest as the day is long. Physically you didn't feel well, besides the fact you were rather hung over, I saw pain. Real physical pain, I sensed it was from your back and your leg. I also saw inner pain from when you were a child. Deep feelings of loss and betrayal "

"And when you touched me?"

Annie smiled, "I knew you liked me, even the colors around you changed when we touched. They seemed to vibrate."

"And now?"

"I know that you have loved me for a long time and that you still love me even though what I have just told you was difficult for you to hear, you still care deeply about me." Her voice faltered, "I think you . . . ." Annie was momentarily without words.

Harry leaned over and kissed her tenderly. "I believe you really can read minds, Annie Bennett, because I really do love you. All parts of you, what you are and what you have been. All of your past is what has brought you here to me and is therefore important."

Eight months later Father Sean Flahrety married Harry and Annie in a private ceremony at Our Lady of Hope Church with only David, Sister Mary Rose and Janet in attendance.

Chapter 7

Janet handed Harry a note when he returned to work after lunch. There had been a visitor while he was out and the woman had left him a brief message. She watched Harry read the note and saw a smile forming as he exclaimed, "I'll be darned!"

Harry stepped into his office and closed the door. In a few moments Janet saw the little light go on signaling he had picked up the phone. For the next few hours Harry tried to keep busy but his thoughts and eyes kept going to the note he had propped in front of him. Finally, he gave in and picked it up again and reread the message.

> *Hey cuz,*
> *I'm in Minneapolis for the next week. Maybe we could get together for dinner.*
> > *Love,*
> > *S. Molly Brown*
> *(Yes, the unsinkable Molly Brown is back)*
> *P.S. You do realize it's high time you reconnect with us notorious Browns. Ha Ha! Call me at 555-3323, at the Royal Hotel, Room 852, or leave a message at the desk as I'm in and out.*
> *P.P.S. When did you start listing yourself in the phone book again? Hmmmm?*

Harry smiled to himself and shook his head. Molly Brown, his crazy cousin was back in town. Well, maybe not totally crazy but highly colorful to say the least. She must have gone back to using her maiden name after her husband died. Actually, he thought, it was her second husband that died or was killed in some kind of a freak accident in Africa. Harry leaned back in his chair and tried to remember the details. All he could recall was her husband had been a photographer for the National Geographic

Society or some other big nature magazine and during a photo shoot an animal had turned on him and killed him. He felt a pang of guilt that he had never tried to contact Molly. By the time he finally heard about his death he believed she had moved back from Africa, and was living out east and not knowing her married name it was easier to justify not doing anything.

A flood of childhood memories engulfed him and he felt a keen sense of loneliness for Molly and the friendship they had shared growing up. Her real name was Sara Cornelia Brown. Since she hated both Sara and Cornelia she somehow adopted the name Molly instead. Sara Cornelia was reserved only for times of grave trouble or monumental exasperation on the part of her mother, Dora. Of course it was also a very effective means of taunting by Harry or Molly's older brother Daniel. "Sara Cornelia, Sara Cornelia, thinks she's such a big fat dealia!" It wasn't poetry but it never failed to get a rise out of her. The teasing usually ended with Harry or Daniel having to fight off her flying fists and take back having said it. He could still picture exactly how she had looked while they were growing up. Her red hair flying in all directions, a generous sprinkling of freckles across her nose, mouth always open and chattering even when she had absolutely nothing to say. In the summer her bare feet were usually dirty but always at least two steps ahead of him. Shoes to her were something to lose and then have to try find under threat of bodily harm. She had been more like a sister to him than a cousin. After his mother and grandma Maria died Harry's care had shifted to his Aunt Dora, and Molly and Harry became inseparable. Newcomers to their small town usually thought they were siblings but the old timers knew differently and usually felt the moral obligation to rectify this common misconception.

Harry pushed his chair back from his desk and rubbed his upper leg. "Damn," he thought to himself, "She could turn an absolutely boring afternoon in little Lowry into a really great time." He could still picture the two of them standing side by side, time after time, in front of Aunt Dora and being scolded for something they had unsuccessfully tried to pull off. She would say something like, Sara Cornelia and Harold you will be the absolute death of me! Why, (big emphasis on the why) can't you two ever behave yourselves and stay out of trouble? I don't know what I ever did to deserve children like you! Harold, why do you listen to Sara? You know she always gets you into trouble. Your poor mother, God rest her soul, would absolutely turn over in her grave. She would make a quick sign of the cross, which Molly would later declare looked as if she was swatting flies. Ha ha! At this point Molly would hang her head and look very remorseful but at the same time she would catch Harry's eye and make a smirking face. He remembered how it would take all of his inner strength to keep from laughing.

Harry's train of thought was interrupted by a soft knock on the door. Janet stuck her head in. "Harry, it's really none of my business but the lady that left you the note, I keep thinking I should know who she is." Janet smiled with an embarrassed expression and added, "Maybe it's none of my business, I'm sorry."

"No, it's all right. She's my cousin Sara Brown. She used to be on one of the local television stations as a roving reporter a few years ago. Actually, that was quite a few years ago. Does that ring a bell?"

Janet looked a little perplexed, and smiled, "Of course, Sara Brown, I do remember her. She's your cousin?"

Now it was Harry's turn to look embarrassed and he answered lamely, "Kind of hard to believe isn't it?" For a few uncomfortable moments he felt all the insecurities of what his life had been before coming to Sullivan Glass come rushing back to him.

Janet smiled and said gently, "I'm sorry, I didn't mean that to sound the way it came out. I just never heard you talk about her before."

"No, it's okay, don't be concerned. I haven't seen her for a very long time. She was the famous one. Sometimes I still cringe when I think about the way I must have looked the day I came in for my interview. Me in my Salvation Army outfit."

Janet giggled and said, "Let's say you were a well kept secret. Kind of like a diamond in the rough."

Harry felt touched by her kindness and said only, "Thanks, I appreciate the fact that all of you were able to look beyond the me you saw that day and had the faith to give me a chance."

"Were you able to reach her? Your cousin, I mean. I could try again if you didn't connect."

"No, she was out but I left a message. Thank you anyway. Please hold my calls. It's been so many years since I've seen her and it has caught me off guard. I think I'd like a little time to myself."

"No problem, you can buzz me if you need me."

Harry turned his chair away from the desk so he was facing the window. It was snowing gently outside creating a storybook panorama.

Propping his right leg up on the heat radiator he started to rub his right knee and ankle that so often gave him pain. He toyed with the idea of having a surgeon look at it to see if something could be done to ease the constant aching but so far he had put it off. He suspected after so many years arthritis was setting in and he would be told to learn to live with it. Annie suggested he take alfalfa tablets and extra vitamin E and fish oils for the inflammation but so far he hadn't taken her advice. It was passive resistance on his part.

The warmth from the radiator helped relieve some of the ache and leaning his head back he closed his eyes and let his mind drift back to his childhood. Parts if it were still so vivid. It was strange for him to think that it had been over fifty years ago. The thought that crept into his mind was the day he broke his right leg, which was probably the original factor contributing to his chronic pain.

It had been a beautiful day in April, still cool enough that they needed a light shirt or jacket that morning but the afternoon had turned into a perfect seventy degree, cloudless day. He remembered how the sun was so bright it made him and Molly both squint when they first came outside to get into the car. Molly had celebrated her eighth birthday two months earlier and her being eight while Harry remained seven for two more days made her even more bossy than she usually was. She had chanted over and over into his ear, "I'm eight and that's great. You're not, you little snot" until he wanted to belt her.

There was no question who was going to be in charge that day. Even though Molly was smaller than Harry, somehow she always seemed bigger. And tougher, and braver, and smarter. She had a big mouth, a big ego and a big imagination. Molly was almost never at a loss for things to do. She could charm almost anyone into seeing things her way and when charm didn't work it was never beneath her to bully them into agreeing with her. Her favorite saying was, "I can't is not in my vocabulary." This could change in an instant if someone told her to do some thing she didn't want to do. After that it became more like "I won't and you can't make me."

That day Aunt Dora planned to take Harry to Nelson's shoe store in Glenwood to get him measured for new birthday shoes. Over the winter he had grown out of his present pair and Dr. Dornot, who Molly referred to as Dr. Doorsnot, or old chrome dome, suggested having his right shoe built up to compensate for his leg-length deficiency.

Before heading to Glenwood, Dora stopped at their Aunt Edna and Uncle Floyd's farm to wish her sister-in-law a happy Easter. Edna and Floyd's farm was on the other side of the road from Grandpa Scarley's. Dora's older stepbrother Floyd had taken over their farm before he married Edna and had proven to be an excellent farmer in everyone's eyes. Edna was a teacher at the Lowry school and after working there for four years finally consented to marrying Floyd and settling down on the second Scarley farm. Her life consisted mainly of hard work and constructive criticism for everyone she came into contact with. She also doted on their only son Clayton.

Edna's birthday was on the same day as Molly's, which, according to Edna, made them birthday twins. This little proclamation didn't set well with Molly who couldn't stand her Aunt Edna. To show her displeasure at the mention of being mutual birthday twins Molly would stick her finger down her throat causing her to gag in a very disgusting way. The only person Molly claimed to dislike more than her Aunt Edna was her sedentary son Clayton whom she usually referred to as Clayton the clod. Even though Clayton was only slightly older than Molly and Harry and a year younger than Daniel, he was never allowed to associate with the Brown children or his cousin Harry. Edna confided to one of their neighbors that she didn't consider the Brown children suitable companions for her Clayton. This didn't seem to be a problem for Clayton whose only interest appeared to be books so Molly and Harry grew up never really knowing or appreciating their cousin.

When they arrived at the farm, Dora gave them strict orders to behave themselves and as usual they both dutifully agreed they would. Edna was in the backyard cleaning out the storage room by the back door. Her mousey brown hair was pulled back tightly into a tight bun giving her face the stern schoolteacher look that had earned her the name Hatchet Face when she was teaching at the Lowry school. Clayton sat reading on the steps with a book propped on his knees and seemed only mildly interested that his cousins had come to visit. Dora and Edna hugged each other and Dora gave her sister-in-law a small Easter package containing a white linen handkerchief with blue edging crocheted around it and a small tin of chocolate treats.

Molly winked at Harry and pointed up at her own nose. They both got the giggles again as they had laughed on the way to the farm whispering the hanky Dora had given her was way too small for a schnozzle as big as

Edna's. Dora turned and opened her eyes very wide and glared a warning for them to settle down or else.

Edna put down the broom she was using to sweep away spider webs and asked Dora if she had time for a cup of coffee and Dora politely accepted. Edna asked Harry and Molly if they would like to come in for a glass of milk and a cookie but they declined saying they would rather be outside.

Molly started snooping around to see if there was anything of interest in the storage room. She would really have preferred to wander through the big old farm house with its polished floors and many rooms peeking into every closet and the big, spooky attic but she knew from past experience Edna wouldn't permit it. Instead, Edna expected them to sit quietly at the kitchen table and drink their milk.

At first there didn't seem to be anything of interest in the storage room and Molly was about to leave to take a ride in Clayton's tire swing when something caused her to let out a quiet whistle. She spied an old wooden wheelchair tucked behind some boxes in the back of the room. It was a large, oak wheelchair with caning on the back and the seat with leg and foot guards to give extra support. Molly glanced at Harry with a big smile on her face and left the storage room and returned to the steps where Dora and Edna were still standing.

Harry shifted in his chair moving his leg slightly to ease some of his pain. He remembered how Molly asked if she could bring the wheelchair out of the storage room to give him a ride.

She spoke in her most charming voice, "Harry's leg has been hurtin' real bad lately. We even had to take him to the doctor in St. Cloud didn't we Mama?" Aunt Dora shot Molly a wrinkled eyebrow look. The look that usually meant "Child, what are you up to now?" but Molly ignored her and added "Pa-leeze?" Edna turned and hesitated saying she didn't think so because the wheelchair belonged to her father and she really didn't want anything to happen to it.

"Please, pleeease! We'll be ever so careful." Molly looked so convincing that even Harry couldn't help but wonder what she was up to.

"Well . . . ." Edna obviously didn't want to give permission but Molly was not about to back down so she continued, "Harry would really like a ride. His leg gets so very tired sometimes, doesn't it Harry?" Molly shot Harry a meaningful look and he gulped trying his best to look tired and hurting. Edna stopped and looked directly at Harry. "I suppose it would be all right. Poor little guy, he can't help the way he is. But mind you, don't go too fast. I don't want anything to happen to that wheelchair. It's one of the few mementos I have to remind me of my father."

When they were sure Edna and Dora were safely occupied inside Molly pulled the wheelchair out onto the sidewalk and taking off her flannel shirt wiped away some of the dust. Harry remembered he was a little surprised she had used her favorite shirt as a dust cloth. It was the one that matched the flannel cuffs of her jeans but he didn't comment. Her white blouse hung out over her waistband but she made no effort to tuck it back in as she was now on a mission.

He remembered crawling into the wheelchair and Molly pushing him up and down the sidewalk twice. Then she stopped and demanded he get out and push her. He refused saying he was the one that had the sore leg and she was supposed to push him. He sat there with his arms folded defiantly across his chest knowing full well he had justice on his side. Molly put her face right next to his and hissed, "Get out of there you little shit, you're no cripple." Then she added with a sinister smirk, "But you just might become one if you don't move that skinny little butt of yours."

Needless to say he got out and she got in. He pushed her up and back on the sidewalk twice before she exclaimed, "This stinks!"

Molly clamped her hands tightly on the wheels causing the chair to stop so abruptly that Harry bumped his chin on the back. She got out and sat cross-legged on the sidewalk sifting the sand where ants had made little mounds between the cracks. After a couple minutes of deep contemplation Molly got up on her knees and pulled a small white packet of Sen Sen out of her jean pocket and dumped the last of the tiny black squares of the bitter licorice into her palm. She stuck out her tongue and licked up some of the small candies. She then realized that Harry was watching her intently and paused to contemplate this new dilemma. Looking down she carefully studied the few remaining slightly damp candies in her sweaty palm, sighed, and reluctantly pushed them up near Harry's face offering them to him. Harry remembered making his most disgusting face telling her in no uncertain terms there was no way he was going to lick up the spit soaked contents of her hand. Molly shrugged and nonchalantly finished them herself. She had gotten into the habit of carrying Sen Sen after a teacher had scolded their class for eating them telling the children with great authority that only drunks ate them to cover the smell of alcohol on their breath. Harry could almost count on the fact that anything anyone told Molly she couldn't do, would be the thing she would do for certain. Molly sat down cross-legged again, and hunched over so her chin was cupped in her hands with her elbows resting on the sidewalk in front of her. She often sat that way when she was concentrating.

"It was your stupid idea to ride in the wheelchair." Harry felt the need to remind her and did so by assuming a false superior attitude.

"Shut up, I'm thinking!"

Harry remembered how serious Molly looked sitting there all hunched over with her forehead wrinkled up, her eyes held in beady, narrow slits. Then she sat up abruptly with a big smile breaking out on her face.

"I've got it!" Jumping up and clapping her hands, she spun around and looked directly at Clayton who was still sitting on the steps with his book. The sun made him drowsy and he was only mildly interested in watching Harry and Molly.

"Dear", Molly said, using her sweetest little girl voice to address Clayton. "Could you please get me a drink of water? I seem to have a very dry throat." She coughed a few times to drive home her point. Clayton didn't move at first so Molly coughed again this time adding dramatic little gagging sounds. Reluctantly, Clayton got up but not before he shot Harry and Molly a suspicious look. As soon as he entered the house Molly grabbed Harry by the arm, "Don't just stand there like a stupid ape. Help me push this chair to the hill by the chicken coop!"

Harry remembered how he weakly protested saying, "Molly, I don't think that's a very good idea," but she cut him off in mid-sentence countering with "It's not just a good idea, it's a great idea. Trust me, this time I know what I'm doing!"

Harry hesitated as past experience caused common sense to momentarily kick in sending a little alarm signal to his brain but it was already too late. Molly jumped behind the wheelchair and was pushing it out of the yard and towards the grassy knoll beside the old chicken coop. Harry remembered standing dumfounded torn between what common sense was trying to tell him and the feeling of loyalty to his best friend. The next thing he knew he was beside her helping to push the wheelchair to the top of the hill. Later, he would rationalize it, desperately wanting to believe it would have done no good to reason with her as the clattering of the wooden foot guards would have drowned out his pleading anyway. In no time at all they stood perched at the top of a steep hill that ended about fifty yards below on the bank of a shallow creek that ran through the farm. Harry remembered how on other occasions they had fun rolling down the hill and sledding in the winter but the thought of her riding down in the wheelchair terrified him. He tried in vain to tell Molly that riding down this hill would be very dangerous but she was already climbing in.

Once she was seated in the chair she grabbed Harry's arm and said, "Not just me, dummy . . . us. Here, I'll scooch over so you can sit beside me. Come on, it's safer if we go down together." About that time Harry thought he heard the screen door slam and Clayton the crier sounded the alarm. Harry still remembered the feeling of panic that gripped him as he struggled with his decision to stand his ground. He would never forget how Molly put her face right into his and uttered the four little words that had so many times previously spurred a reluctant hero on.

"You . . . little . . . chicken shit!!" Her carefully spaced words hissed defiantly at him.

Harry laughed out loud, as he remembered back to that precise moment. It was as though she had slapped him. He had in that brief instant been reduced to mere chicken droppings in the eyes of the person who meant more to him than anyone in the entire world. His frail almost eight-year-old ego couldn't take it and it was as though something exploded in his head. His brain turned to mush and common sense no longer existed. It had flown away into the mythical, totally illogical world that Molly relished and seemed to thrive in.

He remembered thinking he heard someone yelling "No!" in the distance as he threw himself onto the seat beside her and gave a mighty shove. Both he and Molly pushed on the wheels as hard as they could as they started their legendary descent. The last thing he remembered was squeezing his eyes shut as tight as he could and feeling his heart pounding and the tears of fear running down his cheeks.

Molly later told him the great wheelchair ride was, "Probably the most exciting and fun things she had ever done in her entire life."

It wasn't until they were much older she finally admitted it was also probably one of the most stupid things they had ever done and he should have had more sense than to have listened to her. She also told him they made it half way down the hill with no problems and in her expert navigational opinion it looked as if it was going to be a piece of cake. What she hadn't known was that over the winter the rain and melting snow had created a large gully that was out of sight beneath the tall grass from where they had started at the top of the hill. As the wheelchair crashed headlong over the edge it struck a huge rock sending Molly and Harry catapulting into the great beyond while it sank lazily into the mud like some dying creature never to be seen again in one piece.

When Harry regained consciousness he found himself lying on Aunt Edna's back lawn with a cold washcloth on his forehead. He remembered the metallic taste of blood in his mouth and that his head hurt with a vengeance. His Aunt Dora was hovering over him and asking if he could hear her and how many fingers was she holding up in front of him. All he could do was groan and for the life of him couldn't understand why Dora wanted him to count her fingers. This, especially when it should have been obvious to everyone that he was in a great deal of pain and probably on the brink of death.

Finally, when he tried to move his right leg and found he couldn't, he began to cry. Dora comforted him by telling him not to be afraid even though it appeared that his leg was broken. She said they would go to the emergency room at the Glenwood Hospital and everything would turn out fine. She continued to turn the cold cloth on his forehead and after what seemed like a very long time carefully helped him sit up. Once he was sitting upright and some of the dizziness had passed he looked down at his leg. When he saw it was now at a very disconcerting angle he felt a new weakness enter him. Dora supported his weight and quickly laid him down again. Glancing up he saw his cousin Molly hovering over him looking very pale and scared. Her eyes were red and tearful and she was holding a bloody cloth over the bridge of her nose. It suddenly occurred to him that if Molly looked pale and scared it was more than obvious they were both in deep shit. He remembered shutting his eyes and letting out a very loud beller.

Dora put her arms around him and held him close. When he stopped sobbing she reassured him again saying that the doctor would be able to set his leg and that in no time at all it would be as good as new. Even though Dora was not a very big lady she was able to carry Harry to the back seat of her old Ford. She put the pedal to the metal and literally flew over the dusty gravel road arriving at the Glenwood Hospital emergency room in record time. Edna had phoned ahead and as soon as they drove up two nurses came out and helped place Harry on a gurney and rolled him into the emergency room. One of the nurses stood ready with a hypo. Within minutes everything got fuzzy and then turned black. When Harry finally awoke it was dark outside and his Aunt Dora was sitting by his bedside holding his hand. His leg was in a large plaster cast suspended by a rope with a pulley hooked to the ceiling and for a moment he felt as if he was going to float off the bed. For the next couple of weeks Harry was fussed over by the hospital nurses including his aunt Dora who worked part time on the day shift. Molly, who wasn't old enough to visit him inside the hospital perched herself outside his window ledge and gabbed with him while they both ate ice cream. It was a very long time before Harry let her forget what a really dumb idea the wheelchair ride was. Thinking about it now he remembered she had treated him with a new kindness and respect that lasted almost a full week.

Edna never forgave them for what happened to her beloved father's wheelchair but Molly blew it off saying, "It's not like she really needed it. What a selfish old crabby ass!"

Harry picked up the phone and dialed the number on the note that was propped in front of him. The phone rang four times and a very breathless Molly answered.

"Hello, Sara Brown here."

"Hi, Sara Brown. It's me, Harry."

There was a pause and then Harry heard a soft chuckling laugh. "Well, well. The elusive Mr. Scarley. I was finally able to track you down. I checked all the obvious places first, the hospitals, homeless shelters, jails, YMCA and finally just as I reached the point of total exasperation I almost, God forbid, considered the morgue. You can imagine my surprise when I find you tucked safely away in some fancy, smanchy office with your own walnut desk and name on the door in big, shiny letters. Did you marry the boss's daughter?"

"Hey, Molly, I'm fine. Thank you for asking. And to answer your tactless question, no, I didn't marry the boss's daughter, she was his personal assistant."

Molly let out an undignified giggle, and then continued, "Good move Harry! Totally unbelievable! You really got someone to marry you? Will wonders ever cease? God, I should talk, I found two people crazy enough to marry me. I can't wait to meet your wife, except right now I'm running late for a meeting with my publisher but I really do want to see you. I'm staying at the Royal Hotel and since they have a wonderful restaurant I was wondering if we could get together for dinner here tonight. I would love to see you again. I know it's short notice but you could bring your wife and I promise I'll be on my best behavior." She finally stopped for a breath.

"It sounds great, but Annie's busy tonight. She works with autistic and behavioral problem children two nights a week but I would love to see you too. Actually I think my wife would find you very interesting." He paused momentarily, not wanting her to miss the not too subtle implication of his last comment. "Besides, she still thinks I come from a normal, well adjusted family and I may need a little time to prepare her for you."

"Don't break my heart after all these years. Surely you've been able to put our colorful past behind us? Our silly little differences and occasional brushes with the law. All the times you blindly followed me into battle. I was young. How was I to know what a schmuck you were? Oh well, see you at six and don't be late. Ta Ta. There was a pause. "Oh, by the way Harry . . ."

"What, Molly?"

"Nothin'"

Chapter 8

When Harry told Annie about the call from his cousin she was excited for him and encouraged him to go to dinner with Molly. She agreed it might be better if he were to visit with her first, as there was obviously a lot of catching up to do. Annie suggested they could have Molly over for dinner at their home another time so she could meet her. She reminded him not to worry about how late it might get as she had made arrangements with Martha O'Grady to give her a ride home. The child she was to have been working with that night was ill, and instead she would be meeting with Martha and Sister Mary Rose to talk about their plans to redecorate the sunroom at the Seaton House home for unwed mothers.

Harry greatly admired his wife's dedication to helping others and Seaton House was one of her pet projects. It had been founded by the nun who had been instrumental in helping Annie get back on her feet after her car accident. When Harry questioned her why she felt the need to keep herself so busy with all the charitable work she did she answered simply that it was her dharma. At the time he did not know what dharma was, but learned later that it was essentially the opposite of karma. Annie believed the love and kindness one shows others in this life could hasten to break the cycle of reincarnation one's soul must go through in future life experiences. All of this was new to Harry but intuitively he felt very comfortable about her convictions. He suspected she was more spiritually evolved than he, and her determined belief system only reinforced his love and admiration for her.

Martha was the wife of a retired police officer and she and her husband Michael spent many hours volunteering to help keep Seaton House running smoothly with it's never ending parade of pregnant teens and young women who took up temporary residence there. Martha often contributed her sewing and cooking skills and Michael's usual role was that of handyman for the ailing electrical and plumbing systems at the spacious turn of the century residence. Annie reassured Harry she would ask Michael about putting on the new storm windows he offered to pay for and kissed him good-bye as she left for her meeting.

Janet informed Harry the name of the restaurant he was to meet Sara at was The Century Room and was in her opinion, the finest restaurant in Minnesota. The hotel itself was one of the older structures in downtown Minneapolis and housed a beautiful blend of marble and crystal in the old world tradition. The dining room was, according to her, breathtaking and the food was fantastic.

Harry arrived at the hotel at almost exactly six o'clock even though knowing Molly as he did, he was certain she would be fashionably late. The maitre d' who greeted Harry at the entrance of the restaurant was extremely polite and had a polished manner. Harry felt himself becoming somewhat ill at ease as he entered the restaurant and saw the elegant decor. Janet was right, the hotel was beautiful but the restaurant was everything and more than she said it would be. Even though the principle dining room was a huge open space it was arranged in such a manner that the outer areas featured gently curving walls with recesses furnished with candlelit tables for two. This effect of this design created an intimate feeling that immediately engulfed the restaurant's upscale clientele.

At the far end of the dining room a large fireplace made of dark green marble with a polished carved mantle accented with scrolls of cream and gold welcomed its pampered guests. Huge urns of plants and flowers were strategically placed to further enhance the decor.

Harry gave the young man his name and asked if Sara Brown had arrived yet. Somehow, it didn't surprise him when he smiled broadly and replied, "Ah, yes, Ms. Brown . . . no she's not here yet but she did call down to say she'll be arriving soon. Let me have someone show you to your table. Ms. Brown asked to be seated off to the side where it would be more private."

Another polished young man ushered Harry to one of the secluded tables near the fireplace where Harry could hear the crackling fire and feel the comforting warm glow. He thanked the young man and selected the chair facing the door so he would be able to see Molly when she made her grand entrance. He was aware of the fact that he was extremely nervous. Silently admonishing himself he tried to relax by taking a deep breath. After all, this was the same cousin he had grown up with. She was more like a sister, but then, it had been a very long time.

A pretty young waitress in a long black dress with white collar and cuffs approached the table, introduced herself as Taylor, and inquired how Harry was and if he was enjoying his evening. She smiled warmly and to his surprise waited for him to reply as if she was actually interested in what he was going to say. He answered he was fine and thanked her. She smiled again and asked him if he wished to order a drink while he waited for Ms. Brown to join him. She looked directly into his eyes and Harry could feel his face growing red. Clearly, he was not used to so much attention, especially from someone this lovely. His new life that evolved since his employment at Sullivan Glass was far easier than it had previously been. Still, he couldn't help but remember the years after his accident when he'd been just another invisible street person. The type of person most people wished would go away. He ordered a white wine and then quickly changed his mind and ordered a Scotch on the rocks. When she asked if he preferred a certain brand he told her whatever she recommended would be fine. She suggested a brand and even though he was unfamiliar with it agreed to her choice. A few moments later she returned and placing the drink in front of him, smiled once more saying she hoped he would enjoy his evening.

Harry sipped on the Scotch and savored the smooth, mellow flavor as he quietly surveyed the elegant world of the beautiful people that surrounded him. The tables were filled with well-dressed dinner guests even though it was a weekday evening.

The calming influence of the Scotch and the warmth of the fireplace quickly had a mellowing effect on Harry and he began to feel more relaxed than he had in a long time. He was therefore startled as he felt a tightening in his chest as he caught sight of the familiar red hair in the distance. The woman who entered was laughing and appeared to be flirting with the young man who had escorted Harry to his table. Harry could see him offer her his arm. Then he observed with amusement as heads turned to watch Molly sweep past the tables toward him. Harry rose stiffly to his feet as they approached and he too found himself marveling at how stunningly attractive his cousin had become.

Her dark red hair was swept up in a Gibson girl style with a few loose tendrils just touching her beautiful face offering contrasts to the intense green of her eyes. Her skin was smooth and creamy and she had remarkably few wrinkles. She had obviously aged very gracefully, and even in her maturity appeared slim and elegant. Her dark green dress was floor length and although simply cut definitely enhanced her feminine allure.

The young man escorted her to Harry's table and it was obvious he was very taken with the charming vision on his arm. Molly smiled graciously at the young man and said, "Thank you, Marcus. You are much too kind." Turning to Harry she extended her hand and said, "Why, Mr. Scarley, how kind of you to join me this evening." She maintained her formal facade until Marcus exited, then moving closer, threw a mock punch at Harry's arm and said, "Hey cuz, how the hell are you?" She didn't wait for an answer but instead gave him an endearing hug and said, "I've missed you a lot and I'm sorry it took me this long to find you."

Harry felt himself becoming overcome with a flood of emotion but gradually managed to stammer out, "I've missed you too, Molly. It's so good to see you." The words seemed to stall in his throat.

They sat down and a strange deja vu feeling descended on Harry. He felt the instant connection between them as if they had not been apart, and he knew an important part of his life that had been missing slid back into place. Molly had the ability to put anyone at ease and he understood why she had been so successful in her work interviewing people.

Taylor appeared again and Molly ordered a glass of Chardonnay. It arrived promptly and as they sipped their drinks they attempted to recapture their past. Molly told Harry about the years she spent studying at and graduating from St. Cloud Teachers' College. "For your information if you remember, that was Dora's idea, not mine. God, could you even imagine me in a classroom teaching anyone's children?" In the same breath she went on to tell how later, she had switched from teaching to journalism while working on her Master's Degree at the University of Minnesota—Duluth. She explained she had been in several of the plays and even considered dropping journalism for theater but then met this really sweet, hunky guy named Mark in her journalism class. She had temporally fallen in infatuation with him. It was he she felt she owed her life as a journalist to. He had encouraged her to pursue a career in journalism because it offered her more options when she got out into the real world. Without catching her breath, she continued that she then found out the really sweet guy was gay, so right after graduation she packed up her belongings along with her bruised ego and moved to St. Paul where she found a job with a newspaper as a temp for a food critic who was out of commission with a case of food poisoning. "Don't laugh, I'm being totally honest. I hated the job but I did get to eat on a regular basis. While I was finishing up with the food gig I was lucky enough to get a part time job as a reporter covering some of the local political scene. One of the rallies I attended was the campaign for Senator Graham Stone, who by the way, is really kind of an asshole but that's really neither here nor there. At the time I had so many stars in my eyes I thought he was Mr. Wonderful. While I was getting all gung ho over politics I met a very nice man by the name of John Gilman who was one of the lawyers on Senator Stone's staff. John is one of the kindest, most honest men I have ever known. He introduced me to all the wonderful people I read about in the newspapers and saw on television. After about a year of going out with him I married him. In retrospect I know I did kind of love him, but I honestly think I loved where he took me more. Not cool, huh? He took care of me not only socially, but in every way I could have ever wanted. He doted on me, cooked for me and treated me like a queen. John wanted children but I didn't because I was having too much fun. He finally settled for a Basset hound named Daisy, which, by the way, I let him keep in the divorce. Like I needed that anchor around my neck. Mind you, I'm not proud of the way I treated John. He really deserved so much better. When he found out I had spent a night with Senator Stone he asked for a divorce. At the same time Senator Stone's staff informed me I was no longer welcome because they were afraid of a scandal with him being a married man. Don't ask me why I did such a dumb thing, I never did anything like that before but I guess I let the life we were living go to my head.

Since John had given me a very generous divorce settlement I had no choice but to move on. Fortunately I was lucky enough to get a call from a friend who was launching a new magazine called Interview. I flew to Colorado for my interview for the position of chief interviewer and I got the job. For the next few years I was able to fly all over the world on someone else's dime and meet and interview all sorts of famous people. I was free as a bird and got to see all the places you and I said we would visit someday. The pay was fantastic and for a long time I felt I was on top of the world. Then one day it started to sink in to me that with all the people who were constantly around me I felt alone. Does that make any sense at all to you?"

Harry nodded, "Yes it does. More than you would ever know."

Molly continued, "I remember I went home for my dad's funeral and Dora and I had a long conversation. She asked me what I was running away from. It caught me off guard as up to that point I believed I was pursuing my dream and not running from anything. Of course I denied it. She also told me she didn't approve of the way I was living my life and of course that went over like a pregnant pole vaulter. What is that Latin phrase? *Damnant quod non intelligent.* They condemn what they do not understand. We had serious words and I flew off in a big fat hissy fit believing my mother was so small townish. Poor Dora. I don't think she ever really understood me. She was so good and kind and I gave her such a bad time. Are you sure you really want to hear all of this?"

"Absolutely! Keep going." But then couldn't resist adding, "Could I stop you anyway?"

Molly grinned, "No, no one could ever stop me. Not back then, and not always even now. Not even you Harry, and you knew me better than anyone." She started to giggle like she used to when they were growing up. "God you were such a pushover in school. Remember the time in second grade when we were all asked to tell a joke and I convinced you to say, what did one mouse say to the other mouse? Come around the corner and I'll show you my hole."

Harry grinned back. "I believe I ended up sitting outside Miss Grunwald's room with my mouth taped shut crying my eyes out."

"In my defense, if you remember, I really didn't consider it a bad joke and of course I did get punished at home when Dora found out about it. I just didn't think you would be naive enough to tell it."

Harry studied the amused look on his cousin's face. "You were always so unconscionably convincing and I was so damn trusting. Go on with your story instead of airing my youthful foibles."

The young waitress brought their menus and both Harry and Molly declined her offer for another drink.

"Let's see. About that time I was given the opportunity to interview a man by the name of Steven Jensen. He was considered to be the finest wildlife photographers like . . . forever. At that time he was working for The National Geographic Society magazine outside of Nairobi. Since I had never seen Africa, I jumped at the chance. In preparation for my interview I found out everything I could about him, which by the way, turned out to be very little. What I did learn was that he was a very private person and usually didn't give interviews to anyone. He was a shy farm boy from Iowa who developed a love for animals while growing up in corn country. Somehow he became this remarkable photographer who it seemed could literally communicate with the animals he photographed, but when it came to humans he was a man of few words. Kind of the old John Wayne stereotype. 'Yep.' 'Nope.' You get the idea. This sounded like a wonderful challenge and being the stubborn person I am, I immediately vowed to bring back the best interview anyone had ever gotten.

I remember when I got off the plane in Nairobi, how I marveled at the beautiful differences in the people and the country. Even though I had traveled extensively, somehow this place seemed special, remote and exciting. From there I took a small bush plane to the campsite where I was to meet this elusive Mr. Steve Jensen. Well, after a very bumpy, white knuckled two passenger airplane ride, the pilot who kept drinking his medicine from this little silver flask, attempted to land us on this half-assed grass airstrip. I found myself praying with all the holiness I could muster until I felt the wheels of the plane hit the ground with a series of bouncing, hard thuds. There was no brass band to meet me, only one extremely tall, very black African man in his native attire who, as far as I could tell, spoke no English. I learned later his name was Kamau and his father was a murogi, or deviner, which meant he had knowledge of medicine and magic. There was a horse to carry my bags and it was obvious he and I would be walking. He motioned for me to follow him, and for the next two hours we walked in the blazing African sun. Occasionally he would stop and say something and point, but since I couldn't understand a word he was saying I just kept nodding in agreement. I have no idea what I was agreeing to but I knew I didn't want to piss off such a big guy especially way out in the middle of nowhere. By the time we got to the campsite I was hot and sweaty but still determined to charm the pants off this Steve guy. I had dressed to catch the eye of the most stoic man. I remember I had this little green tee shirt on that matched my eyes perfectly and accented my hair ever so grandly. I just happened to not be wearing a bra and my white duck pants were a little bit tight. Unfortunately, I now smelled like a brooder pig, my perky little straw hat was limp and no longer perky, and my cute little tennis shoes were covered in a dark coating of clay. After a quick look-see in my mirror I still felt I would have a good impact. After all, they say ninety percent of success is attitude, right?"

Harry grinned, for he couldn't believe how candid she was being. "I believe that's what they say. Go on."

"As we approached the campsite I saw this tall, lanky cowboy working off in the distance. He turned and waved to us and went back to whatever he was doing in the middle of a pen of cattle. I stood there trying to look casually charming but I didn't have a clue as to what I should do next.

The tall, black man who brought me into this inferno said something to me. Of course, I had no idea what he meant and then he called out to the cowboy saying something in what I learned later was Swahili. The cowboy dropped what he was doing and started toward us motioning for me to follow the tall dude. When I got closer to him he opened a gate and I followed him through it. I tried to look sexy while jumping over huge clods of mud and manure. The cowboy, whom I now recognized as Steve Jensen, walked so fast I could hardly keep up. Before I knew it I was standing knee deep in cow shit and mud. My right tennis shoe and white pant leg were now brown up to my knee. I let out this less than lady like howl and Steve came to my rescue. As I tried to pull my foot out of the crap and muck my shoe came off and stayed sucked down in the goo and I fell back and sat down right in the middle of the whole friggen' mess. Steve leaned over me, reached down and pulled my shoe out of the crap and helped me to my feet. All he said was something like now that really sucks. He handed me my shoe and walked away but then turned back and said, you might consider getting yourself some decent clothes and a pair of sensible walking boots. There's snakes all over this place in case you didn't know. When he handed me the shit covered shoe and I looked into those intense blue-gray eyes and saw the twinkle, surrounded by that rugged tan face, I knew I had met my match. In that instant I fell utterly and hopelessly in love. Of course, I was furious with him but I knew this was a man I could totally admire and respect. Later he admitted to me he thought I seemed a bit high on myself, uppity was a word he used, and decided I needed to be brought down a notch or two.

After we were married he admitted that at that moment he knew he was going to marry me too. Oh God, it was so romantic! I still think about that very special time and it takes my breath away."

Harry gave his cousin a dubious look, "You're sure it was romance that took your breath away and not the smell of the cow crap?"

Molly giggled, "I guess you'd had to have been there to appreciate it."

They gave the waitress their orders and in that short time Molly's demeanor appeared to shift to a more serious mood. In the glow of the fireplace Harry thought he could see tears forming in her eyes. As she started to talk her voice quivered and she paused and wiped the tears away with her napkin. Then she took a deep breath and said, "He was the love of my life. I know that now. He was the man I was meant to be with forever, my soul mate. I sent back the best interview any editor could have ever asked for, and along with it my resignation from the magazine. We were married a month later by a missionary priest and I stayed by his side for the next two years. It was the happiest time in my life and now when I reflect back on those times I think deep down I knew it was too good to last. Steve kept telling me I was being silly, that we were destined to be in love and we would grow old together. He teased me saying we would have matching rocking chairs out on our front porch with our grandbabies crawling all over us as we watched the sun setting at the end of day. Eventually, as time went by, I started to believe it and I threw myself into loving him totally and completely. He was a natural teacher and he taught me about animals and people, and most of all how to care for the land he loved so much. Oh, how he loved Africa! He said his soul belonged there and would always remain there. He taught me about photography and even how to cook. Most importantly, he taught me how to love. To him each person was uniquely important, and each day was a new adventure. He believed that everyone's life was a wonderful gift to be enjoyed and savored because it could slip away in the blink of an eye.

All the people he came in contact with seemed to love him, especially the natives and because of their love for him I was accepted without question. He never let any of his crew shoot animals for sport but followed the rule that you take from the land only what you need to exist. To him animals were as sacred as people and therefore to be revered. Steve was not a religious person but he was one of the most spiritual people I have ever known." She paused and took a deep breath. "I remember the day I lost him. Now when I think back it seems like some kind of surreal nightmare and I still find it hard to believe it really happened.

We were to leave the campsite the next morning to fly into Nairobe so he could send some of his photos back to the States. By this time he was freelancing and we really didn't have any set schedule. I hadn't been feeling well and at first thought I had picked up some intestinal bug from the food or the water so I stayed in bed that morning. Actually I had started to suspect I may be pregnant but I felt it was too soon to say anything and thought I would visit a doctor when we got to Nairobe. It rained the night before and the morning was absolutely beautiful so Steve decided to go out one last time. He kissed me goodbye but I was so nauseated I was glad to be able to roll over and go back to sleep for another hour or so.

That was the last time I saw him alive. A short time later I awakened to hear a terrible commotion outside. All the people were crying and wailing. I'd never heard anything like it before. It was the most horrible wailing sound, like people were in terrible agony. As I came outside I was met by Steve's right hand man Geffory Chanclor. He said I must go back inside that something terrible had happened. I knew at that moment, by looking at his face something horrible had happened to Steve. He tried to restrain me but I pulled away from him and went running in the direction of all the wailing. Kamau, the tall man that met me at the airport several years before stood cradling Steve's body in his arms. They were both covered in blood. I ran to Steve to comfort him but he was already dead. I started to scream and I must have fainted. Later they told me he had been photographing a lioness and her two cubs. He'd been working very close to them and reached down to change the lens when a shot rang out from a distance. The lioness was wounded and she reacted by attacking Steve, the closest assumed source of threat. Within a few seconds she had mauled Steve savagely and fatally before Kamau had been able to put a spear through her heart. Steve bled to death by the time they got him back to camp. After seeing him I think I must have been in shock but I remember waking up on the ground and looking at the beautiful African sky not having a clue as to why I was lying there. It was as though time had stopped and I was suspended in some kind of a weird time warp.

Slowly it dawned on me what had happened and as I looked over at Steve's body I thought how peaceful his face looked even though he was drenched with blood. It was as though he had accepted the fact his life had been wiped out in that one unguarded moment. Rolf, our film crew doctor helped me back to my tent and wanted to give me a sedative but I told him I might be pregnant and I would be fine. I lay down on the bed only a few hours earlier I had shared with the man I loved and wept. When I awoke, the sky had turned dark and I knew something else was wrong. I became aware of the fact that the bed under me was wet and sticky. I reached beneath me and when I looked at my fingers they were covered in blood. I knew I was losing the baby we had so desperately wanted. At that instant my whole world crashed and I knew I had lost everything."

Molly's face contorted with pain as she sobbed in little short pants as if she were trying to catch her breath. Then she wiped the tears away that were running down her face. "God, I'm sorry Harry. I didn't mean to lose it right here in the restaurant." She sniffed loudly in a most undignified way and slowly regained her composure.

Harry reached over and took her hand, "It's alright, no one can see you here. Just me and I don't mind. I've seen you cry before." Molly smiled that bittersweet smile he still remembered from some of the times they had comforted each other when they were children.

"The very saddest part for me was I learned later that the two assholes that wounded the lioness were CEO's from New York who came to Africa on Safari hunting for trophies to decorate their office walls. The sonavabitching poachers had the nerve to come onto our campsite and actually stood near my husband's body arguing about who would get the dead lioness for their trophy wall. Imagine, shooting a beautiful animal with a scope from a hundred yards away! What a couple of cowards. I can't tell you how much I hated them! Kamau grabbed the closest jerk by the scruff of his neck and squeezed him until his eyes bugged out and physically dragged him from the campsite. His arrogant hunting buddy about crapped his pants when he saw the rage in Kamau's eyes. Neither of them got the trophy they wounded. When they buried Steve the natives buried the lioness next to him. Kamau said they needed to meet again in the afterlife and become friends. The poor creature was only doing what her instincts told her to do to protect her cubs. Our crew was able to have the cubs placed in an animal sanctuary until they were old enough to go back into the wild."

Taylor brought their salads and Harry could see she had picked up on Molly's sadness and carefully asked, "Is everything alright here?"

Molly looked up at her and said sweetly as she dabbed her eyes with the napkin, "Oh yes, it's just these insufferable allergies. I think I must be allergic to Romeo's after shave." She nodded in Harry's direction.

Harry had the urge to laugh out loud to break the tension of their intense conversation but controlled himself. The waitress looked a little confused as if she knew she was being teased but maintained her dignity and excused herself but not before Molly asked her to please bring them each another drink. Harry thought about declining but changed his mind as the emotional intensity of the conversation left him feeling quite sober. As he looked at Molly he found himself reflecting how unthinkable it was to see the unsinkable Molly Brown in such a vulnerable moment.

Molly picked up her fork and commented. "The salads look wonderful."

Their conversation was interrupted by the soothing strains of chamber music performed by a group of young people dressed in tuxedos and evening gowns. They listened with enjoyment and after a short while Harry said, "Molly, I know this sharing has been very painful for you. I want you to know, I really do care about you. So, if you feel up to it I would like you to continue with your story."

She smiled a sad smile and took a deep breath. "Well let's see. I lost the baby but Rolf was able to stop the bleeding long enough for them to fly me to Nairobi where they did a D and C on me. By the time I came back to the campsite Steven had been buried. Everyone knew the Africa he loved so much was where he would want to spend his eternity. As I stood at his graveside I remember feeling I wanted the ground to open up and swallow me so I could join him. Of course it didn't, so finally I gathered up the few belongings we had and made preparations for my departure. Steven was not a worldly man and lived a simple, genuine existence among the people he loved. I gave his cameras and equipment to his crew and left Africa and its bittersweet memories behind. I've never been back but someday I may return there. At this point, I haven't decided."

She paused thoughtfully as the waitress returned with their drinks. "I came back to Minneapolis to try to get on with my life. Isn't that what everyone tells you to do? But the truth of the matter is I didn't have the slightest idea how one would go about doing that for I was feeling shattered. Finally I went home to visit my mom and my brother but it didn't help. Mom was already getting old and didn't seem to understand me any better than she had before. My brother Daniel was a highway cop working out of Alexandria. In his quiet way he probably helped me the most. He had been a medic in the Viet Nam War and told me it had been his job to gather up the wounded and the dead and their body parts and bag them to be shipped home. I could see how it had changed him. He's really a lovely, sensitive person now. Not like back when we were kids. He spent a lot of time listening to me and letting me cry and basically said time would help to lessen the sting but I would have to find my own inner strength in my own way."

More composed, Molly continued, "I returned to Minneapolis but I still cried a lot. I cried for the man I had loved and lost and for the children we could never have. By this time my friends were all married and having kids and I started to avoid them because I knew I would never have my dream of matching rocking chairs on a front porch where my love and I could watch the sunset. I cried until I thought my eyes would fall out. I lost weight and looked terrible and soon no one wanted me around because I was such a mess. Part of the time I felt guilty because I thought maybe I should have gone with Steve the morning he died, or that maybe God had taken him away from me as a punishment because I had been such a lousy person. The rest of the time I was mad at God for letting this happen to us. I was making myself crazy. I also hated those two assholes who wounded the lioness, and just about anyone or anything else that happened to piss me off."

Molly paused and took a generous swallow of her wine before she continued. "You may find this hard to believe, but it was my ex-husband John who finally came to my rescue. He sat me down and talked some sense into me. After all those years and how badly I had treated him, I could tell he still cared deeply for me. He was able to find me a part-time reporting job and later I did some work on local television where I interviewed Minnesota people that were leading interesting and unusual lives." At that point, Molly rolled her eyes to show her displeasure with that particular job.

"One day I ran into my old boss from Interview magazine and she offered me a full time job similar to what I had been doing before. I was totally grateful and accepted immediately. For the first time since Steven died I felt a spark of life returning into my soul. I was able to keep my apartment here and I flew to New York or London or where ever I needed to go.

Slowly I was able to pull myself out of the depression and actually start to get on with my life. True to my old form, I jumped back into everything with a vengeance. Looking back now I realized my depression had been replaced with a slow simmering rage. Underneath my smiles and brave talk was a real full-fledged pissed off kind of Molly Brown mad. I'm sure you remember as a kid, when I would rush into a situation with both fists flying, red faced and totally out of control. I was out of control but no one could have told me that. That is, not if they were smart and wanted to live to talk about it. I saw my friends having fun and being happy and I felt cheated out of the life I knew I deserved. For quite a while I had been mixing antidepressants with alcohol and it did terrible things to my head. I started to let myself believe that I was entitled to my own happiness and it didn't matter how I got it or who got hurt in the process. I used people to get what I wanted without a second thought, and I wanted everything.

I know now that I had become a full-fledged prick. Not a pretty thing for a lady to acknowledge about herself is it?"

Molly looked deeply into Harry's face and said, "You look shocked. I'll bet you never thought you would hear me say that about myself did you?"

"No, Molly, I honestly didn't, but don't you think you're being a bit too hard on yourself?"

She was quiet but finally broke the silence, "Let me continue and you can decide for yourself. Somewhere down the road I became reacquainted with Senator Stone. To me every man at that time was fair game and whether he was married or not was immaterial. We quickly rekindled the flame that existed in my mind at least, and our affair took off. He can be a very charming man when he wants to be and he knows how to make a lady feel very special. I needed to feel special at that time and I was eager to show the world just how wonderful I really was. One day I received a dozen red roses with a note asking me to meet for a discreet dinner. The note was signed G. Stone, which was, by the way, the way he signed most of his correspondence so I didn't give it another thought. Naturally, I was ecstatic. Somehow, in my over medicated mind I thought this would be the night he was going to tell me he was finally leaving his wife and wanted to marry me. I dressed up so fine and left my apartment on top of the world because I was out to get me the happiness I so deserved. I sat in the dimly lit restaurant sipping my drink thinking how I would react when he asked the big question. I wanted it to be perfect. Not too surprised but yet confident that I had known all along he would ask me to marry him. Talk about a schmuck! I heard someone call my name and thinking it was the waitress with a message saying Graham might be late, I looked up. There was a young girl standing in front of me, who looked about sixteen. I couldn't help but notice how her face was very white and tight looking. She spoke in a controlled voice as she said, "Sarah Brown, I'm G. Stone, as in Gloria Stone. I know you were expecting my father but you were mistaken. If you want to screw up your own life whoring around that's your business, but stay the hell out of my family's life. I'm sorry I can't stay for dinner but I'm not into slumming." At that point she picked up my drink and threw it squarely in my face. Then, at that very precise moment, a photographer snapped our picture. He captured the moment perfectly, the glass still in her hand and the drink running down my face. Later I would see the photo and the pained look of startled surprise on my face was nothing short of incredible. The great, sophisticated Sara Brown had been set up and snookered by a sixteen-year old girl. I had taken the bait and fallen into her trap like a freshman in high school.

I spent the rest of the night drinking and nursing my wounded pride. Sometime after midnight I went to my ex-husband's home. Even though he was now remarried I still had a key to his townhouse so I let myself in and got him and his wife out of bed. I needed someone to feel sorry for me, and who better than John, my ever so compassionate, long suffering ex-husband. I tried to tell them what had happened making myself appear as if I had been the innocent victim but I was so drunk I passed out on their living room sofa. The next thing I knew I awoke with Daisy the Basset hound licking my face. It turned out she was the only one who was happy to see me. When I opened my eyes, Helen, John's new wife was standing over me with a cup of coffee and let me tell you she was not a happy camper. She informed me it was ten o'clock in the morning, that I should drink the coffee and then get my self-serving ass off her couch and out of her house."

Molly rolled her eyes again and then her voice took on a dramatically sarcastic tone. "Well! I was so pissed off that she had the nerve to treat me that way I proceeded to give her a piece of my mind telling her she had not a clue of what my life was like. I also told her she was a spoiled bitch and had no right to yell at me.

Now looking back and reflecting on the condition of my mind at the time I realize giving her a piece of it could have been a very dangerous thing to do, but what the hell, I did it anyway. After I told her off I grabbed my coat and attempted to make the most dramatic exit I could but not before I shot back with, we'll see what John has to say about your despicable behavior! I was so hung over I almost fell on my face. I remember as I put my hand on the doorknob Helen said my name in a very quiet voice. I thought, ah ha!"

Molly was getting very animated at this point and Harry had all he could do not to laugh.

"The little bitch is really scared now. I turned back expecting to see her groveling at my feet but all she said was, the key please, and she held out her hand. I reached into my purse, threw the key in her face and slammed the door behind me. John's office was only a few miles from their house and as I drove there I angrily rehearsed my lines. I knew that by the time I got there Helen would have called John to warn him and I wanted to be ready. John was now in private practice and he was waiting for me by the front door. Since he knew my temper he had anticipated a gigantic scene and the office had been cleared of everyone. I mean everyone. Not even his receptionist was there. He ushered me in and shut the door. I started to cry copious tears and I put on a performance worthy of an Oscar. He listened patiently to my sad tale of woe and indignation and handed me tissues to blow my nose and to wipe the snot and mascara off my face. When I finally finished he took me into the small half bath off his office and pointing me at the mirror said in a very kind voice, Molly I want you to take a good look at yourself.

I tried to get away because at this point I really looked like hell, but he held me tightly by the shoulders and made me look into the mirror again. He asked me to take a really good look at myself and tell him if I like the person looking back at me. He added that he stood a hundred percent behind what Helen had said, and that I needed to regain control of myself."

Molly set her wine glass down as she continued. "I couldn't believe what I was hearing and I angrily pulled away from him and tried to leave his office but he stopped me and made me sit down. He continued to talk to me and told me the world and the people in it were not there for my amusement or my convenience. He said if he had been more of a man when we were married and put me in my place he might have saved me from some of the pain I had to go through, but because he was afraid of losing me he had let me continue in my selfish ways.

Oh, Harry, it hurt so bad to hear him say that. I guess so often I believed because someone didn't speak up whatever I was doing must have been all right. I was so wrong wasn't I?" She didn't wait for him to answer and continued. "I think it was like that when we were growing up wasn't it? You didn't always agree with me but you let me have my way because it was easier and I suppose you loved me too, in your own way and didn't want to hurt me or have me stop being your friend."

Harry didn't answer as at that moment the waitress brought their food and inquired if they wished anything else. They thanked her and assured her everything was fine.

Molly picked up her fork and took a bite of salmon but Harry knew she wasn't really aware of what she had placed in her mouth.

"John, reminded me of the story of Dorien Grey. Do you remember when we read that in Mr. Paulson's English class? It was by Oscar Wilde.

It was about a young man who had eternal beauty and youth but how the painting of him he kept hidden away showed the man he had become, all ugly and awful. John asked me how I thought my portrait would look if I kept on using and hurting people the way I was doing. It was killing me to listen to what I knew to be the truth. Finally, John gave me a gentle, comforting hug and reassured me I was a very special person. He told me that everything he said he felt he had to because he cared so much about me. He even offered to drive me home so I could sober up. I don't really remember how I got back to my apartment, between the crying and the hangover I'm lucky I didn't wrap myself around a tree or kill someone else. When I got home I pulled the drapes and sat in the dark and I cried again like I had when Steven died. I thought no one could cry that hard without their heart literally breaking apart. My soul was in sheer agony and I finally cried myself to sleep. When I awoke later I found a manila envelope had been slipped under my door with the picture of me with the drink running down my face. You couldn't see who had thrown the drink, only the back of her, but the note made it very clear it would be given to a tabloid if I didn't leave Graham alone. My first impulse was to tear up the photograph but then I hesitated. I studied it for a short while in disbelief, and finally decided to put it up on my fireplace mantel where I could see it as I sat in a nearby chair.

I remembered the sadness and anger in the young girl's face as she confronted me in the restaurant, and I realized even though she was still a child she had the courage to stand up to life and face it, not running and hiding like I had been doing. For the first time I appreciated Dora's wisdom when she asked me what I was running from. I was running from life and I was running from God. It was me who hadn't understood, not her. I began to cry again and for the first time in years I got down on my knees and prayed. It had been many years but I remember I said something like, please God help me to find my way, I am so screwed up." Molly made a face and then said, "Except, I don't think I said screwed up. I may have said something that was a little less reverent like the F word. But you do understand I was in a highly emotional state and speaking from my heart. I said, God I want to change but I'm going to need your help. I don't know where to go from here. Well, God didn't speak to me and in my stupor I must have fallen asleep again while I was waiting for my divine message. How long I spent in this position I don't know for sure but when I awoke to the sound of the phone, I was still kneeling but sort of draped across the footstool. When I tried to get up I realized my legs were asleep and I barely made it to the phone before my brother's wife Lee was about to hang up.

She told me Dora had fallen and broken her hip and they were doing surgery in the morning. She also said she knew how busy I was and they didn't expect me to come home but would keep me posted on how mom, that's what Lee called her, came through the surgery. Now this is the part you probably won't believe. After hearing Lee's message it took me about five seconds to decide what to do with my life. I told her I would be there the following afternoon and hung up the phone. Call it a synchronous fluke or a miracle but I had no doubt that God had given me the answer to my prayer. I threw all the things I needed into one suitcase and called the gal who did my housekeeping and asked her to hire someone to pack all my belongings and get them ready to be moved to Glenwood. I told her I would call her with my new address as soon as I found a place. The apartment I was living in at the time was furnished so it made my decision much easier. I called my boss and asked for a leave of absence telling her only it was a family emergency. I gave notice to my landlord and the next morning I took off and didn't look back. End of story."

Molly grinned and then attacked her meal with gusto. "This is the best food I've eaten in a long time, don't you agree?

Harry sat looking at Molly with an incredulous expression on his face. "You are living in Glenwood?"

"Yes."

"Little, quiet Glenwood, Minnesota?"

"Yes, what's so surprising about that?"

"Nothing!" Then Harry started to laugh. "Or, I should say everything."

"I like it. It's a wonderful town. I'm happy there. So deal with it."

"No need to get defensive about it, but after the story you just told me I find it hard to see you settling down to a quiet life of knitting and fishing for your supper in beautiful Lake Minnewaska."

"I know, it sounds a little weird doesn't it. I think I needed to rediscover my roots. Anyway, I don't knit. I tried it but it just doesn't seem to work for me. I'm dexterously challenged when it comes to crafty things. I write children's books. That's why I'm here in Minneapolis, to see my publisher."

Harry's face continued to express his amazement and disbelief. Sensing this, Molly said, "So, now you know all about me, tell me about you."

"I'm afraid my life is quite pale compared to yours."

"So bore me. I still want to hear about it."

Slowly Harry filled her in about how he had finished college and gone to work for the Sindler Company. When he came to the part about his accident and all the troubles that incident had brought into his life he decided to downplay it and move quickly around the topic.

"Wait! Tell me about this accident. Did you have a major accident like a serious car crash or did you just trip over your shoe laces because you weren't paying attention?"

Harry knew he should've known better than to try to get something past Molly. "I fell down a staircase, a big, long staircase."

"What? Were you drunk or just clumsy?" She stared at him, her eyes in little, squinty slits.

Harry could feel himself becoming exasperated with Molly's questions. "I got hit by a rocket."

"Give me a break, a rocket? Like I'm going to believe that."

"Actually, I was with a girl in my apartment when her drunken, jealous lover showed up and broke down my door and threw me down this very long, steep staircase and broke just about everything in my body that was breakable. Is that better?'

"Now, that's more like it. I knew there must have been more to your life than you were telling me. So, then you spent a long time in the hospital and . . . ."

Harry filled her in on the details of the rest of his life including the awful time he had spent living close to poverty after the accident and right up to his present life with Annie.

"So, no kids either. How about a cat or a dog?"

"Two cats actually, Thomas and Bentley. Annie already had them when I met her. I had a cat named Sasha. I found her when she was a kitten eating out of garbage cans. When I married Annie, Sasha had already died. Before I started working at Sullivan glass I lived in a dinky little efficiency apartment with a cracked sky light that dripped water every time it rained. Later as I started to get back on my feet, I was able to move into a bigger apartment. After we were married we chose to live in Annie's home. It's small but big enough for the two of us. We thought if we ever had kids we'd find a bigger house but since we haven't had any we've just stayed there."

The waitress cleared the dishes and both declined dessert. They ordered hot tea and finally Harry asked, "Is your mom still alive?"

"I'm sorry, I thought you knew. She passed away about five years ago. I guess you didn't get the letter I sent telling you about her funeral."

"No, I didn't. I moved a few times so I guess it never got forwarded."

"After my dad died, mom kept her house on North Lake Shore Drive but when it got too much for her she sold it. My brother built a new home between Glenwood and Starbuck and added a small efficiency apartment in the lower level. He and his wife Lee are such thoughtful people and they anticipated the day when mom wouldn't be able to live alone. She was living there when she broke her hip. After she got out of the hospital we placed her in the Starbuck nursing home. They call it the Minnewaska Lutheran Home and she lived there for several years before she died. I was able to visit her almost every day. I wouldn't have given that time up for anything, and, as it turned out, it was a much needed healing time for me. Dora, or mom, I should say, called Lee her daughter and she insisted I was your mother Mariah. I tried to tell her I was her daughter Sara but she would just smile and say no, you are Mariah. Sara is gone. It hurt at first but I got used to it. I asked her about you and she would always say you were away at school. Toward the end she was very confused but there were little windows of time when she would be lucid. During those times she would say something that made sense and I knew my mother was still there with all her memories tucked away inside her."

Molly went on to tell Harry about her move and how she had happened to run into the real estate lady who sold her the house she was living in. It was a medium size, three bedroom cottage out along the south shore of Lake Minnewaska. She explained it had been built as a summer residence for a wealthy family from Minneapolis that came to Glenwood to spend their summers, but after their only child left home, they decided to sell the house and do more traveling.

"Pat, the real estate lady had just received the call to have the home listed on the market as I walked into her office looking for lakeshore property. After I heard the description of the house I almost bought it sight unseen. Then remembering my experiences with my previous impulsive nature I reconsidered and made an appointment for later that day. It only took a few minutes into the tour to make up my mind it was perfect. I can't tell you how peaceful it is there. Sometimes in the morning I go out early and sit on my neighbor's dock as the sun is coming up. I see the mist rising off the water and watch the graceful gulls calling out and gliding overhead and think how much Steve would have loved it. The mornings are so serene and from time to time I feel I have recaptured the happy, contented feeling I had when I was with him. Even though I'm alone now I don't feel the terrible loneliness I was plagued with when I was living in St Paul. This may sound strange, but I almost feel like Steven is still with me and this helps me to know I belong there."

Harry inquired if she saw many of the people they graduated from high school with and she replied that occasionally she did. As Harry expected only a few had stayed in Glenwood after high school or came back after college.

"I did meet a girl we were in high school with quite by accident when I was still working for Interview magazine. Do you remember Rhonda Wesley?"

Harry shifted a little uncomfortably in his seat, "I think so. Didn't she move at the beginning of our senior year?"

"Yes, she was pregnant and apparently all the rumors about her were true. She moved to St Paul to live with her aunt and to have her baby. You're probably not going to believe this but she is now Rhonda Resser."

"Uh, not wanting to appear dumb but is that supposed to mean something to me?"

"Thee Rhonda Resser!" She accented the "thee".

Harry found himself perplexed wondering why women would say thee instead of just the when they wanted to emphasize a point. "Thee Rhonda Resser." He repeated the words as if trying to get them to make more sense.

"As in the former Supreme Court Honorable Judge John Resser. She is his wife."

"Oh, him. Yes, I've heard of Judge Resser. I thought he retired because of his age. She must be a whole lot younger than he is."

"That's true, he is a lot older. She's also a lawyer and does a lot of work defending women who are without funds but need legal representation. Back when I did the interview with them he was newly appointed to the Supreme Court. All the reporters were trying to get an interview but for privacy reasons she and the judge kept declining. Imagine my surprise when I took a really good look at her picture in the paper and realized she was our Rhonda Wesely. I called her up and after she remembered who I was she agreed to have me interview them. She said I was always nice to her back in school and she admired my spunk. Who would have thunk? Back then she was shy but clearly one of the most intelligent girls in our class. Now she's an absolute knockout. She asked me about you saying that you were so kind to her the morning you found her in the janitor's closet down by the band room puking her guts out because she was two months pregnant. It was right after that she left town and went to live with her aunt. She has a daughter, Cassie.

Her aunt worked part time for John Resser and after Cassie got a little older he helped Rhonda get into the University of Minnesota and later law school. She said that the Judge and his wife adored Cassie and Mrs. Resser often took care of her while Rhonda attended her law classes. I don't know how many people knew it but Cassie was Gary Stanton's baby. When Judge Resser's wife died of cancer Rhonda had just finished law school and she came back to work in John's law firm. About a year later she realized she had fallen in love with John but because of their significant age difference decided to leave the firm. One thing led to another and John proposed to her and they were married that same year. As time passed most people assumed Cassie was John's daughter because he and his former wife had almost raised her throughout the time Rhonda was in law school.

After he and Rhonda were married they felt there really was no reason to correct that misconception. When he was nominated to the Supreme Court, they realized their lives were no longer private and that's the reason they agreed to let me do the interview. They felt it was better to publicly acknowledge that Cassie was Rhonda's daughter from a previous relationship than have it come out in a tabloid. Rhonda felt she could trust my integrity to handle it appropriately and after the interview was published she called to tell me she and her husband were very pleased. I remember I asked her off the record if she ever saw Gary after high school and she said he visited her while she was still in college. He told her how unhappy he was in his marriage and he wished he could change that part of his life. She said as he sat there telling her about his life she saw him so differently than back in high school. Instead of being strong and confident he seemed weak and needy. She said she avoided telling him anything about Cassie because she was afraid he might continue to come around and she knew she didn't want him in her or her daughter's life. Shortly after she learned that Gary had been killed in a car accident and the rumor was it may not have been an accident but a suicide. Rhonda told me she had no regrets about her life. She didn't regret her relationship with Gary after all, he had given her a beautiful daughter and for that she and John were grateful. She reflected on when she'd seen him that last time she realized he was more of a high school infatuation than a true love. Back in high school she was trying to escape from an unhappy home life and no one could have talked her out of being with Gary. She said she had wanted him more than she had ever wanted anything in her life."

Harry looked up at Molly as if he was hearing something he couldn't quite believe. "Rhonda really said that? That no one could have stopped her from being with Gary?"

"That's what she said. Go figure. I always thought he was extremely conceited, and not particularly smart, but what did I know?"

Molly didn't notice the change in Harry's demeanor and continued with her conversation, "Did you know the old high school we went to is no longer a school but has recently been made into townhouses? They consolidated all the little schools in the area into one large school between Glenwood and Starbuck. One of my friends works there in the office and one day on a whim I asked her if she would look up my IQ from back when we were in high school. Of course I couldn't help but ask her to check yours as well. You're probably not going to believe this but yours was a teeny bit higher than mine."

"Really? A teeny bit higher than yours you say. That really does surprise me because the day I looked them up I distinctly remember that mine was quite a bit higher than yours." Harry grinned as Molly's mouth dropped open.

Molly peered at Harry intently with her eyes narrowed into little slits as she had done earlier in the evening. She was feeling flustered as Harry dared to question her authority. "So, Mr. wise guy, when did you look them up?" Her voice had a slightly sinister tone to it.

Harry's voice took on a casual air and he knew he was going to enjoy this part of the conversation. "Oh, I knew that already back in high school."

"Get out of here! How could you have known that back then and not used it against me?"

"Do you remember Mazie Blake?"

"Yeah, wasn't she that kooky girl who dyed her hair green and would walk down the halls singing the Hamm's Beer song in falsetto? I think she's the one who gave me a copy of The Catcher in the Rye and then when I almost got caught with it she stuck it down her underwear."

"Yes, that Mazie Blake and she didn't dye her hair green. She dyed it black and it just turned green when her mother made her wash it out. Anyway, to get back to the topic at hand, her mother worked in the main office and one day when I stopped there she was waiting for her mom to finish with a meeting. The office was deserted and when I asked what she was doing she said she was looking up everyone's IQ score and did I want to know what mine was? I said sure, and of course I couldn't help but ask her to look up yours too." He found a strange sense of satisfaction in parroting Molly's words. "You can imagine my surprise when I realized that academically I was smarter than you. By the way, Mazie was a little weird but she was number two in our class and do you know who was number one? Clayton the clod."

"That's what my friend told me. Not only did he have the highest IQ of anyone who graduated from Glenwood High School, he's like a damn genius, and probably one of the smartest people in the whole world. I still can't believe how badly we treated him back then."

"I also know Mazie is doing research work in the field of genetics. I bumped into her one day a few years ago and she's still quite eccentric but very interesting to talk to. Heck, who knows, she may be one of the people who is responsible for changing the future of mankind. Kind of hard to believe isn't it?

Molly was still pondering the fact that Harry hadn't told her in high school he was smarter than her. "All those years and all the crap I gave you with my superior attitude because I honestly thought I was so much smarter than you and you never told me differently. I can't believe it."

"I may have tested out smarter than you, but let's face it, you were much more street wise than me."

Molly smiled and said, "In so many ways you remind me of my husband, Steve. You are so kind and trusting and always wanting to believe the best about people. Steve was willing to forgive anyone for anything. He said life was much too short to be wasted on holding grudges. He would let me go on about something I thought I knew more about than anyone else and then later I would find out he was just waiting for me to screw up. He called it letting me cook in my own soup. It was his homespun way of saying no matter who we are, life has its way of teaching us the principles of natural consequences. Of course, you remember how well

I took directions or advice from anyone. Since I was young, my attitude has always been, been there, done that, and probably done it better than anyone else in the world."

"Oh, really Molly?" There was a hint of sarcasm in Harry's voice, "I can't say I ever noticed that about you."

Molly ignored Harry's remark and continued, "I remember one time when I had been living in Africa less than a year and I started thinking I was the chief resident authority on almost everything. After all, I had charmed the pants off, and was sleeping with the big boss. I started telling everyone including Steve, how I thought things should be done. As I mentioned, his right hand assistant was Geffory Chanclor and after awhile I know he'd had just about all of me he could take, but was too much of a gentleman to complain to Steve or say anything to me.

I remember on one occasion we were given the opportunity to meet some of Africa's elites. There were several chieftains and other governmental dignitaries and I got it into my head that I was going to make a lasting impression on the guests. Trust me, I did. I especially wanted to make my husband Steve proud of me. Without telling him I convinced Geffory to teach me a Swahili phrase, something like, I admire you and I am grateful to meet you. He suggested it could be, I speak your praise and my heart is full, because Swahili phrases are different when expressed from the English translation but that the meaning would be there. He taught me a phrase all right, which I practiced diligently until I had it down perfectly. When I stepped forward and uttered those memorable words everyone including my husband came unglued. No one would tell me exactly what I'd said but as close as I could figure out it was something like, I am happy my mouth is as big as my ass is wide. I have never been so humiliated in my whole life and I was furious with Geffory. I raged around and told Steve I expected him to fire him and I remember he just stood there looking at me and finally said, I guess you just stepped into the shit again and don't that suck! Molly, it's time you learn that what you put out into the universe will eventually come back to you. Maybe it's you that owes Geffory an apology for the way you've been treating him. He turned and walked away from me. It was a lesson I thought I would never forget but I guess after Steve died I must have. Some of us are destined to learn the same lessons over and over again until we get it right."

Molly checked her watch and said, "Do you realize how long we've been sitting here? I should be getting some sleep. I was up most of the night trying to finish a new story. That along with the wine, I can hardly keep my eyes open. How about if I call you tomorrow? I would really like to meet your Annie before I go back home."

Harry agreed and after giving each other hugs he left the hotel. All the way home he replayed the conversations of the evening. Primarily he remembered Molly's words that Rhonda Wesely had told her no one could have kept her from being with Gary Stanton. Molly didn't realize it but she had inadvertently lifted a weight from his heart he had carried within himself since high school. He remembered a hot July night in 1960 when he had gone for a walk along the lakeshore. It was the summer before their senior year. He and Molly had gotten into an argument and he left the house so he could be alone and have a smoke. For over an hour he'd sat in the dark behind the Lakeside Ballroom listening to the rhythmic sound of the waves hit the lakeshore. He had been thinking about his life and what he would be doing after high school. At some point he became aware he was not alone when he heard laughing and talking down by the shore and off to the side behind some tall bushes. Soon he could make out the silhouettes of two people holding each other very closely. To this day he didn't know why he sat there listening to them. At first he felt it was just idle curiosity but soon realized they weren't aware they were not alone. By that time their embraces had progressed to more than kissing as they were now lying on a blanket. He heard the girl say something like, "No! Don't! Stop it. No, Gary, please stop." The guy countered with "Come on Ronnie, I can't wait anymore!"

He then heard what he concluded to be a struggle and without looking back he bolted into the darkness. All night long he had lain awake wondering if he should have gone to Rhonda Wesely's aid. He had heard about rape but he didn't technically know when an encounter between a man and a woman would be classified as consensual or when it became rape. On the one hand he'd heard her offer what sounded like resistance and he had distinctly remember her saying no but on the other hand Gary Stanton was a tackle on the football team and outweighed him considerably. He vacillated back and forth struggling with his thoughts. Rhonda was laughing and appeared to want to be with him but she'd also said no. The rest of the summer Harry carried a heavy burden of guilt and even Molly had commented on how moody he had become. Dora had taken him to the clinic for a physical because she had noticed a change in his disposition but the doctor had declared him healthy and said maybe he was just apprehensive about his senior year. His guilt became heavier the morning he had accidentally discovered Rhonda puking in the janitor's closet and heard rumors of her pregnancy. Tonight he finally heard those magic words, that no one, not anyone in the world could have stopped her. She had wanted Gary that night after all. There would never be that doubt in his mind again. He smiled to himself and reflected with fascination on human nature.

The following day Harry felt better than he had for a very long time. Annie concluded his visit with Molly had done him a world of good and he heartily agreed. Molly stopped at the office and all of them, including Janet and David, went out for a long lunch. Molly and Annie liked each other immediately and before she left, Molly pulled Harry aside and asked how David had been able to remain single as she thought he was absolutely divine.

Chapter 9

The Friday following Molly's visit, Harry finished all his imperative work by four o'clock and reached for the stack of mail Janet had brought in earlier that morning. He quickly glanced through the pile making sure none of it needed to be attended to immediately. He then opened a newspaper lying next to the stack. He smiled as he realized it was the Pope County Tribune and knew it was Molly's way of reacquainting him with Glenwood. He spent the next hour reading and re-reading the entire paper and was amazed at how most of the names that were mentioned were totally unfamiliar. At five o'clock he cleared his desk and put on his coat. It was only then he realized how quiet the office had become. As he opened his door he could see Janet still at her desk talking on the phone and he sensed from the tone of her voice and the way she was laughing it must be a personal call. A few days earlier Annie had confided to Harry that Janet finally had met someone very special about a month earlier and this accounted for her newly found happiness. The special someone was a widower who just happened to be the new veterinarian to whom she had taken one of her lovebirds to have its beak trimmed.

Harry didn't know much about Janet's personal life as she almost never spoke about it. Annie told him before coming to work at Sullivan Glass Janet had been married to an abusive husband and it had almost resulted in the loss of her life. He remembered on the one occasion she had talked about her past she'd said she owed everything she had to David and Annie but hadn't elaborated.

As Harry entered the reception area he heard Janet cheerfully say "I love you too. I'll see you tomorrow" and then hung up the phone. When she looked up and saw Harry standing across the room she reacted with a blush, quickly looking down and reaching for a stack of papers on her desk.

As Harry walked toward Annie's office, Janet said, "Oh, I'm sorry, I guess I forgot to tell you, Annie's not here. She left around three o'clock after she got a phone call from Doctor Mandel. She said to tell you she would see you tonight at dinner. I hope you weren't waiting for her."

"No, I was catching up on some work before the weekend."

As if anticipating Harry's next question, Janet continued, "She took a cab. I think maybe there was some kind of a situation with one of the children she's been working with but I don't know that for a fact."

"That makes sense. Annie cares about those kids as if they were her own. I wish we could have had a child, but since we can't I guess this is the next best thing. Thanks, Janet, I hope you'll have a very nice weekend."

"Thank you. I'll be ready to leave in ten minutes or so. I have a few more copies to do. I guess I got a little side tracked. I'll see you on Monday."

As Harry walked toward the elevator he thought about the volunteer work Annie was doing. Diane Mandel was the pediatrician who recruited Annie to work in her free clinic with the younger children that were exhibiting behavioral problems. It was her attempt to nip these antisocial problems in the bud before they became too serious. Diane felt if she could prevent the children from having to be medicated at an early age to control their destructive behavior, she might be able to keep them from ending up in the court system later on. She was one of the few medical doctors who was willing to try an unorthodox approach such as utilizing someone like Annie to reach these children, rather than the common practice of writing a prescription and hoping for the best.

Harry rode the elevator up to the third floor and left a packet of papers in one of the lawyer's offices that was doing some work for their company. As he was about to step back into the elevator he realized the two men occupying it were having a heated discussion. His first impulse was to step back and wait for the next elevator but the older of the two held the door open for Harry and said, "It's alright, you can come in. I think we are finished with our discussion." The younger man continued scowling but stepped back to make room for Harry. Everyone was very quiet as they stood staring at the closing elevator door. The younger man suddenly moved closer to the older man and said in an angry but quiet and controlled voice, "How could you let him get away with that? He took the account right out from under our noses and you never said a word. I think you need to get yourself a new set of balls."

The older man glared at him and hissed back, "Quiet! This is neither the time nor the place!" The ride down continued in dead silence but Harry could feel the tension in the air. As he stepped off the elevator he could hear the younger man continue to berate the older man.

Harry got into his car and as he pulled into the heavy Friday evening traffic realized it could be a long, slow trip home. His mind went back to the younger man's words, "I think you need to get yourself a new set of balls." The attack was clearly on the older man's manhood when all he probably meant to say was he should have stood up for his principles.

Harry had a hard time understanding people who found it necessary to verbally chastise someone in the presence of others. To not only express their opinion so publicly, but also feel the need to try to slander or destroy someone else's self image. At that moment Harry recalled an incident that happened when he was about eight or nine years old and living with his Aunt Dora and Uncle Stan in Lowry. He could almost hear the sound of the taunting of some of the boys that hung around the small downtown area. The person usually singled out to persecute was Andy Janak. The taunt was to the tune of Jingle Bells. "Dinky balls, dinky balls. He wears overalls. Some are big, and some are small and some don't fit at all." It was, unfortunately, a too common occurrence and looked upon by most of the adults in town as harmless, boys being boys.

Harry and Molly had gone to Dahl's Cafe, the only restaurant in Lowry to buy some candy and Sen Sen. Outside, two older boys, maybe ten or eleven, were leaning against the cafe eating ice cream cones. Harry never forgot their names and they were forever etched into his psyche. Donny Doopala and Larry Tennent. He too had often been the target of their harassment. The boys were town kids, which meant they didn't have to help on the family farm doing chores or working in the fields the way the country kids had to. Donny Doopala noticed Molly and Harry first and said something rude like, "Well, if it isn't Red and the gimp out for a walk, or should I say a limp?"

Donny was fat, spoiled and homely. He was known to have a mean streak and none of the other kids liked him. Larry was a not so smart follower, and didn't have any friends either so they found each other to be acceptable company. Donny's dad owned a local construction company and everyone thought they were rich mainly because they lived in a big new house. That alone commanded some respect or at least tolerance by the other kids for Donny. Molly stopped and put on the haughtiest smile she could muster and replied in an equally snotty voice, "Why, if it isn't Dummy Poopalot and his sneaky shadow Larry the snitch." Molly could say things like that to Donny and get away with it because he and Larry had tangled with her older brother Daniel when they had tried to intimidate her before.

Donny sneered back and countered with an equally snotty comment about the Grand Canyon being only slightly smaller than Molly's mouth. Molly then made a gesture with her hand as if she was dismissing them and said, "Why don't you and your ugly ape friend go back to the zoo you escaped from." Sparring verbally was a commonly accepted form of entertainment among many of the children. Fist fighting was not.

It was at that point Harry noticed someone standing around the corner in the shadows watching and listening. The person was Andy Janak and he was known and accepted by everyone in Lowry as being simple. He was pale and sickly looking and probably in his late twenties but everyone called him a boy. He seldom talked but when he did he held his head down so you couldn't see his face and spoke in an almost inaudible voice. His shoulders were rounded and his tall, thin frame looked as if it shouldn't be able to support his body. He always wore a flannel shirt and a pair of overalls that were too big and too long.

As Andy stood watching the bantering between Molly and Donny, Harry could see a slight grin forming on Andy's face as if he was enjoying what was taking place. Andy liked Molly and Harry because they were kind to him whereas Donny was a bully of the worst kind.

Donny spotted Andy and angrily commanded, "Wipe that grin off your retarded face dinky balls or I'll do it for you!"

Andy drew back into the shadows but not before he became even more pale than usual. Donny began chanting his dinky balls taunt but Molly interrupted him by pointing at his feet and saying, "Donny, oh my gosh, there's a dollar!" Donny greedily looked down where Molly was pointing as her hand swiftly came up under his double-dip ice cream cone and shoved it up into his nose. Molly let out a triumphant whoop, and said, "Speaking of retards, they should call you dinky brain!"

Harry chuckled as he and Molly ducked into the safety of Dahl's Cafe leaving a very angry Donny outside the window wiping the ice cream off his face with his shirtsleeve.

"He's such an asshole," Molly whispered with great authority as she selected her ten cents worth of penny candy and a small, white packet of

Sen Sen, "That should teach him not to pick on Andy." She smiled sweetly as she thanked Mrs. Dahl and carefully laid her money on the counter.

They sat down in a booth and Molly started chomping on her candy. She favored the chocolate mints and Harry, the black licorice.

Donny and Larry glared through the window planning their revenge. Molly looked up and gave them an even snottier smile than before. She held up her second finger and pointed it at her enemies outside. Carefully she drew a circle in the air and then poked her finger through the imaginary circle. With her finger still pointing at them she slowly turned her hand around so her palm was now facing her and then substituted her middle finger for her second one.

Harry was shocked she would do that and he grabbed her hand. He whispered, "Are you nuts? If Mrs. Dahl or your mom ever saw you do that you'd be one dead duck!" Molly sighed and said, "Oh, Harry, you worry way too much" as she quickly glanced around to see if anyone had been watching.

Harry's attention came back to the slow moving traffic as a small red sports car suddenly cut in front of him attempting to squeeze into an almost non-existent space ahead. He braked slightly and a young woman waved a thank you for letting her into his lane.

His thoughts returned to Dahl's Cafe and he found himself thinking that Molly had the equivalent to balls even back then. What was it his Jewish friends called it? Chutzba? Andy Janek came into this world ill equipped to deal with the harshness it had shown him. Harry felt a feeling of empathy and sadness descend upon him as his thoughts refocused on the life of this gentle young man he never really got to know. To call someone dinky balls was a sad commentary on human sensitivity even if they were only kids. He wondered why no adult had ever stepped in and made them stop.

Andy was a fragile soul who lived with his mother in a small, single story house next to the schoolyard. His father had been a farmer until one autumn several years earlier he suffered a heart attack while out in his alfalfa field. His wife found him later that evening when he failed to return home.

Andy's mother's name was Frances. She was a short, round, Czech woman who, in spite of enduring the tragedy of losing her husband, and raising her young, simple son alone, still seemed to be smiling all the time. She was considered to be one of the best cooks in the Reno area and was unquestionably the finest kolaches and bread baker in all of Pope County. After Frances buried her husband she and Andy moved to the small house near the school in Lowry. Frances sold her farm to a wealthy farmer named Garrett Van Damm whose land adjoined hers. In the arrangement, Frances became the cook and housekeeper for his wife Cora.

Cora Von Damm was kind to Frances and often boasted while shopping at McIver's store that God surely smiled on her family when he sent Frances to work for them. Andy attended Lowry school until he became too tall for the desks, in each case being promoted to a higher grade out of the kindness of the teacher's heart as he did not seem to comprehend his schoolwork and rarely spoke even when called upon.

One day when Andy failed to show up for school no one questioned it but rather accepted his absence as inevitable. He was never able to hold a job and people sometimes seemed suspicious of him. Harry never understood why, but evidently being different was enough to cause people to react negatively to him. Instead of attending school Andy and his small dog roamed the wooded hills on the outskirts of town never bothering anyone but seemingly never accomplishing anything either. Harry and Molly learned that Andy was terribly frightened by loud noises such as gunshots or the motors of heavy machinery. Amazingly he would sometimes be seen standing out in the rain during a thunder and lightning storm with his arms out stretched and his face turned up into the downpour until his mother scolded him to come indoors.

Andy and his mother lived in Lowry almost a year before Molly and Harry finally made friends with him by sharing their candy and playing with his small dog he had named Sphunt. Frances told Harry the dog's name meant cork because the way he jumped up and down it reminded them of a cork bobbing up and down in the water.

Even though he rarely spoke to them Andy would smile shyly and shake his head up and down as if he was saying yes to whatever they were saying. One day, they found him sitting on his front steps drawing a picture in a tablet. When he noticed them approaching he quickly closed the tablet and tried to hide it behind his back. When they convinced him to show them what he was drawing he shyly brought out his red tablet with the words Big Chief written in bold letters across the front. To their astonishment Andy had drawn a picture of an angel, finely detailed and more beautiful than anything either of them had ever seen in their religion classes or in church. Later, Harry came to realize Andy's drawings were similar to the beautiful paintings of angels that could be found in the great cathedrals of Europe.

Molly asked Andy where he had seen a picture of an angel like that and if he had copied his drawing from a book. Andy's only reply was his simple smile and the look he gave her briefly before turning his face away. As usual, Molly was not to be put off and persisted by pointing to the drawing and asking him again where he had seen such a beautiful angel to draw. Reluctantly, Andy looked up at Molly and slowly pointed to his eyes and then into the air in front of him. At that he quickly closed the tablet and went inside the house. An entire week passed before they saw him sitting on his steps drawing in his tablet again.

About a year later Cora Van Damm, or Cora Van Dammit, as Molly referred to her, called Dora saying she was concerned about Frances's health. She explained to Dora that Frances seemed to be tired all the time and often seemed short of breath, especially while climbing steps. When she saw that Frances's ankles were swollen Cora offered to take her in for a checkup, however she refused to see Dr. McIver. The same afternoon Cora sent Frances home early so she could rest even though she kept insisting nothing was wrong. Cora knew Dora was a nurse and called her wondering if she would please stop at Frances's house in the morning to check on her before she left for work. Dora agreed and added that if she felt it necessary would take Frances to the doctor herself.

Early the next morning around four A.M. Dora's phone rang and it was Maynard Mattson the janitor at the school. He told Dora that he found Andy sitting in the dark on the front steps of his house cold and crying and that he had obviously been there most of the night. Upon entering the house Maynard found two dinner plates and cups sitting on the kitchen table. Maynard knew then something was wrong, as Frances would never have left the dishes undone. One of the plates still had food on it but it appeared to have been untouched. When he called out to Frances there was no answer. He entered her small bedroom and found her lying peacefully on her bed fully clothed with her flowered apron still on. Maynard concluded that Frances apparently fixed supper for herself and Andy and as she sat down to eat decided she wasn't feeling well and went into her bedroom to lie down. He felt she had dozed off and died quietly in her sleep. When she didn't return from the bedroom Andy went in to wake her and when she didn't respond he went out on the steps and cried.

Cora Van Damm made sure Frances had a very nice funeral at the Reno Catholic church complete with a lunch of scalloped potatoes, coleslaw, ham sandwiches and plates and plates of cakes, bars and kolaches. During the eulogy Cora said she wanted Frances to be proud as she looked down from heaven and saw what a fine funeral she was having. Andy sat quietly in the church next to the Van Damm family, but later refused to come out to the graveside for the burial or the luncheon that followed. Dora and Stan were finally able to coax him out of the church and into their car. In spite of Harry and Molly's best efforts to cheer him up, Andy refused to speak on the ride to his home and kept his forehead firmly pressed against the side window in the backseat of the car. When they arrived at his house Andy silently stepped out of the car and ignored Dora's question, asking if he would like her to stay with him for awhile or perhaps come home with them for a few days? He entered his house looking gaunt and frightened as if he was carrying the weight of the entire world on his drooping shoulders.

They waited in the car outside Andy's house for a short while until they saw a small light go on in the kitchen. The ride home was unusually quiet as each of them pondered what was going to become of Andy. Everyone in Lowry was quite sure he was not capable of looking after himself and began discussing how Andy's future should be handled.

For the next few weeks as the town's people were trying to decide what they should do with Andy everyone took turns bringing food and checking on him. Andy silently took the food and the next morning the clean, empty dishes always appeared on the steps. Cora Van Damm contacted Frances's sister in Tacoma, Washington only to find out she was in the hospital but said as soon as she was well again she might be able to take Andy to live with her.

Every few days Molly and Harry knocked on Andy's door. He would open it just a crack, acknowledge their presence with a half smile and close it again. One morning after breakfast they went to check on him and when he didn't answer became concerned. They went to both sides of the house and didn't see him. Finally they concluded he may have taken Sphunt for a walk and were relieved when they saw him sitting in a nearby field with his small dog by his side.

Several weeks later, early on a Sunday morning, Dora and Stan were awakened by the sound of loud knocking. It was Tom Peterson the Lowry policeman. His face was ashen gray as he asked Dora if she would be willing to assist him on an emergency call as Dr. McIver was in Glenwood delivering a baby. Dora dressed quickly and left the house without Tom telling her where they were going. Once they were in the car he explained they were heading for Andy's house. His voice broke when he said that at about five o'clock that morning a neighbor walking his dog reported hearing a crash coming from the Janek home. He found the door standing open and upon entering was shocked to find that Andy had apparently hung himself in their garage.

A few hours later a very distraught Dora arrived home with the dreadful news about Andy. Harry and Molly already knew about Andy's suicide because in a town as small as Lowry word spreads quickly. Harry never forgot how grief stricken Dora looked as she had her family sit in the living room and explained what had happened. She cried as she told how Tom cut Andy down and that they had found Sphunt lying dead near Andy's body. Tom figured that Andy suffocated the small dog and after placing him on his pillow, carefully covered him with a small blanket before he hung himself. Dora said the house was spotlessly clean and orderly except for a red Big Chief tablet lying on the kitchen table. When she glanced at it she was astonished by the tablet's contents and she asked Tom if she could take it with her so nothing would happen to it. As Dora showed them the tablet, Harry and Molly were awestruck at the beautiful drawings. There were several of Frances and Sphunt and two of Jesus and Mary. All the rest were drawings of beautiful angels, filling the remaining pages in the tablet. Molly recognized and pointed to the one they had seen before but it was the last drawing in the tablet that made Dora cry. On the very last page was a beautiful angel with arms outstretched as if she was inviting someone to come to her and be held in her arms. The drawing was remarkably detailed as each tiny feather on her wings was painstakingly drawn. The halo surrounding her head was not just a circle but exhibited a very skillfully drawn, intricate design. Harry thought it was the most beautiful picture he had ever seen. What he remembered most about the drawing was that Andy had drawn tears flowing down the angel's cheeks.

When Dora contacted the Reno priest about Andy's funeral she was told in no uncertain terms there would be no Catholic funeral, nor burial in the parish cemetery because of the circumstances surrounding Andy's death. She was sternly reminded that suicide was a mortal sin and Andy would go to hell. Upon hearing the priest go on and on about the sacred authority and rules of the church, Dora became very angry and slammed the receiver down before he could finish. She then fired off a phone call to her friend Cora Van Damm. Dora literally barked at Vera the local telephone operator as she demanded to be connected with Cora Van Damm RIGHT NOW! Harry was sure the whole neighborhood party line had probably rubbered in on that call. After Dora explained what had transpired with the priest, Cora called Father Helm and told him she was on her way to see him but not before she burned his ears with a few sharply phrased parting comments.

Harry had never seen his Aunt Dora so angry and he had to admit it had scared him. Molly on the other hand, was elated as she shouted, "Boy, the shit's gonna hit the fan now! Just you wait and see!" And it did. For years after, people around Reno and Lowry talked about the day Cora Van Damm single handedly took on Father Helm and the Catholic Church. In the end, Cora got her way. Well, sort of. Father Helm agreed to a partial truce but only after Cora threatened to leave the Reno Parish and take her generous contributions with her. This included the funds she had promised for a major remodeling project that had already begun on the rectory. She also alluded to the fact that Andy's mother Frances had accrued a sizable amount of money from the sale of her farm, including savings from her employment with Cora. Frances had lived very frugally making sure there would always be sufficient funds to look after Andy's needs after she had passed on. This money had been placed in Cora's safekeeping and she explained since Frances and Andy were both gone some of that money could possibly find it's way into the church's coffers. If, and that was a big IF, Andy was given a proper burial.

The battle raged hot and heavy for several hours and the way the story was told and retold later was Cora finally rallied in her unrelenting siege by reminding Father Helm, "For God's sake Father, you know the boy was simple. He had no idea what he was doing." She reminded him too, of the several necessary components required to fulfill the Catholic Church's definition of mortal sin, including the full knowledge, intent and desire to grievously offend God. "No way, could that boy have had that kind of motive." At this undisputable revelation, the steadfast priest began to feel his awareness of church theology was being threatened by a uppity woman parishioner. With this realization he became even more obstinate and firmly shook his head no.

Recognizing his continued stubbornness, Cora finally presented the priest with her most compelling argument, Andy's Big Chief drawing tablet. Father Helm looked at the pictures in disbelief. He sat stunned and without saying another word arose from his chair, walked to a nearby filing cabinet and withdrew the necessary documents for the funeral.

The Reno Church received one fourth of Frances's estate, the Lowry public school another fourth, Frances's sister in Tacoma the remaining half and Andy Janak got his Catholic burial. Cora had argued for a Mass with altar boys and the choir but finally reluctantly compromised on a service not inside the church but at the graveside next to his parents' plot in the cemetery adjacent to the church. There would be no church lunch but rather a gathering at the Van Damm farm immediately following the service.

Even though it was near the end of October the day of the funeral was beautiful. The morning started out cool but by ten o'clock when the mourners gathered at the graveside the sun streamed through the remaining red and yellow leaves of maple trees giving the air a misty rose and golden hue. Harry didn't think he ever remembered a more beautiful day. Father Helm kept his word and devoutly conducted a proper Catholic ceremony. It was short but dignified. Following the final prayer he abruptly turned to leave for the rectory when Cora grabbed him by the sleeve and sternly nodded her head in the direction of the casket. Father Helm turned back and was tempted to glare at her but reconsidered. He begrudgingly sprinkled the casket with a generous dousing of holy water and made a hasty sign of the cross over it. Cora sniffed loudly and adjusted her dress over her ample bosom in one triumphant gesture and then made a dramatic sign of the cross as her response. Father Helm soon realized that Cora's checkbook would not open nearly as often as it had in the past.

Dora and Cora, or the dynamic duo in Molly's words, picked out a beautiful granite headstone engraved with an angel and had it placed at the head of Andy's grave. In the early morning hours a week after the funeral, Frances and Andy's house burned to the ground. The cause of the fire was never learned. Dinky balls, dinky balls, he wears overalls. Some are big and some are small and some don't fit at all.

It wasn't long after the funeral that Dora announced they were moving to a larger home on North Lake Shore Drive in Glenwood. She told everyone it was because she and Stan were now both working in Glenwood but Harry and Molly suspected she was still pissed with the

Reno priest. Molly grinned and stated in her most haughty voice that as far as she was concerned Father Helm could just go straight to helm. Hee, hee. Incorrigible. Back then Molly insisted the word meant one who was a free spirit and unwilling to be manipulated but Harry remembered looking up the meaning in Webster's dictionary, and found it meant incapable of being corrected, unruly, delinquent. Incorrigible. That was so Molly.

The traffic on his commute home continued to be unusually slow and as Harry turned into their driveway he was surprised to see the house still dark. As he opened the garage door he felt a twinge of concern but then told himself he was being silly, Annie was fine and would be home soon. He let himself into the house, fed the cats, who by now were very indignant about eating so late, checked the mail, and decided to start dinner. Searching the refrigerator he found some chicken breasts and decided to make lemon basil chicken and baked potatoes. He knew Annie liked Caesar salad and propping the cookbook on the counter carefully followed the instructions. He had just finished setting the table when he heard a car door slam and Annie saying goodbye to Diane. As she entered the house he noticed how flushed her face was and could see she was very excited about something. Tossing her coat on the loveseat she entered the kitchen and put her arms around Harry's neck. She pressed her body close to his and said, "You sweet man, you even fixed supper, I love you so much" and kissed him firmly on the mouth.

Harry looked at her with surprise and when she didn't immediately explain what had happened he inquired, "Problems with one of the children?"

"No, not really, but . . . ." Annie paused as she tried to come up with the right words.

"Dinner's ready. Let's sit down, you can tell me while we eat."

Annie did a quick blessing but Harry could see her mind was clearly not on what she was saying. As Harry dished up the chicken Annie pressed her lips together and said, "Do you remember the special little girl I recently told you about? Her name is Jessie and I've been working with her for about four months now."

"I think so. The one with the big brown eyes who is in perpetual motion?"

"Yes, that's the one. She is adorable and I fell in love with her the moment I laid eyes on her. She's the one the mother abandoned at the free clinic when Jessie was only a few months old. The mother was a very young Hispanic girl probably no more than sixteen or seventeen. She brought Jessie into the clinic with a severe infection in both her ears. She and the baby were both poorly dressed and the staff felt sorry for her. While they were waiting in an exam room the attending nurse instructed the mother to fill out the customary forms but when she came back she was gone and the baby was left all alone. The only information she filled in on the form was that the baby's name was Jessie and her birth date.

Diane was able to get Jessie into a foster home almost immediately but the two times they have tried to place her in a permanent home it hasn't worked out. She's three years old now and I must admit she is quite a handful. The foster mom Jeanette has done a pretty good job with her but in the last six months she can hardly handle her. She has two children of her own and feels Jessie's disruptive behavior and the extra attention required was causing her own children to resent her. Since I've been working with Jessie she seems to be making reasonably good progress and I think all of us feel she is on the road to becoming a happy, normal child. The first night I saw Jessie, Diane put her and me into a viewing room. I sat in the middle of the room on the floor with my eyes closed so I could tune into Jessie. For the first five minutes she ran around wildly throwing things off the shelves and knocking over anything she could. When she realized I wasn't going to react she finally stopped and came over and tried to pry one of my eyes open. I opened my eyes and looked into hers but didn't say anything. Jessie stood there looking at me and she finally reached over and poked me and said, you talk. Her speech development seems to be behind what would be normal for her age and her mispronunciation of words indicates she has a hearing problem. On the other hand, she tests out extremely well on her physical skills. Running, throwing, kicking are all things she does very well. Jeanette says that Jessie doesn't listen and will almost attack if someone tries to physically restrain her. One of her favorite things to do is to turn the radio or the television on as loud as it can go and then stand with her hands pressing on it screaming at the top of her lungs.

As Jessie stood there trying to understand the situation I started to make a chanting sound very quietly, mah-rah . . . rah-mah, which I use to raise the positive energy vibrations and dispel the negative ones. As I continued this rhythmic chant she just stood there not quite sure what she was supposed to do. Cautiously, she reached out and placed both of her hands on the sides of my face and slowly let them slide down onto my throat. When she felt the vibrations of the sound on my voice box she smiled and started to make a mmmm sound herself. It seemed to calm her and in a few minutes she put her arms around my neck and settled into my lap. I held her close and rocked her in my arms almost like I would have a baby. Harry, I want you to know this touched me deeply and in a couple of minutes I was in tears. Thinking back on those moments is very precious to me and somehow I feel they were a breakthrough for Jessie as well.

Diane and I agreed it was important to get Jessie's hearing rechecked as soon as possible. After quite a little tussle during the testing we learned that little Ms. perpetual motion has significant damage within both ears and some permanent hearing loss. We assume for most of her life she's been hearing the world in a very distorted and unfriendly way. She has other emotional problems but we believe most of those concerns will diminish if her hearing can be improved.

From that time on Jessie seemed to be doing very well and showed continuous progress in almost every area. Unfortunately, the last time she came in, it was almost as if we were back to square one. Neither Diane nor I could understand why she had such a dramatic setback. After talking with Jeanette she finally explained that she and her husband were having serious problems and we agreed this could have a bearing on Jessie's behavior. The reason I left so quickly today was this afternoon Jeanette brought her into the clinic and told Diane she could no longer cope with Jessie's behavior and they had regretfully decided to give her up. When Diane questioned Jeanette more closely as to what had brought her to that decision, she broke down and told her that her husband walked out on her and the children. Jeanette also learned they were several payments behind on their mortgage and the bank is threatening foreclosure. She explained they are deeply in debt because her husband hasn't worked for the last four months and has a serious gambling problem that has used up all their savings.

I feel so sorry for her, she's virtually destitute and now has no choice but to go back to work full time and hope she can get back on her feet. I phoned David at his little farm near Faribault to see if he could help. When I explained the situation he agreed to help her with the house payments and also give her enough money so she can go back to school to refresh her secretarial skills. Now you can see why she has made up her mind to not keep Jessie."

Annie was silent for a moment and finally looked into Harry's eyes. For a moment he thought she was going to cry. Then, in a very quiet voice she said, "Harry, Diane wants me . . . I mean she wants us, to take Jessie. She thinks it can be arranged because Jessie has been such a difficult to place child." Once again, Annie paused briefly to gain a sense of Harry's initial reaction to her announcement. Then she continued enthusiastically, "We'll have to apply for legal guardianship for the time being but even with our age as a factor and my vision not being perfect Diane believes in time we should be able to adopt Jessie. I know I'll have to have someone help me with Jessie's care while I am at work, but I'm sure we can find someone. Harry . . . its like all my dreams are being answered. I know this is like a bolt from the blue, but what do you think?"

Harry sat with his mouth full of food but didn't speak. As he chewed he realized he never expected to be a father at his age. He also reflected on his earlier memories of Andy Janak and how his aunt Dora felt that if only someone had taken the time to be there for him things might have turned out differently. At that moment Harry knew what his answer would be. He and Annie would make the time to be there for Jessie and do their very best to see that nothing bad would ever happen to her. He looked into Annie's pensive eyes, swallowed hard and said, "I say we go for it."

Annie jumped up and hugged him, "I knew it! I told Diane you would say yes. We can go over to Jeanette's tomorrow afternoon so you can meet Jessie. I'm so excited! There's a lady who works at the clinic who does volunteer work and said she would be willing to help with Jessie's care. Now all we need a bigger house!"

Chapter 10

The next morning Harry and Annie met with Diane Mandel to start the necessary paperwork and also give Harry the opportunity to meet the woman who would be helping with Jessie's care. Martina Diablo Williams was a forty-seven year old Spanish American woman who was already more than familiar with Jessie and her special needs. Martina's three children were grown and she had been contemplating taking a full time job, but agreed this would be the perfect opportunity to re-enter the work force without having to train for something she might not enjoy. Martina was known by the clinic staff as Tina, and by Jessie as 'Teenie'. Everyone agreed having a caregiver who Jessie was already familiar with would make her transition easier. The plan was to have Annie remain at home with Jessie for the first two weeks with Martina coming by for regular visits. When it was obvious that Jessie was making the transition successfully Martina would come at seven-thirty each morning and stay until Annie came home from work around five o'clock in the afternoon.

Harry and Annie arranged to meet with Jessie's foster care mother Jeanette and her children at four-thirty. The rest of the afternoon they shopped for some of the essentials they would need to prepare Jessie's room. Annie asked each of the store clerks to hold the items they selected until she confirmed the purchases with them on Monday morning and they in return assured her that if she desired the items could be delivered that same afternoon.

Before Annie could proceed with finalizing the commitment she felt it necessary that Harry could meet Jessie in person and feel certain he had made the right decision, even though he assured her several times he had already made up his mind and would not change it.

Before heading to Jeanette's house, Annie picked out a Pooh Bear and Harry a musical Jack-in-the Box that played Pop Goes the Weasel. They had the gifts wrapped with pretty flowered paper and large pink bows.

When they arrived at Jeanette's Harry was stunned to see how shabby the foster parent's house looked but didn't comment to Annie. Jeanette greeted them warmly at the door and introduced them to her nine-year old son Charlie. She explained that her daughter Linda had agreed to work late at McDonald's to earn extra money for a class trip. Jessie was sitting alone on the couch with her thumb in her mouth and her blanket held up to her nose. When she saw Harry and Annie she raised the blanket and covered her eyes. Jeanette explained Jessie had just wakened from her nap and was still drowsy. Jessie kept the blanket pulled snugly to her eyes as Jeanette picked her up and settled in a large granny style rocking chair. Jeanette invited them to sit down and Harry joined Charlie on the couch and Annie sat in a large stuffed chair next to the rocker. Annie offered Jessie the gifts they had brought but she turned away burying her face into Jeanette's chest and refusing to look up in spite of her foster mother's coaxing. After they visited for about ten minutes Jessie slowly turned her face and carefully studied Harry. Observing this opportunity Harry reached into his pocket and pulled out a bag of gummy worms. He carefully opened the bag and passed it to Charlie. "Care for a gummy worm?" The boy flashed a big smile and took one of the worms and holding it over his open mouth carefully chewed on it making sure that Jessie could see what he was doing. After a second worm descended into his mouth he looked at Jessie and said, "Hey Jessie girl, these are really good."

Jessie was eyeing Charlie and the gummy worms and finally her curiosity overcame her shyness. She slid out of Jeanette's lap and ran to her foster brother. "Chardy you got?"

Charlie grinned at Harry and answered, "I've got gummy worms. Mmmm good." He rubbed his tummy. "Jessie girl have one?" He held the bag out to her and looking at Harry she gingerly reached in as if she wasn't quite sure if it was okay. She held the gummy worm away from herself and making a face shook her head back and forth as if she was afraid. "Bite me?"

Charlie laughed, "No, silly! They won't bite you. They're candy. Go ahead and eat one."

Jessie studied the green gummy worm and looked over at Jeanette as if to be reassured. "Go ahead, Jess, you can eat it. Harry brought them for you."

Jessie put the worm in her mouth and her sparkling brown eyes became very large. "Mmmmmmmm good." She chewed and swallowed the worm and looked back at her foster brother. "More, Chardy?"

Charlie passed the bag back to Harry. "You'll have to ask Harry. They belong to him."

Cautiously, she inched closer to Harry holding out her hand. "Hairdee . . . Jessie some?"

Harry held the bag out to her saying, "Here, Jessie, you can help yourself. These are for you and Charlie." Soon Harry was visiting with Jessie as she ran unafraid around the living room. Within the hour she had crawled into both his and Annie's laps as they watched her eagerly as she unwrapped her new toys. By the time they left there was no doubt in their minds that they had made the right decision.

Early Monday morning Annie notified the stores and by that afternoon the furniture and other items began to arrive. On Wednesday morning a white van driven by Diane Mandel stopped in front of Jessie's new home. Expecting them, Annie excitedly ran outside to meet them. Jessie was sitting in the back seat with Martina. They stepped out of the van and onto the sidewalk. Annie and Martina each took one of Jessie's hands and the three walked side by side toward the front door. Diane followed them carrying a single beat up suitcase and pushing a doll buggy with a wobbly back wheel. Harry stood in the doorway waiting and watching the strange little procession. He knew from that day on their lives would never be the same.

Harry and Annie's previously serene household suddenly became a whirlwind of activity. With David and Harry's encouragement, Annie decided to take the entire month off work and Jessie seemed to adapt to her new circumstances amazingly well. The only members of their family who seemed to be suffering distress were their two cats who now spent much of their time hiding from Jessie's quick little hands and piercing screams. For the first two weeks they could be seen only when they were sure she was tucked safely in bed.

With David's assistance Jeanette was able to get back on her feet, and she and her children were able to obtain counseling to help them cope with their changing lives. They stopped at least once a week to see Jessie and it was during one of these visits Jeanette admitted to Annie that her marriage had been broken for a long time and she had filed for divorce. Her husband refused to deal with his gambling problem and she realized it was time for her and the children to move on with their lives. After a few months a new sparkle seemed to be returning to Jeanette's eyes and a gradual renewal of her spirit also became evident.

Annie took to motherhood with such determination that Harry couldn't believe how domesticated she had become. Jessie had only a few minor setbacks and these episodes were not nearly as traumatic as Diane had anticipated. Annie worked tirelessly with Jessie to help her adjust and to improve her speech. Her new hearing aids were probably Jessie's biggest source of frustration and she wasn't at all shy about letting everyone know her displeasure at having to wear them.

Harry had never been around children before and suddenly finding himself the father of a very active three year old daughter seemed totally awesome and something new to be marveled at each day. Since their marriage, Annie had been going to church regularly with Harry attending only on special occasions. Now that Jessie had become an important part of their life Annie encouraged the idea of their attending church as a family and having Jessie baptized. She decided Jessie's baptismal name would be Jessica Ruth and Harry agreed with her choice of names. Annie explained to him that Ruthie had been her doll's name when she was a little girl and she always hoped to use the name Ruth if she ever had a daughter.

Molly came to visit after a few weeks so she could, as she put it, "Check out the new little babe." Picking up on Molly's energy, it took no time at all for Jessie and her to become the best of friends. Harry watched with amusement as Molly held Jessie and read story after story only to have Jessie clap her hands and beg, "More, Lolly, read more, more, more!"

To Annie's dismay Jessie occasionally insisted on keeping her finger in her nose. Coaxing did not seem to help and both Annie and Harry began to suspect Jessie was doing it on purpose to see their reaction and the resulting attention it generated. Molly found it amusing because she said it reminded her of something she might have done at that age. On her next visit as Molly sat reading to her niece she confided very seriously, that she had written a poem just for her. "Listen very closely because Aunt Lolly is going to give you some of her great wisdom.

> *Remember not to pick your nose, it's not the thing to do . . .*
> *But use your hanky daintily until you're sure you're through.*
> *For picking is a practice no one can condone, not at any time . . .*
> *Not even when alone!*

Now if by chance you should be seen with your finger up your nose,
listen very carefully how the explanation goes.
You simply say, it's just a scratch and not a pick, you see . . .
How could you think this awful thought of proper little me?"

Jessie clapped her hands and said, "Lolly's silly! Jessie likes she finger in she nose."

Harry smiled, "That doesn't happen to be an original poem, is it?"

"Actually, yes, it is, but my publisher felt it might be a little too graphic for developing minds so it went into the circular file. Jessie seemed to like it though. The kid's got good taste even if she walks around with her finger up her nose."

Harry rolled his eyes but was secretly pleased how much Molly appeared to enjoy his daughter. His daughter. His and Annie's daughter! The words sent shivers down his spine. When Annie took Jessie up to bed, he and Molly sat in the living room sipping tea and visiting about nothing in particular. As they talked Harry noticed a kind of sadness engulfing Molly's usual upbeat demeanor. When she looked up and saw him studying her she grinned and said "What now? Don't even try to psychoanalyze me like you used to do when we were kids."

"I'm not. It's just that you seem a little sad."

"Yes and no, I guess. I see you and Annie and you both seem so happy. Now you have Jessie and your life seems complete and of course that makes me happy. Then I think about my life, and I'm not sure I like it very much. Now don't get me wrong, I'll be O.K. but I can't help thinking about the fact that I'll probably never have a child of my own and that makes me sad. I find myself wondering what our lives could have been like if Steve had lived and our baby could have been born. It's silly I know, because part of me knows that was never meant to be, but . . . ." Molly stopped mid-sentence and after pausing briefly took a deep breath and continued, "Actually, our cousin Clayton has helped me a lot. Did I tell you he lives in Glenwood now?"

"No, I think the last I heard about him was he had some remarkably important high security job working in the Pentagon in some space lab. What in the world is he doing in Glenwood?"

"He's retired now, but you're right, he has had some truly remarkable jobs. He doesn't talk about his past much because not only is he a genius but also a very humble and modest man. A little eccentric but I guess if you're a genius you see the world differently then the average person. For instance, one minute he'll be telling me about the Ma Sum Mara in Kenya and how the big cats attack the Wildebeests. A few moments later he will go into a detailed account of the NosGa Plateau in Peru, and something about weird spider monkey shapes and how eight hundred straight lines cover one thousand miles and converge at sixty-two points, or some damn thing. I get lost in some of the conversations and as you know, I always thought I was quite intelligent but he makes me realize what intelligence really is. He has a remarkable memory for details and I don't think there's a worthy book he hasn't read and retained all the facts. Anyway, as I was saying, he's helped me to understand everything that happens to us in this life is not just a series of random events but a specific path the soul has chosen to follow. He's also been helping me with meditation and teaching me about yoga. He told me if I want to feel better about myself I need to be more careful about what I think about and the foods I put into my body."

Molly looked up at Harry and continued, "I didn't recognize him the first time I saw him in Glenwood. He was in the grocery store and while I felt I should know him, it took me three more aisles to figure out who he was. Even then, I still wasn't absolutely sure until I heard him speak. It's funny how a person can always recognize a familiar voice. Back in high school I remembered him as being physically larger. He was kind of pudgy when we were growing up, and so much of a bookworm I don't think he ever played any sports or joined any clubs. He always wore those big, thick glasses, nerdy clothes, and had a funny haircut. Not ducktails and black leather jackets like the really cool guys who wanted to look like bad boys.

When I saw him in the grocery store and he came over to visit with me I'm sure my amazed expression made me look like a complete fool. I stood there with my mouth open and for once Molly big mouth Brown was speechless. He looks a little like Ben Kingsley did when he played Gandhi in the movie. He's, how can I say this? He's changed so much he actually looks smaller and he's very trim, probably because he's a vegetarian. He's totally bald, with little round glasses. When he talks to you he looks directly into your eyes and he has the softest, kindest looking eyes I have ever seen. When I'm with him, it's almost as if he radiates a calming presence."

Molly's words had taken on a reflective, almost reverent sound and Harry couldn't resist rolling his eyes and giving his cousin one of those, yeah, sure, looks. He added dryly, "You sound very taken with him."

"Damn you, Harry, put a sock in it and don't you give me one of those looks. I'm trying to tell you how much he's changed." Molly's eyes flashed and he could see how embarrassed she was about her emotional description of their cousin. "Can't you ever be serious with me?"

Harry immediately regretted his attitude and he apologized, "I'm sorry, I had no right to act that way. I guess when I'm with you my mind goes back to our childhood days when we always seemed to have a pissing contest going about who could give the other the most crap. I really am sorry. Getting back to your comment, Annie tells me that certain people do send off very strong vibrations, especially people who have attained great spiritual growth. It sounds like Clayton may be one of those people."

Molly didn't initially react to his apology so he continued. "I don't know if you are aware of this but Annie is one of those unique people who can tune in on people and read their vibrations." Immediately Harry wished he hadn't made this statement but like it or not, he had. To his surprise it seemed to bring Molly back into the conversation.

"What are you saying? That Annie is psychic?"

Harry shifted his gaze and finally said, "Yes, I guess in a way you might say she is. It's like she can look inside someone and see what kind of a person they really are."

Molly put her head down as if she were studying the contents of her cup and very quietly said, "So, what does she say about me?"

Harry hesitated as Annie's observations of Molly had been shared in a private conversation, but he felt not to answer now would only complicate the situation. "She said you have wonderful energy and a zest for life. That you are straight forward and honest, but have had to learn some hard lessons because of your impulsiveness. Let's see, she also said you have had to bear a great sadness but you're a much stronger and kinder person for having gone through that pain. She feels some of that sadness is leaving you as you have grown spiritually. I know she likes you a lot and admires your sincerity. I can honestly tell you, I really haven't discussed many of the details of your life with her. Even if I had, it wouldn't change her opinion of you. Annie is a person who doesn't judge people by their past. After all, she married me, so what does that say about her?"

Molly grinned and Harry knew she had forgiven him for his insensitive behavior. He was relieved the tension between them had eased. A little later Annie joined them and offered to bring each a piece of her famous cheesecake. The rest of the evening was full of laughter and light-hearted fun but after Molly left and they were putting the dishes in the sink Annie turned to Harry, "Did you and Molly have some kind of a disagreement before I came in?" Harry told Annie what happened and then said, "I don't know why I acted like such a jerk and hurt Molly's feelings. I don't usually do things like that and I'm still feeling badly about it."

Annie put her arms around Harry's neck, "I could be wrong but I think for one unguarded moment the little child that still lives inside you, the one that lives inside each of us, felt a little jealous of Clayton. At least the Clayton Molly was describing. In some small unconscious way you possibly wanted to discredit him in Molly's eyes. Molly was your best friend through all the years you were growing up. You shared hundreds of experiences as well as your innermost thoughts. Now that you have rediscovered her friendship and because you value her family connection, I suspect for one brief moment you felt her admiration for Clayton somehow threatened to lessen her feelings about you. Not to mention the fact, as the result of some form of warped logic, you two seem to feel the need to give each other grief and derive your own form of nostalgic pleasure in doing so."

Harry wanted to protest but knew it was true. He had felt a little twinge of jealousy as Molly described Clayton, with that almost adoring tone in her voice. "That was pretty childish of me, wasn't it?"

"Not really, I think many adults are unconsciously motivated by the child that continues to dwell within all of us. The child who never felt adequately loved, or pretty or handsome enough, or guilty for something that was completely out of his or her control. It seems impossible but I think it affects us all more than we would ever care to admit." Annie took Harry by the hand and as she turned out the kitchen light whispered, "Let's go peek in at Jessie and then I know something you can do to make my inner and outer child very happy."

Harry followed her upstairs and once again felt he was the luckiest man alive.

Chapter 11

Minneapolis, 1997

Louis Welheim read the business section of the morning paper as he ate the breakfast his housekeeper, Ethel Danner had prepared for him. When he was convinced he hadn't missed any major developments in the business world he casually flipped through the rest of the paper. He did this last part of his routine with very little interest and as he was about to fold the paper and get on with his day, a photograph of a woman receiving an award from the Mayor of Minneapolis caught his eye. He stared at the picture with rapt curiosity, carefully studying the woman's features. Beneath the photograph the caption read, Sister Mary Rose, founder of Seaton House was honored yesterday at a reception given by the Mayor of Minneapolis in recognition of her life-long dedication to helping the underprivileged.

His thoughts were interrupted as Ethel entered the room and stated, "Excuse me for interrupting your breakfast, Mr. Welheim but Estelle didn't sleep well last night. I don't think those sleeping pills Doctor Priester prescribed are strong enough."

Louis looked up as he folded the paper in half, leaving the photo exposed and said in a matter of fact voice, "Call Roland and have him change the prescription. Tell him I feel it needs to be stronger. I don't want her getting up at night. She needs her sleep as well do you. You can't be expected to stay awake all night watching her." He spoke with a crisp German accent and had the air of a man who expected to be listened to. "I appreciate the excellent care you give my wife. I'm leaving for the office now and I should be there all day. Call me if anything unexpected should arise."

Work for Louis was a business he owned known as Delta Developments, Inc. If one knew where to inquire, they might be informed that the

President and CEO of Delta Developments was a self-made millionaire who acquired the bulk of his money in real estate and the rest through astute investing. He was considered to be not only one of the most successful businessmen in Minnesota but possibly the entire United States. This, however, was a little known fact outside the business community as he was also a very private man and rarely in the spotlight of the public eye.

Delta Developments' main office was located on a corner on the outer edge of the business district in a stately old landmark built at the turn of the century. The outside facade of the granite structure was architecturally ornate and extended one-half block in each direction and was a classic example of the quality of construction Louis most admired. Delta's offices occupied the first floor with most of the remainder of the building being occupied by prominent law, accounting and architectural firms. The entire top floor was leased to a real estate firm known as Crown Realty. A little known fact was Crown Realty and several of the law offices were actually subdivisions of Delta Developments and answered directly to Louis.

Louis parked his Mercedes and as he entered his office asked Geesela, his personal assistant, if Tom Blake had come in yet as he wished to see him immediately.

Tom Blake, a distinguished, impeccably dressed gentleman, checked his silver gray hair and his expensive, exquisitely tailored suit before he entered Louis's private office and quietly closed the door behind him. He found Louis seated at his massive desk studying the newspaper in front of him. At fifty-five, Blake had spent most of his legal career working directly with Louis and made it his business to be sure he was available whenever Louis summoned him. He had never considered working for anyone else and was regarded as Louis's most trusted and loyal employee. He sat in one of the heavily carved chairs in front of Louis's desk and waited for him to speak. Louis finally looked up and acknowledged Tom's presence.

"Good morning, Tom. How are you today?"

"I'm fine, thank you sir. How may I be of service?"

Louis returned his gaze to the newspaper in front of him. "Have you seen today's newspaper?"

"Yes I did. Was there something special?"

"Did you happen to see the photograph of the nun, Sister Mary Rose?"

"Yes, as a matter of fact, I did. I believe she's the one who received an award from the Mayor for her unselfish dedication to helping the underprivileged."

"What can you tell me about this Seaton House she established?"

"It's a home for unwed mothers. One of my colleagues in this building does some of their legal work, pro-bono of course. I hear she takes in any young woman whether she can pay or not. She appears to rely on God for the finances to run the place and it seems that sometimes he's a little slow in providing the funds."

Tom was careful not to let his sarcasm show in his voice. "He said the nun has a reputation of being a character, really quite charming, and able to talk almost anyone into contributing to her many charitable causes."

"Show me exactly where Seaton House is located."

Tom pointed out the neighborhood on a city map. "Seaton House is actually quite a lovely old place, with a stone carriage house in back surrounded by a big yard and old trees. It's well constructed but in need of major restoration to bring it back to its original beauty. The equally large home on the adjacent lot is in terrible shape and needs to be taken down but the absentee owner is resisting selling it until he can get his asking price. Which of course, he never will because he is asking way too much. Whoever finally acquires that property will be buying the location and nothing more."

Louis studied the map and then sat back in his chair. "Does the order the nun belongs to own Seaton House?"

"No, I understand they lease it from a private party. The only reason I know this is because it's a prime piece of property and we checked it out last year with the possible idea of purchasing it."

Louis removed his reading glasses and continued, "I want you to buy the house on the corner and put a Crown Realty sold sign on it. Then leak an announcement to the press the house is to be torn down immediately. Of course the historical and preservation folks will be in an uproar, which will give it the attention we need. Do whatever it takes to make it happen, I'll trust your judgment."

Tom Blake was careful his expression wouldn't convey that he couldn't believe what he was hearing as he knew better than to question his employer's judgment. "Consider it done."

Louis continued, "Once you have it secured, contact Sister Mary Rose, informing her that Crown Realty has a buyer who is very interested in purchasing Seaton House. Also, emphasize that property taxes are going up and their landlord is thinking of selling. Get her shook up by casually letting her know there are possible code violations at Seaton House and the roof and upper floor windows need to be replaced. Do it gently, but do whatever it takes to unnerve her. You know the drill. Discrepancies in the lease agreement maybe, and, oh yes, go ahead and buy Seaton House too, but make sure the current owner agrees not to tell anyone he has sold it, especially Sister Mary Rose."

Tom Blake was tempted to frown but controlled his impulse. He knew his employer to be a cut throat, ruthless master of manipulation but the thought of him harassing a nun seemed a little out of character.

Observing Tom's miniscule reaction, a cunning smile broke across Louis's face, and he said, "Relax Tom, we're about to make friends on this one. We're not out to destroy some charitable cause that helps mankind, or in this case womankind. Be sure you deal with Mary Rose directly. When she calls Crown Realty have the office secretary give her the run around, but at some point let her realize Delta Developments is the party behind the purchase of Seaton House. Then, direct her to me but don't give her my name, I'll handle it from there. And, of course, as always, let's keep this between you and me." As he rose to leave Louis's office the lawyer couldn't help but notice how intently his employer was studying the image of the nun in the newspaper.

Tom did exactly as Louis had directed him to do. By evening the wheels were set in motion. Tom had seen Louis dramatically change people's lives before and he couldn't wait to see how this little scenario would play out. Never in all the years he worked for Louis had he seen him do anything to make friends.

That evening Louis sat at his desk in his home office with the door closed after giving Ethel explicit instructions not to disturb him under any circumstances. He didn't wish to take any phone calls and she was to keep his wife quiet even if it meant sedating her. It was Louis's pattern to retreat into his office each evening after dinner to complete unfinished work, read or plan strategies, but more often than not, it was to escape having to deal with Estelle.

The warm satin glow of the recessed wood panels gave his office a feeling of quality and endurance. Louis never tired of gazing at the patterns in the expensive walnut paneling that lined his favorite room. He also deeply cherished his magnificent antique desk that he had purchased on his one and only trip back to Germany. Its massive legs and side panels featured intricately carved characters from German mythology and the craftsmanship was of the finest he had ever seen. His office fireplace was much more masculine than the one Estelle had chosen for the living room and was made of fieldstone that extended the length of the wall across from his desk. The stones were of earth tones, rusts, umbers and dark browns that complimented the elegant dark brown carpeting on the floor.

Louis had selected Wagner's Prelude for tonight and he savored the music playing softly in the background. In his reverie he turned his chair around and studied the huge painting on the wall behind his desk. He had commissioned the work by a well-known German artist named Hans Gunther shortly before Gunther's untimely death. Now the painting was worth many thousands more than he had paid for it, but that was neither here nor there, as Louis knew he would never part with it.

The painting portrayed the two great wolves of Woden. One of the wolves, the magnificent white wolf known as Freki, was lying in a passive pose. The equally impressive black wolf, Geri was standing fully alert as if ready to spring into action at his master Woden's command. The painting never failed to be a great source of inner pleasure and comfort to him. It was as if the animals now belonged to him and not Woden.

Turning back and facing his desk he extracted a small key from the key ring he always carried, and opened the upper right desk drawer that contained private papers and personal items. Louis pulled the drawer completely out until it reached a stop. He extracted and placed the documents it held on his desk, then carefully reached back into the drawer until his fingers felt a small lever that released with a clicking sound. With the click the bottom of the drawer popped free revealing a small storage compartment beneath it. Lifting the divider out he began examining the contents of the secret storage space. The items included a small paper bound book he had handwritten as a child when he was living in Berlin with his grandmother and his aunt. He spent no time looking at the book but instead picked up the pale pink envelope beneath it. It was a letter addressed to him in a carefully executed feminine hand. He had received it shortly after he graduated from high school in Germany. Louis was never sure why he had kept the letter all these years. He opened the envelope and took out the letter written on matching pink stationary, a black and white photograph and a small gold ring. Studying the photograph he couldn't help but notice how handsome he had been back then, but also how visibly intense and serious he looked for a boy of eighteen. The girl with him in the photo was smiling and appeared to be very much at ease. Her face bloomed with a happy, joyful expression. The young woman's smile revealed perfect white teeth between full lips and her beautiful blond hair flowed around her shoulders. He studied her face and could almost see the sparkle in her eyes. She could have been the perfect Aryan wife for him and the devoted mother to their superior children. Louis, now in deep reflection, pondered yet again why she had rejected him and his offer of marriage. The gold band he held in his hand was engraved with a wreath of ivy. He remembered how he had searched a long time for the right jeweler who could inscribe the ring to his exacting expectations.

The young woman's name was Ivy Stockel. They were the same age and had been classmates and closest friends throughout their last two years of high school back in Berlin. Louis had loved Ivy and believed she had shared the same feelings for him. Never once did she indicate she may have other plans for her future. He smiled in bittersweet resentment as he reread her letter in which she explained she had promised herself to God. She would become a nun and had chosen to become a bride of Christ for all eternity. For a brief instant Louis felt the pain, anger and bitterness sweep over his heart once again. He shuddered for he was not used to having his emotions tilt him off guard this way. "Promised herself to God," he spit the words out as if all these years later they still left a vile taste in his mouth. He turned the photograph over and read the fading words inscribed on the back, "I will love you forever, Ivy." It had not been forever. She betrayed him and left him for another. A God he considered to be an invisible, nonsensical figment of a young girl's overactive imagination. Carefully, Louis replaced the photograph, ring and letter into the envelope and picking up the small book, returned them to their secret hiding place. He replaced the false bottom back into the drawer and gently pressed down until he felt the click. Almost absent-mindedly he placed the stack of papers back into the drawer and locked it.

Today, after all these years, seeing Ivy's picture in the paper and the article referring to her as Sister Mary Rose had brought back a flood of memories and feelings he had never expected to deal with again. His strong emotional response had caught him off guard. The reaction was mixed with an element of pain and disbelief and he quickly concluded he wasn't comfortable with this combination of feelings. He recognized that for a moment he had felt out of control and to him this was synonymous with weakness. The awful realization that a portion of his nature was still vulnerable somehow both frightened and excited him. Secretly, he relished the new feeling of excitement he had not experienced for a long time. With a keen sense of challenge and ironic amusement he welcomed this new chapter into his otherwise totally organized and predictable life.

Usually Louis bought and sold real estate without giving a single thought as to how it might affect the people who were involved. To him every purchase or sale was strictly a business transaction. This time it was different. The Seaton House acquisition was not an impersonal transaction, but rather a second chance to find closure to a part of his life he now was forced to realize had been left unresolved. It had taken him a long time to get over Ivy. He had left Germany shortly after his twentieth birthday and immigrated to the United States. When he settled in Minneapolis his exclusive focus in life had become a singular devotion to amassing great wealth. He would create a fortune that would surpass what most men only dream about.

By the time he met Estelle he was already well on his way to realizing his dream. The fact that Estelle's family was wealthy was certainly not a detriment. In the beginning she had been very different, gracefully elegant, cultured and of course, rich. Pampered all her life, she was used to getting what she wanted. She was a strong, confident and independent woman and Louis had great admiration for all these qualities. Estelle graduated from Vassar and had earned a Master's Degree in Economics from the Harvard School of Business. Back then her superior education made her seem only more desirable to Louis. When he proposed to her she surprised and delighted him by being willing to give up her aspiring banking career and free lance work as a fashion model, to stay at home and raise a family.

Within a few months following their marriage Estelle announced she was pregnant. Both were thrilled and immediately began making preparations for their firstborn but the new found joy quickly turned to sorrow when Estelle suffered a miscarriage in the second trimester of her pregnancy. They waited a year before attempting to have another baby and when Estelle told Louis she was sure she was pregnant they exercised every precaution to ascertain she would carry this baby to full term.

Louis thought back to the night their son was born. Estelle's labor began while she was shopping for a few last minute items for the baby. Her driver took her directly to the University Hospital where she was immediately admitted and taken to the obstetrics floor to prepare for the delivery.

Louis had been in Chicago at a business meeting when he received the call that Estelle had been admitted to the hospital. Even though the baby was two weeks early everything seemed to be proceeding normally. Estelle's obstetrician, Dr. Terrel Hartman, a seasoned veteran who headed the Department of Obstetrics and Gynecology at the University, telephoned Louis and after explaining the situation, assured him everything was going well. By the time Dr. Hartman returned from the phone call, Estelle's labor had slowed down and she was drifting off to sleep from the pain medication they had given her. Since her water had not yet broken, Dr. Hartman felt it would be awhile before the baby came.

Later, Louis learned that Terrel had left the hospital at about nine P.M. and even though Estelle was still having mild contractions, he was confident there was nothing to be concerned about. His orders had been to call him if there was any change and he would immediately come back to the hospital. From there the story became somewhat muddled. The young intern on duty claimed by the time he was summoned to the delivery room Estelle was in heavy labor and about to deliver. The nurse on duty who had only started working in the delivery room that week, had a different story. She contended she had been instructed by the intern not to call Dr. Hartman and when she finally did Estelle had already delivered and was bleeding profusely.

By the time Dr. Hartman finally arrived at the hospital, Louis's apparently healthy son had been born but Estelle was in shock and there was great concern they could lose her. After several blood transfusions she appeared to stabilize but was still very weak. Louis took the first available flight back from Chicago and arrived at the hospital in the early hours of the morning. By noon Estelle's condition had improved dramatically and she was awake and out of danger. Even though she was very weak and unable to nurse her newborn son, he had been assured she would be fully recovered within a few weeks.

For reasons Louis was never able to explain or accept, Estelle was never the same. She went from being his beautiful, exciting wife and lover to becoming a nervous and over-protective mother. All of her attention was focused on their son, who she named Eric Louis. While Louis was initially overjoyed to be a father, it soon became apparent Estelle didn't trust him with the baby and he was never able to establish the bond he knew would be important to their son's development.

Estelle fussed over baby Eric night and day and agonized over his slightest whimper. She became obsessed with the baby's needs and slowly Louis felt himself being pushed away. Their sex life apparently died the night their son was born. When Louis suggested they make love she would find excuses why she couldn't. When he persisted she would submit but it usually ended in disaster with her crying and complaining the pain was unbearable. Finally Louis's pride would not allow him to keep asking. Over the years several gynecologists had examined Estelle but none were able to find a physical cause for her discomfort.

Louis saw to it the attending intern and the nurse on duty in the delivery room the night of their son's birth were never permitted to work in the medical field again. In his mind it gave him very little satisfaction for the price he had been forced to pay.

Eric Louis quickly grew into a bright and sensitive youngster. He seemed healthy enough but was not at all interested in athletics or any form of competition. Soon it became evident to Louis that Estelle's constant hovering had affected the child. Unlike his athletic father, Eric appeared to be a sissy and a mama's boy and Louis found it difficult not to be critical of his behavior. By the time Eric was fourteen he appeared to exhibit certain effeminate mannerisms which Louis found to be increasingly irritating and eventually avoided his company whenever possible.

Against Estelle's protests Louis enrolled Eric in a very expensive private school in Zurich and with that decision a final rift occurred in their relationship. With his son out of the picture Louis had hoped he and Estelle might rekindle the love they had once known but Eric's absence from their life only complicated matters. Estelle seemed heartbroken and lonely. For weeks she sat in sullen silence refusing to acknowledge Louis's presence. She spent hours talking to Eric on the phone. During one of their lengthy conversations, he mentioned he had taken up tennis and encouraged her to do the same. Estelle decided this would allow her to spend more quality time with their son when she visited him and she arranged to begin lessons at the country club. When word got back to Louis regarding his wife's interest in a certain handsome young tennis instructor he put a stop to her lessons by having the instructor fired, but not before he had suffered an unexplained broken arm.

After this incident, their frequent arguments escalated and it was not uncommon to find Estelle drinking in the middle of the day. On more than one occasion Louis came home from work to observe her staggering around and having to hold onto furniture. She slurred her words and repeated statements over and over until he couldn't stand it any longer. Louis became furious and after a serious argument threatened to have her placed into treatment. That night she tried to kill herself by taking an overdose of sleeping pills. He had no choice but to have her committed to the psychiatric ward of St. Mary's Hospital. This was to become the first of many stays.

Louis hired Ethel Danner, a private duty nurse who had previously worked on the ward where Estelle had been a patient. Although Ethel had been under suspicion of stealing narcotics from the medications room at the hospital, she was later exonerated when it was proven it was another nurse who often worked on the same shift. By moving her and her ten-year old daughter into their home Ethel was available to supervise Estelle twenty-four-seven.

The arrangement proved to be the best solution for all concerned and under Ethel's constant watchful attendance, and the proper medication Estelle was kept in a manageable state of limbo. Every two months for the next several years Louis arranged for Estelle, Ethel, and occasionally her daughter, to fly to Zurich to visit Eric and spend time in their home near Basel. Louis looked forward to the times he could spend alone and not have the ominous feeling of being the caretaker to a houseful of dependents.

Glancing at the clock he realized it was getting late and that he had an important meeting in the morning. As he entered the living room he found Ethel watching television by herself now that her daughter was away at college. She assured him Estelle was sleeping soundly and he headed for his bedroom. He showered and went directly to bed but he found sleep did not come easily that night.

Four days after Louis's meeting with Tom Blake, a very upset Sister Mary Rose entered the Delta Development Building not knowing who she was looking for, and determinedly stated that no matter what it took, nobody, regardless how important they thought they were, was going to close down Seaton House. She sat stubbornly in the waiting room even though she'd been informed earlier that no one could see her for at least an hour. Finally, the stern looking receptionist ushered her down a long corridor and into an office and directed her to take a seat where a man sat in a chair behind a large desk with his back toward her.

Mary Rose sat patiently waiting for the man to acknowledge her. When she could no longer contain her anger she stood up, "Excuse me, but I need some answers and I believe you're the only one who can provide them. If you would be so kind as to face me maybe we can get this whole situation cleared up. You have no right to put my life's work in jeopardy simply because you are in the habit of gobbling up real estate for your own gratification. Seaton House is important not just to me, but to every young woman who comes to us while she is waiting to have her baby. Many of these women are alone and have no one else to turn to. Tell me, where will these girls go if you close us down?"

Mary Rose's voice trembled but she had no intentions of giving in to her emotions. She took a deep breath and in a very controlled voice continued, "I'm not in the habit of talking to the back of a chair and I consider it very rude behavior no matter how important you may think you are."

The man in the chair slowly turned to face the nun and in a very polite voice said, "Please forgive me. My intentions were not to be rude to you but rather to give you a chance to speak your thoughts on this extremely important matter."

Mary Rose peered into the face of the man in front of her and he heard her gasp. "Gerhard Louis Welheim, is that you? Oh my goodness! It is you! It's me, Ivy Stockel. We went to school together in Berlin."

Louis smiled, got up and graciously extended his hand to Sister Mary Rose. "Of course I remember you, how are you? I see you are still not afraid to speak your mind."

Mary Rose studied him in total astonishment. She was immediately impressed by the fact that he was still a very handsome man. His blonde hair was now graying and even though he was heavier, he still maintained the body of an athlete. His manners were polished but there was the same stoic German carriage he had back in high school. As he stood with his hand extended she said, "Oh no, I don't want to shake your hand. I get a hug from you!" She moved around to the side of the desk and gave Louis an affectionate hug. Later, she would recall how stiff his response had been but for that moment she didn't care. She was a hugger and he would just have to accept that. As she pulled her chair closer to the desk she continued, "I came here expecting to have a big confrontation with the enemy and instead I find one of my very dearest friends. God certainly works in mysterious ways."

Mary Rose went on to explain the dilemma she was having with Seaton House and at the end of their conversation Louis promised he would help her find a solution to her problems. Shortly after, Mary Rose left Louis's office thanking God for his intervention, but not before she extracted a promise from her former friend to visit Seaton House as soon as he could find the time.

Chapter 12

Annie sat at the small dining room table Harry had draped with a large blanket to create a tent for him and Jessie to play under. Harry assured Annie her sitting at one end would not interfere with their special playtime and she enjoyed listening to Jessie giggle as she and Harry climbed around on their hands and knees.

As she finished licking the last envelope on the stack of bills she had been paying she could hear Jessie laughing and demanding "Coco Puffs, daddy. Jessie wants more Coco Puffs!" Jessie had developed an intense liking for the chocolate cereal at her foster mother's and Annie had been reluctant to change Jessie's eating habits too quickly hoping to make the transition to her new family easier. She sat back and watched Harry scoop Jessie up into his arms and head for the kitchen on their quest for Coco Puffs.

"Juice too, daddy, Coco Puffs and apple juice too!"

Annie loved their home but it had become painfully obvious it was now too small for the three of them and all of Jessie's belongings. She laid the bills on the buffet and reached behind the clock and took out a picture of a lovely old Tudor home. The house was located a few miles away and it had been the house Annie had dreamed of owning ever since she first met Harry. She remembered the day she had first taken special notice of the house with its huge, beautifully landscaped yard and wrought iron fence surrounding it. Sometimes, as she drove past slowly, she would wave to the older couple that owned it but hadn't felt it proper to ask if they ever planned to sell. One day just for the fun of it, she snapped a picture of the home and made a habit of repeating to herself that someday it would be theirs.

When Harry and Jessie reentered the dining room she tucked the picture back behind the clock but not before she silently reconfirmed someday she and Harry would own that house. A few weeks later David stopped to pick Annie up for an early meeting that Harry didn't have to attend. On an impulse Annie asked David to drive by 'her' house. David was explaining to her about their upcoming board meeting and as they passed by the house Annie let out a shriek and yelled, "Stop the car!"

David hit the brakes not knowing what caused this sudden outburst and Annie, who had already unbuckled her seat belt, was thrown up against the dashboard. Before David could regain his composure Annie bolted from the car and was sprinting through the gate of her dream house. As David looked down he noticed Annie had not bothered to put her shoes on as she made her grand leap from the car. He glanced back and saw she was now approaching a young man who was attempting to place a For Sale sign on the front lawn. Annie was waving her arms wildly and David could hear her yelling, "Stop! You can't do that! Don't you dare put up that sign!"

Seeing the woman descending upon him the young man stepped back but not before Annie had grabbed the sign and attempted to wrestle it away from him. David could hear him yelling at Annie, "What the hell are you doing lady? I gotta' get this sign up, my dad is already pissed at me and if I don't get it up I'm gonna' be in big trouble!" He pulled the sign from Annie's hands and held it in front of him like a shield. "Back off before I'm forced to defend myself!"

Watching with great amusement, David got out of his car and approached the confrontation on the front lawn. When the young man spotted him he yelled, "Do you know this woman?"

David stood chuckling to himself as Annie attempted to regain her composure. Then moving in very close to the young man she said in a very determined voice, "Put the sign down, and move away from it. You can't sell this house. It belongs to me. Well, it doesn't belong to me yet but it will. I want to buy this house and you can tell your father that you sold it to me. I'll even see to it you get the commission for selling it. Even if I have to pay it myself."

The young man cocked his head and said, "No way, a commission? That would be totally awesome." Then he wrinkled his brow and looked at David. "Is she serious?"

David had all he could do to retain his composure, but recognizing the urgency of the matter replied, "She is totally serious. She definitely wants to buy this house and she can afford to do it. If I were you I would take your sign and put it back in your van and consider this to be one of the luckiest days of your life." He couldn't resist adding, "I would also suggest you might not want to antagonize her. She may be little but she can be pretty aggressive when she wants to be."

Annie shot David a dirty look and mumbled under her breath, "Get serious, this is a life and death matter. We're talking about our future home."

David reached into his billfold and handed the young man his business card, "My name is David Sullivan. I own Sullivan Glass. This slightly disheveled lady is Ann Scarley. She works with me at Sullivan Glass. She and her husband will call the realty office as soon as we get to our office and confirm the purchase of the house. Let's see, Bantom Realty? Is that the Les Bantom Realty Office?"

"Yeah, Les is my Dad. I'm his son Kevin. Did she really mean that about my getting the commission?"

"Absolutely, now put the sign back in your van, before my friend decides to do something drastic."

At three o'clock David, Annie and Harry walked through the house and gardens and by five o'clock they had signed the purchase agreement. That night when Annie lay in bed she felt for the first time in years her period of atonement had come to a close. A month later they moved into their new home and Annie began the joyful task of decorating and furnishing it.

Chapter 13

David heard the phone ring as he stepped out of the shower and grabbing a towel stood drying himself as he picked up the phone, "Hello".

"Hi, David, it's me, Annie. I was . . . oh shoot, Jessie don't . . ."

David held the receiver away from his ear as the phone on the other end clattered to the floor. This was accompanied by a scuffling sound followed by Annie saying, "Oops, sorry David," and then another clattering sound, and a scuffle. "Gol dang it, Jessie, let go of the phone. All right, just say Hi."

"Hi, Daybid." The sweet sound of Jessie's angelic voice chirped over the phone.

"Hi, Pumpkin."

"I not punk in, I Jessie."

"Oh, that's right, I forgot. Hi Jessie, how are you?"

"Fine." There was a pause. "I eat worms."

"Yuck, that doesn't sound like a good breakfast to me."

David could hear the phone being wrestled away from Jessie's tight little grip. "Oh, gosh, I'm so sorry, I guess I don't quite have this mother thing quite figured out yet."

"You feed the kid worms for breakfast?"

Annie giggled, "Gummy worms. She loves them and you can blame Harry for that. Jessie has him wrapped around her little finger. All she has to do is raise her voice and he folds. What a wuss! I was wondering if you would pick me up for work? Harry has a doctor's appointment and I'm not up to hitchhiking."

"I think I can do that but I do have to stop at Seaton House for a minute on the way. Mary Rose has a picture of some wicker furniture she's picked out for the sunroom and wants me to see it before she orders it. I told her I trust her judgment but she insists I approve of it since I'm the one who is going to be paying for it."

"And the Lord always provides." Annie was mimicking Sister Mary Rose's favorite saying. "She really has your number, you do know that don't you? She can always count on you to come through for anything she needs. Do you really think we can have a short visit with Mary Rose? We probably won't get to work until ten."

"No, problem. She assured me she has another appointment at nine this morning so we should be fine. Anyway, I don't think the boss will care."

"No, probably not. I'll see you shortly. Oh, and David," she cleared her throat. "You really should put some clothes on when you answer the phone."

Annie could almost feel David's astonishment so she quickly added, "Relax nature boy, I'm just jerking your chain. I'm good but not that good, see you soon."

"You're really evil sometimes, but I'll pick you up anyway." David hung up and made a mental note not to answer the phone naked again.

As Annie slid into the front seat of the car she grinned and said, "Had you going for a minute there, didn't I?"

"And to think I used to encourage you to use your special talents. Thank God you don't have a criminal mind. At least I don't think you do. Quite frankly, I don't know how Harry puts up with you. Let's hope he never decides to stray from the marital bliss he's now enjoying or he will suffer big time."

"Quit your whining. You know you love me and Harry and you'd be lost without us. Speaking of love, I can't believe how much love Jessie has brought into our lives." The rest of the conversation centered around Jessie and before they knew it they were at Seaton House listening to Sister Mary Rose tell them about the latest turn of events.

"Here I was anticipating the very worst scenario for Seaton House and voila! A miracle happens. Instead of losing Seaton House to some urban redevelopment project, it is quite possible, well almost for sure, it is going to be donated to our Order. It also looks like the soon to be empty lot next door may also be given to us for some future add on, or for now, the much appreciated extra yard space. I think a gazebo would be charming don't you?" She didn't wait for a response and continued talking as she led them up to the second floor sunroom and pointed out where the new furniture would go. By the time the discussion was closing Annie and Sister Mary Rose agreed the old drapes would have to go. David concurred and agreed to pay for new window treatments as well.

As they started down the stairs Mary Rose mentioned their new benefactor was her next appointment and he was expected at any moment. She explained he was an old friend from back in high school and she was eager to have them meet him. She interrupted herself again to ask David if he was sure it was all right to order new window treatments and he reassured her it was a necessity. In her usual enthusiastic way of showing her appreciation Mary Rose gave him an affectionate hug. "I love you to pieces David, and I know God sent you to watch over my girls and me. Then she added playfully, "Who knows, if I wasn't already promised to God, and if we'd met sometime earlier, and if you were a few years older and I wasn't so happy doing what I do, things might have been different."

David grinned and replied, "And if you weren't already promised to God and you were maybe a little more than a few years younger and we had met sooner who really does know what might have happened?"

"Oh, you're such a heartbreaker, reminding an old lady how ancient she really is." She put her arm around his waist and held her other hand out to Annie. "Such wonderful friends God has blessed me with."

As they descended into the foyer they were surprised to see the new Seaton House benefactor already waiting. Mary Rose introduced David and Annie to Mr. Louis Welheim and they all shook hands. David watched with particular interest as Annie put her hand into Louis's. For an instant he was sure he saw the color drain from Annie's cheeks as she quickly withdrew her hand.

On their way back to the office, Annie was noticeably quiet so David tried to initiate conversation. "That's one smooth man Sister Mary Rose has for a friend. He's really good looking, don't you think?"

Annie didn't respond, so David questioned her. "What did you feel when you touched him?"

"Nothing." Her voice was trembling.

"Annie, it's me. I saw your face when you shook his hand."

Annie looked at David and he could see the troubled look in her eyes. "I'm sorry to say this but I believe he's not a nice man."

"Not nice, how? Can you be a little more specific?"

"He's very dangerous. That man controls people and destroys them. He is evil and Sister Mary Rose needs to be very careful. He's not the man she believes him to be. I think he has another agenda going on that Mary Rose is a part of and totally unaware of."

David reflected in silence for a moment. "I'm sorry to hear you say that. Mary Rose seems to trust him and she certainly deserves only the best."

They agreed not to tell anyone about Annie's observations at least until they could find out more about Louis Welheim.

After lunch David knocked on Harry's office door. Annie had gone home early complaining of a headache and David felt the need to talk to Harry. "Did your doctor's appointment go okay?"

"Yes, thank you, I'm feeling better. Sometimes my leg hurts where I broke it not once but twice. The doctor gave me some medication to take the edge off the pain. I also took Annie's advice and got some alfalfa tablets and vitamin E."

"Good."

Harry could sense David had something else on his mind. "Anything else?"

David entered Harry's office and shut the door. "Is it difficult living with Annie being the way she is?"

"How she is? Oh, you mean about her special gift? No, not really. I never knew I could love anyone so much. She's hell on light bulbs when she gets upset. You've probably noticed that if you get her mad enough light bulbs kind of explode when she walks into a room. Thank God she hardly ever gets mad or it could get a little expensive."

Harry looked serious again, "She knows a whole lot more than she lets on to you and me. You are aware of that aren't you?"

"I am now, and I'll keep that in mind the next time I answer the phone with nothing on."

Harry grinned, "Oh, yeah, she told me about the shower thing. Between you and me I'd suggest you keep a towel handy just in case. See you tomorrow."

Chapter 14

David invited Harry to have lunch with him the following Friday before leaving for a week's vacation. Harry knew David had not been feeling well and wholeheartedly agreed a week in the country might do him good. In the country meant David would go to the small farm outside of Faribault he had purchased about five years earlier. He was looking forward to spending some time by himself with only his dog Greta to keep him company. The farm was actually less than forty acres, consisting partly of woods and swampland, but it gave David and Greta a place to stretch their legs away from the hum of the city. Over the past several summers David remodeled the house with the help of his neighbor and turned it into his own little hideaway. It was located near Lake Mazaska and provided a place to fish as well as an opportunity to photograph the abundant wildlife. Annie christened the farm David's Ponderosa, and she and Janet teased him about becoming a farmer. Their housewarming gift to him had been a pair of bibbed overalls and a tool belt.

After ordering their food David slid a check over to Harry and said casually, "I have something for you." Harry picked up the check and was astonished to see it was for twenty thousand dollars.

"Remember on your last birthday when you said you didn't want anything and I told you I'd have Baxter invest some money for you? Well, he did, and this is what you've earned. That guy is a regular King Midas. Bottom line is he made us both a lot of money."

Harry pushed the check back in David's direction and countered, "I can't take this. I wouldn't feel right about it."

"I thought you might say that so I have an idea. About three months ago Father Sean was telling me Our Lady of Hope needs a new roof. Father Sean is retired now but he still helps out every so often. Father Tom Aston is the full time priest and as you know, he and Father Sean never got along very well. Father Sean was telling me Father Tom runs around turning off lights and shutting off the air conditioner in the rectory when it's one hundred and ten degrees outside. It seems part of the reason Father Tom stays on at Our Lady's is because of his frugal ways. By the way, did you know it was Father Sean who recommended you for the job with us?"

"I thought it was my former boss, Mr. Sindler."

"He gave you a very good recommendation, but it was Father Sean who really went to bat for you. He even called the morning of your interview to say you were a wee bit under the weather. That maybe you had a touch of the flu, but he wanted us to know that you were a good man."

"I was hung over and he knew it. It was Father Sean that gave me a wee bit of the hair of the dog that bit me to get me through the morning. I almost ralphed on his desk."

"Annie knew it the moment she laid eyes on you and she thought it was hilarious that Father Sean tried to cover for you. I already told him I'd donate money for the roof and I had a pretty good idea you might want to also. He was thrilled of course but then asked if we might keep the new roof a secret from Father Tom for the time being and I said I thought that would be fine. From the twinkle in his eye I'd say he has something up his sleeve but I'm not really sure what it is. He's already made arrangements with the roofers to start. So, would you like to go in on the new roof with your share of this unexpected windfall?"

"I do. If it wasn't for Father Sean I might still be living in that walk-up apartment with the cracked skylight sucking my thumb and feeling sorry for myself. God knows I owe him a lot."

A few weeks later Harry got a call from Father Sean and at first thought the good Father might have been imbibing in a wee nip. He soon realized Father Sean was in an extraordinary good mood as he let the story of the new roof unfold. It seems that Father Tom had been out of town attending a retreat and had reluctantly left Father Sean in charge. According to the old priest, before Father Tom left he'd lectured him as if he were daft.

"Like I was some kind of a feeble minded old fool. Do not, he had said to me, do not spend one red cent while I am gone. Is that very clear to you? Well, I just walked away from him as I wasn't going to validate what he was saying by answering him. By the time he arrived home from the retreat the boys already had a good start on the new roof. When he spotted them up there hammering away I thought he was going to rip the handle off the car door. As you can imagine, he started yelling at the roofers to come down saying it was a mistake but I had told the boys to ignore him.

Paddy O'Rourke, one of the guys that came over with me from Ireland when we were lads being the crazy fool he is, started yelling back at Father Tom, saying, what did you say? I can't hear you. By this time Father Tom turned kind of a pasty white and he started waving his arms to get the attention of the other boys but they just continued to ignore him. Then Paddy, the crazy fool, starts strutting back and forth with his arms folded under like wings, flapping them up and down and crowing like a rooster. At this point Father Tom turned red and the veins in his forehead and neck started bulging out like balloons and he looked a lot like a demented chicken as he stood there waving his arms. Paddy is lovin' the whole scene and he crows all the louder. He's not real fond of Father Tom for giving him a whole rosary for penance when he goes to confession because he won't give up the drink.

At this point, I make my entrance, for as much as I am enjoyin' it the same as Paddy I felt the good Lord tapping me on the shoulder telling me this is probably enough. I didn't want this God fearing lad, good Father Tom, to have a stroke so I come forward holding the invoice out to him that is marked, paid in full. The minute Father Tom sees me he starts yelling at me and shaking his finger in my face saying that he knew I was the one responsible for this. I think his exact words were, you crazy old fool! We can't afford a new roof! There's no money! How many times do I have to tell you that before it sinks into that feeble head of yours? I stood there in front of him, and continue to hold the invoice up for him but he pushes my hand away telling me that nothing I am going to say is going to make him forgive me. I shook the invoice in front of his face and finally he sees the Paid in Full across the bill and the next thing I know he's on his knees crying like a baby and thanking God. He finally got control of himself long enough to come into the rectory but he still wasn't talkin' to me."

Harry laughed so hard he could hardly talk but finally he asked, "How's Father Aston doing now? Has he forgiven you?"

"The last time I saw the lad he was lying face down on the altar begging God to forgive his lack of faith. Mark my words though, it won't be long before he starts turning the thermostat to sixty-five in the rectory to cut down on the heating bills. He's a career penny pincher. He thinks finances are all columns of black and red. I think God sent me to him to bring a little excitement into his life. Where else is anyone going to get a return on their money like you gave me? God bless you Harry. You and your family will always be in my prayers."

"Goodbye, Father Sean. Enjoy your new roof and don't forget to give my regards to Father Tom."

Chapter 15

Annie replaced her magazine on the coffee table and looked around the family room in the new house they now called home. She could hear Jessie and Harry laughing in the kitchen and suddenly felt such a powerful rush of emotions flow through her it caught her completely off guard. She couldn't remember being so happy in her entire life and realized she must have been given what some people refer to as a peak experience. For an instant she felt such total and complete joy as if she had experienced a glimpse of what heaven must be like. Jessie and Harry strolled back into the room each with an ice cream bar in hand and Annie groaned as she said in a half joking voice, "Harold dear, you are turning our little girl into a junk food junkie. I think the three of us need to have a serious talk about nutrition."

Jessie climbed behind the couch where she had put her dolls to bed and invited Harry to follow. The phone had been laying on the davenport and when it rang it startled Thomas the cat who had fallen asleep on it. Annie reached for the phone and said hello while trying to pacify the indignant feline for disturbing his nap. She was delighted to hear Molly's voice. "Molly, how are you? We haven't heard from you for such a long time. You must be enjoying living in Glenwood." Molly and Annie had become great friends and Harry had been teasing Annie that Molly enjoyed her company more than she did his.

"I'm fine, thank you, but I'll bet you'll never guess how I spent the last two days."

"You had a garage sale."

"Yes, how did you know?" Molly sounded a little disappointed that Annie had guessed her secret so quickly.

Annie paused and said, "I think you may have mentioned it to us the last time we talked and it somehow stuck in my mind."

"Well, you're right. I had one super, fantastic garage sale. I think every person from Glenwood, Starbuck and Villard showed up to look and buy. I made over five-hundred dollars."

"Super! Here, let me give this phone to Harry and I'll take the one in the kitchen so we can all visit."

"Where is the proud papa?"

"He and Jessie are sitting behind the couch with all of her dolls and indulging their sweet tooth. Here he is."

Annie, Harry and Molly chatted for about ten minutes when Jessie became too noisy and Annie said good-bye and took Jessie upstairs for Martina to give her a bath. Since they had moved into the bigger house it was not uncommon for Martina to stay overnight rather than go home to an empty house. When Annie came down Harry was still talking to Molly and on an impulse she caught his attention and whispered, "Tell Molly you like her shoes."

Harry looked puzzled but said, "Hey cuz, I really like your shoes."

There was a long pause and then Molly said suspiciously, "You dumb shit! Why did you say that?"

"Say what?"

"The crack about my shoes. Why did you say that?"

"No reason, except that I like your shoes."

"How do you know what kind of shoes I'm wearing? Do you have some kind of a see all phone. Oh God . . . I hope not . . . I look like hell."

"Just kidding." Harry looked at Annie and shrugged. "I said it to get a rise out of you."

There was another pause and Molly said, "I'll have you know my shoes are very nice. I have white tennis shoes on." Then she added a little sheepishly, "With Tweety Bird and Sylvester embroidered on them."

Harry laughed out a loud, "Good fashion statement. This from the girl who ditched school every time she had a bad hair day."

"You ass! Never mind. I won't say another word. I've been trying very hard to be a sensitive and compassionate person who acts and not just reacts. I'm learning not to judge anyone even when they are being a total asshole. Clayton says I need to try a little harder and slowly it will come naturally to me." There was another pause and she added, "Damn, it's a hard go. About the time I think I'm finally making progress I get hit with the nasty stick and I find myself having to bite my tongue. Take today for instance. The people around here are very nice and I really like them, so don't get me wrong, but at about two-thirty today I was about ready to hang this garage sale thing up, but people kept showing up even though the ad in the paper stated very clearly it was over at two o'clock. You know me, when I get tired I have a tendency to get a little cranky."

"Golly gee, I never really noticed that." Harry couldn't resist his need to comment.

"You! Put a sock in it! Anyway at about a quarter to three, I'm giving all the leftovers away because there is no way in hell I'm dragging all this shit back inside. Let's see where was I going with this? Oh yes. This really nice, middle-aged, couple shows up, you know the kind, a little bit like the Jehovah's Witnesses who come ringing your doorbell as you're about to step into the shower. Not that I have a problem with them, but here I am giving away boxes of clothing, and about everything else anyone seems even vaguely interested in, when the husband picks up this really great looking dress. I mean this had been one expensive dress. It might have been a Vera Wang, I can't really remember. Anyway, he starts asking me all these irritating questions about the dress. Is the size accurate or does it run small? Is it natural fabric or is it a synthetic? Quite frankly about this time he was really starting to frazzle my nerves. Oh, and did I mention that it had been about four hours and six cups of coffee since I had a chance to pee? So he keeps following me around dress in hand and finally says to me, does this dress have to be professionally cleaned or is it washable? I stood there looking at him and didn't dare say anything for about thirty seconds as Clayton's words pounded through my mind. Act . . . do not react. I want you to know it took every smidgen of my self-control but I finally said in a very polite voice. Sir, the way Dora used speak when she really wanted to get some man's attention, the only difference being this time I was actually trying to be a little sarcastic. Sir . . . I'm really not completely sure . . . but considering the fact that I paid a lot of money for that dress, and considering the fact that it is free to you, I can't see you have anything to lose now do you? I turned and walked away but what I really wanted to do was grab him by the front of his shirt and say, listen, Jack, I don't know if it is washable or dry cleanable but I do believe it might just be stick it up your assable!" She paused, then continued in a more quiet, polite voice, "But I didn't, so aren't you proud of me? Just call me Saint Sara the sarcastic! Hell's bells I'm not sure there's any hope at all for my salvation."

When Harry told Annie about Molly's Vera Wang dress they both had a good laugh about his cousin's quirky and nontraditional quest for spirituality. Later that night in bed, Annie curled up around Harry and they lay together in the silence and darkness of their bedroom. Finally Annie whispered to Harry, "Go ahead and ask. I know you won't be able to fall asleep until you do."

"Ask what?"

"Don't play innocent with me. You know exactly what I mean. About Molly's Tweety Bird shoes."

"You're right. How did you know?"

"It's hard to explain. When I think about someone really hard, it's like a picture pops into my head. It happens more often now, and sometimes I can't seem to control it."

"Like David coming out of the shower?"

Annie giggled. "I knew you'd bring that up. Trust me, that one really surprised me too. It's not like I expected to see him standing there with nothing on but you do have to admit it was kind of funny. You have to believe me on this. It's not like I go looking for these things to happen."

"Yeah, I guess so. Things like that are pretty harmless, but what if you tune into something that isn't funny? Then what?"

"I don't know. I've thought about that a lot."

Doesn't it scare you sometimes?"

"Yes." Annie's voice was so soft he could hardly hear her answer.

"Are you alright?"

"No, I need you to hold me tight. I want to feel your arms around me so I'll know you'll always be here for me no matter what."

Harry turned and faced his wife and felt her body melt into his. Long after Harry had fallen asleep Annie lay staring into the empty darkness above her. Her explanation seemed to satisfy Harry and she knew he would always love her in spite of her strange gift. What he didn't know was how much her unique gift was starting to scare her.

Gradually sleep overcame Annie's thoughts but at some point she felt herself being shaken. In a state of panic she struggled to get away and it took her a few moments to realize she was safe in her bed and the person shaking her was her husband. The voice that seemed so frightening in her dream was in reality Harry's voice calling her name.

"Annie, wake up. Are you okay? It's me, Harry".

Annie opened her eyes and realized she was gasping for air as if she was choking. "I'm okay. It was only a nightmare. I'm fine now." She struggled to sit up and in the early light could see Harry's ashen face.

"You were moaning and then you let out this scream as you started thrashing around like you were fighting with someone. I tried to wake you but you kept pushing me away and saying you needed to leave."

"Don't worry, I'm okay . . . really, Oh my God what a nightmare! I haven't had one of those since right after my accident."

Annie got up and went into the bathroom. She turned on the light and glanced at herself in the mirror. Then, pulling back the hair from her forehead peered at her reflection intently. She used the toilet and took a drink of water. Before she turned off the light she inspected her forehead again. As she climbed back into bed she realized Harry was still awake.

"Are you all right?"

"Yes."

"Do you want to talk about it?"

She didn't respond immediately but lay quietly trying to reconstruct her dream. Finally, she spoke. "When I was little I used to tell my parents I had a friend who would come and visit me. My mother immediately labeled it as an imaginary playmate and informed me it was a normal childhood phenomenon. I was only about five at the time and I didn't know anything about childhood phenomena, normal or abnormal. Her analysis meant nothing to me. All I knew was that I had a special friend who came to visit me. This went on for several years until one day my mother overheard us talking in my bedroom. She confronted me and told me I was much too old for that kind of nonsense. When I insisted I really did have a friend she called me a liar and slapped my face. I was told in no uncertain terms never to mention my imaginary friend again. I never did and slowly my friend's visits became less frequent. One day she told me even though I wouldn't be able to see her anymore she would always be with me.

In this dream, I saw my friend again. Her name was Onna and I recognized her immediately. I was so happy to see her and even though we were both grown up, it was as though we had never been apart. I hugged her and said how glad I was she had come back to me. She assured me she had never left.

I remember everything in the dream was so beautiful, not just the colors and the surroundings but I had a feeling of lightness and completeness. Even the air smelled wonderful. She took my hand and we walked through this beautiful countryside filled with flowers and trees laden with fruit. Finally, we came to a wooden bridge and as we started across I looked down and I could see there was writing on each board. One said, Broken Promises, another, Lost Opportunities, and the next one, Unfulfilled Dreams. I started to laugh as I felt quite giddy with joy and I pointed to the boards and said they reminded me of a picture in one of the piano books I had as a child that said the road to hell is paved with good intentions. My friend smiled at me as we crossed the bridge.

Soon I became aware of a magnificent building made of polished black marble and she indicated we were to enter. Since the sunlight had been very bright outside it took my eyes awhile to become accustomed to the indoor light. As my eyes readjusted I gasped in astonishment at the beauty before me. We were in a huge palace lavishly furnished and filled with magnificent music and wonderful smells. Hundreds, no, thousands of elegant people were laughing and enjoying every kind of pleasure you could imagine. As we entered the ballroom we were greeted by a handsome young man who welcomed us to what he referred to as the Pleasure Palace. He motioned for us to come closer as he explained there would be no desire that would go unconsummated, and no wish that wouldn't be immediately fulfilled. I stared into the gigantic ballroom, with crystal chandeliers and exotic birds hanging in gilded cages. But mostly, I studied the beautiful people. As I looked closely, I could see some were lavishly dressed and covered in jewels and sequins as if they were royalty. Others were naked but I knew they wanted to be that way because of the provocative manner they were acting. Others were eating and drinking at tables piled high with exotic food and many kinds of liquors. I guess I could say they were all engaged in very hedonistic activities.

My friend and I declined the young man's invitation and he in turn sneered at us and his whole attitude appeared to change, becoming quite hostile. We turned to leave and my friend quoted the verse from Corinthians. I remembered it because I won an award for memorizing it when I was a youngster. 1st Corinthians, 9-12. *'For we know in part and we prophesy in part; but when that which is perfect has come, that which is imperfect will be done away with. When I was a child I spoke as a child, I felt as a child, I thought as a child. Now that I have become a man, I have put away the things of a child. We see now through a mirror in an obscure manner, but then face to face. Now I know in part but then I shall know even as I have been known.'*

As we started down the path that led us back to the bridge, my friend handed me a silver mirror and told me it was the mirror of illumination. When I held it up and looked into it I saw my face but I didn't have any scars and I was unblemished. My skin was clear and shown with a beautiful soft light. As I studied my reflection an eye opened up in the center of my forehead and even though it hadn't been apparent seconds before, it now stared back at me from the mirror. The color of the eye was magnificent. It was an intense azure blue, so bright and clear it caused me to gasp at its beauty. The eye then closed and there was no evidence of it having been on my forehead.

My friend told me not to be afraid and everything was as it should be, and then she motioned to me to look into the mirror again, but this time I should gaze beyond my reflection and into the darker background. At the same time she cautioned me not to, under any circumstances, turn around. Truthfully, I wanted to keep looking at my own reflection but I did as she told me and looked into the darker area surrounding my face. Oh God, Harry, it was so awful! The black marble building was gone and instead it looked like some kind of a toxic waste dump. The young man that greeted us at the door was now half man and half beast and covered with terrible sores and snot and slime dripped from his nose and mouth. He was so sinister and disgusting that when he glared at me I felt a coldness enter my entire being. I could also see strange looking beasts prowling around behind him and some of them seemed to have blood dripping from their mouths and I knew they were demon predators looking for victims. The same people who had been dancing and enjoying themselves earlier were now rolling and writhing with pain and they resembled maggots feeding off each other. I became aware that each of these souls had lost any shred of its former human identity and the uniqueness they had strived so hard to develop in their former lives was gone. It was as though they were destined for all eternity to be alone and yet one in their misery and suffering, but I can't explain that contradiction. I was consumed with a feeling of total despair and hopelessness and I screamed and dropped the mirror as I started to run. I think that must have been when you tried to waken me. It was the strangest dream I've ever had."

For several minutes Harry didn't speak as he reflected on his wife's nightmare. He held her close, comforting her by stroking her hair and kissing her forehead. It was Annie who broke the silence when she whispered, "What do you think the awful dream was trying to tell me?"

"I'm not really sure. There's certainly a lot to think about. I know in my heart you are not like other people, you seem to have been given talents or gifts that need to be used to help humanity. How, I'm not sure. Maybe you need to wait and see what the future brings."

Chapter 16

Michael O'Grady could hear his wife preparing supper in the kitchen as he watched the five-o'clock news. The phone rang and Martha spoke quietly so her husband wasn't able to hear the conversation. After a few moments she appeared in the doorway, "Danny is coming over to have supper with us. Will you put the yard light on and watch for him? I'm still frying chicken."

Michael took off his glasses and laid them on a small end table and inquired, "Isn't Doreen home again tonight? It's the second time this week and it's only Wednesday."

"He said 'she' is home but has fixed another one of her casseroles for supper and he didn't feel quite up to it."

Michael grinned, realizing the 'she' Danny was speaking of was the boy's mother. Neither of their grandsons referred to their mother as mom, but said her or she, as if referring to an interfering outsider.

"The old deadly casterole, eh?" He purposely mispronounced the word the way Danny did, "Well, I'd say Danny is using his head by eating here."

Michael flipped on the yard light and glanced across the dark street. Danny was their youngest grandson and only recently had celebrated his eighth birthday. Doreen and her third husband Lenny, and Corey, their twelve year-old grandson lived across the street and two doors down. After the breakup of her second marriage, Martha and Michael moved Doreen and the boys into the house nearby so they could help with the care of the boys. A move Michael now questioned the wisdom of more and more in recent months.

"He's already here and I think he plans on spending the night since he has his school books, backpack and Dixie."

Martha gave a worried glance at Michael as she said, "I hope that doesn't mean what I think it means." She didn't finish her comment as

Danny was already coming into the house accompanied by his miniature dachshund, Dixie.

"Hi, grandpa and grandma, it sure smells good in here."

Michael put his hand on Danny's shoulder, "Hey guy, nice to have you here with us. Looks like you're planning to spend the night judging from your baggage?"

"Can I, grandpa?" Danny had a pleading look on his face.

"I guess so. Grandma and I get pretty lonely around here since all our kids are gone. Grandma will call your mom later. So, I hear you escaped the deadly casterole tonight."

Martha frowned at Michael, "Don't encourage him. It's probably a very delicious casserole."

Michael followed Martha into the kitchen and leaned up against the counter. "Martha, you have to face the truth. Doreen might be a pretty fair schoolteacher and a fairly good daughter but she is one hell of a poor cook."

"Shhh! Don't forget that little boys repeat what they hear."

"He isn't even listening to us. He's all wrapped up in his television show."

Michael reached across the stove and took a small piece of chicken off the platter. "If you remember on our last anniversary she insisted on bringing something, and you let her bring cake because you said no one could ruin a cake. She brought a beet cake. Holy mother of God! Martha, you know I like beets but no one in their right mind makes a beet cake. It tasted like dirt. None of us could eat it and we all sat around looking like we wanted to puke."

Martha started to protest but Michael put his finger to her lips. "I could be slowly starving to death but I would have to think long and hard before I would even consider eating one of Doreen's devastatingly delicious casteroles."

She pushed his hand away, "Shame on you." She turned away quickly and Michael could see she was having a hard time keeping from laughing. "Call Danny into the kitchen so we can eat."

After supper Martha called Doreen to ask if Danny could spend the night. Doreen said it would be fine, as she needed a break from her youngest son anyway. Mother and daughter shared a short conversation and Martha hung up the phone not relaying her conversation to her husband. She silently cleaned the table, clicked on the dishwasher and sat down at the dining room table to help Danny with his homework.

Later, as Michael settled Danny and Dixie into the bedroom that had been Doreen's room he turned to leave when he heard Danny call to him. "Grandpa, don't forget to put the night light on . . . and, do you think you could stay with me until I fall asleep?"

Michael looked at Danny and couldn't help but notice how small and vulnerable he looked. "I guess I could stay for a little while. Us guys have to stick together. Something you want to talk to me about? You were awfully quiet at supper?"

"No."

Within a few minutes, Michael could feel himself drifting off to sleep when he heard Danny's soft voice ask, "Where's shit creek?"

Michael's eyes flew open. "What did you say Danny? Shit Creek? Where did you hear an expression like that?"

"She said it."

Knowing Danny was referring to Doreen, Michael asked, "She did? When?"

"Tonight, before I came over here. She was yelling at Lenny and told him if he wasn't careful he would wind up in Shit Creek without a paddle."

Martha's assumption was accurate. Doreen and Lenny were at it again. "I think it just means your mom and step dad are having a few problems."

"That ain't a good place to be is it?"

"No, I guess not."

"I didn't think so. Goodnight, grandpa. I love you."

"Good night Danny. I love you too."

Sleep was out of the question now, and Michael lay awake staring up at the pattern the nightlight cast across the ceiling. Martha was right when she suspected Doreen and Lenny were fighting again. It didn't surprise him at all. With Doreen it was always a matter of time before she found a reason to fight with someone. Doreen was their middle child and Michael thought he remembered reading somewhere that life was often more difficult for a middle child. Familial placement. No, that didn't sound quite right but he knew it was something like that.

His thoughts drifted to their oldest child and only son, Thomas Michael. He had followed in his father's footsteps and chosen law enforcement as his career. It had been the proudest day of Michael's life when he saw Thomas Michael graduate from the Police Academy. He had worn his badge proudly and served with honor and dedication until the afternoon a suspected drug dealer shot him in the face with a sawed-off shotgun and ended his life. In spite of the years that had passed, Michael continued to feel a deep ache in his chest thinking about that day. Their youngest daughter's name was Kathleen and he couldn't help but smile every time he thought about her. In his mind he always pictured her full of life, laughing and giggling while most of the time Doreen sat in the background pouting.

When Kathleen told Michael she was going to follow him and her deceased sibling into law enforcement he had all he could do to keep from pleading with her to walk away from it. The thought of losing her too was too much to deal with.

Danny whimpered in his sleep and Michael's thoughts came back to Doreen. He didn't really blame Lenny or the other two husbands for not being able to get along with her. It was true, in Michael's opinion, Lenny was a bit spineless but a stronger man would never have put up with Doreen's disruptive behavior. Michael had been brought up to cherish and protect women, especially women who were being abused. Now, after all his years on the police force he'd come to realize that some women, his daughter included, took advantage of this, and as a result, they themselves became the abuser.

Deep within his heart Michael knew it had been more difficult for him to love Doreen than the other two children. She hadn't inherited her mother's quiet, gentle ways and she always had to have the last word. He loved his grandsons with all his heart and it pained him to see what their daughter was doing to them. Danny was so gentle and at times almost wimpy. Michael knew Martha would scold him if she heard him use that word but he felt it was accurate. Maybe vulnerable was a better word. Corey was a different matter. At one time he too had been gentle and vulnerable but the years of living with Doreen was taking a heavy toll on him. If the saying is true what you see day after day you eventually become, Doreen's influence was slowly creating a smaller version of herself. It took real effort to look beyond the hard, cynical shell to see the frightened little boy Corey really was.

At first the signs were subtle. Corey had been a bright, healthy baby from the first day he was born but shortly after he left the hospital he had developed croup. Later his pediatrician would say that Corey was high strung and that he had a nervous stomach. As he got older Doreen would tell people that Corey was strong willed, probably because of his higher than average intelligence and that he was bored. Her favorite line was she was a schoolteacher so who should know better than her? Doreen always knew better than everyone else. She was an oracle of wisdom and a fountain of unlimited knowledge. Her favorite words were, "I know" and let's face it you couldn't explain anything to someone who is convinced they already know everything.

Even though Doreen's past track record didn't validate her exaggerated opinion of herself she would simply say it wasn't her fault that everyone always let her down. As Corey got older Doreen called him the pill, and mother's little juvenile delinquent. As he grew older Corey began to believe all the labels she so casually tacked on him. Doreen dragged him to school counselors and psychologists in an effort to find out what might be wrong with him. Later she fed him Ritalin and other drugs but to no avail. What never seemed to occur to her was that she might be a big part of the problem. If a hint of that reality was brought out during a counseling session Doreen would cry and carry on so pathetically the counselor ended up comforting her and shifting his or her attention away from what the real issue was.

The part that made Michael the saddest was throughout all the years Doreen was growing up and into her early adulthood, this same behavior was going on and he and Martha hadn't really done anything to stop it. They had been there for her and the boys, picking up the pieces when her life fell apart. Babysitting so she could continue working and helping her buy the house after her second husband walked out on her. They had even paid off her credit cards when the finance company came after her. He winced as he thought back on several occasions when they had covered her bad checks so she wouldn't be prosecuted, all the time telling themselves those were the things caring and responsible parents might do for a child who was having problems. No matter how many times he and Martha went over her situation the bottom line remained obvious. She was no longer a child and they had unintentionally become part of the problem by allowing her to continue with her destructive and selfish behavior. They could only hope and pray it wasn't too late for Corey but both knew it would be a difficult task to win his trust back.

As Michael stared at the ceiling his thoughts went back to the night he knew had been a pivotal point in their relationship with their eldest grandson. The phone rang at eleven-thirty at night. It was Doreen and she was screaming hysterically into the phone that they had to come over because Corey had attacked her and she couldn't go on living with this monster. They couldn't understand any more of what else she'd said because of her yelling and crying into the phone and threatening her son at the same time. Michael and Martha dressed quickly and without speaking drove to Doreen's home not fully knowing what to expect. When they arrived the door to the apartment was wide open even though it was late in December. As they entered they could see the Christmas tree lying on its side and broken ornaments scattered everywhere. Obviously there had been some kind of a struggle and a policeman was unsuccessfully trying to take a statement from a very hysterical Doreen.

Danny was crying but Corey was sitting in a corner looking very frightened and all Michael could make out of Doreen's conversation with the policeman was she wanted the little monster out of her house and never wanted to see him again. As soon as Doreen saw Martha she broke into hysterical sobs and ran toward her pointing to her scratched face saying Corey had attacked her and she had no idea what provoked him.

Between the officer, Martha and Michael they were able to gradually calm Doreen down. After more tears and accusations it was decided that for his own safety Corey would be taken from the apartment and placed in a safe home rather than juvenile hall for a few days. The incident was written up as a domestic dispute that had gotten out of hand. Normally, the police might have let Michael and Martha take Corey home with them but Doreen objected, saying it was time the little bastard learned some serious lessons. The policeman apologized to Michael but said judging from Doreen's state of mind it might be better if one of them stayed with her and Danny through the night.

As the officer took Corey's arm to lead him away the boy turned to Michael and looked directly into his eyes saying, "In case you don't know it, your daughter is a psycho bitch! You're afraid of her like everyone else." Then Corey was gone. A nine year old boy being placed in a police car and taken to some strange house to keep him safe from the very person who should have been protecting him.

Two days later Michael picked up Corey at the safe house but he was now a different child than he had been before. This Corey was sullen and pulled away from Michael when he tried to touch him. As he got out of the car he looked at his grandfather and said in a cold voice, "She'll never make me cry again, not ever."

When Michael was sure Danny was sleeping he slipped out of the bedroom making sure a second nightlight was left on and the door remained open.

Chapter 17

Harry sorted through the papers in his desk drawer where he kept most of his personal items trying to find a list of phone numbers. Upon finding the elusive list he also noticed three obituaries. One was for Peter Brentwood IV, who had died unexpectedly at the young age of thirty-six, the second for the double funeral of Ruth and Jacob Freedman who had died within two days of each other, and the third for his old friend Betty Bartusek. Betty's funeral had taken place on November 4, 1993, and he was a little surprised to realize how quickly the time had passed. Harry wished he could have spent more time with Betty the last year of her life but he hadn't. What was the phrase Molly so often used? In the blink of on eye everything could change.

Mercifully, Betty's life ended rather quickly. Her constant coughing turned into pneumonia and in September she was unable to continue her work at the Salvation Army. Coupled with her progressing emphysema and the stress of living in her very small home with her son Bubba and ex-husband Dom, Harry was not surprised to receive a call informing him she'd been admitted to the hospital. The nurse who called said Betty was critically ill and needed to speak with him as soon as possible.

Harry left work early that Monday and went directly to Abbott Northwestern Hospital. Betty was in a double room on the side by the window. Her roommate was an elderly woman who was so pale and lay so still, Harry wasn't completely convinced she hadn't already expired. Fortunately the nurse at the desk had warned him Betty's roommate was also very ill but was indeed alive, just not responding to the outside world.

A curtain separated the two beds and as Harry entered the room he could hear Betty's labored breathing and coughing. She appeared to be dozing and as Harry looked down at her he was shocked to see how bloated and puffy she was. Her face and hands were swollen and distorted, and from the rattling sounds coming from her throat and chest he felt death couldn't be far away. He called her name softly and she slowly opened her eyes but appeared dazed and confused.

"Hello, Betty, it's me, Harry. I came as soon as I could."

She turned her head slightly and tried to smile and he could see she recognized him. The tube that supplied oxygen through her nose was not enough to relieve her labored breathing. She opened her mouth to speak but her parched lips stuck together and were coated with a white sticky substance. She motioned toward the water glass on the table next to her bed. Harry gently offered her a sip and she took only enough to wet her mouth and lips before she pushed the glass away. "Buddy, I've got to tell you something. I'm dying. I know it and that's okay with me."

Harry wanted to protest but he knew she was right so he reached for her hand as if to reassure her.

"You've always been good to me but now I have to ask one more favor of you. I've got no one else to turn to." She started to cough and Harry could see how difficult it was for her to struggle to get enough air to sustain her life. He found himself praying silently she wouldn't die while he was visiting with her.

"I've got no one but those two dumb shits at home and you know very well I can't expect anything from them. Bubba, well, I can understand him being the way he is, it's not his fault, poor kid. But Dom, he ain't never been worth the powder to blow him to hell. Buddy, will you see to it I get a proper funeral?" Her eyes had filled with tears. "I wouldn't ask this but I've got no other choice. The money I have saved should go for Bubba's care when I'm not here to look after him."

Her voice still had the soft southern drawl but the years of cigarette smoking had ravaged it and made it raspy. She continued, "A nice funeral with some flowers but not too many. A spray of roses on the casket and a ribbon that says mother and wife but make sure it's not too heavy. I wouldn't like that weight on me."

Another bout of coughing ensued and she seemed to choke on her own saliva so Harry gave her another sip of water. He waited for her to stop coughing and then reached for her hand again. "Don't give it another thought. I'll take care of the funeral and be sure there is always enough money for Bubba's care for the rest of his life."

Betty seemed relieved as she looked into her friend's eyes. "I knew the first time I laid eyes on you that you had a heart of gold. I always thought . . . ." She seemed to drift away for a moment and then said, "I always thought my funeral should be at the St. Paul Cathedral with a choir. I remember seeing a movie once that took place somewhere down south . . . this Negro housekeeper for some rich family died and they gave her the grandest funeral I ever saw. They had horses with plumes pulling the burial wagon and a big band playing as the funeral procession made its way down the main street. It made me cry it was so beautiful and that's when I made up my mind no matter how lousy my life was I was going to have a nice funeral. I don't expect nothin' like that, but maybe there could be a white limousine for Bubba and Dom to ride in. Bubba has never been in a limousine and I know he'd really get a big kick out of that."

Harry silently breathed a sigh of relief thinking that plumed horses and a marching band could be a little hard to come up with in November or December in Minnesota.

After another coughing spell she continued with her voice taking on a more dreamy tone, "And Bubba and Dom would be standing by my casket in tuxedos looking like royalty. And a top hat, they would each have a top hat to wear. They would come to the Cathedral in the white limousine with red and silver balloons tied to the antenna and the balloons would be set free at the graveside just like my soul being set free . . . ." She lay with her eyes shut and Harry thought she had fallen asleep as her face looked much more peaceful. Betty opened her eyes and added thoughtfully, "And a new dress for me. Something real pretty, for God knows I've not had pretty for a long time. Probably not since you brought me those pink roses."

Harry continued to hold her hand as he assured her all of her requests would be honored. She fell asleep and Harry could tell the conversation had completely drained her. He left the hospital but not before he asked that he be notified if she needed anything or if she were to pass on. That night at about eight-thirty he received the call she had died alone peacefully. The nurse explained the family had been called earlier but they hadn't made it in.

The next morning Harry called Dom to express his condolences and to tell him he would be handling the funeral arrangements according to Betty's wishes. He asked if the Lexington Funeral home would be satisfactory, to which Dom mumbled something like "yeah, sure" in reply. Harry arranged to have the visitation to be held on Wednesday from four in the afternoon until eight in the evening. Since Betty had never actually been a parishioner at the St. Paul Cathedral, Annie used her connections with her friends at the church to arrange for Betty's funeral. It was to be held at the Cathedral at ten on Thursday morning. With this already being Tuesday it gave them only one more day to complete the arrangements. Annie and Harry had requested Friday but since it had already been reserved for something else they assured the pastor Thursday would be fine.

In gratitude for their cooperation for Betty's funeral Harry provided a very generous donation to be made in the memory of Elizabeth Dufoe Bartusek. In turn they were assured a choir would sing at the funeral mass even though it was on very short notice. The flowers were ordered and a spray of pink roses that was not too heavy, complete with ribbons was chosen for her casket. A white limousine with red and silver helium balloons was reserved and an appointment was set up for Dom and Bubba to be fitted for their tuxedos.

Harry instructed Dom and Bubba he would be picking them up at one-o'clock to have them fitted for their tuxedos, get haircuts, and buy them sensible outfits for the wake. He also instructed them to take a bath and put on clean underwear before he got there. When Harry arrived at Betty's tiny home he found Dom and Bubba red-eyed and reeking of smoke and beer. The usually tidy house was in disarray with dirty dishes and beer bottles stacked in the sink and on the kitchen counter. Harry had wisely alerted the clothing store about Bubba and Dom so they would be somewhat aware of what to expect. Bottom line was he had explained they would be expected to outfit two mourners who could easily qualify as the Gentleman Quarterly's worst nightmare.

The clerk at the clothing store was an elderly gentleman who appeared to have been employed there forever, and assured Harry he was quite up to handling the task. In spite of this Harry was sure he'd heard a tiny, yet audible gasp as he presented Bubba and Dom. Dom was not difficult to fit as he was small and thin but Bubba presented a much greater challenge. Later, as Harry described the scenario to Annie he would say "Picture a large, overstuffed sofa about to be hauled to the dump ground. Then try to wrestle a tuxedo around it. What more can I say?"

When the task was done and Dom and Bubba stood side by side, top hats and all, the clerk maintained his very dignified composure but Harry had to turn away to keep himself from breaking into hysterical laughter. Finally, he was able to choke out, "Very good, sir!" Harry couldn't guess where they found the top hats, but agreed Bubba would do well to have suspenders and both gentlemen would probably need dress overcoats as the weather on Thursday was to be windy and rainy, with a slight chance of snow flurries. An outfit for each of them to wear to the wake was also selected and the trio quickly exited the store.

That evening Annie showed Harry the pink lace dress she had picked out and both agreed it would help to compensate for all the years Betty had gone without pretty. Earlier, Annie questioned the wisdom of putting Dom and Bubba in tuxedos but now agreed it seemed important to Betty and it was only right that Harry honor her deathbed wishes. When Annie cautiously asked if they really looked as bad as Harry described his reply was, "Dom looks like a sleazy river boat gambler villain in a melodrama . . . Bubba, well, what can I say? Try to imagine a comedy called, The Phantom of the Ape Ra?"

Annie declared him evil for saying that, but recanted by adding he was a good friend for following up so thoroughly with Betty's wishes.

On Wednesday evening Harry and Annie arrived at the funeral home at about six-thirty and Harry noticed with sadness fewer than ten names were recorded in the guest book. He justified it by saying many of Betty's friends were elderly or poor and didn't have cars and of course, the weather had turned cold and raw. He looked around at the small gathering of people trying to pick out Dom and Bubba but was unable to locate them. As he and Annie approached the casket Harry was relieved to see how nice Betty looked and that some of the puffiness had left her face allowing her to look more like her old self. The funeral director approached them and asked if the bereaved family had arrived and Harry realized with a sinking feeling Bubba and Dom had not yet shown up. Harry excused himself leaving Annie to visit with the few mourners and finding a telephone dialed Dom's number. Dom answered and Harry could immediately tell he had been drinking. He could also hear Bubba blubbering in the background and when he demanded to know why they weren't at the funeral home Dom explained in a slurred voice that Bubba was sick. He continued by saying he thought it must have been something Bubba had eaten and now he had the runs. For this reason Dom decided he had better stay home and take care of him.

Harry felt the anger flaring up inside of him and it took all of his self-control not to yell into the phone. He took a deep breath and spoke in a very precise, overly controlled voice, "Listen you ingrate, you both be ready at eight-thirty tomorrow morning, bathed, dressed, and sober waiting by the front door. Do you understand the fact that I am not suggesting you be ready, I am ordering you to be ready. If for some reason you're not ready when I arrive, you'll regret it for the few short seconds that will remain of your pathetic, selfish, useless lives. Am I making myself sufficiently clear? Do you understand? What part of what I am saying do you not understand?"

There was a long pause, which prompted Harry to repeat himself, "DO YOU UNDERSTAND?"

"Yeah." The line went dead.

When Harry reentered the small funeral home chapel Annie couldn't remember seeing him so angry. He didn't speak but knelt where the family should have been as the priest led the mourners in praying the rosary.

The next morning Harry woke up feeling cranky and irritable. The temperature had dropped dramatically during the night and the gusting wind had picked up even more, making the wind chill bitterly cold. As he looked out the window he realized it had snowed during the night. It was arranged that Martha would pick up Annie, and Harry, Dom, and Bubba would ride in the limousine and meet them at the Cathedral. Annie wanted to be sure all the preparations were in order and Harry wasn't completely convinced he could count on Dom and Bubba to be ready on time.

Shortly before Harry left, the priest called asking if it would be all right to say the prayers normally said over the casket at the cemetery in the church because of the dangerous wind chill. Harry agreed this was a good idea and as he put his coat on joked with Annie about the drive-by burial Betty was getting. Both were greatly relieved they would not have to stand outside in the biting cold.

The limousine arrived at their door at exactly eight o'clock, complete with six red and silver balloons, banging crazily from the antenna. Harry gave the driver the address to Betty's house as he sat back in the comfortable leather seat and found himself wishing the day was already over. The morning was overcast and dreary and the morning commuters were moving slowly with several stalled vehicles stopping traffic and diverting cars into alternate lanes. The driver apologized to Harry for the delays and they agreed the sudden drop in temperature had caught people off guard. The snowfall intensified and as they approached Betty's house he could see the yard was already white with snow and the sidewalk had a small drift forming. Harry tried to step carefully through the drift but ended up with his shoes and socks getting wet. He wished he'd taken Annie's advice when she had suggested he wear overshoes and realized he would have aching feet for the rest of the day.

When Harry knocked on the door Dom opened it immediately as if he had been waiting for him. He was dressed and ready but Harry could smell the cigarettes and alcohol on his breath. Even though he averted Harry's scrutinizing look Harry could see how glassy and blood shot his eyes were. Harry stepped inside and couldn't help commenting, "Needed a little liquid courage already this morning?" Dom silently retreated to the safety of a wooden chair by the kitchen table as Harry glanced around and noticed how Betty's neat house now looked like disaster area. He also became aware of the stifling smell that permeated the air and made his stomach turn uncomfortably. The fact that it must have been at least eighty-five degrees in the house only compounded the stench.

Harry spotted the thermostat and turned it down to seventy-four degrees and asked, "Where's Bubba?"

Dom pointed to the bathroom and mumbled, "In the can. Like I told you, he's been sick . . . he's been in there most of the morning."

Harry could hear the toilet flush and Bubba came out of the bathroom zipping up his pants. As he pulled his suspenders up and tried to untangle them he mumbled, "Shit, these are all wet. They must've fallen in the toilet." The suspenders were indeed all tangled and wet but Harry couldn't bring himself to helping Bubba untangle them.

"Put your coat on and maybe nobody will notice." Somehow, it didn't surprise Harry to see that Bubba's' crisp white shirt was stained with coffee and some other unidentifiable substance. Bubba dug under the couch and retrieved his shoes and put them on as he assured Harry he was ready. Harry looked into Bubba's face and realized the person inside that large body was still a child. As Bubba pulled on the black topcoat Harry couldn't help but think how much he resembled an unmade bed. As they stepped outside Harry cautioned Bubba to hold onto his hat but it was already too late and a gust of wind sent it sailing across the lawn. The driver who had stepped outside to open the limo door made a sprint across the yard and put his foot onto the brim of the runaway hat. He returned it unscathed to a very confused Bubba.

The limousine was warm and comfortable and Bubba immediately chose the seat by the window leaving Dom to sit in the middle. Bubba was holding his top hat in his lap and his hair was standing straight up in the air. A big grin spread across his face and he was obviously delighted with the vehicle. He kept saying "Cool" and "Neato" as he rubbed his hands over the white leather upholstery. Harry found himself wondering how it must feel to be Bubba seeing the world through his child's mind and having the world expect him to behave like the thirty something year old body he inhabited. He remembered his conversation with Betty that ever since the car hit Bubba on his bike he didn't seem to fit in anywhere. A low, unmistakable rumble interrupted Harry's thoughts, followed by Bubba noticeably fidgeting in his seat. A big, stupid grin flooded across Bubba's face. The limousine quickly filled with a disgusting odor and Harry groaned, "Oh God, Bubba was that you?"

Bubba kept grinning as if he had done something special, "It ain't my fault, ever since ma died 'bout all we've had to eat is beans. I told Dom they go right through me but he said I had to eat 'em anyway."

Harry put his hand over his nose but not before he gave Bubba a stern look, "Don't do that again . . ." His admonishment came too late as Bubba shifted to one side in his seat and the limousine was again filled with the unmistakable stench.

Harry tapped on the window that separated the chauffeur from his passengers and requested he roll the right back window half way down. The cool, crisp air filled the back seat and cleansed the polluted air away. Bubba immediately started to whine, "Geez, I'm freezing, gimmie a break."

Harry glared at Bubba, "Do that again, and I'll make you run behind the limo the rest of the way."

When Harry felt sure Bubba had learned his lesson he tapped on the glass and signaled to the driver to roll the window back up. Bubba muttered under his breath, pouting like a small child. All the while, Dom remained mute and stared straight ahead obviously not wanting to get involved. Bubba continued to mutter and Harry could pick out several obscene words and part of a sentence containing the words dick head and grouch. Leaning forward and glaring at him Harry said only, "Bubba, shut up."

Bubba sat quietly for a few minutes and then proceed to explore his surroundings. He quickly discovered the small bar and was delighted to see it was stocked with several single serving bottles of liquor as well as imported beer. As Bubba held up a bottle Dom leaned forward and for the first time showed some interest in what his son was doing. Harry didn't move but said in a low, controlled voice, "Put it back."

Bubba looked at Harry and said, "Can't we just have . . . ."

"Don't even think about it. Put it back."

The rest of the trip preceded in silence with Harry looking out the window at the swirling snow and wondering how Betty ever put up with these characters so long. Death seemed an acceptable option.

When they finally arrived at the Cathedral Harry noted sadly there were only a handful of people there. David and Michael were visiting off to one side and Martha and Annie were standing by Betty's casket.

Harry asked if Dom and Bubba wanted to see Betty one last time before the casket was closed. Bubba grabbed for Dom's arm but the unwilling father moved away quickly averting his son's grasp. Harry saw the look of confusion in Bubba's eyes and took him by the arm and led him to the casket reminding him to take his hat off.

Annie smiled at Bubba and said softly, "Robert, your mother is at peace. She looks very nice, doesn't she?"

Bubba stood staring down at his mother and started to cry. "Why can't she come home? I want her to come home. I'm so lonesome. Ma! I need you to take care of me." He reached down to touch her face but quickly pulled his hand away as he felt the coldness of her skin. The funeral director appeared and suggested they close the casket, as the service was about to begin. As Annie led Bubba to the pew reserved for the family, he started to sob out loud. Annie tried to comfort him but she being so small, and him so large, it created a strangely pathetic sight. By the time the choir sang their opening song and the service started there were maybe thirty people in attendance. Harry and Annie were deeply moved by how incredibly beautiful the music was. The priest celebrating the funeral mass delivered a touching eulogy even though he'd never met Elizabeth Dufoe Bartusek. Harry felt his spirits lifting knowing his friend Betty was leaving this world just as she had imagined she would. As he looked around at the huge Cathedral he was filled with a sense of awe at its beauty, and made a silent commitment that he and Annie would come back to have a closer look at its splendor.

They rode to the cemetery in silence except for Bubba's sniffling and nose blowing and when the undertaker unloaded the casket only the priest and his altar boys got out of their car and hurriedly sprinkled Betty's resting place with holy water and made the closing sign of the cross. Luckily the ground had not yet frozen so Betty could be laid to rest before winter set in.

The driver of the limousine got out and released the red and silver balloons, which immediately shot straight up into the air as a great gust of wind caught them. Harry smiled as he envisioned Betty's soul shooting up to the heavenly reward she so rightly deserved.

As soon as they left the cemetery Bubba started complaining how hungry he was. Dom tried to hush him up but the conversation ended with them bickering over who was the boss now that Betty was gone. Harry tapped on the glass partition and motioned for the driver to put the window down. Handing the driver a hundred dollar bill he told him he needed to be dropped off at Sullivan Glass. He asked him to take the other passengers to a Kentucky Fried Chicken drive-through and purchase two large buckets of chicken and all the trimmings, adding he could keep whatever money was left from the hundred dollar bill.

Harry explained to Dom and Bubba they would be contacted by Betty's attorney about her Will and he and Annie would provide them with money and groceries until then. He further explained as far as he knew Dom would inherit the house minus the things Bubba would want for himself. Bubba would then be moved to the group home Betty had chosen for him where he would probably live for the rest of his life. Bubba sat grinning and Harry wondered how much of what he had said was understood. He looked directly at Bubba. "Do you understand what I'm telling you?"

"White or dark?" Bubba was looking very happy.

"What are you talking about?"

"Do we get some white meat and some dark meat, 'cause I like 'em both. And mashed potatoes too. And gravy but I don't like that green cabbage stuff."

Harry sighed and said, "Yes, you'll get both white and dark and mashed potatoes too."

The rest of the trip Bubba and Dom argued about who would have to shovel the walk when they got home and if there really were two snow flakes that were exactly alike. The driver stopped the car in front of Sullivan Glass and Harry reminded Dom to hang the tuxedos on a hanger and a man from the clothing store would be by the next day to pick them up.

He saw Dom's eyes dart over to the limo's bar and his parting words to him were, "Touch what's in the bar and I'll see you inherit nothing."

The day after the Will was read, a For Sale sign appeared in front of Betty's tiny house.

Chapter 18

Harry awoke with a start as he became conscious of Annie telling him to wake up, that the phone was for him. He struggled to clear his head of the deep dream state he'd been in and responded by whispering, "What time is it?" He felt slightly confused and needed a few moments to gather his thoughts before he took the phone.

"It's a little after two." In the dim light she looked apprehensive.

"Who is it?" He whispered again as he felt his own fear starting to kick in. He couldn't remember any time when good news came at this hour. In his dream he'd been lost in a long, dark hallway. He opened door after door but each room was dark and empty. He couldn't remember what he'd been looking for but knew he was scared. He took the phone from her and said cautiously, "Hello?" He could hear a lot of noise in the background, almost as if the person on the other end was at a party.

"Harry, old friend, how the hell are you?"

"Who is this?"

"Gil Meyers. You remember me don't you? Or are you too successful now to have forgotten your friend from the good old days?"

"Where are you, and do you have any idea what time it is?"

"Hey, I'm in Las Vegas. You know, the city that never sleeps and I guess we forget some parts of the world still go to bed with the chickens."

For obvious reasons Harry could feel his apprehension was being replaced with growing irritation but he made an effort to be pleasant. "How did you find me?"

"I called Robin, the girl that used to work in the office at Sindlers. Remember the homely one with the great ass? She knew right off where you were. I think she always had a sweet spot for you. Anyway, she gave me your phone number."

Harry could feel his irritation turning to anger. "What could be so important that you needed to find me at two in the morning?"

"Harry, to cut right to the chase, I need a little favor from you."

"A favor? What kind of a favor?" Something inside had now changed and he felt a little threatened. Almost as if a tiny voice inside him was cautioning him to be on the alert.

There was a pause on the other end. "Harry, we go back a long way, both as business partners and good friends. You put your feet under my table and broke bread many times. It's true we haven't kept in touch but I knew if I could count on anyone it would be you."

"How much?"

In the background Harry could hear the sounds of slot machines and people shouting. Harry repeated the question. "How much money do you need, Gil?"

"Ten thousand dollars. It's kind of hard to explain over the phone but if you'd wire it to me I'll explain the whole thing in detail in a couple of days. You see, I owe this guy and he won't wait. He wants the money now and . . . ." There was another pause. "Hell, Harry, remember the whole time you were in the hospital I broke my hump holding the business together. It was me who met with Texas Instruments trying to get them to buy our power cell."

Harry cut in. "There were no meetings with Texas Instruments. I checked. There was no business for you to break your hump over. You left with all the money and my car. By the way, what ever happened to my Hawk?"

There was another pause and Gil countered. "Look, it wasn't my fault you got mixed up with that ditsy waitress and ended up in the hospital. I had a family to support."

"The car?"

"It was a piece of shit. The engine blew and I sold it for scrap, but that's water under the bridge. I need your help now man, let bygones be bygones."

"I loved that car. It was the first car I ever owned. I think, no I know I liked it even better than I liked you." Harry glanced at Annie who had a slightly amused look on her face. He continued, "You know Gil, there is the belief that everything in life happens for a reason, and I know it was important for me to have you come into my life at exactly that time. I guess I had to learn some hard lessons from you. There is also the belief that out of each situation we learn from these lessons and if we don't we're destined to repeat the same ones over and over until we get them right."

"I have no idea what the hell you're talking about." Harry could hear the mounting anger in Gil's voice. "What the fuck are you saying? That you won't loan me the money?"

Harry took a deep breath, "Gil, on the ship of life there are those people who are captains and navigate the course a ship will follow. There are also the sailors or the workers who keep the ship sailing. Then there are the barnacles, those who are hanging on for the free ride. Let's say I am finally willing to let you become the captain of your ship and not continue being a barnacle. Good night Gil."

"You son of a bitch."

"No, actually, I think it was something else you called me. It seems you once referred to me as a simple bastard and an easy mark."

Harry handed the phone back to Annie, and when she placed it back on the receiver he said quietly, "Did I do the right thing?"

"Yes. You've learned that lesson and you don't need to learn it over again. I love you, Harry. You're a good and kind man. It sounds as if Gil is a person who takes advantage of everyone He's the kind of person who'll spend his entire life looking for decent people like you and using them for his own gain. You did the right thing. Good night my dear one."

Chapter 19

David and Sister Mary Rose sat on the sprawling porch of Seaton House sipping iced tea and enjoying the warm weather.

"Tell me a little more about this new patron you have for Seaton House, what's his name again? Louis Welheim wasn't it? He seems like a nice enough man. He's very German isn't he? I met him when Annie and I were here checking out the sunroom." David tried to sound casual but he was really fishing for more background information on Louis.

Mary Rose placed her iced tea on the small wicker table between them. "Very German is an understatement. His real name is Gerhard Louis Welheim. I suppose he started to go by Louis when he came to the United States. I first met him when my father was teaching in Berlin after the war. We lived there for two years and Louis was one of my best friends. World War II had ended but there were still a lot of hurt feelings existing, especially among the young people. For some reason I didn't completely understand, Louis felt the need to protect me from anyone who might resent Americans."

She laughed and picked up her glass again. "Not that I really needed to be protected. I've always been pretty much able to take care of myself." Mary Rose flashed one of her winning smiles at David and continued. "I think he was the first young man I met at school and since he was one of the most popular boys his attention was very flattering to me. You know how teenage girls can be. We became close friends. He was dashingly handsome and charming and also a great athlete. He had an extremely competitive nature about sports to the point where he was not at all gracious when he lost. It seemed as though winning was everything to him. When I tried to tell him it was only a game he would become very serious and say, "Ivy, you don't understand. Winning is everything to me. Looking back now I realize he'd shown signs of a dark side for such a young man. His mother had been married before the war but was unable to get a divorce from her husband even after she became pregnant by a high ranking officer in the German Army. That officer was Louis's father. That's all I ever learned about his parents because I quickly realized this was a very touchy subject and Louis didn't like talking about them. His mother, I think her name was Ava, and the officer, were both killed in a car accident when Louis was a small child. He was raised by his grandmother and a maiden aunt. Since Ava never married Louis's father, he went by her maiden name, Welheim. I remember asking him if he missed his parents and he said he hardly even remembered them. Interestingly though, he told me when he learned Adolf Hitler died he felt a light had gone out in his world and he had cried for him. April 30th was the anniversary of Hitler's death and every year Louis took that day off from school in Hitler's memory. I thought that was very strange even then and that part of him scared me. How could such a bright young man feel that way? Wait! I think his father's name was Goebbels but he wasn't a relative of Josef Goebbels the man Hitler had appointed Chancellor. I could be wrong about that but for some reason that name sticks in my mind. Adolf Hitler became Louis's hero and even though his grandma Gerta made it very clear she could never understand what her grandson saw in that man or his philosophy, he continued to idolize him."

Mary Rose stirred her iced tea and then continued, "I think . . . in fact I know back then, Louis had a serious crush on me. You know how it is, that first love seems so important, but I tried to pretend it didn't exist. I only wanted him to be a friend. I remember a few nights before my family was to return to the United States he gave me a friendship ring and tried to kiss me. By that time I'd already decided my vocation in life was with God, and when I gently pushed him away and tried to explain to him I wanted to become a nun he reacted very strangely. He was furious and threw the ring on the ground and stormed off. I was hurt by his anger because I honestly had no idea his feelings for me were so serious. I remember his parting words were that it wasn't right for me to give myself to a God who didn't exist! I was stunned and hurt and I cried for a long time. I picked up the ring and when I was back in the states I returned it to him with a note trying to explain about my love for a God who really did exist and that I would always care and pray for him as a friend but he never answered my letter. I had neither seen nor heard from him all these years until he recently surfaced and is willing to become a patron for Seaton House. He was able to straighten out the whole tangled mess and now my Order owns it free and clear plus the extra lot next door. God surely does work in mysterious ways."

David sat quietly wondering if Mary Rose would regret her alliance with her former friend. He really had nothing to base his thoughts on, only what Annie had told him after she touched Louis's hand. If Louis had the ability to upset Annie then he knew in his heart the matter required further investigation.

Chapter 20

Michael was lying on his back on the kitchen floor of Seaton House with his head under the old kitchen sink. He had initially stopped by to drop off a maternity dress Martha had altered for one of the young women living there, but soon found himself being escorted by Mary Rose into the kitchen. She had beseeched him to check a drip under the sink that was increasing every day. She also assured him he would only need to look at it and if it appeared at all serious she would call a plumber. Then she added quietly even though she knew their tight budget couldn't afford to call a plumber she was confident God would provide as He always did.

From his recumbent vantage point Michael could see that rust had eaten through the U-trap and whenever anyone used the sink the drip became a steady stream. He noticed a new U-trap lay conveniently by his left elbow along with a pipe wrench. He groaned when his knee joints cracked as he crawled out from under the sink and headed for the basement to turn off the water. As he started down the rickety wooden stairs he heard the doorbell ring. It rang several more times followed by Mary Rose's voice, "Michael, would you be a dear and get the front door? There doesn't seem to be anyone around except you and me, and I'm in the middle of a long distance call."

Michael retraced his steps as he muttered that maybe next time he would bring his butler's uniform. Wrench in hand, he opened the front door and found a pleasant looking woman standing next to a large box of what appeared to be used clothing.

"Hello." The woman greeted him warmly. "Is Sister Mary Rose here? I have some clothing I thought some of her girls might be able to use."

Michael made a quick assessment of the woman. Mid-forties maybe, pretty in a sort of plain way, but with a warm smile. She impressed him as the kind of a person you could trust if you needed help in an emergency, even if you didn't know her. The woman smiled again as Michael opened the screen door and invited her in. "Sister Mary Rose is in her office but she's on the phone and if you're a friend of hers you know it could be a little while." He grinned as he made a gesture with his hand that signified Mary Rose's notorious ability to talk and talk and talk.

The woman put out her hand, "My name is Veronica Sanders and I'm not really a friend of Mary Rose. Someone at the church I go to mentioned she's always able to use good, clean clothing for the girls living here after their babies are born, so I thought I would bring some over. Most of the items are almost new and it would be good if someone could find use for them."

Michael picked up the box of clothing and brought it into the foyer. The woman looked around and asked, "Do you work here?"

"Well now, that all depends on which way the wind is blowing for Mary Rose. No, not really. My wife and her are good friends and I help out once in awhile. Today I happen to be the plumber and tomorrow I might mow the grass or repair the garage door." They could hear the animated rise and fall of Mary Rose's voice and her laughter as she chatted on the phone. Michael motioned to Veronica with the wrench he still held in his hand, "This could be a bit of a wait. If you have time I'll be happy to pour you a cup of coffee and we can visit while I fix the sink."

"Thank you, I do have some time and that's very kind of you. I've heard so much about Sister Mary Rose and I'm really looking forward to meeting her."

Michael poured the coffee and invited Veronica to sit down. "Mary Rose is Minnesota's very own little Mother Teresa . . . with a healthy bit of a liberated twist." He chuckled as he pushed the sugar and creamer closer to her and handed her a spoon from an old cut glass spooner on the table. "I think you'll see what I mean after you get to know her. By the way, my name is Michael O'Grady and I'm pleased to meet you Veronica."

"What do you do when you're not plumbing or mowing grass?" The woman had such a polite and friendly manner Michael found himself instinctively liking her.

"Well, let's see." He let a little of his Irish brogue surface, "I'm a retired police officer. Thirty-five years I worked right here in Minneapolis trying to keep law and order."

"Do you miss it? The work I mean?" The woman seemed very interested in what she was hearing.

"Yes and no. I still do a small amount of private investigative work now and then, kind of off the record. Usually for friends and old acquaintances from my years on the force. I helps me keep my finger on what's happening in the Metro area without the daily danger factor. My wife is glad I'm retired. She used to worry about me." He thought about his son but didn't continue. The woman leaned forward as if she was going to ask Michael another question but was interrupted by Sister Mary Rose sweeping into the room.

As Sister Mary Rose and Veronica introduced themselves, Michael slid back under the sink for the second time and tackled the problem of replacing the rusted U-trap. Removing the old pipe had turned out to be more difficult than he had thought and he concluded as charming as older houses were, antiquated plumbing and furnaces were a constant source of problems. Seaton House was in need of a full time maintenance man and he wasn't sure he wanted the job. Finally, he was able to free the old trap and as he reached up to attach the new one he was shocked by a cold blast of water in his face. "Holy Mother of God!" he sputtered as he jerked himself from beneath the sink and struggled to sit up. He found himself face to face with a very startled Mary Rose.

"Oh my goodness! What have I done? You poor man! I'm so sorry, dear Michael. I accidentally turned the water on without thinking . . . by mistake, of course. I wasn't thinking. I was talking to Veronica and reached over and . . . . it was such a dumb thing to do. Here's a towel. Can you forgive me?"

Her bright blue eyes were so wide with astonishment Michael had all he could do to keep from laughing. Putting on his most stern face he said quietly, "Please don't ever do that again." He carefully spaced each word, and it was only mid sentence he realized he'd been interrupted by the doorbell as he was about to go to the basement to shut off the water.

"Oh my, no! Of course not, dear, Michael." Mary Rose attempted to wipe off some of the water that was still dripping from his face with the kitchen towel she held in her hand. At that point Michael couldn't help himself and burst into loud laughter. In surprised relief, Sister Mary Rose also started laughing. Their laughter seemed to feed off of each other and she ended up sitting on the kitchen floor next to Michael, both with tears streaming down their cheeks.

Veronica sat by the table and viewed the scene with wonder and amusement. It had been a long time since she'd seen people who seemed so comfortable with each other. Michael finished his project uneventfully and when he left he could see the two women still sitting in the living room chatting as if they were old friends.

About seven o'clock that evening Michael received a phone call.

"Michael O'Grady?"

"Yes."

"This is Veronica Sanders. Do you remember me? We met this morning at Seaton House. I was there for your Baptism."

He could hear her giggling softly and smiled knowing for sure he was going to like this lady. "Yes of course I remember you. How can I help you?"

"I hate to bother you, but . . ." She paused, and started again trying to choose her words carefully. "I'd like to talk to you about a little project I'm working on. It's very private but I believe I could use some help and I think you might be the right person. Would you be willing to meet with me? Of course I will pay you for your services. I'm not wealthy but I'm sure I can pay whatever you might ask."

"Are you at home?"

"No, Please don't think me presumptuous but I'm at a pay phone quite near your home. I found your address in the phone book. I prefer not to use my home phone and I feel I need to be very careful not just for myself but for anyone who would choose to help me. It's difficult to explain."

Michael had to admit his curiosity was definitely piqued. He felt the rush of adrenaline he became so familiar with when he was still on the force and he knew he missed that feeling. He'd been bored during the last few months and felt it was only a matter of time before his daughter Doreen would again be asking for money. "Would you like to come to my house? I have a small office and we could talk privately."

"I you wouldn't mind. You're very kind and I promise I'll not take up too much of your time. As I said, I have your address already so I'll be there shortly. Thank you."

Michael put the porch light on and stood waiting by the front door. Less than five minutes later he saw a dark green Honda drive up. Veronica Sanders got out and walked quickly up the walk. Michael opened the door before she had a chance to knock and quickly ushered her into his office. It had been their children's playroom when they were small, then a television room when they were teenagers, and now it served as his office.

As she entered she stopped and admired the aquarium that was home to one large fish.

"That's quite a fish you have there. It's a piranha isn't it?"

"Yes, I keep him in here because my wife Martha isn't fond of him, especially when I feed him. She thinks it's cruel and unnatural to feed him goldfish. She said there is no reason why he shouldn't be able to eat fish food like all the other fish. According to her all fish should be pretty to look at and not be aggressive."

"I think I agree with your wife, but I must say he is rather handsome in a cruel sort of way." She took off her jacket and sat in the chair Michael offered her. "First of all, I don't want you to feel obligated to help me, please be clear on that. What I'm going to tell you needs to be kept totally confidential. I'll be honest with you, I don't know for sure if I'm even on the right track. I believe I am but I can't be one hundred percent sure. So, if at the end of my story, you think I am barking up the wrong tree please feel free to say so.

By now, you are probably wondering what in the world I could be so concerned about, so I'll get right to my story. About a year ago, my half-brother was murdered. He was a cross-country trucker, mostly bringing freight from Texas or Arizona to Minnesota, and then back again. His name was Juan Rodriguez, but after my mother left his father she called him John Rodriguez. You see, my mother married my father when she was only eighteen and living on a ranch in Texas. The marriage didn't last. She was a wealthy American and he was a poor Hispanic ranch hand. There were simply too many cultural and economic differences and they split after two years. My mother left Texas with their year old baby boy and moved to Colorado. When John was about six my mother married my father. I was born a year later and when I was about seven my parents decided they couldn't handle John and sent him back to live with his natural father. I knew he was a wild child and he and my father didn't relate at all. But we were kids and he was the only brother I had, and I missed him terribly. I had grown up with him and I couldn't understand how they could just send him away. We kept in touch, more at first and then as he got older less often, but enough that I knew most of what was going on in his life. John suffered from what he used to call itchy feet. He needed to be on the move all the time and that's why the trucking job seemed so perfect for him.

The evening he was murdered, I got a phone call from him. For some mysterious reason, he sounded really scared and for him that was unheard of. By that time John was no kid, he was fifty-one years old and he was very streetwise. He had been in a few scrapes with the law when he was younger but nothing serious. He told me he needed to talk to me, and that he was about to leave Douglas, Arizona and would call from somewhere on the road later that night. He said he thought someone was trying to kill him because he found out something he wasn't supposed to know. He added he would explain later but was worried someone might be watching him.

That was the last I heard from him. The next day his father called from Texas to tell us that John had been killed in an accident. At first they believed he had fallen asleep at the wheel but later they discovered he had died from a single gunshot to the head. The Texas Ranger who investigated the case tried to tell us it might have been a stray bullet from an elk hunter's gun, but dead center through his forehead? Of course I remembered John's phone call and it sent chills up and down my spine. Not long after his father called my mother and told us not to come down as the body had already been cremated and there would be no funeral service. My mother said he sounded strange and refused to elaborate. A few days later his dad called again and said the police had picked up a man that had the same kind of rifle that killed my brother but while he was being held in the local jail he hanged himself. When I insisted I wanted to come down because I didn't think the story made sense he begged me to leave it alone. He finally said if I tried to find out the whole story a lot of innocent people could be hurt. At the time I didn't know what else to do so I just backed away from it. I regret I didn't go to Arizona immediately. My mother is getting up in age and seemed to fall apart after John's death and I felt anything I would try to find out might only make things worse. Then, about three months ago, I got this in the mail . . . ."

Veronica took a plain white envelope from her purse. Her name and address was typed on the front but there was no return address. It bore a Texas postmark. Inside was a plain piece of white typewritten paper with a short note.

To find out who killed John, you will first need to know why.

> *Ask yourself, what else might be in those trucks that would be important enough to kill for? Go back to the source, but do not involve the police, or you could end up joining your brother.*

"For the life of me, I don't have a single clue as to who may have sent this letter. At the time I was living in Colorado. I'm a legal secretary and was working for a lawyer who, let's say for all practical purposes, uses less than traditional methods to get information when necessary. For this reason I showed him the letter and told him my story. He had someone look into the trucking company John worked for. The company is based in Texas and has another smaller office in Douglas, Arizona. The company goes by the name Tru-Star Lines. My employer was able to cut through some of the legal red tape and found the real owner is one E. Truman and not Fritz Mueller, the man most people assume owns it. Fritz Mueller only manages it for E. Truman. Originally the company was founded and owned by a Mr. Edward Truman who owned several profitable trucking lines in the states but upon his death the company was inherited by his wife and then by their only daughter, Estelle Truman. After some additional back door digging my boss was able to find out that Estelle Truman is now Estelle Truman Welheim, and that she and her husband live here in Minneapolis. When I learned that I quit my job and moved here. As the letter said, go to the source. So to me this could be the source the note was talking about. I believe destiny must be guiding me because after a month I was able to get a job as a secretary in Mr. Welheim's office. His name is Gerhard Louis Welheim, but he goes by Louis."

Totally intrigued by now, Michael frowned as Veronica continued with her story.

"Oh, don't worry, Mr. O'Grady, he has no idea who I am. He had me checked out as he does all his prospective employees and to him I am just some plain Jane secretary who moved to Minneapolis because the cost of living was too high in Boulder. My former boss figured he would get a call on my past employment so he made sure we had the same story. Remember, my half brother John was half Hispanic, and as you can see, I look very Scandinavian with both my parents being Caucasian. So far, my job at Louis's office has been a total dead end and I'm starting to get desperate. The one thing I have learned is that Louis has a way of controlling people. He's extremely charismatic but he's also manipulative, and it's not beneath him to buy loyalty when necessary. He also has a private secretary, or I should say, personal assistant, Geesela, who probably knows more about Louis than anyone but for what he pays her she can afford to keep quiet. Plus, I think she has some kind of weird crush on him. Not that I think there's anything going on between them but her job seems to be her life. It's obvious to me he uses her but she doesn't seem to mind."

Michael gently lifted his hand and the gesture momentarily stopped her discourse. "So, Veronica, what do you think might be in those trucks?"

She looked into Michael's face with complete sincerity and replied quietly, "Drugs. It has to be drugs. I think someone is bringing drugs in from Mexico or South America to the Texas or Arizona area and then they are being transported north by Tru-Star Lines trucks to their distribution destination probably here in Minnesota.

When I first met Louis he struck me as being an exceptionally nice man and I was almost convinced I was wrong about his involvement in this whole scenario. Now, however, the longer I work for him I've come to realize there's another side to him that almost no one appears to knows about. A very dark side. I also believe most, if not all the drivers, like my brother John, are unaware of what they're hauling in addition to their obvious cargo. I think my brother may have inadvertently stumbled onto the truth and they had no choice but to eliminate him.

"Why do you feel that the man the Texas police said was supposedly responsible for John's murder and later committed suicide wasn't really the man that killed him?"

"My ex-boss had his private detective check that out. It turned out the guy was a local drunk, crazy as a loon but completely harmless. I believe John was killed by a professional using a high powered rifle. The person who killed him was a true marksman not some shaky old alcoholic. The detective also found out that John was actually the third driver to die that worked for Tru-Star Lines in the previous two years. The first one supposedly fell asleep at the wheel. No one questioned it mostly because the guy had a history of drinking and didn't have any family to question the findings. The second one supposedly committed suicide but not before he killed his new wife. They claimed he found out she was having an affair while he was on the road. Again, it seemed logical enough to the people around there and no one really questioned it. After all, being the wife of a cross-country trucker must be rather lonely, right? The police said the night before my half-brother was killed he and the man they believe killed him had an argument during a card game. One of the local officers claimed he was called to a bar to break it up. The odd thing was no one else seemed to have witnessed the argument."

"That's quite a story. Now, exactly what is it you think I might be able to do for you?" Michael was quite sure he already knew what her answer would be but he wanted to hear it from her.

"I want you to find out everything you can about Louis. See if you believe he's capable of doing what I believe he is, or if I'm wrong. If I'm careful maybe I can help you some from the inside but as you might expect, if I were to go poking around in his personal life I would most surely arouse suspicion. As I said, he's a very private person and if I do anything to offend him in any way, I know I would be out of a job. You have experience in this area and you can be objective. At this point I am too emotionally involved and I may be seeing things that aren't really there."

Veronica sat back and took a deep breath while she studied Michael's face for his reaction. She admired that he was an exceptional listener but also she admired his detached professionalism. Finally, she continued. "I do know a little bit about his family. Not a lot, but it might prove helpful. The other day his assistant, Geesela left her desk to use the rest room. I was in her office putting some papers on her desk when the phone rang. Normally, I would never think of answering her phone, but it kept ringing . . . maybe eight or ten times, like someone wasn't about to give up until it was answered. I could see by the little red light on her desk phone that Louis was on his private line, so glancing around to see if I was alone, I picked up Geesela's phone and before I could say anything this woman started blubbering into the phone. She was very distressed and said there was an emergency at Louis's home and that Estelle, Louis's wife, had been hurt. It turns out the woman was Ethel Danner who's their housekeeper and also Estelle's full time private duty nurse. She kept saying she was sorry for calling Geesela's desk but Louis's private line was busy as well as his other line and she didn't know what else to do. It seems Estelle had somehow gotten into the Scotch, a lot of Scotch, according to Ethel, and had found Ethel's car keys. She had backed Ethel's car out of the garage and proceeded to deliberately ram and smash into the other cars in the garage, especially one of Louis's prize collector cars. It was some special car that supposedly was used to haul Hitler around in during World War II. Anyway, upon the last impact she struck her head on the steering wheel and Ethel had to call an ambulance to take Estelle into the E.R. for stitches. Right now, Estelle is tucked away in St. Mary's Psychiatric unit where, I'm starting to realize, they have a room she calls home quite often. Even there she has her own private duty nurse instead of the regular staff. It's almost as if Louis doesn't want anyone around her and needs to control who has contact with her. One of the staff nurses who works there goes to the same hairdresser that I do. It's amazing what women tell their hairdressers. When I opened the door to tell Louis there was an emergency at his home and he should go to St. Mary's Hospital he hung up the phone and immediately left his office. When I was sure he was on the elevator I pushed the Star 69 and recognized the number as being that of Fritz Mueller who manages Tru-Star Lines in Arizona. Louis's other phone had been taken off the holder and was beeping, so I suspect he did that on purpose so he wouldn't be interrupted. I don't know that for sure but I think it seems reasonable. Later, Geesela questioned why I answered her phone and exactly what Mrs. Danner had told me. I said only that there had been an emergency and she wanted Louis to go to St. Mary's Hospital but both his phone lines had been busy. Geesela then told me in her very deliberate German commando voice that in this single instance it was all right to have answered her phone but not to do it again. She also told me Estelle's health has been very delicate for the past several years and the reason she needed a full time nurse. I also found out from my hairdresser there's a son, but for reasons no one seems to be able to explain, he's never around. He has a home in Basel, Switzerland and four or five times a year Ethel Danner and Estelle go to visit him. They usually fly into Zurich and then take the day train to Basel. That's about all I know about him. I realize it's a long and complicated story and one that may carry a genuine risk for you. However, in the short time I've known you, I feel I can trust you completely. To be truthful, I felt the courage to ask Sister Mary Rose about you. Now, there's one thing I know. I've got to hand it to you, that dear lady is ready to recommend you for canonization as a saint. I think fate or divine providence must have guided me to both of you."

Michael had been sitting quietly with his arms folded over his chest as he listened to all the information she had shared. Veronica paused and retrieved a hanky from her purse as tears were welling in her eyes, "Please, can you help me? Frankly, I'm desperate and I don't know what else to do or who else to turn to."

Michael uncrossed his arms and watched his guest closely as she wiped her cheeks and blew her nose quietly. As far as he could tell she seemed completely sincere and not some crackpot who would make up a sensational story. He also remembered his wife Martha mentioning she had met a very smooth Mr. Welheim previously at Seaton House and for some strange reason she hadn't cared for him at all and couldn't understand why Mary Rose thought he was so wonderful. Good, sweet, non-judgmental Martha, who liked virtually everyone, had not liked Louis. He reached over and reassuringly touched Veronica's hand, "I promise I will do everything I can to help you find out what happened to your half-brother and I'll start tomorrow by learning all I can about Louis." He paused and then added, "and I will use my utmost discretion so as not to arouse his suspicion"

She breathed a sigh of relief and said, "Thank you, from the bottom of my heart. If there is ever anything I can do for you I promise I will."

After discussing fees and how payments would be handled Veronica got up to leave, which prompted Michael to ask, "How did you happen to pay a visit to Seaton House this morning? Was it a coincidence that you happened to have some used clothing to drop off?"

Veronica smiled and she seemed to blush ever so slightly. "I think I made the right choice picking you to be my detective. No, it wasn't a coincidence. You see, I was working in a side office next to Louis's the day Sister Mary Rose came in to find out who was behind the idea of Seaton House being sold and all the other problems she was confronted with. She didn't see me but I saw her and I heard some of their conversation. None of that was a coincidence either, it was engineered from the get go. From what I can gather so far, Louis doesn't do anything just because he's a nice guy. I admire Sister Mary Rose but from the little I now know of her, I believe she has way too much faith in the intrinsic goodness of mankind."

After Veronica left Michael sat thinking about what she had said about Louis and Mary Rose. If this seemingly questionable man had manipulated his way into their friend's life, he must have an ulterior motive. And now, from what Veronica had been suggesting, he didn't think Louis's reason was necessarily a benevolent one. Michael felt he might find it very interesting to poke around a wee bit and see what mischief he could uncover. Yes, there it was again, that old familiar rush of adrenaline.

Chapter 21

The next morning Michael awoke with a renewed sense of purpose. Something inside told him he was about to take on an assignment that could make a genuine difference in several people's lives. He had enjoyed his retirement at first and remembered how he'd been looking forward to it. However, it hadn't taken long for him to realize he could sweep the garage and mow the lawn only so many times before it would become a major source of monotony in his life. He left the house whistling but not before Martha reminded him of the meeting later in the day with their grandson Corey's school counselor. He rechecked the address in his notebook and drove toward the neighborhood where Louis Welheim lived. He was not at all surprised to see Louis had more of an estate than a traditional home. The house was large and with its stone exterior and slate roof was distinctly European in appearance. The home was surrounded by a beautiful and well cared for lawn with a professionally attended garden in back. It was elegant but not ostentatious, certainly suitable for a wealthy man, but not outrageously so as to call attention to his wealth. After all, there was perhaps good reason not to draw undue attention.

Michael parked a short distance from his destination and set out on foot. Protected by tall shrubbery, he stood watching the house. After about fifteen minutes one of the doors of the six car garage opened, and a man who Michael assumed to be Louis, drove off in an immaculate, black Mercedes. After the car was out of sight Michael walked to the front door and rang the bell. Within minutes the door was opened by a large, middle-aged, unattractive woman. She peered suspiciously at Michael but made no attempt to unlock the screen door that separated them. Michael smiled and using his most friendly Irish brogue said, "The top of the morning to you Madame! I hate to be botherin' you but I need to ask if you might have seen this wee bit of dog around here?" He purposely held the photograph of Danny's dachshund at an angle where she would have a problem seeing the picture closely. "He belongs to my grandson and seems to have wandered off. The poor lad is crying his little eyes out over him, so I thought I would ease the child's misery by trying to locate it."

The woman attempted to see the picture and hesitated. She carefully looked Michael up and down and reluctantly opened the screen door a crack and took the picture. "It's a lovely little dog, I can see why your grandson is so upset. I can't say I've seen any dogs around here for a while. We used to have a dog, her name was Fluffy but she's gone . . . ." The woman seemed to hesitate. "She got lost too, so now we don't have one. I know it hurts to lose a pet and I hope your grandson finds his dog. I'm sorry I can't be of more help."

Michael was afraid she was about to close the door so he quickly said, "Say now, that's one heavenly smell coming from your kitchen."

The woman smiled and Michael noticed she had several crooked teeth, which didn't do anything to enhance her appearance.

"I'm baking chocolate chip cookies. I make really good cookies. It's probably one of the things I do best". She appeared a little wistful and then brightened as she added, "We buy the chocolate in Switzerland."

"Well then, I would have to say your husband is one lucky man."

"Oh, no, I don't own this house, I only work here." She paused again and then added cautiously, "Would you like to come in and have a cookie and a cup of coffee? The house is so empty since Est . . . I mean Mrs. Welheim isn't here, and I'm sure I can't eat all these cookies by myself."

As Michael entered the house he couldn't help thinking to himself that judging from her ample size she must have eaten more than her share of chocolate chip cookies. They walked directly to the kitchen and she invited him to sit at a round marble topped table. When the timer on the stove dinged the woman bent over to remove the last sheet of cookies from the oven, and Michael was more than a little amazed by her very broad back end. Again he had the uncharitable thought that the good Lord must have hit her with the old ugly stick and then hit her again for good measure. She placed several of the hot cookies on a dainty china plate and placed it directly in front of Michael. "Would you like some coffee, too? I made a fresh pot and it would be nice to have someone to talk to. I get lonely with the lady of the house in the hospital. Her name is Estelle and her husband is Louis Welheim. You may have heard of him. He's a businessman downtown. I'm the housekeeper and Mrs. Welheim's personal assistant and private nurse. She is also my friend."

Michael noticed a certain amount of pride in her voice. "And you are?"

"I'm sorry, I guess I forgot to introduce myself. My name is Ethel Danner. I've worked for the Welheims for many years. They're like my family. They've been very kind to me, and my daughter. She doesn't live here anymore because she's in college, but I live right here in the house. I have my own private quarters in the back and have a wonderful view of the garden. They even gave me my own car. Except . . . it's being fixed now. That's why I'm here all by myself. Until my car is repaired I can't really go anywhere."

Michael finished a second cookie and remarked sincerely, "Ethel, these are about the most delicious cookies I've ever eaten. You weren't exaggerating when you said you bake wonderful cookies."

Ethel smiled and Michael felt his heart go out to her. She obviously was very lonely and to have someone compliment her and make her feel appreciated meant a great deal to her. He felt a little guilty when he found himself thinking she resembled an old mongrel dog looking up at her master with sad eyes, grateful for even the slightest little pat on the head. For over forty minutes Ethel talked and Michael listened. By the time he left the house Ethel Danner felt she had found a new friend and Michael had a much better understanding of Louis and his family without having to ask a single question. He had given her his first name and phone number if she were to see his grandson's lost dachshund.

Shortly before six that evening Michael pulled his car into their driveway and turned off the ignition. For a moment he put his head down on the steering wheel as he tried to put the events of the afternoon out of his head. He felt sad and disturbed about the meeting he had attended. It had included his daughter Doreen, Lenny, Corey, and Becca Rhodes from the Hennepin County Family Services. Martha hadn't attended at Doreen's request because their daughter felt it was better for all concerned. This request was a typical Doreen power play to exclude one of her parents simply because she could.

The purpose of the meeting was to decide what would be best for Corey since he appeared to be having more behavioral problems each day. His latest episode involved threatening another student at school and later at home attempting to punch Doreen when she confronted him about his deplorable conduct. Today, Doreen had been on her best maternal behavior, explaining as usual, that she was a teacher and had worked successfully with hundreds of other people's children, but her own son was more than even she could handle. At one point with tears in her eyes she almost broke down as she related how she had tried over and over again to understand Corey's behavior, but regardless of how much effort she put forth she hadn't been able to reach him. Michael found himself almost wanting to believe his daughter. Lenny sat next to her as mute as a bump on a log but it was Corey who really broke his heart. He sat pale and stone faced, with no emotion except for the hatred that flared in his eyes as Doreen pleaded her case. When 'she' as the boys called Doreen, reached over to touch Corey's hand in a motherly gesture of concern, he pulled away and told her to fuckoff!

He was now becoming his own worst enemy, Michael thought, as this response only made Doreen's story seem more plausible. As much as Michael loved Corey he felt he owed it to his daughter not to say too much. After an hour the meeting ended in a stalemate with Becca calling a truce between mother and son and explaining she would review the case and make a recommendation in a few days. Until that time Corey was to return to a foster home. Doreen cried copious tears and Corey left without protest but not before he stated to Becca and Michael he didn't give a shit where he stayed as long as it was far away from 'her'.

Michael struggled to get out of his car and realized how stiff and sore his body was becoming. He felt old and worn out and wondered how many more years he would have before his end would come. He felt pain deep in his chest and wondered if a person could die of a broken heart. He was glad Martha wasn't home yet because he wasn't ready to tell her about the meeting. As he went to put his key in the lock of the side door he noticed the screen on the kitchen window adjacent to the door had been removed and the window had been forced up. At that instant he forgot his aches and pains as he prepared himself to check the house for an intruder. He silently unlocked the door and peered into the semi-darkened house. Nothing seemed to be out of place or unusual. As he entered the kitchen he looked for something he could use as a weapon and chose a long butcher knife from the counter. He no longer carried a gun and the only one he owned was in his dresser drawer in his bedroom. He listened before he proceeded into the living room and the silence was deafening. He was entering the hallway that led to the bedrooms when he thought he heard a voice coming from his and Martha's bedroom. At first he couldn't identify the voice, only that someone seemed to be talking to someone else. Quietly, he approached the door and noticed it was slightly ajar. He felt the rush of adrenaline and could feel the blood pulsing in his temples. His mouth was dry and his heart pounding. As he held the knife in an attack position he heard the person speak again. With a surge of relief he recognized the voice as that of Danny. He lowered the knife and peeked into the bedroom but was not at all prepared for what he saw. Danny had taken Michael's revolver from his dresser drawer and was pointing it at Dixie's head. With horror Michael listened as Danny, his sweet little Danny boy who was afraid to sleep at night without a nightlight, spoke menacingly to his dog.

"I said, shut your mouth you spineless bastard or I'll shut it for you." Danny's face was hard and cruel and Michael suddenly felt as if his own body had turned to stone. His first impulse was to shout to Danny to stop but he found himself unable to speak or truly comprehend what he was seeing. Danny spoke again in the same cruel and demanding voice, "You heard me . . . I said shut up or I'll blow your friggen' brains all over this room!" The tiny dog reacted to the strange tone of his master's voice and jumped back drawing his lips tightly over his teeth. He growled and barked sharply at Danny. The boy reacted violently to his dog's uncharacteristic demeanor. He swayed backward as a jerking spasm shook his small body. He pointed the gun at the dog again and his face became distorted with rage, "You've just made my day you stupid bastard!"

Michael threw himself into the room but not before he heard the click of the gun. At the same time he heard himself yelling, "No, Danny! No! Oh, God, no!" Michael's voice had a strangled quality to it. Danny spun around and pointed the gun at Michael. His small face was white with terror and his entire body shook with fear. He held the gun out in front of himself but his arms and body were shaking uncontrollably. Michael dropped the knife he was still clutching and gently approached Danny and took the gun from the frightened boy's hand. When Michael held out his arms to hold his grandson the boy fell into his arms. As Michael held him close he felt Danny's body still convulsing with fear and he became aware of how much his own body was shaking. The confused dog continued barking sharply and Michael tried to quiet him and comfort Danny at the same time by saying, "It's okay Dixie. Danny is fine. You go in the other room and be quiet. It's okay, Danny, Dixie is fine, nothing happened. Grandpa took the bullets out of the gun so you didn't hurt anyone." The whole time he was holding Danny he was thanking God Martha had taken the ammunition and locked it away as a safety precaution. Michael spent the next several minutes sitting on the floor holding Danny close and gently rocking the child as he did when he was a baby. Danny's shaking gradually subsided and he was sobbing softly as Michael repeated over and over, "It's okay, Danny. It's okay. We love you. We love you more than you'll ever know."

"I'm s-s-ssorry, grandpa. I-I-I didn't mean to hurt anybody. We were j-j-just playing." Both were sobbing as they sat together in the fading light of the day.

Michael didn't know exactly how long he sat holding his now passive grandson in his arms when he heard Martha's car in the driveway. He heard the back door and Martha calling his name. He didn't turn around but could feel her presence and he knew she was standing in the bedroom doorway. She was silent as she studied the scene of her husband rocking their grandson with the gun lying on the floor beside them. He turned slightly and saw her face was filled with fear and he heard her gasp. Michael said softly, "Everything is fine, nothing happened." He put his finger up to his lips to signal her not to say any more. Looking down at his grandson's tear stained face he saw his eyes were closed and he appeared to be asleep. Michael carefully got up and laid Danny on the bed and covered him with the bedspread.

Dixie came cautiously back into the bedroom and climbed up on the bed next to his master and laid his head on the pillow next to Danny's face. Michael backed out of the room and as he was about to close the door he heard Danny's small voice, "Don't shut the door grandpa. I'm still afraid of the dark."

"I won't shut the door, Danny."

"Grandpa?"

"Yes, Danny?"

"Make her go away. I hate her."

"You mean your mom?"

"Yes, I hate her. She hurts people and she lies. All she ever does is yell and hit us."

When Michael entered the kitchen Martha was shocked to see her husband's pale and tightly drawn face. As he started to tell her what happened with Danny they heard someone opening the front door and Doreen came barging in without warning. She slammed the door behind her and made no effort to conceal how angry she was. Before either

Michael or Martha could say anything, Doreen shouted, "Is Danny here? The little s. o. b. left his baby sitter's house without permission and now we can't find him. Of course that spineless bastard Lenny can't be bothered to help look for him. What did I ever do to deserve such ungrateful brats in my life?"

At that instant Michael felt something snap inside. He stepped directly in front of Doreen blocking her way. She was smoking a cigarette and Michael grabbed her arm as she was about to inhale. He held it firmly above the wrist and squeezed as hard as he could and at the same time stared directly into her eyes. Doreen let out a cry of pain and surprise. As she struggled to break away her cigarette fell to the floor. "Are you crazy?" she screamed and continued to pull away from her father but he didn't release his grip on her arm.

Michael's voice was low and overly controlled as he said, "You did nothing to deserve having those children in your life except give birth to them, and if I have my way you'll not have them in your life much longer!"

Doreen struggled harder to free her arm but Michael refused to relinquish his hold. "Don't you ever call either of my grandsons a son of a bitch, or a little bastard, or any of those horrible names ever again. Do you understand me?"

The color had drained from Doreen's face and for once in her life she was speechless. She had never seen her father so angry. His face was red and the veins on his forehead were protruding. His clear blue eyes had taken on a grayish cast and were filled with rage. Doreen opened her mouth to speak but Michael cut her off.

"To answer your question, no I'm not crazy, but I think you are. You are a self-centered, manipulative, self-serving, spoiled brat and I will not let you go on hurting those two boys anymore. No more pills and no more abuse. Do I make myself perfectly clear?"

Doreen's face became ugly and she pulled her arm free. She stood rubbing her arm staring at Michael and spat out, "Who the hell do you think you are to judge me? You have never loved me! It was always wonderful Thomas Michael or sweet little Kathleen, never Doreen. Neglected little Doreen never got your attention. Neither of you ever had time for me when I was growing up. Well, I've got news for you, I don't have time for you and your sanctimonious judgments now. You can go straight to hell, both of you. And stay the hell out of my life from now on. I'll take Danny and then you won't ever have to see me again. Where is he?" She moved in the direction of the bedrooms but Michael stepped in front of her.

"Doreen you need serious help, you're not well. You take pills to go to sleep and pills to keep you awake. You live on pain pills and anti-depressants and I suspect most of the time you have so many prescriptions you have no idea what they're doing to your head.

Doreen put her hands up to her ears, "I don't have to listen to this shit. Who the hell do you think you are? You're no Sigmund Freud! All you are, is some has been flat foot cop who doesn't know enough to keep his nose out of where it's not wanted. I'm a teacher. I have . . ."

Martha had been standing silently watching the altercation between her husband and daughter when she cut in, "Doreen, your father is right. We are your parents, the two people who love you more than anyone else in the world. We only want to help you."

Doreen spun around and raised her hand and for a moment Michael thought she was going to slap her mother.

"Shut up! You shut the hell up!" Doreen backed away and moved towards the door still holding her hand up in front of her. "This time you've gone too far. There won't be a Doreen for you to pick on. You mark my words, you'll be sorry. This was a great big mistake and you'll both be sorry for the rest of your miserable, goddamn lives. I'd call the police and have you both arrested for assault and kidnapping but we all know how they always protect their own." She stomped out and slammed the door.

Martha stood quietly twisting a dishtowel in her trembling hands, as Michael sank into the nearest chair. They were silent for a while and then Martha spoke the words that expressed the awful thoughts they were both entertaining.

"I'm so afraid she is going to do something foolish. Something to hurt herself."

Michael tried to comfort her, "Don't you go thinking like that. You know Doreen. She'll cool off. I'll go over in a little while and check on her. Lenny's truck is parked out in front of their house. He'll be with her."

Martha started to cry softly. "I don't know, Michael. Doreen's not like other people. She's our daughter and I love her but she's not like other people. No one has ever been able to love her enough. She feels everyone is always taking advantage of her and is angry all the time. I'm not sure what we could have done to make her feel that way but somehow, regardless of how hard we've tried, we couldn't give her what she needed. Even before she started with all the pills she seemed to be unusually needy. Sometimes even when she was younger, I found her so hard to love, and maybe she picked up on that from me. I used to pray all the time about her and I still do but . . ."

Michael got up and put his arms around his wife. "Martha, dear, you know we did our best. We loved all our children in the same way but I guess sometimes love isn't enough. We couldn't save Thomas Michael from someone else's greed and hatred, and we can't save Doreen from herself if she won't let us. But we can try, and keep on trying and keep on praying."

They sat by the table and Michael told her what happened at Corey's meeting and how he had walked in on Danny holding the gun to Dixie's head. He explained that when Danny asked him to make his mother go away because he hated her for yelling and hitting them, it was as though something snapped inside him which probably triggered his outburst with Doreen.

The telephone rang and both Michael and Martha jumped and looked at each other with dread in their eyes. Michael picked up the phone and said softly, "Hello." There was silence and Martha saw her husband's face turn ashen white. "Oh, God! I'll be right over." He handed the phone to Martha, "Call St. Mary's emergency room and tell them we're bringing Doreen in. Sure as hell, she's taken an overdose. I'll load her up in my car and we'll drive her there. At this hour there won't be much traffic and it will be faster than an ambulance."

"I'd better wake Danny."

"Let him sleep, he's been through enough today. I'll have Lenny come and stay with him. I can't see Lenny wanting to be anywhere near the emergency room with Doreen."

As soon as Martha hung up the phone from talking to the emergency room nurse she grabbed her coat and peeked in at Danny who was sleeping soundly. She left the house and could see Michael and Lenny loading a screaming, very uncooperative Doreen into the back seat of their car. As Martha opened the car door to sit next to Doreen, Michael started the engine and held up a large plastic bag filled with bottles and vials of pills. "We're going to need these. I think she took sleeping pills but I'm not sure. Hold onto her so she doesn't try to jump out of the car."

The trip to the emergency room took only about twenty minutes but it seemed much longer. Michael kept checking the rear view mirror and found himself worrying about his wife almost as much as his daughter. Doreen was amazingly docile and appeared sleepy but also slightly disoriented.

Michael pulled the car into the emergency room entrance and was met by an orderly with a wheelchair. Between the two of them they were able to move Doreen into the waiting room. The orderly explained it would be only a few minutes before there would be a treatment room available. She offered no resistance and only mumbled incoherently.

Martha stayed at the admitting desk providing Doreen's personal information and Michael sat with his daughter until the orderly returned and pushed her into a treatment room. A petite, red haired nurse joined the orderly and with Michael's help were able to lift and transfer the now almost non-responsive Doreen onto a treatment table. The orderly began strapping Doreen's left arm down and at the same time the nurse reached for Doreen's right arm to confine it. The moment Doreen realized she was going to be restrained she swung her right arm and caught the nurse sharply across the face. Only moments before her body had been limp and dead weight but now she was screaming and thrashing her free arm menacingly at those who were attempting to restrain her. The orderly ducked in time to avoid being hit by her forearm and instinctively the nurse threw herself across Doreen's chest to hold her down. Michael grabbed for Doreen's legs to keep her from arching her back as he heard the nurse cry out, "Oh no, she's trying to bite me! Hold her head down!" The orderly pushed Doreen's head back and firmly grabbed her right arm. The nurse had just enough time to secure a leather strap across Doreen's chest as the orderly struggled to hang onto her thrashing arm and head. Michael held firmly onto Doreen's legs and heard the orderly say, "Holy Jerusalem! She's as strong as a horse! Are you sure she took an overdose?"

The nurse didn't comment but quickly took Doreen's blood pressure and pulse. She had already prepared the room and set a out tray of supplies and the other items they would need to perform a gastric lavage. Her cheek was red and starting to swell where Doreen hit her. Michael could feel his heart breaking as he watched his daughter struggle against the restraints that now held her prisoner. She had lost her human qualities and now looked more like a desperate animal that had been caught in a trap. He stepped closer and tried to comfort her but she cut him off, "Get away from me! I'll never forgive you for this!"

Michael looked into her eyes and saw the fear and anger, and part of him wanted to tell the nurse it was all a mistake and that he would take his daughter home. Then he recalled Danny's words as he held the gun to Dixie's head and knew the words that came from his grandson's mouth were only echoes of what he probably heard Doreen spew out over and over again. He bent over and said, "Doreen if we don't do this now, we'll never forgive ourselves." She continued to thrash and struggle but the restraints prevented her movements so instead she raised her head and spit at her father as she screamed. "Get the hell out of here! I don't need you! I don't need anyone."

Michael turned to leave and saw Martha standing in the doorway. She studied her husband's ashen face and gently wiped the spit from his nose and cheek with her hanky. "We're doing the right thing." She walked over to Doreen and said firmly, "Stop it, Doreen. They have to wash the pills out of your stomach. You're only making it worse for yourself by struggling so you might as well behave. Our minds are made up and the only way you'll leave this hospital is if you are clean and sober."

Amazingly, Doreen stopped struggling and the nurse motioned for Martha and Michael to leave. "She'll be fine. The intern is here and we'll take good care of her. Thank you for your help, but you really don't want or need to see this. A gastric lavage is not a pleasant thing to watch. From here she will be admitted to the psychiatric ward and once she's up there you'll be able to see her for a few minutes. After that you should probably go home and try to get some rest. Tomorrow her doctors will evaluate her and notify you of their findings. Right now the most important thing is to get rid of whatever she took. Do you happen to have the empty bottle or the meds she may be taking?"

Martha held up the large plastic bag of prescription bottles and vials of pills. "I assume it was sleeping pills but it could be anything from this bag."

"The nurse took the bag and said only, "That's quite an impressive amount of pills isn't it? Do you have any idea how she managed to get all these drugs?"

Michael shook his head and added, "There could be more. These are the ones from her medicine cabinet and the bedside table. I'm quite sure there will be more in her purse. I'm really sorry she hit you."

"Thanks for your concern, but it goes with the territory. It's probably not the last time someone will take a swing at me." She reached up and touched her bruised cheek. "She does have a powerful right hook. I didn't really see it coming. Usually if someone has taken an overdose and is as unresponsive as she was when we moved her to the treatment table they don't recover that quickly."

Michael studied the nurse's face, "So you're saying it could be possible she didn't really take as much as she wanted us to believe she did?"

"We won't know until we complete the lavage, but judging from her vitals and how awake she is now, my guess is she may not have. Sometimes in these situations it's more of a cry for attention or help than wanting to die."

Michael and Martha sat in the almost empty waiting room grateful that emergency rooms in private hospitals were usually less crowded than some of the others like Hennepin County. Martha reached over and placed her hand on her husband's wrinkled hand. "We've been through a lot together, haven't we? I think losing Thomas Michael was still the worst of all. To have him taken in such a violent way was an unthinkable tragedy, but we got through that, and we will get through this. Doreen is an adult and needs to know there are natural consequences. We both knew this could happen but she is our daughter and somehow we just kept hoping it would never come to this. These last months she's been like a walking time bomb waiting to explode. We have to think of what she's been doing to her two boys. Today the gun Danny held wasn't loaded but tomorrow it could be, and you might not be there to stop it."

Michael looked into his wife's eyes and thought she never looked more lovely than she did at this moment. She was kind and accepting of whatever happened in their lives. "I wish I hadn't lost my temper but when I heard Danny calling Dixie, the dog he loves so much, a spineless bastard, I knew that wasn't him talking. It was Doreen spewing out her vicious anger and he was probably trying to make some sense of it by repeating it. He knew it was wrong and he tried to tell me he was only playing, but it could have been a deadly game that no little child should have to take part in."

Martha wiped her nose with her handkerchief. "As painful as this is I know in my heart we're doing the right thing. We ignored the warning signs for a long time and hoped and prayed Doreen would get better, but she didn't. I think this is one of those times when God expects us to take responsibility for our child. She took the pills and now she'll have to be on the psych ward until she gets her problems straightened out. Maybe someone else with more experience with this kind of thing will do better than we did."

Michael sat quietly and finally said, "Did you see her eyes? It reminded me of one time when I was still on the force and we got a disturbance call. We went to this old shed behind a house and found this guy whose neighbor's complained he'd been beating a dog with an iron rod. This dog was skinny and malnourished and it was very obvious the guy had been mistreating it for a long time. When we got into the shed we saw the guy lying in the corner covered with blood. He was trying to hold the dog off with the iron bar. As we stood there the dog spun around and leaped at us, his teeth were bared and there was blood all over his face from how he had ripped the guy's arm apart. I froze. All I could see was his bloody fangs and the whites of his eyes as he made an explosive leap toward me. My partner shot the dog in the throat while it was still in the air. The dog let out a yelp and fell bleeding to death at my feet and I remember I stood there looking at its eyes and the blood gushing out of the wound. A golden retriever is usually such a kind and loving dog and this guy with his cruelty and meanness had turned it into something vicious and evil. I felt no sympathy for that guy. I wanted to hurt him for what he'd done to that poor dog. And, yet . . ." Michael paused and looked at his hands, "When I looked into Doreen's eyes tonight when she was struggling in the emergency room I couldn't help thinking about that poor dog. Doreen had so much hate in her eyes. Where did that come from? We never mistreated her. We tried to treat all the children the same but somehow she ended up feeling neglected and mistreated."

Martha sighed, "I don't know. I've thought about it and prayed about it but I just don't understand what goes on in her head. I suppose with all the pills she takes everything gets all mixed up. Hopefully someone else who deals with this more can help us find the answer."

It was late by the time Doreen was admitted to the psychiatric unit and all the fight had gone out of her. She wouldn't look at or speak to either of them and finally the nurse suggested it might be better if they went home and got some rest. Martha cried softly when they left the hospital but seemed to recover on the way home. Neither of them spoke until they turned into their driveway and could see Danny sitting by the kitchen table. He had fixed himself a peanut butter sandwich and given Dixie a left over hamburger patty he found in the refrigerator. Lenny was sound asleep in front of the blaring television still holding an empty beer can in his hand.

Martha gave Michael a disgusted look and then shook her head as if to say, don't say anything to Lenny, just tell him to go. As Martha took Danny and helped him get ready for bed Michael woke Lenny, turned off the television and gathered up the five other empty beer cans. Lenny didn't say anything as he opened the door to leave, so Michael volunteered. "Doreen's going to be alright. She has to be in the hospital for awhile for some counseling and to help her get off the drugs she's been taking, but she shouldn't have any serious after effects from tonight."

Lenny shrugged but didn't turn around to continue the conversation. Deep down Michael wanted to follow Lenny outside and kick him in the ass but he knew it wouldn't change anything and it might make things worse than they already were. Instead, he let Dixie out to make one last trip outside. While he waited for her he stepped out on the porch letting the cool air clear his head. He didn't tell Martha that Lenny had gotten into his truck and driven away without going back into his house. That night, Michael, Martha, Danny and Dixie all shared the same bed but in the morning it was evident only Dixie had slept well.

Danny awoke complaining of a tummy-ache and Michael and Martha decided it would be better for him to stay home from school and spend the day with them. By nine-thirty Michael had visited with Becca Rhodes and she assured him he and Martha should have no problem getting temporary custody of both Danny and Corey until Doreen was well enough to resume their care. Michael hung up the phone and glancing out the window noticed Lenny loading his belongings into his truck. As Michael walked across the street Lenny waved weakly to him. After he finished loading his belongings he turned and faced his father-in-law, "I'm really sorry but I t can't take this any more. Tell Doreen she can have everything. I don't want nothin' but the few things I took. Tell the boys good-bye for me." For a few minutes he stood silently studying his feet. Then he looked up into the sky so he didn't have to make eye contact with Michael. "They're telling you the truth. The boys, I mean. She is crazy." As he got into his truck Michael inquired where he could be reached but Lenny didn't answer and instead started the engine. Michael watched Lenny drive down the street and out of his daughter's life. He couldn't help but feel like one more person had failed Doreen, but in all honesty he knew she had driven Lenny away the same way she did everyone who was unfortunate enough to come into her life. Michael went into his garage and took his gun down from the high shelf where he had hid it last night before he went to bed. He studied it knowing he could give it to one of his friends on the force but remembering Danny's face when he held it to Dixie's head made him feel sick inside. He placed the gun in the jaws of the vice on his workbench and reaching for his hacksaw began the task of destroying it. He was amazed at the hardness of the metal but he persevered. When he finished he took the pieces and tossed them into the garbage can. The thought of raising two boys at his age lay heavily on his mind. As he entered the kitchen he heard Danny laughing out loud as he and Dixie were in the middle of having a tug of war with one of Martha's kitchen towels. Somehow, at that moment he knew everything would be fine. What was it Martha always said? It would all come out in the wash. He had to believe she was right.

Chapter 22

Shortly after Harry arrived at his office he received a call from Molly asking if he and Annie would like to go to lunch with her about noon. Harry explained Annie had a business luncheon but he would be delighted to dine with his favorite cousin. She replied that her publisher's office was not far from Sullivan Glass and since she'd planned to meet with her most of the morning, and since it was such a glorious day, she would pick up sandwiches and they could eat in the little park a block from Harry's office.

Molly arrived about ten minutes after noon and as they walked to the park Harry noticed how quiet she seemed. He inquired if her meeting went well and she nodded affirmatively. "The publisher has even agreed to using my illustrations which is a really big surprise to me. You were always a better artist than me. Do you still draw?"

Harry shook his head no and they continued walking in silence. As they arrived at the park a young couple was leaving so they sat down on the newly vacated park bench. Molly took sandwiches out of a bag and without a word handed two to Harry with a bottle of water.

Finally he couldn't stand the silence and he asked her gently, "Molly, are you alright? I'm not used to being with you when your mouth isn't moving."

She grinned at him, "You devil. You always did know how to sweet talk a girl."

Harry bit into a sandwich and said, "Umm, good Reuben sandwich. I haven't had one of these for a long time."

Molly held her sandwich poised in front of her and said, "Did you ever wonder when we started to grow apart?" Harry stopped chewing and said, "Not really. I suppose it was when we left for college."

Molly took a small bite of her sandwich and chewed it with a thoughtful look on her face. "No, I think it was before that. Do you remember the big fight we had at the breakfast table one morning? I think we were in tenth grade."

Harry tried to think back to the tenth grade. "I don't think so. We had quite a few blow ups back then so why don't you refresh my memory."

"You kept doing that thing to me. You know, when you would draw a circle in the air and then put your finger through the imaginary circle."

Harry started to laugh and drew the imaginary circle in the air and poked his index finger through it. "You mean that thing?"

"Yes!" Her eyes flashed. "It still gets a rise out of me when you do that along with that same stupid smirk on your face."

Harry took a drink of his water and peered at his cousin, "Why should that bother you? It didn't mean anything. I made it up so I could bug you."

Molly looked closely at him and narrowed her eyes, "Are you sure it didn't mean anything? Her voice had a suspicious quality to it.

"Cross my heart and hope to die." Harry grinned mischievously as he quickly crossed his heart.

"See, that's it!"

"What's it?"

"That look! That damnable smirk I was talking about. You still do it and I still don't believe you!"

Harry sat back and looked at his cousin with a serious expression on his face. "So what did you think it meant?" Then he added very slowly, "Asshole?"

"I knew it! Just the way you said it now, with that arrogant little taunt in your voice. You knew it all the time and you did it to make me mad. Whenever Dora would ask you about it you got that innocent little boy look on your face, but it didn't fool me for one minute."

"Seriously and truthfully, on my Boy Scout's honor. It didn't have any meaning, I made it up."

"Oh well, big hairy deal, Mr. truth and honesty. If I remember correctly you were a Boy Scout for only about four hours until you fell in the river and quit the troop."

Harry unwrapped the second sandwich and said, "Anyway, some fat kid pushed me in that creek . . . and your point of this whole earth shaking conversation is . . . ?"

"The point is . . . I think it was at that time I consciously realized you were a lot smarter than me, even if I never would have been able to admit it."

"I don't have the slightest idea what the point is you're trying to make. You used to do that sign to other kids."

"I know, but it was still your sign. You created it and it belonged to you. Let's face it, that sign was pure genius. After all, it was good enough to get a rise out of me. I think it was that day at breakfast, for the first time I started to feel you slipping away from me. Before that you always were so open to any of my suggestions and all of a sudden you seemed like you didn't need me any more. I remember, I tried to do the sign back at you and you looked at me like I was the most pathetic piece of crap in the whole world. The worst part was I knew I was pathetic. I was plagiarizing your original work and I wasn't smart enough to come up with something more original on my own. I think it hurt my ego."

"Excuse me, Ms. injured ego, but I seem to remember you were a bit of a ball buster yourself. Correct me if I'm wrong, but weren't you the girl who told Georgie Kopala you'd rather die than be with him, even if it meant the end of the entire human race? Seems to me that wouldn't really be an ego booster for any guy."

Molly took another small bite of her Reuben and a piece of sauerkraut fell in to her lap. Absentmindedly she picked it up and put it back in her mouth but not before she muttered, "Pig slopped again." It was the taunt they used to hurl back and forth when they were small children, but this time there was no self-consciousness or embarrassment connected with it.

"You're absolutely right. I wasn't always very nice to other people when I was growing up. Seriously, I've been making a real effort to be nicer to people. In retrospect, I see now even when you were young you were innately kinder to everyone than I was, and that's my point. I mean about you being smarter. You seemed to understand that concept, but I had to learn it the hard way. My parents tried to point that out to me but noooo, I had to find it out on my own. I guess I was too stubborn or too dumb to take their word for it."

"I think you're being a little hard on yourself. It probably might be more appropriate for you to take into consideration the differences in our personalities. You tended to be more animated and your open nature is part of what made you such a good reporter. I, on the other hand, was quieter and more content to follow your hair-brained plans and schemes. I guess I've always been self-conscious about not having a father and the fact that I was kind of an orphan and taken into your family out of the kindness of your mother and father's hearts made me an easier target for other people's meanness. When we were growing up one of the things I liked most about you was that you always had the courage to speak your mind and bear the consequences, no matter what they might be. I would hear you rant and rave and call people names and more often than not I wished that I'd been the one that had the courage to stand up and fight, but with you around, I didn't have to because you usually did it for both of us."

"Nice guy! Now that really makes me feel good about myself. Kind of like I was the evil twin." Molly picked apart the last crusts of her sandwich and threw them to the pigeons that had gathered around their feet. "I don't know, somehow you seemed to be naturally good and I always felt the need to kick the old sacred cows . . . test the limits . . . see how far I could push without getting into trouble. I remember back in high school when we had to write or recite a poem pretending to be a famous person. You did George Washington Carver and I did Mae West. Mr. Paulson said yours was sensitive and poignant and you got an A."

"Yeah, I remember that. We did pick very different people to portray. I'm starting to get your point. Whatever possessed you to recite that poem?"

Molly grinned, "Mr. Paulson said mine was entertaining but questionable and I got detention." She repeated the verse in her best Mae West impression:

> *"I hear you knocking but you can't come in.*
> *I'm in my nightie but it's oh so thin.*
> *I need the money but it's such a sin.*
> *Oh, quit your knockin' and come on in."*

She giggled mischievously and it was only then she noticed two young boys intently watching her performance. She momentarily studied them and added, "Boys, when I'm good I'm very, very good. But when I'm bad I'm even better." She turned back to Harry and grinned. "What the hell, all the worlds a stage . . ."

Harry shook his head and couldn't help but laugh. The boys grinned and waved as they walked on. Molly dropped back into her serious mode. "I still talk a lot with Clayton and I know he's helped me more than any shrink could have. When I was living in Minneapolis shortly before I moved back to Glenwood I realized I had filled my life with distractions so I could avoid looking at what kind of a person I had become. I sought out people who were used to using other people because it seemed to reassure me it was perfectly fine to hurt others. People like my ex-husband and his wife were a source of real irritation to me because they reminded me what I was doing was wrong. Now that I have time to reflect on how my very existence affects the people around me and it is quite remarkable."

Molly paused and continued, "Of course, now I know that us growing apart was a normal thing to have happened but at the time it still threatened me. It felt like I was no longer good enough to be your friend and it made me sad and angry. Somehow, I always had the feeling I had to be in control and when I couldn't be I got mean spirited. I talked with Clayton about this and somewhere in our conversation he commented that the sword of spirituality is double edged and it can cut both ways. It must be tempered to be strong, and justice and goodness must be treated with common sense and forgiveness. I wasn't really sure what he meant by that remark and I'm not sure I still do, but it got me thinking about some of the people I had hurt.

The one that has really bothered me was Graham Stone's daughter, Gloria. Remember the young girl who threw the drink in my face and told me to stay away from her father? I kept thinking of the pain on her face and knowing that I was responsible for putting it there haunted me. It bothered me so much that one day I sat down and wrote her a letter asking for her forgiveness. I told her she'd been right to do what she did and that if there was any way I could make up for all the pain I had caused her and her family I would try to do it. I explained at that time I'd lost my husband who I loved very much and I was angry with God, but I know now I had used his death as an excuse to selfishly hurt other people. I also told her how her confronting me had been what I needed to turn my life around and I would always be grateful to her for having the courage to do that. I put the letter in the mail and hoped and prayed that she would accept it in the right spirit. Well, you know how I am. I waited for awhile and then forgot about it. Last week, much to my surprise, I got a reply. Oh my God! I need to tell you it took all my courage to open it and I found myself preparing for the worst. Harry, it was the saddest letter. She thanked me for writing to her and said my letter arrived at a time when she'd been at one of the lowest points in her life. She said it helped her to finally admit to herself that her father was not a very nice man and to blame me and the other women he had affairs with was foolish. All the years she was growing up she had witnessed her mother's suffering and yet somehow defended her father, believing it was her mother's fault for not being the wife he needed.

She went on to say she had been living with a man and found out he was so much like her father it almost drove her to ending her life. She said the day she got my letter she was so depressed she felt she could no longer go on living. After reading it she realized to let someone else take away your will to live or decide how you would live your life is completely wrong. She thanked me and asked if maybe we could start over again. It seems over the past years she'd been so critical of her mother they drifted apart but now they were working at rebuilding their relationship. It kind of reminded me of that story where the wise man talks about how a butterfly's wings fluttering in one part of the world can affect the weather in another part of the world. It was so awesome to me to think I may have made a positive difference in her life by sharing my feelings with her."

Harry sat studying his cousin and finally replied, "That's a pretty remarkable story and once again I need to tell you how I admire your courage and candor. I want you to know I'm not really smarter than you. We just have different lessons to learn and I believe you've made some giant steps."

"Thank you, kind sir! I appreciate your vote of confidence but before you get all dewy eyed over my conversion to sainthood, I must confess on my way up here some guy flipped me the bird because he thought I cut him off so I did this to him . . ." She drew the imaginary circle and put her index finger through it. "And, I want you to know that was when I still thought it meant something really bad."

Harry laughed and threw his sandwich wrappers into the trash. Molly picked up her wrappers and as she carried them over to the basket paused, "So often, it seems to me I take one step forward and two backwards. About the time I think I've got a handle on this goodness thing something questionable pops out of my mouth and I blow that myth all to hell. Well, Slick it's been good but I've have to run. Thanks for being such a good listener."

Harry looked at his cousin, "You just called me Slick. You haven't done that since we were really little kids. Where did that come from?"

Molly stared at him with mock look of puzzlement, "I don't know. What did I just say? Stuff pops out of my mouth and I have no idea where it comes from. Oh, and by the way, one of the things I notice when I'm driving to Minneapolis is how many people pick their noses when they drive. Yuk! It's so gross! Like they think when they get into their car or truck the good manners fairy puts some invisible shield around them so no one else will notice their disgusting habits. Yeah, fat chance!" She rolled her eyes. "Oh, and I almost forgot, I might be coming up next week so I'll give you another jingle but for now I'm off and running full tilt into the great world of psychological and spiritual enlightenment."

As she turned to leave a small dog on a leash barked at her. She stopped and eyed the dog and carefully drew the imaginary circle and put her finger through it. She smiled and winked at Harry. He watched her walk down the sidewalk and melt into the crowd and wondered how she could be so serious one moment and so irreverent in the very next breath. All her life she'd done that and Harry wondered if that irreverence was her attempt to cope with the uncertainty of life and the painful issues she seemed destined to obsess over.

As he entered the office Janet greeted him and handed him several messages. "How was lunch in the park with your cousin?"

"Good." He paused as if still reflecting on his conversation with Molly. "But I'm quite sure I know how Alice must have felt after she had lunch with the Mad Hatter."

The following Sunday night as Harry sat reading the newspaper the phone rang. He glanced at the clock and as he held the receiver to his ear said, "Hi, Molly, what's up?"

There was a brief silence and Molly said, "So, how'd you know it was me?"

"Because no one else calls me at this hour just to chat."

"God, it gives me the creeps when people seem to know things before they happen. What are you doing?"

"I'm sitting here eating an Eskimo bar reading the funny papers. How about you?"

"Actually, for the last half hour I've been sitting here contemplating our human fragility."

"Whoa, I'd have to say we were not exactly on the same wave length. You mean like yours and my fragile mortality?"

"Not just us, everyone's mortality. The whole friggin' world's mortality. Humankind."

"I'd say that's pretty heavy thinking for a Sunday night and I'm not sure I'm up for this conversation."

She ignored his comment, "Aren't you going to ask me what brought these thoughts on?"

Harry knew she wanted him to ask but for once he wished she would just volunteer the information and not have him drag it out of her. Her obsessing on her spiritual growth was starting to wear on him. "So, Molly, what brought on these heavy thoughts?"

"Thank you for asking Harry. How very thoughtful of you. "Do you remember Monty Taterra?"

"Your brother Daniel's friend? Monk, the terror?"

"Yes, he was about four years older than us. Bennie Benson, Monk and Slider Hrdlichka and Daniel all chummed around together. You probably remember Monk and Slider were older than Daniel and Bennie but they were inseparable. Bennie, Slider, and Daniel all had black leather jackets and ducktail haircuts but Monk wore a red nylon jacket because his hero was James Dean. *Rebel Without a Cause*, remember? Monk said he saw that movie at least ten times when it first came out. He even looked like James Dean. He was so gorgeous."

"Yes, I do recall all of this. I was there with you, remember?" He sighed audibly hoping she would get to her point before his Eskimo bar expired.

"I know you were. I needed to go over the facts to get it straight in my own mind, so bear with me. Eat the damn ice cream but listen. If you remember they all signed up to join the army together but Monk was rejected because of some kind of heart murmur. He stayed behind and helped run his dad's repair shop. I bring my car to him now whenever I need something done. God, when we were young I thought he was so handsome and I had the biggest crush on him. Bennie and Slider didn't like it when I tried to hang around but Monk was always nice to me. Bennie would say, get lost fart blossom but Monk made him stop calling me that and that's when I think I fell in love with him. I even gave your bike two flat tires and a broken chain just so we could bring it into his dad's shop and have Monk fix it."

"My bike? You mean to tell me you broke my bike just so you could moon over Monk? How come you didn't wreck your own bike?"

"Duh, that would have been a little transparent, don't you think?"

"Oh silly me, even I should have been able to figure that one out."

"Anyway, to get back to my original point, Monty, no one calls him Monk anymore, Monty lives in Lowry and is still a mechanic. Yesterday morning he was helping Slider repair a flat on his car. They were working in Slider's driveway and Monty was under the car and somehow it slipped off the jack and almost crushed him. He said it was weird because he's used that jack and done that very procedure so many times he doesn't even have to think about it. I don't know all the details but Slider said they had taken the tire off, and were trying to put the new one on when the jack slipped and the car came crashing down. He said if Monty had been only an inch or two to the left it would have crushed his head. Monty is going to be okay but it shook them up. I think back in high school they all thought they were invincible. I went to see Monty in the hospital and that's what started me thinking about how tenuous life can be."

"That's true, none of us know when we're going to . . . ."

She cut him off mid-sentence. "So it's really important to have your life in order, not to wait until it's too late."

"Yeah, live each day as if it was your last one on earth, because it could be."

"Exactly. I keep thinking about all the crazy things those guys pulled off and how many times they could have been killed when they were teenagers but they all survived. Think about it, all three of them got sent to fight in Viet Nam and they all came back. Then the time Slider's car got stalled on the railroad tracks and how they pushed it off before a passenger train came blazing through. You just never know do you?"

"Nope. No one knows."

"Do you remember when they chained Perdy the cop's squad car to a telephone pole when he was asleep inside? Then they went speeding through downtown Lowry honking the horn so when Perdy took off after them it almost tore out his transmission. That was so awful!"

Harry wasn't entirely convinced Molly really thought it was awful or just plain funny. He knew her sense of humor. "How about the time they caught a big warm cow pie in a paper bag and put it on Mr. Doopla's front step? Then poured lighter fluid on it and set it on fire, then rang the doorbell and ducked behind the bushes. When old man Doopla came out and tried to stomp out the fire he slipped and fell in the cow crap."

"Totally terrible." Molly agreed sincerely. "He could have broken his neck. They could have gotten themselves into big trouble but Perdy played his cards right and got Mr. Doopla to back off. After that the boys pretty much left Perdy alone." There was a slight pause before Molly continued. "I hate to admit it but it was me who suggested the cow crap in a bag trick to Monty."

"I wish I could say that surprises me, but it doesn't."

"I kind of feel bad about that. But, you remember old man Doopla was a real grouch. What you put out into the universe will come back to you."

"My point exactly."

"Oh, God, that's true. Maybe that's why I stepped into that cow crap when I was in Africa."

"Good night, Molly. Tell Monty I said hello and hope for his speedy recovery."

"Harry?"

"Yes, Molly?"

"I sincerely hope God can overlook some of the things we did when we were growing up. We were just dumb little kids."

"We?"

"We. Bye. Love you."

Chapter 23

Early Thursday morning Michael called the St. Mary's psychiatric unit to check on his daughter's progress. The ward secretary explained Doreen was doing as well as could be expected. She let Michael speak to the charge nurse who relayed the same information, but qualified it by saying anyone who had taken large quantities of pills over an extended period of time as Doreen had, would experience a period of withdrawal. She also expressed it would be in everyone's best interests to postpone visiting until Doreen's doctor suggested it would be appropriate. Doreen's psychiatrist was Dr. Suzen Shepherd and Martha had already spoken with her. Michael and Martha felt Doreen might relate better with a woman doctor as men appeared to be a difficult issue for her to deal with.

Dr. Shepherd requested she meet with Martha first and the following day with Michael. He suspected with Doreen's obvious antagonism toward men the new doctor wanted to see how her patient and her mother related without Michael's influence. This was understandable and he spent the rest of the day trying to get more information on Louis. After school he and Danny worked until suppertime building a birdhouse.

The following morning a few minutes before ten o'clock, Michael entered the downtown office of Dr. Suzen Shepherd and introduced himself to her receptionist, Gladys Davis. He found the office to be comfortable and tastefully decorated. He was further impressed that the magazines were actually current and of interest to him. He selected one on woodworking and settled back in a comfortable leather chair. He began reading an article on building go-carts and was becoming engrossed with plans that would tentatively include his grandsons when an office door opened and two women stepped out. The younger lady was dressed in a soft tan suit and the older woman was wearing a full-length chinchilla coat even though the day was obviously too warm to be wearing fur. Exquisite diamond rings adorned many of the older woman's arthritic fingers. Several were set with the largest and most brilliant gems Michael had ever seen.

Gladys stood up and ushered the older woman to the door and assured her that her chauffeur would be waiting at the outside door. Michael laid the magazine down as Suzen Shepherd approached him extending her hand to introduce herself. As was Michael's habit, he made a quick assessment of his daughter's doctor. She was about forty-five years old and by Michael's standards, a very attractive woman. Her brown hair was cut short in a stylish manner and Michael admired that she was a professional person that looked comfortable being a woman. He had come to notice it was not uncommon for some professional women to be dressed in attire resembling that of a man. He knew some would interpret this feeling as sexist but it was the way he'd been brought up. She gestured for him to enter her office and Michael realized during the same time he'd been assessing her she had been doing the same to him.

Dr. Shepherd smiled warmly and he immediately understood why Martha had spoken so favorably about her. As they sat down she opened a manila folder that lay on her desk and adjusted her glasses. She looked directly at him and said, "Thank you for coming in. Your daughter Doreen requested that I meet with you and your wife to help get her situation sorted out. As angry as she was with you she has come to realize she still needs your help. I hope we'll be able to help your daughter recover and lead a happier and healthier life. Normally I would be working more directly with her husband but I understand he is no longer around, is that correct?"

"Yes, that's correct. Lenny left the morning after Doreen was admitted to the hospital and we're not really sure where he is." Michael resisted the urge to tell her what a worthless piece of work Lenny Dickerson was.

"There are two children, Corey and Danny but I understand Lenny is not their biological father"

"No, he isn't. In fact, he's Doreen's third husband. Her first husband is the boys' father and presently lives in Florida. The second husband is no longer in the picture."

"Do the boys spend any time with their father?"

"No, they don't. Doreen would never permit it. George has remarried and has a new family. He's a wonderful man and I believe if permitted he would enjoy being a part of his sons' lives."

"Are both boys living with you now?"

"Danny is but Corey is in a foster home. Becca Rhodes, from court services, thought maybe by tomorrow I should be able to bring him home to be with us."

"Michael, how do you feel about the idea of raising two boys at this stage of your life?"

Michael grinned, "Well, now, if I said I didn't have a few concerns I'm quite sure you'd know I was lying. Both Martha and I have known for a long time this could become a possibility. We feel since we have come this far by admitting there is a very real problem we're also prepared to accept this responsibility. Martha is good with children and I always felt she did a wonderful job of raising our three. Now that I am retired from the police force I'll be there more to help with the boys as well. According to Doreen, a major source of her emotional problems was that I was never there for her. She felt I always put my work before my family."

"Do you think you did?"

Michael seemed to sink lower into his chair but replied, "In all honesty, I don't think so. It's true I worked extra jobs sometimes so Martha could be home as a fulltime mother. Back then that was the way it was done. The father worked as the sole breadwinner so the mother could be home with the children. I asked our youngest daughter Kathleen if she ever felt neglected like Doreen did. She has repeatedly assured me both she and her brother Thomas Michael felt we were always there for them. She feels that I could never have fulfilled Doreen's needs even if I'd stayed with her twenty-four-seven."

"Kathleen is your daughter who is in police work out in San Francisco and Thomas Michael your son who was killed in the line of duty. That makes Doreen the middle child." She said it more as a statement than a question.

Michael knew from his years on the police force sometimes you could make a situation worse by divulging too much information. He observed time after time where a person had dug themselves into a hole by trying to be too helpful but he felt with his daughter and grandson's future at stake, if he was to blame, this was the time to step forward and take responsibility. "Maybe I wasn't the kind of father Doreen needed. I tried hard to be but it seemed no matter what I did, it wasn't enough for her." There was pain in his eyes, "For some reason, Doreen was always more difficult for me to love. I tried to pretend I loved all my children equally but deep down I knew I couldn't. When Kathleen was born, Doreen was three and she seemed to resent her from the first moment she laid eyes on her. Later, as they got older, she would say that sweet little Kathleen was my favorite."

"And . . . . ?"

"I honestly tried not to have favorites. Both Martha and I made a distinct effort to be sure one child never got more than the other, right down to the last toy or piece of birthday cake. Somehow, Doreen always saw it differently."

"Tell me about Kathleen."

"She has always been a joy to behold. I think she came into the world with a smile on her face. I would take the children to the park and Kathleen would skip and dance wanting to know about every bird and flower. Thomas Michael would be quietly watching a squirrel or a bug but Kathleen wanted me to tell her about everything she saw. Doreen, on the other hand, would be dragging behind pouting because she was hot and the bugs were biting and whining about why she couldn't have ice cream. Kathleen and Doreen were as different as night and day. For Kathleen, life was always an adventure and a down hill ride whereas for Doreen, it was always as if she was struggling to push a great boulder up a steep hill with no one to help her."

"Do Kathleen and Doreen communicate at all?"

"No, Doreen may send Kathleen a card at Christmas but that's about all. Kathleen on the other hand, always sends presents for the whole family but Doreen thinks she's doing it to get closer to her boys so she can take their love away from her.

Kathleen moved out to San Francisco after she graduated from the Police Academy and lives with her significant other who is also on the police force. We would prefer it if they were married but then I know things are different than when Martha and I got married. At this point they realize with their demanding careers, children are not a real good idea. I guess these are things you learn to accept as a parent." Michael didn't notice how Dr. Shepherd smiled slightly at his last statement. He looked up at her, and asked, "Do you have children?"

"Yes, I do. Twins, Brandon and Barbara."

"Do they have similar personalities?"

"Yes and no. Even though they're twins I think in some ways they are completely different. He is a racecar driver and she is a librarian. How different is that? But sometimes they seem so close I think one can feel the other's pain."

"Not so for Doreen and Kathleen. Its almost like they came from different planets. What is it they say about two men looking through prison bars? "One saw mud and one saw stars. Doreen is not only not a fun person to be with but she seems to suck the life out of everyone around her." Tears threatened to spring into Michael's eyes and he said quietly, "Please forgive me, I had no right to say that."

"Michael, I need you to be honest with me and if that's how you really feel about your daughter, that's what I need to know. I'll make my own observations about Doreen as I work with her. Obviously, whatever is going on in her life isn't working or she wouldn't have done what she did. Don't ever feel you need to hide your feelings because you think I won't approve of what you're telling me."

Dr. Shepherd then shared some of her preliminary observations regarding Doreen. She discussed the possibility of Doreen being bipolar and how her low self-esteem probably contributed to her escalating drug use. They discussed codependency and how, over the years, with each of her various episodes of crisis she allowed her parents to come to her rescue and later accused them of meddling in her life. Her ambivalence being reinforced when she felt she had again failed and needed to ask for more help. She mentioned the importance of tough love and the future of Doreen's children.

After an hour of emotionally draining discussion Dr. Shepherd took off her glasses and pushed her chair back from the desk. "My hope is that through the process of exploring the things we've talked about we'll be able to have Doreen accept herself as a special person who has a loving family who will always be there to love and support her, unconditionally. Hopefully in the process she will come to realize she is responsible for her choices, and how the consequences of these choices directly affect her family."

She sat back and added, "Martha told me the frightening story you shared with her about your grandson and his dog. She also told me about how you compared the look in Doreen's eyes in the emergency room to a mad dog you saw your partner shoot. She mentioned you wondered if people would judge you harshly for having a daughter that was so totally out of control and the concern that you didn't recognize the seriousness of the problem sooner. I just want to reassure you most parents have a difficult time admitting their sweet little babies can have serious problems as teenagers or adults. It's very natural to want to look the other way and give them the benefit of the doubt. As parents, I feel we are all guilty of that at times. I'd like to share something with you. If you were my patient I probably wouldn't feel it appropriate, but I think this could be of some help to you as a parent.

My husband is a wonderful man, kind, soft spoken and intelligent. He runs a family owned wholesale nursery business with his twin brother. The bulk of their business is to supply shrubs and other supplies to the larger landscape companies around the Metro area. Like most families we've had a few ups and downs. Our twins have always seemed to be close emotionally and when they were children they really gave us very few problems. When they became teenagers we had some of the usual problems, There were several speeding tickets for our son, and considering his occupation now, he still insists he was just trying to qualify. He was also arrested for a DWI during his first year at the University but other than these incidents there has been very little cause for concern.

For their first year of college both Brandon and Barbara attended the University of Minnesota. Barbara did especially well academically and Brandon was holding his own. Because every day I hear about the pain and struggles in other parent's lives, I was feeling quite smug about the wonderful job we'd done raising our own children. At the end of her second year at the U. of M. Barbara expressed a desire to transfer to Concordia. Brandon was satisfied staying at the University and while we discussed his transferring too, he declined. After thinking about it more and wanting to respect our now young adult children's wishes we decided it might be good for them to go to separate colleges.

Barbara had always been rather quiet but whenever we talked about her future plans she seemed to become even more reserved. Occasionally I would tease her about marriage or make a remark about having grandchildren, but she would only smile and say that we would have to wait and see until the right person came along. I got the shock of my life one Saturday morning when Brandon and I were having breakfast and I commented on how I wished Barbara could find a nice boyfriend. I still remember that incredulous look on my son's face. He stared at me for the longest time and then said, you are kidding aren't you, mom? I looked at him with surprise and replied no, why would you say something like that? He sat back in his chair and finally exclaimed, what planet do you live on, Dr. Shepherd? I was totally confused and said, what on earth are you talking about? His expression changed to one of great concern as he said, mom, you really don't know? Barbara is gay. You of all people must have known. There won't be any boyfriends and there may never be any grandchildren. As I tried to collect myself, Brandon just sat there and finally said, I think you and your daughter need to sit down and have a long, serious talk."

Michael could feel the empathy Dr. Shepherd was offering and was grateful for her candor.

"Of course, it was true, our daughter is a lesbian. My husband had suspected it but waited for me to say something. After all, wasn't I the trained professional? Then of course, I went through all the stages a parent goes through. I denied it, blamed myself, felt like I was a failure and spent way too much time obsessing about what everyone would say. It took my sweet and understanding husband to point out this was not about me, not directly anyway. Rather, it was about Barbara and how we needed to support her by accepting her lifestyle and reconfirming what a wonderful person she is.

It took a little while but we now realize our daughter is the person she is supposed to be. It's a different lifestyle than we would have chosen for her but it's obviously something she must go through. Looking back, I realize there were subtle signs but I didn't allow myself to see them. So, Michael, please don't chastise yourself for not addressing your daughter's problems sooner. From what Martha has described you have helped and supported Doreen in every way you could. We need to remember yesterday is gone, and we must move forward and focus on the present. Doreen has a different way of viewing her life experiences. To her the world is a threatening and hostile environment and over time we'll try to help her see it in a more friendly and favorable light. Even as professionals, we don't always know why each individual perceives the world so differently. The one thing you can count on is that we'll do all we can to help her cope. Our immediate primary task is to get her medications straightened out and when she's willing to share from her heart, we will be there to listen."

Michael got up to leave and reached across the desk to shake hands with Dr. Shepherd. "Are you and your daughter close?"

"Yes. I am happy to say we are. I still have times where I find myself asking God why, but this experience has made me stronger, and I hope wiser. It certainly has given me a much greater understanding of what other parents go through. Thank you for coming in today and I hope you and your daughter will find a common ground to share. I really believe it will be possible."

Chapter 24

David awoke with a terrible headache. His doctor had prescribed several different medications but none of them seemed to help. This morning he felt nauseated and thinking it was possibly a side effect from the newest medication he called his doctor's office. After being put on hold for what seemed an inordinately long time filled with jangling music, the receptionist relayed that Dr. Rassmusson suggested if David was willing, they would schedule him for a CT scan. He agreed and an appointment was set up for the following Monday. A new prescription was called into the pharmacy and she assured him it could be picked up in an hour. He called his office and explained to Janet he would be coming in late as he'd decided to stop at Seaton House to inspect the newly redecorated sunroom. After, he would swing by the pharmacy to pick up his medication.

He found Mary Rose on the front porch admiring a beautiful bouquet of flowers her friend Louis had sent in honor of her birthday. David handed her a small wrapped package and she eagerly tore off the paper and appeared totally delighted with the small mosaic icon of the Blessed Virgin Mary. When he explained it had been his mother's she protested saying it should stay in his family. Upon hearing that remark David gave her a hug and told her she was very much a part of his family.

As Mary Rose led the way to the sunroom she chattered about how much the girls were enjoying the new furnishings. Several young women in various stages of pregnancy were sitting at a small table playing cards but stood up to leave when David and Mary Rose entered. Mary Rose made it clear they could stay but one of them explained they were due to attend their parenting class that was about to begin in the library. In her usual enthusiastic way, Mary Rose put her arms out and then brought her hands together in praise saying, "Isn't this just about the most gorgeous room you've ever seen in your entire life?"

David couldn't help but smile at her zest for living and her ability to enjoy all the aspects of her life of loving service. Somehow, she accepted the good she experienced with unmitigated joy, and the problems she might encounter were to be considered as gifts, and should be confidently accepted as opportunities to grow. She continually lived the principle that whatever transpired, whether perceived as good or otherwise, be immediately turned over to reside in God's hands. In spite of his headache he had to smile at her enthusiasm for the newly decorated sunroom.

"I have to agree with you, it is one of the most beautiful rooms I have ever seen."

Sunlight filtered through the new window blinds that gave the room a bright and airy look and also kept it from becoming too warm in the afternoons. The colors Mary Rose and Annie picked were soft, pastel shades of pink, green and off white giving the room a look of perpetual springtime. The new furniture was white wicker with floral cushions, and the carpet, a soft shade of pale green.

"I think you may have missed part of your calling. It seems you could have a little decorating business on the side and do very well."

Mary Rose brushed his compliment aside but he could see how pleased she was with the way the room had turned out. Now beaming with excitement she continued to explain how Louis had suggested he would be willing to not only provide a new heating system but that he felt it would be wise to install central air conditioning at the same time. As they continued to enjoy their visit a young blonde woman appeared in the doorway carrying a tray with two glasses of lemonade and a plate of cookies. She entered and placed the tray on the table and stepped back and said, "I thought you might enjoy some refreshments so I . . . why, my goodness, is that you David Sullivan? I can't believe it's really you." She stepped back as if to give him a better look.

David stared at the young woman and said, "Jezzie, is that you? Oh, my goodness, Jezebel Smith!"

"It's me alright. I guess you've probably noticed I've grown up a whole lot since the last time you saw me." She turned around and struck a little pose as if to show him the new Jezzie Smith.

"What in the world has brought you back to Seaton House? The last I heard you were headed out west to start a new life." Then he added cautiously, "You're not . . . ?"

"Oh, God no, don't you dare even think that! I learned my lesson the first time. One mistake like that was enough in my life. No, I'm just passing through Minneapolis long enough to complete a little unfinished business and then I'm on my way to Europe. The problem is the airline lost my luggage so I stopped here to say hello to my dear friend Sister Mary Rose. She mentioned she was behind on her bookwork so I've offered to help in return for her letting me spend a little time here. I'm an excellent accountant now, thanks to the help you gave me after my baby was born." She smiled again and fanned herself with the front of the jacket she was wearing intentionally revealing her low cut sundress and very ample breasts. "My, it's warm in here! Won't it be nice to have air in here?"

David was amused as it was very obvious Jezzie was indeed all grown up and was flirting with him. "You look wonderful. Where have you been living?"

"Mostly Vegas, I was working as a full time accountant for one of the casinos. My boyfriend works there too. He had to finish up with his job and then he's flying to Minneapolis and we'll go on to Europe together."

Mary Rose interrupted, "Thank you, Jezzie. It was very thoughtful of you to bring us refreshments but don't you think you'd better be getting back to our books?" David picked up a not too subtle hint of disapproval in her voice.

"Yes, ma'am . . . I will, but I only wanted to say how nice it was to be able to see you again David." She smiled sweetly showing her perfect white teeth. You and Mary Rose were the two people who were there in my time of need and I'll always be grateful."

"Jezzie . . . ."

"Don't worry, Sister. I'm on my way, but before I go I have a question for David. What would you give me for a basketful of kisses?" She smiled provocatively at David.

"Jezebel!" Mary Rose's voice sounded shocked.

David grinned, and replied, "It's okay. If you remember, it's part of the game Jezzie and I used to play. We both love old movies and we'd try to stump each other by quoting a line from one of them. To get back to your question Jez, I'd give you a basketful of hugs. Rhoda Penmark from *The Bad Seed.*"

"Very impressive! I never could stump you and I see you're still as good as ever." She flipped her long, frosted blonde hair over her shoulder and started to exit the room.

"Jezzie?"

"Yes, David?"

"Do you stay in contact with your family?"

She smiled slightly, "Only my grandmother. She lives up north. Her name is Bessie Dankers. Bye now." She winked at David as she made her departure.

"That girl!" Mary Rose's voice was now full of disapproval. "If you ask me, I think she's still looking for trouble. She may think she's learned her lesson but I'm not so sure. I think it may have been a mistake letting her stay here this time, but she really has been a dear helping me with the bookkeeping. Heaven knows that's clearly not one of my strong points."

David reached for his glass of lemonade and commented, "She really has changed from that fifteen year old runaway the police brought here a few years ago."

Mary Rose was still visibly irritated, "She was flirting with you. You do know that don't you? She should be ashamed of herself. You were like a father to her. Getting her front teeth restored after that no good boyfriend knocked them out. You also paid for her classes so she could learn accounting and then she stands here brazenly flashing her chest at you . . . which, by the way, is not at all what the good Lord gave her. What would ever possess a mother to name her daughter Jezebel? It's like giving her permission to be promiscuous."

"Her real name is Jennifer Smith. She chose the name Jezebel when she ran away from home."

"Well, at least she keeps in touch with her grandmother. Maybe she can influence her granddaughter to get her life in order."

Since Mary Rose seemed to take comfort in that thought David didn't have the heart to tell her Jezzie had found perverse humor in using the name of the woman who committed all the murders in the book *The Bad Seed*. Bessie Dankers was the person who passed her murderous tendencies onto her evil granddaughter.

He sat silently looking at the empty doorway, "I wonder if she ever thinks of the little boy she gave up?"

"Probably not. I'm not sure it's in her nature." Mary Rose sipped on her lemonade. "From the little she has told me she's been leading a rather active life in Las Vegas. She was a showgirl in one of the casinos for awhile, but said it was too hard on her feet and back so her boyfriend got her a job in the accounting office. Against my better judgment I let her share a room with Ellen, the quiet, dark haired girl who was in here earlier. Jezzie has been helping some of the girls by showing them some grooming tips and I think she has been good for Ellen. They seem to relate well."

"I remember how sad Jezzie was the whole time she was here. That's probably the reason I got to know her, I felt so sorry for her." David picked up a cookie and took a bite. "I noticed how interested she was in watching all the old movies and that's how we started that little game of challenging each other with lines from them, and seeing if the other could recognize it."

"Even back then she was very secretive about her background, and I don't think she's changed much."

David looked at his friend and said, "What makes you think that?"

"Well, as you know, I try to respect my girls' privacy but when Jezzie showed up the other night with no bags it seemed a little strange to me. I checked with the airline she said she came in on and there was no report of lost luggage for Jezebel Smith. I also noticed she seems to carry quite a bit of cash in her purse so it wasn't like she couldn't have afforded a hotel. I don't know David, it seems as if there is something going on in her life besides what she is telling me. Almost every evening she goes for a walk and Ellen tells me she has started to flirt with some guy who plays tennis in the courts next to the park. I think there could be some hanky panky starting there."

David chuckled at the nun sitting next to him and said, "Hanky panky? Mary Rose, I haven't heard anyone use that expression for at least forty years."

She took an imaginary swipe at him and said, "Are you trying to tell me again that I'm getting old? Just because today adds another year to my age doesn't mean I'm ready for the retirement home."

An extremely pregnant young girl appeared in the doorway and said someone was on the phone asking about the new furnace and she had answered it because Jezzie was outside having a cigarette.

David hugged Mary Rose goodbye and headed for the pharmacy to pick up his new prescription.

Chapter 25

Suzen Shepherd was surprised to receive a phone call from Dr. Roland Priester. She was even more surprised when he asked if she would be available for the next few days to check on one of his patients who was presently in the St. Mary's psychiatric unit. Suzen had never met nor spoken to the man before but having read many of the articles he'd written for the various psychiatric periodicals and journals, was extremely flattered he would call her. He explained he would be unavailable for personal reasons, which she learned later meant he'd suffered a gall bladder attack and was facing the possibility of surgery. Roland Priester was almost seventy-two years old and considered to be a bit of an eccentric but brilliant scholar in the psychiatric field. For all practical purposes he was retired but continued to treat a few private patients.

When Suzen assured him she would be pleased to help he explained his patient, Estelle Welheim, was the wife of a long time friend of his. She was suffering from chronic melancholia and depression and occasionally would enter St. Mary's to rest and have her medications re-evaluated. He explained that Estelle had been in a slight car accident requiring a few stitches in her forehead, but a uterine tumor had been discovered and her husband felt it important to have it taken care of immediately. She would, he continued, go from a short stay on the surgical unit, then return back to her private room in the psychiatric unit until they were sure she was emotionally and physically stable enough to be released. He made it clear that at all times she would be accompanied by her own private duty nurse and Suzen's only role as her temporary psychiatrist would be to be available if there should be an emergency, or if Estelle's husband should need to speak with a doctor. He cautioned her not to change any of her medications or any of her routines unless she consulted directly him or her husband.

Before he hung up he thanked her and asked if she had any questions. When she stated she was comfortable with his instructions he concluded by cautioning her that because of Estelle's husband's position in the community, his patient's privacy was to be protected with the utmost discretion. Suzen assured him she would be careful and thanked him for considering her to look after Estelle in his absence.

As Suzen hung up the phone she was aware for some unexplained reason she had developed an uneasy feeling in the pit of her stomach, and yet was unable to pin point what part of the conversation with Dr. Priester had triggered her discomfort. Later, as she sat in her office sorting through her patient's notes she found herself trying to recall an article she had recently read on fibroid tumors of the uterus and the significance the author had attributed to them. She remembered the author associating uterine fibroid tumors with a particular type of woman who often suffered from feelings of being emotionally unfulfilled. She wondered if this might be an appropriate topic to add to a book she had recently started writing.

The following morning as she made her rounds on St. Mary's seventh floor she noted with satisfaction that each of her patients had shown some indications of progress. Doreen Dickerson was sitting at a table in the day room drinking coffee and appeared to be the picture of health. She was confiding to the woman next to her that she expected to be leaving the seventh floor very soon. Suzen greeted Doreen and wasn't surprised she appeared to be trying a little too hard to convince her how well she was doing. She also noted how Doreen appeared to pout when Suzen was unable to tell her exactly how long she would have to remain on the psychiatric unit. After their brief visit she left Doreen and her new friend and as she was walking away she wasn't totally sure but thought she heard Doreen say something under her breath that sounded very much like go to hell. She smiled and realized she would certainly have her work cut out for her in the clinical management of Doreen Dickerson.

When Suzen completed her visits with her other patients she made her way to Estelle Welheim's private room and had to admit she found herself more than a little curious to meet her newest patient and wondered why a man like Dr. Roland Priester found her to be so special. As she entered Estelle's room, Suzen was met by Carole Flint, one of three private duty nurses employed by Louis Welheim. Suzen introduced herself to Estelle and nodded a greeting of familiarity to the nurse whom she'd met several years before when they had worked together as part of the regular hospital staff. She had always felt Carole's demeanor to be rather arrogant, but reluctantly had to concede that as far as nursing skills were concerned she was one of the more competent nurses. Suzen hoped Carole would leave the room so she could speak privately with Estelle, but even when she obviously hesitated before engaging in conversation with Estelle, Carole made no effort to leave and instead appeared busy with her charting.

Suzen began casually visiting with Estelle and found her to be an attractive but sad looking woman. She appeared to lack spontaneity and came off as rather noncommittal and flat. After observing her body language and indifferent responses to simple questions she suspected Estelle was being over sedated and this was probably interfering with her cognitive processes. At one point Estelle acknowledged she was bored and when Suzen suggested she might enjoy writing a poem or short story Carole Flint turned and stared directly at Suzen. Estelle replied she didn't think so and Carole turned back to the notes she had been working on. They continued to visit on a superficial level and after about five minutes one of the regular staff nurses poked her head in and informed Suzen she had a phone call at the desk. Suzen asked Estelle if there was anything she needed and Estelle shook her head no, and then asked if she would be in to see her in the morning before they took her to surgery. Suzen assured her she would and excused herself.

The next morning Suzen came in a little earlier than usual so she could visit with Estelle before they gave her the preoperative hypo. Again, Carole Flint stood awkwardly close to Estelle but with her back to them as if she was giving them permission to speak but was clearly unwilling to leave Estelle alone. Once again, the conversation was superficial, and when Suzen inquired if Estelle was nervous about the surgery she replied no without any facial expression and that she could care less about what the outcome would be. As Suzen was preparing to leave, Estelle held out her hand for Suzen to inspect and told her there was a spot that itched and whether she felt it would be helpful to put some hand lotion on it. Suzen inspected the pale abrasion Estelle was pointing to. Looking directly at Estelle she thought she caught the hint of a slight smile forming on Estelle's lips. She smiled back and agreed that hand lotion probably would help.

"Dear, would you mind getting my lotion from the bathroom?" Estelle was addressing Carole but her eyes never left Suzen's. Carole hesitated before she put down her notes and walked swiftly into the bathroom as

Estelle's hand shot out and deftly knocked a small African violet off her table.

"Oh dear! Call me butterfingers. Carole, please be a dear and find the janitor. I would hate to cut my feet on the glass."

The nurse looked suspiciously at her ward and then glanced at Dr. Shepherd before reluctantly leaving the room. Quickly, Estelle pulled a water-stained paper from her robe pocket. She smiled mischievously at Suzen and said, "Sorry about the plant thing but how else was I going to get rid of nurse Rachad? I wrote this last night but you must promise me that no one else is to see it. Not blowhole Priester either. Just you. I like you. I wrote it when I was soaking in the tub. As long as I keep saying 'yes boss' and she knows I'm not trying to drown myself she leaves me alone. Hide it before she gets back."

Suzen quickly stuffed the paper into her lab coat pocket before Carole Flint returned with a dustpan and small brush in her hand. After assuring Estelle her vital signs were normal and that she should do just fine in surgery, she promised to look in on her again in the evening and excused herself. As she turned to leave she found herself face to face with an imposing looking gentleman who introduced himself as Louis Welheim. In response she started to introduce herself, but was immediately assured he already knew who she was. After a pleasant but very brief conversation, Louis made it quite clear their meeting was over.

After she had completed her rounds and was back in her office she remembered the paper in her pocket. She opened it and studied Estelle's wispy penmanship. The letters slanted forward almost to the point where they appeared not to be able to support themselves. She had titled her writing The Unguarded Thought.

> *I am sitting in a dismal room with only one window. There is no door. The room is stripped of everything. There are no ruffles or frills or things that could have been or how they ought to be. It is filled only with the reality of how it is. I am sitting on a straight backed chair and I'm very uncomfortable but I dare not slump. Above me a light bulb burns brightly and the glare hurts my eyes but it cannot penetrate the black shadows in the corners of the room.*
>
> *As I sit here, a thought comes into my mind but I know I must not allow it to remain for it is forbidden. I turn my eyes*

to the window and try to discover a way out but I see there are bars preventing my escape. As hard as I try to avoid noticing the shadows, I cannot, for coming out of the depths of blackness I can hear voices softly calling to me. Out of the corner of my eye I catch a subtle movement. Something is watching me from under a pile of long discarded regrets, things that might have been different if only I had been stronger. Then, the accusing eyes are gone and I sit alone with my confusion about the voices that torture my thoughts.

I do not know how long I sit here as my room has no clock and time seems to have stopped for me before I see movement and something evil slithers out of the blackness and glares at me. This time I cannot avoid seeing it so I stare back. It taunts and teases me seductively, and pretends to be harmless but I know better. The eyes are cruel and the mouth whispers forbidden words about justice and revenge. I shut my eyes and hope that when I open them the unguarded thought will leave me alone but it refuses to give me peace.

Suzen carefully placed the paper on the desk in front of her. She studied the wispy handwriting and thought back to her first impression of Estelle. Her demeanor had been flat and almost emotionless and yet today she had shown a spark of independence. It was obvious that Carole Flint's nursing duties included staying close to Estelle and making sure she did not do or say anything she wasn't supposed to. As Suzen re-read Estelle's writings she felt a chill enter her body.

Chapter 26

Michael reached for the telephone to call his daughter Kathleen and tell her about Doreen being admitted to the hospital and the possibility of having a family intervention to confront her about her drug use. As he touched his hand to the receiver the phone rang causing Michael to involuntary jerk his hand away and jolt his mind from the heavy thoughts he had been mulling over. On the second ring he picked up the receiver and cautiously said, "Hello".

"Dad? Is that you?"

"Yes, Kathleen, is that you?"

"Yes it's me . . . is something wrong? You sound kind of strange."

"No, we're all fine. I was surprised to hear your voice because coincidently I just reached for the phone to call you."

Kathleen chuckled and her voice relaxed, "Well then, I guess I saved you some money didn't I? I'm actually at work so this one's a freebie so you don't have to worry about me spending my money recklessly. How's mom?"

"She's fine. We're both fine."

"Then why do I get the impression everything is not fine?"

Michael knew she wouldn't believe him when he said they were fine and would not be satisfied until she had more information. All the years when she was growing up he and Kathleen had been so close they used to tease each other about being able to read the other's mind. "Your mom's busier than ever but should you be calling from work? I don't want you to get into trouble."

"No, dad, I won't get into trouble. As a matter of fact this week I think I could do almost anything around here and they would think it was all right . . . but I'll tell you about that later. On the other hand, for you to call me during the daytime, that's not at all like you. Getting kind of extravagant in your old age, aren't you?" She had a teasing quality to her voice.

"You know me too well for me to try to fool you. Actually, I was calling to tell you about Doreen."

"So why doesn't that surprise me? What's she done now?"

"She . . ." He paused and took a breath and for just an instant he felt like he wanted to choke. "She took some pills and now she's in the hospital." He hated the quiver in his voice.

"Let me guess, just enough to scare the life out of you and mom but not enough to hurt herself, right?" He could hear the total disgust in her voice and he thought about all the times Doreen had hurt her when they were growing up.

"I guess that's about right."

"What a piece of work. So now what? I suppose she is lolling on some private psych ward like a queen bee while everyone scurries around trying to understand poor, little, abused Doreen. I can't believe how one person can be so selfish."

"You don't like your sister much, do you?"

There was a silence while Kathleen tried to compose herself. "I'm sorry dad. I know how hard this must be for you and mom. I don't want to add to your pain by bad mouthing your daughter. I love my sister but I don't like the way she manipulates everyone around her. The warm fuzzies that sisters are supposed to share got lost a long time ago. How are the boys taking this?"

"They're fine. We have them here with us until Doreen gets out of the hospital." He felt like he was lying about them being fine and wondered if his youngest daughter would pick up on this feeling.

"I'm glad you and mom have them now but do you ever wonder how much damage Doreen will be able to inflict on them before they reach adulthood?"

"Yes, we do. Your mom and I have had to do a lot of soul searching about that very question. I talked with Doreen's psychiatrist about this. Her name is Suzen Shepherd and I think you'd really like her. She thought a family intervention could be a beneficial thing to do at this point. You grew up with Doreen and probably know her better and can be more objective than we can. What do you think?"

There was a long pause and he heard Kathleen sigh. "I think . . ." There was another pause, "I think whatever you and mom need to do I will support, but I don't want to be part of it, at least not at this time. What is it they say? If you can't say something nice about someone then at least don't cause them any harm. I'm sorry dad. I'm too angry with Doreen. She hurts people. Doreen's not dumb, she's very astute and when she goes after someone she goes for the juggler. She doesn't fight fair. When we were growing up anything I might have shared with her in confidence became ammunition when she wanted to hurt me. She's into character assassination big time and isn't satisfied with just getting even, she wants to annihilate whoever gets in her way. Remember what Thomas Michael used to call her? He referred to her as the sisty ugler and wicked witch of the west. Tommy was one of the kindest, sweetest brothers in the whole world and even he had to admit what a brat Doreen was."

"You still miss him a lot don't you?"

"I do. He was the best brother anyone could have ever wished for. Not a day goes by that I don't think of him. I talk to him whenever I need help with my life."

Michael felt the twinge in his heart that he always experienced when his son's name was mentioned. He thought how Tomas Michael had pulled someone over for a simple traffic violation and the man, who later was identified as a drug dealer, put a sawed off shotgun in his son's face and pulled the trigger.

Kathleen continued, "Please, dad, I hope you'll understand. I'm so sorry. Tell mom I can't come. Actually Ross and I are leaving tonight for a short vacation at a resort in Mexico. Our bags are packed and sitting in the front hall. I really need to get away. It's been very stressful here at work."

Kathleen paused and Michael could hear her fidgeting with the phone as she continued. "Don't tell mom but do you remember the night I called to talk but kept saying nothing was wrong? Well, the day before I had to shoot a guy. For the only time in my entire life I almost killed another human being. Don't worry he didn't die. I shot him in the chest but I honestly did try to miss his vital organs. I only wanted to get his attention." She giggled uncomfortably and continued, "He's okay now. Well, he's not really okay, he's in prison."

Even though his younger daughter was telling him something that was already in the past he felt the sting of fear for her safety. "Oh my God, Kathleen! What happened?"

"The puke was a drug dealer. I'm part of a special task force to crack down on drug trafficking. We don't just go after the pushers on the streets and in the schoolyards, but our job is to eliminate the big boys that are pipelining it into the U.S. I told you I think about Tommy every day and I know he would be really proud of what I am doing."

"Do you think it's wise for you to be part of a task force like that? It has to be one of the most dangerous things you could be doing on the force." Michael couldn't bear the thought of losing another child.

"I'm sure it's what I have to be doing. We did good, dad. We did really good. In the last twelve months we've been able to put away five of those miserable scumbags. I know we can't stop them completely but we sure have messed up their operation.

"How did you end up shooting this guy?"

"It happened during a drug transaction. For weeks we had been planning this major sting operation and when the big night finally arrived we moved in and thought we had them cold. One of the main players took off running with most of the evidence. I bolted after him while the others rounded up the rest of his honchos. I chased him into a dark alley where he seemed to vanish into thin air. I've never been so scared in my entire life. I remember saying to myself, Thomas Michael, at this moment you can see this situation much better than I can, so tell me what to do. I can't really explain it, but at that instant, the thought came into my mind so vividly it was almost as if someone was telling me to look up. I did, and as I lifted my face, I saw a flash of light and felt a bullet whizzing past my chin and ricochet off the brick wall behind me. Honest to God, if I had kept my head down he might have shot me in the face. I pointed my flashlight up in the direction of the flash and there was the guy hanging by one arm from the fire escape like a big ugly monkey. I think the beam from my flashlight temporarily blinded him and I shot him in the chest. The doctor in the emergency room said if the bullet had entered a half-inch over it would have killed him. We kept him in intensive care under heavy guard so nothing could happen to him while he was in the hospital. As you know from previous experience anyone who could prove to be a liability in the drug trade has a very short life span. There's some very strong suspicions the drug lords or the slime at the top have infiltrated our police force. I hate to believe that but there are too many leaks and coincidences not to. To make a long story short we almost lost the guy before he could testify. About the time he was well enough to be moved from the hospital an attempt was made on his life and it was a weird fluke that he lived. Get this, one of the cops that was stationed outside his door noticed a nurse who entered his room had really bad legs. Now, this cop prides himself on being a leg man and when he saw her ugly legs it got him thinking the nurse might not really be a nurse but a man disguised as one. He caught the nurse just as she/he was about to inject something into our star witnesses.

Here's the really neat part . . . We let it leak to the media that we'd lost him. They took him out on a gurney with a sheet covering him and kept him under wraps until the trial. Before I went into court to testify I passed their dickhead lawyer in his expensive three piece suit in the hall, and the arrogant S.O.B. sneered at me and whispered something like, little lady, before I finish with you you're going to wish you'd stuck to being a crossing guard. I have to admit he was good but we were better. When we brought out our star witness I thought he was going to soil his expensive suit. I couldn't help whispering to him on the way out, little man, you probably wish you'd stuck to fixing traffic tickets. Oh, dad, it was sooo sweet."

Michael laughed with mixed emotions as he pictured the scenes Kathleen had described. "Good for you! I wish I could have been there to see you in action. I know Thomas Michael is so very proud of you and so am I. Please be careful, Kathleen. Those are people without souls. You know that don't you?"

"I will be careful and I do know that dad. That's why I'm doing what I'm doing. Tell mom I love her and give her a big kiss for me. I have to go now. I have a call on the other line. And tell Doreen I love her and the boys, and that I wish her a speedy recovery."

Chapter 27

Everyone was relieved when the results of David's CT Scan came back negative. David's doctor, Marty Rassmusson assured him the headaches, though annoying and painful, were probably nothing serious and likely the result of stress. He ruled out cluster headaches and migraines and though he reluctantly admitted he hadn't really been able to find the exact cause, concluded the right combinations of drugs should be able to give David the relief he was seeking.

Molly stopped to see Harry at his office earlier in the day and when he suggested she come to the house later in the evening she decided it would be the perfect time to give him the present she had for him. When she arrived she was pleasantly surprised to find the house quiet, with only the sound of piano music playing softly in the background. Molly looked around the living room and not seeing any toys scattered around couldn't resist asking, "So cuz,, where's Annie and the munchkin? Did they dump you for greener pastures?"

Harry grinned at his cousin's usual lack of tact, "No, they didn't leave me, they decided to spend the night with Jessie's former foster mother. She's moving her family to Portland next week and her kids wanted to see Jessie one more time. David helped her get back on her feet after her husband walked out on them and now she has an excellent job opportunity, but it means they need to move out west. Annie thought a sleep over would be fun and make the emotional adjustment of the move a bit easier for all of them."

Molly sat on the couch across from the fireplace with her legs curled beneath her.

Harry smiled, "I can't believe you can still sit like that. You look like a little girl sitting there, like I remember you when we were kids."

"Yeah, well, that was a long time ago. I feel like we were different people back then. We were sheltered, naive, and relatively innocent. You know what I mean?"

Harry sat down in an adjacent recliner and clicked the footrest in place. "Yes I do, and yet I think deep down we're still those same two people. Hopefully a little wiser and stronger."

"Collectively we've been through a lot, and yet we seem to have landed on our feet. You have such a lovely family, and I believe even if I'm alone, I'm where I'm meant to be. Maybe someday I'll have a family of my own, but even if I don't, I still have yours and my brother's family. I think I can be satisfied with that. There's also our cousin Clayton and he's been a good friend and gotten me through some stressful times. Contrary to the way I appear I'm not always poised and self-confident." She made a face at Harry to show him she was joking about her last statement. "When I think how rotten we were to Clayton when we were kids it makes me feel ashamed. He's such a unique person it's almost like he doesn't belong in this sad old world. He seems to have evolved from a fat little nerd to a highly advanced spiritual being who should be living on another plane."

It never ceased to amaze Harry when he heard Molly speak of their cousin in such glowing terms. She seemed to have a reverence for Clayton that puzzled him. He realized he hadn't seen him since high school and although he never disliked him, he never felt any real connection with him.

"So, you feel Clayton has helped you to change."

"I hope so. There were many years I really didn't like myself. He helped me to realize in spite of the way I had lived my life there's still a great deal of good inside me." She turned and looked at Harry and wrinkled her nose as if she was about to say something funny. "Would you like to hear something really weird? I'll tell you this but only if you promise you won't laugh at me."

Harry was amused at her ability to suddenly shift the conversation to a totally different subject, "Weird? How weird? Like you being abducted by strange blood sucking aliens?"

"Put a sock in it! I'm being completely serious now. Not like when we were kids and I used to make up those bizarre stories about Bigfoot and Dracula."

"I'll be serious. Tell me about weird."

"Well . . ." Molly leaned forward and narrowed her eyes, "I had been back living in Glenwood less than a year when I confessed to Clayton how empty I felt and that sometimes I was still angry with God. Then, in a kind of round about way, Clayton suggested maybe if I was willing to put my spiritual life back in order it might help me. He suggested it might be helpful if I were to clarify in my mind the distinction between religion and spirituality. I hadn't really thought much about that since my husband died. Steve was a very spiritual man but we never really talked about religion. Being raised Catholic the two words were understood to be synonymous. Clayton suggested that because I was brought up to equate my religion with spirituality and possibly judged myself as being bad or evil because I had broken the commandments and precepts of the church. I guess old habits die hard and Dora did such stellar job of pounding that old time religion into me, I felt I would never be able to believe God had forgiven me unless I went back to my Catholic roots. Let me tell you, the thought of having to go to confession after the way I'd been living made me want to barf, but the more I thought about it, the more I knew I had to do it. Since I was too embarrassed to go to the priest in Glenwood I decided I needed to go somewhere else. You probably are aware that now they expect you to sit face to face with your confessor and spill your guts.

That may be fine for some little old lady who goes to confession on a regular basis but somehow the thought of facing that same priest every Sunday and having him think about me and my sinful life didn't sit well with me. One day on an impulse, I drove to Alexandria and found the Catholic church. It was during the week so there were no confessions being heard but I think I was making a trial run to get my courage up. I sat in the church and for the first time in years I did a real, honest examination of conscience. I was so relieved the church was empty and as I sat there I suddenly felt a connectedness. I really don't know how to express it in any other way, but the tears started to flow and I felt sorry for all the bad things I had done. When I looked up there was a kind looking old priest walking toward me. I hadn't heard him come into the church so it took me by surprise.

He sat sideways in the pew in front of me and we started to visit and before I knew it I was confessing the long dismal tale of my sordid life. It seemed like it took a long time but he sat there listening patiently with a loving expression on his old, wrinkled face. When I finally finished he put his hand on my head and gave me absolution and at that moment

I felt as if the weight of the world had been lifted from my shoulders. I even told him about the time I fed brownies laced with Ex-Lax to Donny Doopala."

"No way." Harry grinned, "I'll bet that impressed him all to hell."

Molly continued as if she hadn't heard his comment. "We talked for awhile longer and he told me to meditate on Mary's Immaculate heart. He said to put myself in her place, and try to feel her pain as she watched the soldiers nail her son to the cross, and then think about how she must have had an undying faith in God to be able to forgive the people who had crucified her son. He also said to meditate on the wounded heart of Jesus and try to understand how he could have so much love for the world that he would come to save us, knowing he would be rejected and put to death. The little old priest said sometimes he even tries to imagine the pain Jesus must have felt in his hands and his arms and his whole body as they hoisted him up on the cross. He said if Jesus could forgive all that, then I should be able to find forgiveness in my heart. One of the last things he told me was when I said the sign of the cross I should say, In the name of the Father who created me, and the Son who redeemed me, and of the Holy Spirit who sustains me, I open my heart and my soul to you. Oh Harry, I felt such faith and strength coming from him it just overwhelmed me. As he was leaving I asked him his name and he said it was Father Anton Pavak."

"That's quite a story."

"Wait! I'm not done yet. I did what he said and slowly I felt something inside of me changing. The anger and the depression seemed to be leaving and finally I threw my antidepressants away.

After I quit the drugs my night dreaming started to come back and seemed to be more normal. One night I had this very vivid dream where I was up on the altar of the Sacred Heart church in Glenwood. There were three little pools of water on the floor in front of the altar. When I looked into them the water seemed very black and deep and I remember I felt so frightened. One of the pools was labeled Blessed Virgin Mary, one as Saint Jude and the third one, Holy Spirit. I peered into the Holy Spirit pool and slowly out of the blackness the water rose up like a fountain and gently flowed over me and seemed to envelop my entire being. I've never experienced anything that could even come close to this feeling of total connectedness in spirit. I experienced the incredible sensation of total ecstasy. It was warm and soft and a loving embrace filled every cell in my body. I think I experienced what it must be like to be in the presence of God. I knew I had been baptized in the Holy Spirit and when I awoke I was so excited I needed to tell someone. I tried to call Clayton but he didn't answer his phone so on an impulse I decided to call the priest in Alexandria. I got the rectory number from the operator and I made the call and asked for Father Pavak. The priest who answered the phone said, excuse me? Who did you wish to speak to? I told him that I had spoken with Father Pavak a few days before, and I wanted to share something with him that had happened to me. That's when the priest asked me if this was a crank call and did I think I was being funny. Well, you know me, that kind of pissed me off a whole lot and I said no, it wasn't a crank call and I was not trying to be funny. I'll never forget what he said next. He very curtly informed me that Father Anton Pavak had been a priest at that parish many years ago but had passed on to his heavenly reward in 1980." Molly leaned back on the couch and crossed her arms over her chest.

Harry looked at his cousin half expecting her to break out in laughter but she didn't. "This is all true? You're not trying to bullshit me?"

"So help me, God." Cross my heart, hope to die, stick a needle in my eye."

"Well, you're right. That's pretty weird. In fact, big time weird."

"I told you it was weird. And I swear to God it really happened."

"Did you tell Clayton?"

"Yes."

"And he said what?" He hated it when Molly made him dig for answers when she could have just come out and tell him.

"He just smiled. Harry, I felt that priest put his hand on my head to give me absolution. He was very real but I can't for the life of me explain it."

"Dee-dee-dee-dee." Harry hummed the theme from the *Twilight Zone* and started to laugh.

"You dumb shit! You promised you wouldn't laugh at me and now you are." Molly had a defiant look on her face.

"I'm not laughing at you. I really don't know what to say. It's very strange. Anyway, one minute you're telling me you were in the presence of God or the Holy Spirit and the next minute you're calling me a dumb shit. Am I to believe the baptism of the Holy Spirit you so dramatically experienced didn't stick?"

She stared at him and slowly started to smile. Putting the back of her hand to her forehead she said in a melodramatic voice, "Alas, I fear not, dear cousin. It would seem I am destined to wander lost in this barren wilderness called earth until my Lord comes to take me home." She unwound her legs and stiffly got up. "God, I hate getting old. I'm going to use the restroom but not before I say that you are a piss poor host. Here I am bearing my soul to you and the least you could have done is offer me a glass of wine, and please, put an ice cube in the glass if you don't have the wine chilled. Anyway, the real reason I came here is not to talk about myself, but rather because I have a special present for you that I think will blow you away.

Harry sat looking at his cousin and said, "Have you recently given serious thought to the possibility you might be schizophrenic or maybe suffering from multiple personality syndrome or something bizarre like that?"

As was typical, Molly appeared to be giving his question serious thought and after a moment of reflection said, "No, definitely not. The wine . . . ."

When Harry returned he noticed Molly had taken something from her purse. As he handed her the wine she held up a packet of what appeared to be letters.

"These are for you. I found them in an old cardboard box my mother had stored at my brother's house. They must have forgotten it was there and came across the box last week when they were cleaning out the crawl space in the basement."

Harry took the packet and stared at it. "From your mom?"

"No. Look again. You'll be able to tell by the address."

Harry turned the letters over and could see they were carefully addressed to Mariah Scarley. The return address bore only the name Russ C. His hands trembled slightly and he spoke in a hushed voice, "These were letters to my mother?"

"Yes, to your mother from your father. These are the letters he wrote to her and you'll also see there are letters she wrote back to him. Apparently, grandpa Scarley collected all the letters and purposely kept her and your dad apart. You remember that old gal that ran the Lowry post office? I'm sure good old grandpa made it worth her while to intercept the comings and goings of their correspondence. I'm positive your mother never knew the letters existed."

"Did you read them?"

"Duh . . . What do you think? I said I've changed but I'm not ready to be canonized. Of course I read them. You know me."

Harry looked up at her. "You know who my father was?"

Molly could see how emotional Harry had abruptly become and immediately regretted her flip attitude. "Yes, I know who your father is. He's still alive and he wants to meet you. His name is Russell Cassidy and he lives in New Mexico. He's a well-known professional artist and never even knew you existed. No one ever told him. Our grandpa hid the letters he wrote to your mother and made sure her letters never got mailed. Your father was part of a threshing crew that worked on grandpa's farm. He and your mom fell in love and when he left her that autumn, he continued working with the threshing crew but promised to come back and marry her. Somehow, at the end of the harvest season, he was involved in a farm accident and lost one of his legs when a hay wagon rolled down a hill and pinned him against a barn. He was seriously injured and it was months before he recovered. When he finally did come back to get your mother as he promised he would, grandpa sent him away. That crabby old man told him Mariah had fallen in love with someone else and didn't ever want to see him again. He also said Mariah heard about Russell's accident and knew she could never be happy having a cripple for husband. Of course, your father's heart was broken and he nearly gave up. He struggled for a long time believing life was over for him. Finally he made up his mind he needed to talk to Mariah even if she was married to someone else. As you might suspect, by the time he made his way back to Lowry it was too late. Your mom had already died.

Oh, Harry, it was so sad, almost like Romeo and Juliet. They really and truly loved each other but our grandpa kept them apart and broke both of their hearts."

Harry sat in quiet reflection for several moments. "Where did you say he's living?"

"New Mexico. Somewhere near Albuquerque. I called him and he said if his health was better and he was able to travel he would come to see you, but he's in a wheelchair now and his heart isn't good. When he asked if I thought you'd be willing to come to Albuquerque, I assured him you would. Oh, and I also found this with the letters." She handed him a small pencil sketch of a beautiful young woman. "It's your mom. He must have drawn it that summer before he left."

Harry studied the drawing for a long time and finally said, "She looked so much like you when you were a teenager. I forgot how much you resembled each other. No wonder grandpa had such a hard time being around us. We must have been a constant reminder of the pain he carried in his heart. I was the illegitimate reminder of my mother's sins and you were another Mariah he couldn't control."

Molly could see tears starting to well up in Harry's eyes and her heart went out to him. "Oh, God, Harry. I'm so sorry mom never gave you these letters. I suppose grandpa made her promise never to tell you about your father. You know how sensitive and obedient she was. I'm sure she was afraid for you. She probably believed grandpa's lies that your father really had abandoned your mother and she didn't want you to get hurt. Mom was one of the kindest people in the world and I know she would never have done anything to intentionally hurt you. I think I told you before she died I would go to visit her at the Starbuck Nursing Home and in her confused state she called me Mariah. I tried to tell her I was her own daughter Sara and she would look at me and smile sweetly and say, "No, Sara is gone. You're my dear, sweet, sister Mariah. Of course at first I felt badly that she had erased me from her memory but as time passed and she persisted in her belief I came to believe she probably had unfinished business with Mariah. It seemed to comfort her to believe they were together again. I remember how painful it was for her after Mariah's death, and to make her grieving even worse grandpa had forbidden everyone to mourn your mother's loss. He wanted us to act as if Mariah never existed."

Molly sniffed loudly and took a big swallow of wine, "After your mother died grandma really started acting very strange. She seemed to go crazy after the funeral and refused to accept that Mariah was dead. I know that was the reason my mom kept you with us most of the time. I think she knew grandma was losing it and grandpa didn't help her at all. He was such a crabby old fart all the time. Remember how he would glare at us at the kitchen table and then abruptly get up and leave the house without saying a word?"

She stopped talking and looked directly into Harry's eyes and was deeply touched by the pain he seemed to be in. He was hunched over the letters but made no effort to open them. "I'm sorry, Harry. Here I am babbling on like a fool and you probably wish I'd shut my mouth and go back to my hotel room so you can read the letters."

He looked up at her as if he'd temporarily forgotten she was in the room and she realized he had been lost deep in his own thoughts. "I did hear you, and actually, I'm glad you're here with me. I don't think I'm quite ready to read the letters, at least not yet. Even though I've thought about meeting my dad almost every day of my life, I'm not sure I'm brave enough to take that step. I think I'll be needing a little time to get over the shock." He tried to smile but Molly couldn't help but notice how pale he looked. "Before you go, tell me some more about your mom before she died. I wish now I had taken the time to go back home to see her. She was always so good to me."

Molly studied her cousin carefully and noticed how tightly he clutched the letters. She leaned back into the couch and said, "The time I spent with my mom before she died was very precious to me. Even though by the time I'd moved back to Glenwood she had failed so much both physically and mentally that she had to be in the nursing home, she never complained. She was one of those rare people who seemed to accept everything life handed her, no matter how good or bad things were without being angry or depressed or blaming God for her troubles. As it got closer to her death the night staff would push a big old recliner into her room so I could spend the night with her if she was restless. At the very end her caregivers were careful to turn her every two hours so her skin wouldn't break down and cause her pain. When she refused regular food the cooks would make this white cereal stuff they called rommegrot. It was made from sugar, flour, cream and butter and it was the only thing we could coax her to eat.

"Your mom was the only mother I really ever knew. Somehow, when I think about Mariah it seems as if she was only a dream or an older sister who went away one day. She was only seventeen when she got pregnant with me, and twenty-two when she died, so I have a hard time remembering her. During the time I was recovering in the hospital after I took the dive down the staircase, I would try to picture her face as I lay in my drug induced stupor. Sometimes I could, but more often than not I would draw a blank. Most of those days were very dark for me and I often ended up hating my father and wishing I could get even with him."

"I think the fact I physically resembled your mother was hard on everyone, and became even more painful because I was such a little brat all the time. I suppose they couldn't help but wonder if I would end up like Mariah and maybe that's why Dora tried extra hard to keep me on the straight and narrow. She wanted me to have a better life than her younger sister had."

"Even though I was young I vaguely remember how we would wait for the mail and she would tell me how my daddy would come to take us away with him. She would weave dandelion necklaces and crowns, and make up little stories about princes and princesses and act them out for me. Now I understand why the letters never came. After she became ill, she would still sit by the window looking out at the road but finally towards the end of her life, she gave up hope and often stayed in her room crying."

"I remember when you told me about the day she died."

"Yes, and you called me a big fat liar and poked fun of me."

"Tell me again."

"I was five and grandma made me sit by my mom because she had to go somewhere. I sat in that big old flowered chair next to her bed because by that time she was dying of tuberculosis. I remember thinking she already looked dead because she was so thin and pale and the only reason I knew she wasn't was because of her terrible coughing spells that shook her whole body and cause her to throw up. I was afraid to be alone with her and I would cry real quietly so I wouldn't disturb her. When I got older I looked up tuberculosis in an old medical book and they referred to it as the white plague. That only made me feel worse that God had taken my mother with such a terrible disease and somehow I ended feeling ashamed of her even though I knew better. Dora explained my mother was already dying when they finally realized what was wrong with her and grandpa decided she should die at home rather than sending her to a sanitarium. I believe she died of a broken heart and the tuberculosis was secondary, because she had given up on life. Anyway, getting back to that day, it was pouring rain and the sky was really dark. When it started to thunder and lightning I was so scared that I started to cry. When all the noise and lightning finally stopped, I must have fallen asleep. I don't know how long I slept but when I awoke the rain had stopped and the house was very quiet. I thought the sun had come out because I could see this ball of light over my mother's bed. It hung there for a little while, and then got kind of pointy at the top, and finally moved out the window leaving the room dark again. When grandma came home she found me curled up sleeping in the barn with Buster the dog. They buried my mother a few days later."

"I remember I called you a liar and said you were dreaming or you had made up that story because you heard Dora say a light went out in the world when Mariah died."

"You were right about grandma Maria, that was when she started to act strange."

"I was going to ask you if you remembered how, on windy nights, she would open the windows a crack and put a sprinkle of flour on the window ledge? There was this little poem she would sing to us about somebody's children crying. Both Daniel and I tried to remember it but neither of us could."

Harry thought for a little while before he replied. *"Listen, do you hear what I hear? 'Tis not the wind but rather Mezzolena's children crying for they have a never ending hunger. Come to me my children and I will feed you, for I am the bread of life.*

Grandma Maria said the flour was to feed Mezzolena's children and keep them from crying."

"That's it! You're right. Those are the words. One night I got this call from the nursing home that Dora . . . well mom, I should call her mom, had somehow gotten out of bed even though she could hardly move by herself, and had sprinkled sugar from one of those little packets on the window ledge. She told the nurse it was for somebody's children who were crying and were keeping her awake. I tried to explain to the nurse about the poem but I couldn't remember the verse. I often wonder who Mezzolena was but we'll probably never know since the explanation is gone with mom and grandma."

They sat quietly and stared into the fire. Finally Harry broke the silence, "Would you like some more wine?"

"I'll get it. You sit there." She returned with the nearly empty bottle and divided what was left into each of their glasses and sat back down.

"Do you think I imagined seeing that light over my mother's body?" Harry was still clutching the letters.

"Before I saw my phantom priest I would have said yes because there's no way I could have believed something like that could actually happen. Now I think I know better and even though I'm sure most people wouldn't believe me, I know it happened and has had a definite impact on my life, so that's what counts. Clayton said if you're open to the idea of such experiences happening, they're more likely to occur, but if your mind is closed to the idea of supernatural phenomenon, you might never experience them. He said children experience them more commonly because they don't know they aren't supposed to."

"That's what Annie said too. When she was a child she had a little friend who would come to her who she believes was her angel. That was a regular occurrence until her parents scolded her and made it clear she was being childish and such things couldn't happen. So, did you ever find out how Father Pavak happened to be in the church?"

Molly giggled, "You do know me very well. Yes, of course I went back. By that time I sort of convinced myself he might have been some person who was dressed like a priest and did it as a joke. The thought of me spilling my torrid past to some guy who gets his jollies from dressing up like a priest and hanging out in churches really bugged me. I went back to the church and sat for over an hour, but the ghost Padre was a no show. I finally went to the rectory and at the great risk of humiliating myself knocked on the door. A nice, older lady answered the door and said the priest, Father somebody or other was not in, and she had come to do a little housework. I asked her about the history of the church and if she knew anything about a priest named Anton Pavak. She told me she had known him but only in the latter part of his life. When I asked her if she knew where I might find a picture of him she showed me to the parish office and sure enough, much to my relief, there was a black and white photograph of dear old Father Anton Pavak."

"Was he your phantom priest?"

"Yes, and I must say I was totally blown away but really glad it was him. She said he was a wonderful man and a kind and holy priest. Apparently, it was well known that he had a special devotion to the Immaculate Heart of Mary and the wounded heart of Jesus. When I asked her if there were any stories of anyone saying they had seen him in the church after he died, she didn't really give me an answer. She smiled and said it wouldn't have surprised her to hear he might still be trying to help people. The more I think about it now I don't really know what to think. I know in my heart he was real and he was there with me."

Harry didn't say anything so Molly finally asked, "Are you thinking about your dad?"

"Yes, I was wondering what he looks like and if I resemble him. There were a lot of years I wasted hating him for what I thought he had done to my mother and me and now I find out he never even knew that we both wanted him in our lives."

"So, are we going to go meet him?"

Harry grinned at Molly, "What's this we stuff? He's my father."

"Yes, but I found him for you."

"True, and yes, as soon as I tell Annie, and after I call him to make some arrangements, we, you included, will fly to New Mexico to meet him. Does he have a family?"

"Not really. He did marry a lady who'd been his nurse while he was recovering from another accident. This was after he found out Mariah was dead. His wife has since passed away and there were no children. Now he said his only family is the lady who helps with his care and her family. I think he said the lady was married to his best friend who has also died. We didn't really get into too many specifics because I think this whole thing came as one big assed shock to him. Look, I'm going to go now so you can read the letters. I have a feeling you're going to cry and I don't know if I'm up for any more tear-jerkers this evening. I'll let myself out so you can work on reading the letters."

It was after four when Harry finally fell asleep. He had read and re-read each of the twenty seven letters several times. When he finally started to cry it was as though a dam had burst after many years of holding back emotions he'd been unable to deal with. He was extremely grateful to be alone.

Chapter 28

Michael made a point to keep in touch with Veronica Sanders but as a result of all the commotion with Doreen, and now with Corey and Danny living with them, he had to admit he hadn't really learned much more about Louis. He agreed with Veronica in that although the man was well known in the business world, he had been very successful at keeping his private life out of the public eye. Veronica tried to give him small bits of information but these didn't seem to be of much significance.

One thing she shared with him that he felt could prove to be helpful was whenever something important was happening in the office, Louis always used a California lawyer by the name of J. T. Blessing. Blessing was known to be one of the heavy hitters in the legal profession, very ruthless, extremely effective, and obscenely expensive. It was a known fact that he was willing to defend anyone regardless of innocence or guilt, as long as enough money was involved.

Michael's was doubly intrigued when David Sullivan contacted him and asked if he would do some checking on Louis because of his recently renewed relationship with Mary Rose and Seaton House.

During Michael's next visit with Veronica they discussed David's affection and respect for Mary Rose and her work with unwed mothers at Seaton House. He explained that David had been a long time benefactor for her cause and knowing of her perpetual economic struggles was also very curious about the positive turn of events at Seaton House since Louis had entered the scene. Michael suggested since David also had an uneasy feeling about the man, it could be in their mutual interests to share their findings in the investigation of Louis. Promising complete secrecy, Michael requested Veronica's permission to share with David the confidential information she had provided about her half-brother's murder. Based on her growing trust of Michael and her passion for finding the truth, Veronica agreed. In turn Michael explained that David would shoulder most of the expenses of the investigation, therefore giving them both a much better chance of discovering useful information.

Early the next morning Michael made an appointment to meet David in his office at which time he divulged Veronica Sander's incredible story of her half-brother's death and her suspicions of it's possible link to Louis's trucking enterprise. In return, David revealed his concern for Mary Rose and about the conversation he'd had with her about Louis's childhood background, their high school friendship and Mary Rose's rejection of his offer of love. David agreed with Michael when he suggested they discreetly investigate Louis's family connections in Berlin. Since Mary Rose mentioned Louis's parents were both killed in an accident David suggested the probability of locating the grandmother and aunt. Michael did some mental arithmetic and finally said, "If Louis is sixty, his grandmother would have to be at least a hundred and the aunt maybe in her seventies or eighties. By some miracle, do you think they could still be alive? It seems like a long shot but probably worth checking into."

David looked thoughtful and then smiled, "Let's hope they are alive and at least one of them still has all her buttons."

The men sat in quiet reflection reviewing a possible strategy when David added, "Hopefully, by tracking down some of his family we can learn something meaningful about what motivates Louis. Perhaps we can get started on it right away. Why don't you make the phone calls from here in my office and that way you can keep me informed about what you learn." As David got up to leave he added, "Michael, there's one more thing, I don't want Mary Rose finding out I'm checking up on her friend. She's quite adamant about the fact she's an independent woman who can take care of herself."

Michael dialed the number for the overseas operator and in about twenty minutes came out of David's office with a smile on his face. "Bingo! The old lady is still alive and lives with her daughter, not in Berlin, but right here in the states. They live in Phoenix, Arizona and I was able to obtain the number for her daughter's residence, do you want to listen in while I call her?"

"No, I'll let you handle it for the same reason I stated before. If Mary Rose gets suspicious I want to avoid one of her direct confrontations. See if they would be willing to meet with you and I'll provide you with a plane ticket and the expense money you'll need. Can I make you a cup of herbal tea?"

Michael responded with a little chuckle, "Thanks, but I'll pass. I'm a coffee man myself. That herbal stuff tastes a little too grassy for me but you go ahead."

Michael returned to David's office and dialed the Arizona number. It rang several times before he heard someone pick up. Michael felt his hopes rising, "Hello, may I speak with Gerta Welheim please?"

"I'm sorry, Gerta isn't here right now. She's in the hospital. May I take a message?"

Michael paused briefly, unwilling to have the conversation come to a close so quickly. He cleared his throat and inquired, "Are you, by any chance, Gerta's daughter?"

"Yes, I am. To whom am I speaking with please?"

"You must be Marianna Welheim, is that correct?"

"Yes that's right . . . but if you wish to continue this conversation I must know who is calling." The woman spoke with a distinct German accent but her English was excellent and something about her manner told Michael she was not someone to toy with. He knew he risked having her hang up so he quickly decided honesty would be the best policy.

"I'm sorry, I wanted to be sure who I was speaking with before I identified myself. My name is Michael O'Grady and I would like to be able to visit with you and your mother about her grandson, Louis. I assure you I will be as brief as possible and will keep anything you wish to share with me confidential."

"Is Louis in trouble?"

"No, ma'am, not that I know of. I represent someone who is contemplating doing business with him and it's my employer's standard policy to find out about all his prospective clients."

Marianna hesitated before she continued, "Is there a question in your employer's mind about Louis's character? That he may not be honest or may be capable of harming someone?"

Michael had not expected her to ask such a direct question and was caught off guard. "My employer hasn't made any judgments yet. He needs to have some background on Louis so he can make the proper decision."

"Is this man you represent an honorable person?"

Again, Michael was surprised by the directness of Marianna's question. "Yes he is. He is one of the finest men I've ever met and he just wants to know a little more about Louis.

"Are you a private investigator?"

"Yes, I am."

"You understand neither my mother nor I have seen Louis for many years."

"That may not be important. We're more interested in his earlier life. When he was still living in Germany."

Following his last remark there was an awkward silence. Finally Michael broke the silence, "Marianna? Are you still there?"

"Yes I am. I was only thinking. My mother is not well. Her kidneys are failing but her cognitive skills are still excellent. She may be willing to meet with you but I can't guarantee she would be receptive to sharing anything with you. You do understand you'd have to come to the hospital here in Phoenix?" Michael responded that he understood and would be willing to do so. "And, considering my mother's health is precarious, you'll need to do this very soon."

"I could be there by tomorrow morning."

"Very well. As long as you understand I guarantee nothing." Marianna gave Michael the name of the hospital and the room number and ended the conversation by saying she would inform the desk nurse and meet him outside her mother's room at ten o'clock the following morning.

Michael's flight was uneventful and he was able to find a motel near the hospital. The room was clean and quiet and he slept well despite the fact he had not spent a night away from Martha for many years. He missed the warmth of her body and the soft little sounds she made that reminded him of a kitten purring. In the morning he ate a leisurely breakfast and took a taxi to the hospital. Upon his arrival he went directly to the gift shop where he purchased a single pink rose in a crystal vase, and headed for Gerta Welheim's room. Outside Gerta's room he was greeted by an attractive older woman who introduced herself as Mariana Welheim. Michael shook hands and was very much aware how carefully she was scrutinizing him. Marianna explained her mother was feeling a little better this morning and she would be willing to meet with him. After her initial assessment of him she would decide if she wished to continue the conversation. She also cautioned Michael not to start asking questions right away, but rather allow her mother to initiate the conversation.

As they entered the room Marianna introduced Michael to a frail looking woman propped up against several pillows and Michael couldn't help but marvel at the striking resemblance between mother and daughter. Despite her age, which she would confide later was just a little over one hundred, she still possessed a sparkle in her eyes even though her body was obviously succumbing to her advanced age. Graciously, she extended her frail hand and greeted him. She looked directly at him and said, "Please forgive me but you will need to tell me your name again," Her accent was slightly more noticeable than her daughter's but Michael was clearly impressed with her English and the clarity she seemed to maintain.

"Michael O' Grady." He placed the vase and flower on her table but didn't mention them.

"My daughter tells me you are a private investigator."

"Yes, that is correct."

"I imagine you'd prefer not to share with me who it is you have been retained by?"

"That is also correct, but I assure you anything you choose to tell me will never be used in any way to harm Louis."

The older woman slowly closed her eyes and Michael wondered if she had fallen asleep. He glanced at Marianna and she nodded as if to say everything was fine. After a few moments the older woman opened her milky blue eyes and looked directly into Michael's face. "Michael O'Grady. That is indeed a fine Irish name. I think I like you. You see, my time is drawing near and I need to tell my story to someone. I have kept silent for most of my life and now before I die I believe I must share this information with the proper person. I have serious concerns about Louis's wife Estelle, and my great grandson Eric. I'm not sure my concerns are totally warranted but I feel before I can rest in peace I must tell someone. What you don't know Michael, is that I have been praying to God that He would send someone to help me with my concerns, and now I am hopeful you might be the one. Since time is running out I feel I have no choice but to trust you. Before I begin, you must promise me you will listen with your heart and not only your mind. Please don't condemn Louis before you understand the circumstances that shaped my grandson.

As you would expect, my daughter Marianna knows the story but she is Louis's aunt, as well as being his godmother, and has mixed feelings about this meeting. It may be painful for her to hear me share this with you, but she has the same concerns about Estelle and Eric as I have. Since your call, we've talked it over and believe it may be a good idea to tell a stranger who can be more objective."

She smiled and patted the bed, indicating to Michael that he should sit next to her. "Come and I'll tell you about Louis when he was young."

Michael sat and listened intently as Gerta began her story. "We were living in Berlin and my husband Gerhard was a wealthy businessman in the banking business. Even during the war we were fortunate to have a good income so we were never deprived like many people were. Now looking back, I regret to think that inadvertently that may have contributed to some of our problems. Maybe we had too much, but, of course, you never feel that way at the time. We had only our two daughters and in spite of the war, I wanted them to have every opportunity we could give them. Marianna was two years older than Ava and they were both such beautiful young girls. Ava was always more high spirited and by the time she was sixteen had already married a young man who was to serve in the German army. We were very much against such a young marriage in the time of war, but of course she went ahead anyway.

The frail woman looked up and took her daughter's hand. "Marianna was always the sensible one. The war was in full force but we rarely suffered any hardship, not like some of our friends who not only lost their fortunes, but also their sons in combat. At first everyone was caught up in justifying the war effort, but gradually, being that my husband was higher up in the banking industry, we came to recognize what was really going on and what Hitler was doing, but we kept silent. We wanted to believe it was out of our control and if we were to survive we had to remain quiet.

When Ava's husband left for the army she couldn't tolerate being alone and within a few months she started seeing a young German officer who was working in our local chancellery. After a while the circumstances of her affair got back to her husband and he wrote to her demanding she stop seeing this other man. He also told her he would never give her a divorce.

Of course, she didn't discontinue her relationship with the young officer and soon found she was pregnant with his child. The young man's name was Louis Goebbels but he was not a relative of the Josef Goebbels that worked directly for Hitler. Our little grandson Gerhard Louis was born in 1937. Ava adored her son but by this time her personal life was totally out of control. Her days and nights consisted of drinking and wild parties and she soon became very popular with the high-ranking German officers. Louis's father didn't seem to mind because he was well aware of her spirited nature and selfishly believed her casual liaisons with these men of power could help advance his own military career.

My husband and I tried to reason with Ava but she only pushed us away and for the first few years of our grandson's life we rarely saw him. I shudder to think how he may have been raised. I do know there was a heavy and steady Nazi indoctrination by his father. I learned this later, after Louis came to live with us. He would tell me stories his father had told him and as I listened I often wanted to cry.

But wait . . . I'm getting ahead of myself. Shortly before he came to live with us Ava insisted she wanted to marry Louis's father. Within a very short time we received word that Ava's husband had been killed. It seemed like a strange but convenient coincidence, because at that time he wasn't fighting on the front lines but was working behind a desk. At first we didn't question his death because things like that sometimes happen during wartime, and we also knew that much military information and activities were being withheld from regular citizens. I realized later we were programmed by fear not to ask questions. Ava and Louis's father planned to be married immediately, but were killed in an automobile accident outside of Berlin. That was when our grandson came to live with us. Even though he was acutely aware of his loss, he seemed strangely unaffected by his parents' deaths. He was a beautiful five-year-old boy with blonde hair, fair features, and intense steel blue eyes. He was physically sturdy and it soon became apparent he was bright beyond his years. Later he told us his father and fellow officers referred to him as the perfect Aryan child. Unfortunately, as he grew older we were to learn there was another darker side to his developing personality."

Gerta closed her eyes and remained silent as if in private reflection. In a short while she opened them and smiled, "Most of the time Louis was extremely well mannered but we soon became aware he also had a terrible temper. During the next few years we began to observe he never forgot nor forgave anything that was done to him. In school he excelled at everything but he also developed a great interest in the writings and philosophy of Adolph Hitler. Are you familiar with Hitler's writings?"

"No, not really. I only know he was a crazy man."

"Yes." She looked pensively, "He was probably crazy, but unfortunately also very charismatic. Many people don't realize this, but his ideas were not new nor original but could be traced to earlier writers who were the commonly accepted shibboleths of Viennese right-wing radicalism."

"Shibboleths?"

The older woman smiled and her daughter replied in understanding of Michael's inquiry of a word that would clearly not be a part of his regular vernacular. "A speech or custom that distinguishes a particular group or class of people," Marianna interjected. She then continued, "Hitler regarded inequality between the races and individuals as part of an unchangeable natural order and exalted the 'Aryan Race' as the sole creative element of mankind. The natural unit of man was the 'Volk' of which the German was the greatest, and the state only existed to serve the Volk. All morality and truth was judged by this criterion, whether it was in accordance with the interests and preservation of the Volk. For this reason the democratic government of the time stood doubly condemned, as it erroneously assumed an equality within the Volk that clearly didn't exist. It also supposed what was in the interest of the Volk could be decided by discussion, development of a consensus and finally putting the question to a democratic vote.

As it turned out, and as has history now records, the unity of the Volk found its incurvation toward Hitler and his Nazi movement. Hitler was now referred to as the Fuhrer, for it extolled the supremacy of his leadership and endowed him with absolute authority. Below the Fuhrer came his political party, which Hitler often called 'the movement' to distinguish themselves from the traditional democratic parties, which drew upon the best elements of the Volk and in turn became its perpetrator and its safeguard."

Michael was totally amazed at how articulate and intelligent Marianna's recall remained after all the years, and her knowledge of the world and its ways was most impressive. Finally, after about five more minutes of discourse that yielded significant insight regarding an insider's understanding of the rise of Nazi Germany, Gerta waved her hand and said, "That's probably enough, Marianna. Mr. O'Grady doesn't need to know the whole history."

Marianna smiled and said, "Yes, mother, you're right. I do tend to get carried away. I'm sorry. Please continue."

"My grandson embraced these ideas. I suppose his own father brainwashed him. We attempted to undo some of the damage that had been done but it was too late. I also learned that at night his father would read to him from the Nibelungenlied."

Michael shook his head, "I'm not sure what that is."

Again Marianna interjected, "It's an old German epic which tells the stories of wrathful and violent heroes and heroines, Sigurd, Brunhild, Gudrun, and others. The work is full of supernatural events and pagan sentiments. It inspired many operatic and literary works in its later years."

Gerta continued, "The one superior Aryan race and its powerful and vengeful women, all of these images in a small child's mind must have had a great influence on him. I know Ava wasn't much of a mother and my grandson was often locked in his room alone sometimes for days when she went out. If he cried he was beaten severely. He told me at first he was afraid but later he would make up stories to amuse himself. Of course these fantasies were likely to have been influenced by the stories his father told him. He said his favorite ones were the ones of Woden. Marianna you go ahead and explain. I'll rest now as I am growing very weary."

"Oden or 'Woden' as the Germans called him was king of the gods and of men, and also the reputed progenitor of the Scandinavian kings. As a god of war, he would hold his court in Valhalla surrounded by all his warriors who had fallen in battle. The great king Woden, was attended to by two large and fearful wolves, Freki and Geri. When Woden sat on his throne overlooking heaven and earth the two wolves would be at his feet ready to do his bidding. Louis also spoke of the Hyperboreans who he described as a fabulous people who lived beyond the north wind in a land of perpetual sunshine."

Gerta lay peacefully against the pillows, her eyes now closed, but Michael could see the conversation was draining her strength. After Marianna's discussion concluded she reopened her eyes and continued, "Michael, thank you for being so patient with us. I am sure by this time you're wondering why two babbling old women have brought you all this distance to teach you some German history and mythology but please bear with us a little while longer. I believe you'll see how these factors influenced my grandson's behavior in his developmental years and later his attitudes as an adult.

One day when Louis was about twelve, I was putting some clothes away in his dresser and I came across a short story he had written. It was neatly printed in English and he had bound it into a small book. At first I put it back thinking I should respect his privacy. For some reason however, my thoughts kept being drawn back to it and as I still had so many unanswered questions about my grandson's past, I felt that maybe his story could help me better understand him. I told myself it was for this reason I went back and read it. I don't recall all of what the book was about but I do remember its main theme. It was a tale of a mythological kingdom called Volkland. The ruler was a king much like Woden who had absolute power over all the other gods and men. This king had two wolves that lay at his feet, a large white wolf and an even larger black wolf. The duty of the white wolf was to destroy the weak and the aged. These were the people the king felt had no significance or use in his court. The black wolf was to destroy the enemies of the king. In Louis's story, all those subjects the king viewed as unworthy or a threat, would be eliminated by 'das wolf'.

As I was finishing reading the book my grandson entered his bedroom and when he saw what I was reading he became very angry. Much more angry than I'd ever seen him and for a moment I felt he might harm me. He may have too, except my husband heard him chastising me and called up the stairs to learn what the trouble was. I have never forgotten the hateful look in his eyes as he tore the book from my hands and ordered me out of his room. I never saw the book again and after that he seemed to emotionally distance himself from me. Later, when Marianna tried to gently question some of his harsher beliefs he separated himself from her as well.

As he grew older he developed a great intolerance for anyone he considered to be weak or undesirable. At times he would boldly express in the end the Aryan race would eventually triumph and all of the undesirables would be eliminated. He also believed it was a great pity Hitler had not been able to execute his final solution.

In many ways he seemed to blame the United States for interfering in the war and so it came as a total surprise to us when he announced he was moving here. Are you familiar with the term hyphenate?"

Michael shook his head yes. "It sometimes comes up in police work. I think it means when a citizen of the United States feels an obligation to another country so keenly his loyalty to the U.S. may be questioned."

"Exactly! I believe my grandson could fall into that description. Well, Michael, you have been a good listener. That's most of what we can tell you of Louis's early life. After he moved to the United States we rarely heard from him. In earlier years when his wife Estelle was in better health we would occasionally hear from her. She shared that he was very successful in his businesses but their personal life appeared to be less than ideal. I believe Louis sees the world as a big disappointment when it comes to his very high expectations and frankly, we're fearful his perception of his morganatic marriage to Estelle could put her and their son in danger."

Michael seemed somewhat surprised. "Why would you see them in danger from him?"

"As you may know, Estelle is not well. She's not the woman he thought she was when he married her. She's weak but in spite of that, somehow I believe he's unwilling to let her go and feels the need to control her. My great grandson Eric is a fine and intelligent young man, but has an alternative lifestyle that Louis could never accept."

"Are you saying he's gay?"

"Yes, that's why Louis sent him away to attend school in Switzerland at a young age. He couldn't tolerate having his son around and I believe it broke Estelle's heart."

Throughout all this time Michael sat patiently holding Gerta's hand. His mind was racing amidst all the information this frail and elegant old lady and her daughter had shared with him. He knew it would be a while before he could assimilate it all.

"So, Mrs. Welheim, it's my understanding that you fear Louis could possibly hurt someone, even those he cares about, including his wife and son?"

"I don't know anything for sure. I know when he was a young man he was very volatile and had a lot of unresolved hatred in his heart. Of course as he matured he could have changed but when you called, it all came rushing back to me, and I know I would feel guilty remaining quiet and finding out too late that he was capable of expressions of violence that I might have prevented."

"What about someone who rejected him romantically, even if it was a long time ago?"

"As I've stated, Louis doesn't forget and he doesn't forgive. I would be very wary of that fact. I hope what we've shared with you will help your employer and the people you are concerned about. Thank you once again for listening so patiently to our ramblings. I needed to unburden my soul. Maybe, if I would have had the courage to speak up when Louis was born I could have spared him his painful childhood. Back then, it was not uncommon for people to disappear for no logical reason and my husband and I were both very fearful of the Third Reich. I was afraid Louis's father might hurt us if we tried to take our grandson away from them. Now I am an old woman and I will soon be gone. No one can hurt me more than the pain I've been carrying in my heart. Good-bye Michael O'Grady and Godspeed."

Gerta Welheim lay back on her pillows and closed her eyes and Michael could almost feel her great sense of relief and how she now appeared to be at peace with herself. He thanked her for her honesty and for all the information she provided. He hoped that when her final resting time came, it would now come more easily for her.

Marianna walked with him into the hallway and shook his hand. "Thank you, Michael, this burden has weighed heavily on our hearts. We really had no idea it might turn out this way. Somehow though, we both felt one day perhaps someone would come along wanting to know about Gerhard, or Louis as you know him. Now that it's happened we feel blessed and our prayer has been answered. From what you have learned, you are right to be concerned. There's a great deal of anger and intolerance in Louis. Please be careful and tell your employer to think about what we have shared with you very carefully before forming an alliance with him. Goodbye and good luck."

Michael sincerely thanked Marianna and gave her his phone number and asked her to contact him if they wished to share additional information they felt could be helpful, or if he could ever be of assistance to them in any way.

He left the hospital with the mixed emotions of being grateful for his progress in the investigation but also frightened about what he'd learned. He was pleased to catch an earlier standby flight back to Minneapolis and hoped he could arrive home in time to visit with David yet that evening. Throughout the flight he was unable to shake the uneasy feeling that had lodged deeply in his gut.

As soon as he left the plane he called home to check on Martha and the boys. He then called David's house and arranged to meet with him to share the helpful information he had learned. As Michael entered David's home he noticed his employer didn't appear to be feeling well but David assured him it was nothing more than his now nearly constant headache. He invited Michael to sit and appeared anxious for him to relay what he had learned.

Forty-five minutes later as Michael finished his story David sat back on his couch and shook his head not knowing what to make of this new information. Michael continued, "All the way back on the plane I kept thinking about what these two remarkable ladies shared about Louis. At first I thought it was a pretty strange story and part of me wanted to dismiss it as being too simplistic. However, as I pondered over the conversation I kept thinking that these are extremely bright women. In fact, talking to Marianna is like visiting with a living encyclopedia. She's a true history buff and both of them are well educated and appear to be totally honest and trustworthy people. I'm positive they're not blowing smoke and making up some halfcocked story, as there would be no logical reason for them to do that. I'm sure they honestly believe the guy could be dangerous. Then I think about the Louis everybody here knows, and the concept that this wealthy, highly successful, intelligent, powerful man could be still operating from ideas he concocted when he was ten years old is more than a little difficult for me to wrap my mind around. I have to be honest I'll need to give this more serious thought.

"So our assumption is that if Louis's childhood had been traumatic enough to scare him emotionally, he could still be operating from that level, at least when he feels threatened or provoked. Under these circumstances he may operate at a level he feels more able to control. Intellectually he excels, but emotionally he may be stunted."

"I suppose that could be a real possibility. After all, we do see signs of that around us. Take road rage for example, grown men taking out their personal frustrations on little old ladies they believe aren't driving up to their expectations. My daughter Kathleen says when someone gives you the finger, they're just showing you their emotional IQ. The more I think about it we often do act like a nation of overindulged children. We want instant gratification and when we can't get it immediately we show our displeasure in some pretty strange ways."

"If Louis has remained stuck at that early emotional level, the safe little fairy tale he created is now perhaps being acted out on an adult level. Strange but interesting, wouldn't you say?"

"Gerta mentioned Louis's morga . . . something marriage. I don't know what she meant but she felt it could be risky for his wife Estelle."

"Morganatic?"

"Yeah, that's the word she used. What does it mean?"

"Usually it refers to cultures where a caste system prevails. Like when a man of high nobility marries a women of inferior rank. A left handed marriage, so to speak. The children are considered legitimate but they don't inherit the rank or wealth of the husband. It's very interesting she would allude to that."

"She also said he'd probably never forgive someone who had rejected him emotionally. For example, even though he may not love his wife he considers her more of a possession than a partner."

"Which brings us back to our dear Sister Mary Rose and perhaps why Louis has come back into her life. I'm not sure I like the way this is unfolding, Michael. I think we need to do some more serious searching into the true nature of Mr. Louis Welheim."

Chapter 29

Harry finished watching the ten o'clock news and after turning off the television headed into the kitchen for a glass of juice. He knew he was putting off going to bed because he wasn't sure he was ready for what the next day would bring. As he opened the refrigerator the phone rang and he quickly answered it on the first ring so it wouldn't disturb Annie and Jessie who had gone to bed shortly after nine. He knew it would be Molly as lately she had gotten into the habit of calling at this hour so she could visit with him undisturbed by Jessie's incessant demands to talk to Lolly.

"Hello, Harry. It's me. Of course you already knew that. So, are we still on to meet dear old dad tomorrow?"

"I guess so. Janet is coming to the house early in the morning to stay for the weekend with Jessie and Martina. David gave Janet tomorrow off because Martina doesn't like to be here alone at night and Jessie can be quite a handful when she wants to. David was concerned for her with all the bouncing around she's had. He felt it was necessary for her to be in her own home especially since Annie and I were going to be away from her for the first time."

"You're lucky to have him for your boss and best friend. Maybe I should get to know him better, hmmm?"

When Harry didn't reply she continued, "So, are you a little nervous about tomorrow?"

"I wish I could say only a little nervous but the truth is I'm scared stiff. I've thought about this day all my life and now it almost seems more than I want to deal with."

"Your dad sounds very nice and there's no doubt in my mind he's anxious to meet you."

"I know, but I keep thinking about whether or not he'll like me and if I can be the son he would want. I don't want to disappoint him. Let's not talk about that now. How come you're still up? It takes over three hours for you to get here and at least an hour and a pot of coffee for you to face the world."

"I know that. I'm definitely a night person but I'm so excited about meeting your dad I'll probably not sleep anyway. God, I can't even believe it! You actually have a father! And all those years I'd been thinking you'd crawled out from under some rock and we had pity on you and took you in. Who'd ever believe you have a real dad who is a famous artist to boot?"

Harry felt a twinge of irritation but chose to ignore his cousin's crass sense of humor. "Well, dear cuz, the plane does leave at two and contrary to what you may want to believe, it probably won't wait for you."

"Now don't get your grundies in a bundle. I'll be standing on your doorstep with my luggage in hand before you know it. I want to leave my car at your house instead of at the airport. Anyway, dear heart, for your information I'm already in Minneapolis. I got in over an hour ago and I'm sitting here in my nightgown ready to jump under the covers but I felt the need to check in with you. It's such a huge step you're going to be making tomorrow."

Harry was quiet for a moment and finally asked, "What if he doesn't like me?"

"For crying in the jug Harry, give it up already. You know he's going to love you. After all, you're every father's dream, Mr. straight and narrow, successful and all around nice guy. You have a beautiful wife and daughter and the ability to do his taxes for free. What's not to like? Which reminds me, I was going through some of my mom's stuff and I found my old diaries and notebooks I used to put all my profound little observations in. I was reading all the things I thought were so terribly important back then, and realized throughout all the years we were growing up I could always count on you to be there for me. It was very touching. Would you like to hear some of them?"

"Sure, I could use some positive reinforcement on how nice I am."

"Remember how I would sit up in that big old apple tree at the far end of the garden when I wanted to be alone?"

"Yeah, I guess so. You were always kind of a tree sitter and if I remember correctly it was usually where you sat when you were plotting revenge on someone."

"True. This time I was mad because Addie Benson and Jenny Cross told me I had hair like a hedgehog and a bunch of kids laughed at me. I left school early and went home and sat up in the apple tree. You came down about seven because I missed supper and Dora was starting to worry where I was. I remember you climbed to the branch below where I was sitting and I wouldn't talk to you because I was so pissed off. Finally, I handed you my notebook with this little poem in it. I'll read it to you:

"DON'T TALK TO ME!!" in big letters, exclamation mark, exclamation mark! I'm sitting here in my favorite tree, I hate the world, the world hates me. I plan to sit here until I die, and that will make Addie and Jenny, their names I put in parenthesis, the assholes cry! Giant size exclamation mark! You sat there for awhile and then you motioned for my pencil and notebook. Which, by the way, you told me was totally disgusting because I had chewed on it and it had spit on it. Anyway you wrote this: I know you're better at writing a p-o-m-e, (she incorrectly spelled poem for Harry) But your mom sent me here to bring you home. So climb on down, your sadness will pass or good, sweet Dora will whup your ass. Exclamation mark, exclamation mark!

I remember I had all I could do to keep a straight face and I replied in my most haughty voice, what the hell kind of a word is whup? You looked at me with your evil little grin and said, the kind of word that makes you laugh. I lost it and almost fell out of the tree. I also remember what you said next. You asked me why I let people hurt me, and that just because someone said something, it didn't necessarily make it true. I remembered that specifically because I thought it was so smart of you to say that. Then you added my hair didn't really look like a hedgehog, maybe more like a porcupine, but definitely not a hedgehog. As we were walking back to the house you told me it wouldn't hurt for me to pay a little more attention to my grooming . . . and if I did that, just m-a-y-b-e (she stretched the word out) I might even be considered pretty. That night I let Dora wash and brush my hair and she ended cutting some of the underbrush out. That's what she called the snarls that formed underneath from when I was sweating. I might have been about ten or eleven and probably the hormones had started kicking in. Anyway, I think that was when I first realized I was kind of attractive and started to pay attention to my appearance . . . all thanks to you."

"And your point of sharing this touching little scenario is?"

"That you're a very nice person who was always there to help me when I needed a kind word . . . or a much deserved kick in the butt. By the way, Addie still lives in Glenwood and she's really big. I mean like boxcar big and she can hardly walk. Now, I can hardly believe myself saying this, but I really do feel sincerely sorry for her. Anyway, after that, I found it a lot easier to not let what people said about me hurt my feelings. The only problem is after I got older I think I went too far the other way. For a while it was as though I had no regard for anything anyone thought or said about me. You know, like I wanted to believe I was so great I didn't need to listen to anyone else. I talked about this with Clayton, who, by the way, thinks the world of you and said he knows all will go well for you and your dad. Let's see, where was I going? Oh yes, Clayton thinks I developed this disregard for other peoples' opinion to protect myself from pain and rejection and maybe that's why I also developed the 'I can run with scissors attitude'. He also very gently reminded me if people choose to run with scissors they can often fall and get hurt . . . and even get killed. Mind you, he never criticizes me." Then she added with a teasing tone in her voice, "Not like some people I know."

Harry broke into her one-sided conversation, "Excuse me, Molly . . . but don't you ever get tired of constantly rambling on and on and on about yourself?"

He thought he heard her make a quiet little gasping sound and then she apologized, "Oh my God, I'm so sorry. I called to find out how you were doing and I rattle on about me. That's so very typical and selfish of me. Please forgive me."

He could hear the remorse in her voice and almost wished he could take his harsh remark back but damn it, this was his dilemma and the world didn't always have to revolve around Molly Brown. Finally he recanted, "I'm sorry I said that to you. You know I always love to hear from you because you are my family. I don't know why I said that. I guess I'm really scared. Maybe more scared than I've ever been in my entire life and I don't know how to handle these mixed feelings."

"It's okay. I had it coming. The next few days are all about you and your father. I guess by now you know me well enough to realize things like this, where we are forced to sit down and really examine our feelings and emotions aren't easy for anyone. I blow them off with smart-ass jokes but you take them out and honestly look at them and I really admire that. Your father will see that in you and admire and love you for the man you are, his son. Well, I'd better let you go, it's getting pretty late. See you in the morning. Be sure to bring lots of pictures of Jessie so he gets to know his granddaughter."

"Oh, I will, you can count on that! Annie has a whole photo album packed and ready to go."

"Try to get a good sleep. I love you, Harry."

"Good night, Molly. I love you to." He waited for the final words she always had to get in.

"Harry? I promise to brush my hair. God forbid I should look like a porcupine and embarrass you. Oh, and don't forget the duct tape for my mouth."

Harry hung up and even though he felt relieved Molly had forgiven him for being rude he had to admit he was still in a terrible mood. He felt a darkness inside that seemed to go beyond depression. It was almost as though the deep feeling part of him had been disconnected. He tried to focus on his jumbled emotions and as he did he felt the tightness moving from his chest into his throat. The thought that came into his mind was it was as if his spirit or soul was trying to disconnect and was now whirling inside him like a dry leaf in a wind tunnel. His heart was pounding and he was short of breath and he realized he was having a full-blown anxiety attack. Common sense told him he should drink some orange juice but instead he reached into the cupboard and took down a bottle of brandy. As he poured a glass half full he noticed his hands were shaking and he was aware of a tingling feeling in his fingers. He took a large swallow and felt the brandy burn in his mouth and throat. He coughed and felt the urge to gag but shut his eyes and concentrated on keeping the liquid down. He sipped the brandy and could slowly feel relaxation seep into his mid section. Refilling the tumbler half full again he made his way into the dimly lit living room and sat down in his comfortable old recliner.

As the tightness in his throat and chest began to release his mind drifted back to his early childhood and the man whose absence had been such a dominant presence in his life. He realized what he was thinking was an oxymoron, an absence being a great presence, and he smiled at the inconsistency. Tomorrow he was finally going to meet the father who had never given him a word of encouragement, a hug, or a present on Christmas or his birthday. Probably his mother had mentioned his name but it became a forbidden topic for the whole family, even by the aunt who loved him as much as she loved her own children.

One of the few times he remembered asking about his father he had been sitting in the kitchen with his aunt and grandma and grandpa. Grandpa had come in for noon lunch and Dora and grandma were sitting by the table with a large tan and blue bowl between them as they shelled peas. When he asked if his daddy was coming to get him, Dora and grandma exchanged horrified looks. Grandpa Scarley glared at him and then brought his fist down hard on the table and thundered that he had no father. In his extreme anger he almost added the damning words that Harry was a sp . . . He hadn't finished his tirade but instead got up so abruptly he tipped his coffee over spilling it into his plate of food. He then stormed out of the house. He remembered Dora holding him as he cried and explaining that he must never ask about his father again. Over the years he had agonized over the unfinished proclamation and as he grew older wondered if his grandfather's unfinished sentence would have labeled him as a spawn of the devil. As might be expected even grandpa Scarley's anger could not stop him from thinking about his father. He vaguely remembered his mother telling him his daddy was tall and handsome like a prince and how he would come and take them away but as the summers and winters passed and she became ill she spoke less and less of him. The last time he remembered asking her about him she whispered she didn't really know, and his daddy must have been a dream. After she died Harry made up his own dreams but his father never came.

Harry sipped the brandy and his thoughts now flowed easily. He recalled how he and Molly watched an old melodrama at the Glenwood Theater. The tickets were twelve cents each and Uncle Stan always found at least a quarter to get Harry and Molly out of the house for the afternoon. Harry was frightened of the villain because he thought the damsel in distress looked like his mother. That night he had a nightmare about his imaginary dad trying to kill his mother but in his dream there had been no fair-haired hero to save her and he had awakened screaming and crying. From then on his father seemed to have taken on a darker image and as he got older and other children teased him he felt a growing resentment toward him. One day, when he was a little older, Dora sat him down and explained what was done was done and things are not always as they seem. She went on to say the important thing was for him to live his life in a way that would make everyone proud of him. She said dwelling on his past and his father would only bring him sadness and if he were smart, like she knew he was, he would forget about his father and move on. At the time he wasn't sure what moving on entailed but somehow he'd come up with a fairly workable solution to go on with his life.

Tomorrow all that would change when he finally came face to face with Russell Cassidy. From that moment on he would be expected to take the earlier part of his life and set it aside, acknowledging his old perceptions were no longer valid. He would need to formulate a new reality that now included the man who had helped create him. As he savored the last sip of his brandy he heard Jessie cry out in her sleep, followed by Annie's footsteps as she crossed the hall to comfort her. He set the empty glass down and suddenly a surge of emotion filled his whole being with the overwhelming desire to be there for his wife and daughter. He rose slowly from the recliner and went to them with complete conviction that this is where, and how his life was meant to be.

Before he entered Jessie's room, he paused momentarily and listened to Annie softly comforting their daughter. Annie looked up at Harry and said, "Jessie said Kipper byded her but Cha Cha byded Kipper." Harry smiled as Kipper was Skipper, the little terrier dog Jessie's foster mom owned, that had the bad habit of showing his enthusiasm for Jessie by knocking her down and nipping at her. Cha Cha was Sasha the calico cat Harry had before he and Annie were married. Jessie had never seen Sasha, and only heard about the mischievous cat in bedtime stories. Annie yawned and Harry reached for Jessie as he whispered, "You go back to bed. I'll see that she goes to sleep."

Annie gratefully handed Jessie to Harry and he sat down in the rocker cuddling his daughter. Jessie smiled sleepily at him as she murmured, "Hi daddy, big Cha Cha save me."

"Yes, I heard that. You're a pretty lucky girl to have Sasha look after you."

Jessie looked up at Harry with complete trust and solemnly said, "Yes, I am." Then she added "I love you, daddy."

Harry put his face down into his daughter's neck and smelled the delicate fragrance of baby shampoo and powder and he felt a surge of unconditional love. "I love you too baby and I will always be here to take care of you."

"I too, daddy. You bring me gummy worms?"

"I will if you promise to share some with your mom and me."

"I do. Good night, daddy."

"Good night Jessie. Sleep tight." He laid her down in her bed and checked her covers and the side rails. As he left her bedroom he felt the need to add, "I promise you'll never be alone."

He went downstairs and after he turned out the lights and returned upstairs, he found a note in Annie's handwriting taped to their bathroom mirror. It said simply, "I love you."

As he climbed into bed he heard Annie's voice, "Tough night?"

"Yeah, I guess. I think Jessie was too warm."

"I think you're right. I have the habit of needing to be sure she feels secure and warm. Not cold like I often did when I was growing up. Actually, I meant was it a tough night for you?"

"For a little while I guess, but just having you and Jessie here helps me realize regardless what happens tomorrow, my life is still complete." He pulled Annie close and feeling the warmth of her body against his, drifted off into a peaceful sleep.

Chapter 30

As they boarded the plane to Albuquerque, Harry found himself experiencing excitement instead of the horrible dread he so vividly felt the night before. His nighttime demons had faded with the morning light and he welcomed the new chapters that would be opening in his life. His irritation with Molly had left as well, and he was grateful to have her with them. From past experience he knew if there was ever an awkward moment, Molly would step in and carry the conversation without missing a beat.

Glancing around the plane he felt more than a small amount of satisfaction as he noticed that Annie and Molly were by far the prettiest women on board. Some of the looks and smiles from the men around them told him that others shared his assessment. Shallow on his part? Maybe, but he secretly found great satisfaction in it. Annie chose the window seat and asked if he and Molly minded if she caught a quick catnap to make up for Jessie's early morning reverie. At four-thirty she had appeared at their bedside asking for juice and Coco Puffs and Annie had gotten up so Harry could sleep a few more hours.

As they taxied down the runway, Harry couldn't resist leaning over and whispering into Molly's ear, "You look rather un-ugly today, not your usual porcupine-hedgehog look. I might even be tempted to say pretty, but that might sound a little patronizing."

She appeared to ignore him and continued to stare at the fashion magazine in her lap. Finally she turned to him with a disdainful smile. "You do know that sometimes you can be a total ass. Granted at times a rather nice ass, but nonetheless a total ass. How you ever found such a lovely, wonderful wife is beyond me . . . and why your beautiful, kind, sweet, intelligent and eternally tolerant cousin puts up with you is a total mystery equal only to the black holes in space and the Bermuda Triangle."

Annie sat back and closed her eyes as she heard the familiar bantering between her husband and his cousin commence. She thought of her own childhood and wondered how it would have been growing up in a family where you were not expected to be the poster child for perfection. The last thing she remembered before falling asleep was hearing Molly's infectious laughter as they were reminiscing about two rabbits they had on the farm called Whiskers and Sparky and how they had refused to eat them when grandpa butchered them and tried to convince them they were no different than eating chicken. Annie awakened some time later and continued lazily gazing out the window at the soft white clouds and thought about how beautiful and inviting they looked. She could almost imagine how soft they would feel against her body. Her thoughts turned back to Harry and Molly as she heard them laughing out loud as they reflected once more on their high school years in Glenwood.

"Harry, remember the kid called Pete PeCar? Whenever Dallas Schmedstad and Donny Doupala wanted to pick on someone they always had Pete to torture. They used to call him Pecker Pete. I remember one day when you weren't in school, I think you might have been sick that day, since you and I were usually the only ones who tried to defend Pete and you were absent, our cousin Clayton stood up to those two before I could say a word. You know how everyone considered Clayton to be a bookworm mama's boy . . . but that day when Mr. Paulson was out of the study hall Dallas started to call Pete Pecker Boy. Clayton stopped reading and put his book down. He looked up and quietly told him to quit picking on Pete. Just like that, out of the blue, he told Dallas to stop! The room got deathly quiet because as you remember Dallas was one big, dumb ass, jerk. Dallas turned on Clayton and grabbed his book and threw it up against the blackboard and said something like, oh, yeah? And whose gonna' make me, you little faggot. I'll show you! Clayton stared at Dallas and then said very quietly, then I suggest you zip up your zipper before you show the rest of us your little pecker . . . and by the way, his name is PeCar, which is probably too difficult for your miniscule mind to remember. Poor Dallas grabbed for his zipper, which was wide open, and the classroom exploded in laughter. It didn't stop Dallas from being a bully but after that he seemed to have a whole new respect for Clayton."

Annie turned back to the window and decided she'd like to meet Clayton sometime and then refocused her thoughts on the hypnotic cloud formations. She awoke again to the pilot's announcement that they were

271

about to start their descent and would be arriving in Albuquerque shortly. As she glanced over at Harry she saw he appeared pale and tense so she leaned over and kissed him on the cheek and whispered, "Take a deep breath and try to relax. Remember to enjoy the next few days because this is something you have waited your whole life for." He smiled and took her hand as the plane continued its approach.

The landing was smooth and as they entered the airport Molly took the lead and seemed to be looking for someone. She threaded her way through the waiting crowd and soon was speaking with a distinguished looking Native American gentleman. Molly motioned for Harry and Annie to join them and excitedly introduced them. "Harry and Annie, this is John Crow. He's a friend of your father and he'll be driving us to his home."

John Crow extended his large hand to each of them and greeted them warmly. "I cannot tell you how happy I am to meet all of you. I'll try my best to make your stay here enjoyable and I want to assure you that Russell is anxiously looking forward to meeting you. Learning about you has been the best medicine for him and I am sure you'll get along fine."

John Crow guided them through the airport and helped them collect their luggage. Annie and Harry each brought one suitcase and Molly two. As they left the airport Harry couldn't resist winking at Annie as they listened to Molly justifying her need for having two suitcases even though no one had mentioned it. John Crow easily carried the ladies' luggage and none of them could believe it when he told them he would be celebrating his sixty-eighth birthday in less than a week. He stood straight and tall and his body was well muscled like that of a much younger man. His long black hair was pulled back into a ponytail and only showed signs of graying at the temples which enhanced the contour of his chiseled features. When Molly suggested he could easily be a movie star he only smiled and said, "My wife Isabella is fifteen years younger than I am. I have no choice but to stay fit." As they approached John Crow's car Harry let out a low whistle of appreciation. Before them was a 1958 Studebaker Golden Hawk in mint condition. Harry circled the car and finally said, "Now this is what I call a real car. It reminds me of the first one I owned."

John put the luggage in the trunk and Harry told him about the 1960 Studebaker Hawk that had been his first prized car. Molly and Annie sat in the back seat and Harry up front with John Crow who pointed out the various landmarks and historic sites on the way. Harry couldn't help but notice that John seemed to be repeatedly glancing at Molly in the rear view mirror. When he became aware Harry was watching him, he explained, "You might not know this but the old man Russ, your dad, has a painting of Mariah in his house. He painted it after his wife Sophie died. Now, don't get me wrong, he loved Sophie but deep down we all knew how much he continued to love your mother. I know Sophie was aware of that but she loved Russell so much she didn't care. She had been his nurse in the hospital and I know it was her who was responsible for keeping him alive when he found out your mother had died. Anyway, your cousin Molly could have posed for the portrait of Mariah. Old Russ may have a bit of a start when he meets her and let's hope his old ticker can take it. I feel I should share a little history before you meet Russ. Tom Crow was my older brother and he and Russell grew up together. The summer after they graduated Tom took a job here helping on a ranch, but as you know, Russell was an artist and he couldn't wait to see the country. He traveled all over until his money started to get thin and that's when he took the job on the threshing crew that worked on your grandpa's farm. He fell in love with Mariah and planned to come back and marry her as soon as they finished their last job of the harvest season. I suppose you already heard this but Russell was almost killed when a hay wagon rolled down a steep hill and pinned him against a barn. His legs were so badly crushed they ended up amputating one above the knee and barely saving the other one.

The impact also broke his pelvis and at first they weren't sure if he would ever walk again but he proved them wrong. It took him a long time but he walked out of that hospital with an artificial leg and a lot of determination. He and my brother Tom finally went back to find Mariah but your grandpa told him she had someone else in her life and she didn't want half a man for a husband. He also told him if he ever came back he'd shoot him, even if he was a damn cripple. Russell seemed to give up on everything after that. He and my brother Tom spent a lot of time drinking, playing cards and letting their lives go to waste. Somewhere along the way Tom met Magda, the lady who now works as Russell's housekeeper and after a few months they got married and took off so Tom could work in the oil fields. Russell suddenly found himself without a drinking buddy so he sobered up and started drawing and painting again. I think that was about the time he met Sophie. She was his nurse and at first considered him to be just another one of her patients who needed a lot of therapy. It wasn't long before she took a shine to Russell but when he finally confessed he still had feelings for Mariah, she backed off. After a year or two she told Russell how she felt about him and how even though she was aware of his love for Mariah she would always love him. It was Sophie who convinced him to find Mariah even if she was married to someone else and see if she still loved him. He thought about what Sophie suggested and finally agreed he needed to hear the words from Mariah's own lips. He sold some of his paintings and made a down payment on a fairly new truck and drove to Minnesota to find his true love. Even though it had been several years and he clearly remembered what her father had threatened, he felt he needed to see her one more time. He pulled into the gas station in the little town of Lowry where she had lived and asked the attendant if he knew where he could find Mariah Scarley. The guy was polite but told him she had died a few months before. At first Russell didn't believe him but the man gave him directions to the Reno cemetery and Russell found her grave.

He came back here and after that he went downhill again. He resumed his drinking and after about a week he decided his life wasn't worth living. He told me he drove himself up into the canyons and his intention was to end his life by leaning forward over the edge of a precipice and letting himself fall to his death. He'd been drinking all day and when he started out he was so drunk his truck got hung up on a small boulder so he had to get out and walk. By the time he finally got near the top of a steep cliff he started to sober up. He slowly made his way to the edge and in order to check if the canyon was deep enough he took off his artificial leg and threw it over the side. After hearing it clatter down and the echo that it made he got to thinking maybe it wasn't such a good idea. Since he no longer had his leg he had to climb down on his hands and knees. At one point he lost his balance and tumbled the rest of the way down. He ended up several hundred yards down the mountainside bruised and unconscious. The next thing everyone heard was some hikers found a leg at the bottom of a canyon and called the sheriff. I guess it scared the livers out of them until one of the deputies retrieved it and recognized it was Russell's artificial leg. A little later they found his truck and a day after that they found poor old Russell, who by this time was almost buzzard bait. The desert sun is very hot around here but the nights can get mighty cold and he ended up back in the hospital and that's when he had to part with his other leg. Sophie stayed by his side and wouldn't let him give up.

About six months later they were married and they stayed together until she died of breast cancer about four years ago.

By then my brother Tom and his wife Magda had moved back here and she helped Sophie with the housework and also learned about Russell's nursing care. Eventually she took care of both of them when Sophie got sick. After Tom died, Magda made Russell and Sophie her first priority and now serves as his housekeeper and physical therapist of sorts. Don't get me wrong, those two bicker and go around like two cats in a bag, but somehow they seem to need each other.

Isabella and I moved back here about three years ago. I'm a retired engineer and Isabella runs an art gallery and gift shop in Albuquerque. You'll meet her later today. Magda and Tom had one daughter Star, but she never stayed around these parts very long. She married young and her husband was a nice guy but the two of them were always on the go. They seemed to be always looking for that pot of gold at the end of the rainbow. I'm not exaggerating because those two have searched for gold in Alaska, buried treasure from a Spanish galleon at the bottom of the ocean, and even for diamonds in Africa. Somewhere along the way they had a daughter Skylar, but being on the move all the time was hard on the tyke. Finally Magda took her in and raised her so they could continue their adventures. Russell and Sophie took a real shine to Magda's granddaughter and treated her like she was their own. Now, of course that was quite a few years ago. You'll meet the grown up Sky and her husband and little boy tonight. I think Russ loves Sky like she was his own daughter and he adores her husband and little boy Cody."

John Crow turned the car down a winding dirt road and said, "I know this is a lot of information to dump on you at one time but I think it will be easier for you when you meet the old man." He pointed to the area around them, "This is all Russell's land and he likes to keep it natural like it was when he first moved here. That little house over yonder is Magda's. He built it for her after my brother died. Tom wasn't much of a provider for his family but the old man saw to it they never wanted. Well, this is it."

Nestled back in the hillside was an adobe house with rounded walls that complimented the shapes of the surrounding area. The house was a combination of rock, wood and adobe and the colors blended beautifully into the hillside. As they approached the house, John Crow pointed to the yard and the small gardens he said he had created and tended. As he took the suitcases from the trunk he noticed how nervous Harry had become and he put his hand on his shoulder.

"Russ is probably in there dozing in the sunlight. You go on in and enjoy meeting him. He's one of the nicest people in the world and he can't wait to see you. I'll take care of the luggage." He motioned to Molly to join him and after speaking briefly to her, they stood together while Harry and Annie started up the flagstone path to the ramp that covered half the steps. The door opened as Harry was about to knock and an older Native American woman greeted them and motioned to them to come in. The room was decorated as Harry had expected for this part of the country with hand loomed weavings, painted pottery, and antique ranch memorabilia.

At the far end of the room sat an older man in a wheelchair, sleeping in the sunlight. In front of him stood an easel with a half finished landscape painting and a small table with tubes of paint and large container of brushes. A palate of paint had slipped off his lap and lay where his legs and feet should have been. The woman who introduced her self as Magda called his name softly but he didn't stir. She called again and he lifted his chin from his chest and looked in their direction. Harry felt his heart jump as he stared at the older man he knew to be his father and he awkwardly lifted his hand in a slight wave. Annie moved across the room and Harry felt his legs becoming weak as if they didn't want to support him. As Harry approached his father he was surprised to see how small and fragile he appeared. His hair was thick and white and a small beard and mustache covered the lower part of his face. Russell adjusted his glasses as they had slid down his nose while he was sleeping and as he peered through them to see his guests, a large smile broke out on his face. "Come here Harry and Annie, I've been waiting for you. I had a hard time sleeping last night so I guess I dozed off a little while. Let me look at you." He held out his hands for Harry and as he took them into his, said, "This is the second most wonderful day in my life . . . the first was the day I met your mother."

Harry felt all of his emotions become tangled and stood silently.

Annie spoke first, "Thank you for letting us come to meet you. We've both been so excited that Harry has finally been able to find you."

Harry knelt by the wheelchair and put his arms around the older man but he didn't speak carefully searching for the words he wanted to say. He felt tears coming from his heart and into his eyes and he only wanted to hold this man and feel his presence. As they held each other he felt his father's body shaking and Harry knew they were sharing similar emotions. The room was completely silent for several minutes as they continued to hold each other. Tears from each man's eyes were flowing and blending as they coursed down their cheeks. Finally Harry relinquished his embrace and was able to say, "I think this is the second best day in my life too, the first was the day I met my wife Annie." With that exchange they all began to laugh and the tension that Harry had been feeling so acutely left immediately as Annie bent over and hugged Russell. John Crow and Molly entered the house and came over to join the others. John spoke first saying, "Well, Russ, this lady will probably bring back some memories for you. As Molly took Russell's hand the older man looked into her face and said only, "Oh, my!"

"Russell, I'm very pleased to finally meet you. I'm Harry's cousin Sara, or Molly as everyone calls me. We've spoken several times on the phone."

Russ Cassidy put his head down for a moment and then looking up at her said, "My dear girl, I'm so glad you warned me how much you resemble my sweet Mariah. Even at that you gave this old heart quite a start. Oh, my goodness gracious! If I had seen you on the street I wouldn't have believed you're not her. It's almost like God chose to make another Mariah because she was so beautiful and her life was cut short. How very nice it is to meet you . . . the last I knew of you, you were only an anticipation."

"That's true. I think my mother Dora had just found out she was expecting me when you came to grandpa's farm with the threshing crew."

Russell smiled warmly and tears again began flowing down his cheeks. He reached out with his hands taking Harry and Molly's into his. He gave each an affectionate squeeze and said, "A little more than three weeks ago I was sitting here alone thinking about my life and I realized how lonely and sad I had become believing my life had very little meaning. Today, I sit here with a beautiful family and I want you all to know I'm the happiest man in the world. Please make yourselves comfortable. I want you to feel totally welcome in my home. Now, let's all get to know each other better."

As they sat down to visit, Russell and Harry shared more of the details of their lives. Russell introduced them to Magda, and finally to her great grandson Cody who had been sitting quietly in the kitchen. As Cody was being introduced to Annie she commented that she and Harry had a daughter about his age. He smiled and shyly shook her hand as he said hello. Cody then suddenly turned to Magda and said something in his native language. She responded by saying something back to him as if she was questioning him and he replied affirmatively. Magda stepped forward and took Annie's hands into hers and peered into her palms. She took her knurled hand and rubbed it across Annie's palms and started to laugh. She shook her head up and down and left the room laughing and saying, "Si, Cody, Si!"

Annie looked bewildered, "What was that all about?"

Russell grinned, "Who knows? You'll get used to her. Your great grandmother is a little different isn't she Cody, my man? Cody was calling you Natashka, and that's the kachina that helps erring children. I'm not sure why he called you that. Why did you call her that Cody?"

The boy smiled shyly and shrugged, "I don't know why. I just like her."

Annie smiled at Cody and said, "I guess I'll consider that a compliment since I do work with small children who sometimes are having a hard time fitting in. I like you too, Cody. Thank you."

Magda prepared a lovely dinner serving some of Russell's favorite dishes for the occasion of this celebration. As they were finishing dessert, they were joined by Magda's granddaughter, Skylar, who apologized for being late, and commented that her husband would be joining them later. After kissing her son, grandmother and Russell in that order, she warmly hugged each of the guests. Annie liked her immediately and could sense this was a family where a great deal of love was shared.

Sky accepted the plate of food her grandmother handed her and explained that her husband Bill was a lawyer who did a lot of work to preserve the ecology of the seacoasts. This evening he had been detained at his office on a matter that had to do with a tanker leaking oil off the coast of Alaska. She jokingly added with all his travel activity he was becoming more and more like her wayward parents but that she would always support him in whatever he felt he had to do to preserve the planet.

As they continued to visit in the living room Russell had Magda bring out the old sketchbooks he'd carried with him the summer he met Mariah. Harry and Molly admired the many beautiful drawings he had made of Mariah, which once again, resulted in tears forming in the eyes of their host.

Annie felt an immediate bond with Sky and was surprised and impressed to learn she had created many of the beautiful pottery pieces that were displayed throughout the house. Noticing Annie's interest in her work Sky asked if she would like to see her kiln and her studio. Annie nodded yes and Sky suggested she slip on her jacket and they left the house together walking toward the setting sun and into the rapidly chilling air. Once they were a few yards from the house Sky lit a cigarette and apologized saying she needed to have a few quick puffs and wanted to avoid her grandmother's wrath. "I'll show you the kiln tomorrow in the daylight if you're really interested but tonight we can be out here for awhile and enjoy the beauty of the night sky, if that's alright with you."

As they walked Annie felt herself being enveloped by the beauty of the earth all around her. The sunset was breathtaking and she felt a sense of serenity she had never known before.

"I thought you could probably use a little fresh air." Sky walked a few yards farther without speaking and then remarked, "Annie, I also wanted you to myself for a bit. You see, Magda pulled me aside and told me what Cody had said to you."

Annie looked into the young woman's dark eyes and for an instant was reminded of her daughter Jessie. "I really don't know what he said. Something about a kachina, Natasha or something like that."

"Natashka. He called you Natashka. I really don't know why he did that. Cody is a sweet little boy but sometimes I think my dear old grandmother has had way too much influence on him. My grandparents are Hopi Indians as are my parents and my husband Bill and his parents.

Once you grow to know her better you'll realize my grandmother has made it her mission in life to keep the Hopi tradition alive in her great grandson. She wasn't able to do it with her own daughter and I think she only succeeded in having it drive her away. She was only partially successful in keeping it alive in me as I'm carrying on at least a part of the tradition in my pottery. Now she seems to have great plans for her great grandson Cody, but in a different way." Sky lit another cigarette and inhaled but hesitated as if unsure of how to continue the conversation.

"Why did Magda study my palms and start to laugh?"

"I'm not really sure. She didn't really say. She told me Cody had recognized something in you she should have seen but didn't. You're probably starting to see by now my grandmother is rather different. I love her with my whole heart because she took care of me and raised me when my own parents couldn't.

She was a godsend in helping me finish my education and especially when I found out I was expecting Cody." Sky grinned and drew deeply on her cigarette. "You've probably noticed we tend to marry rather young around here. I grew up with my husband Bill. We were best friends and we always knew we would eventually marry, even when we were in grade school. When we announced our decision to our families no one was surprised. Bill is very passionate about our heritage so he encourages Magda's influence on our son. Right now, Cody is more Hopi Indian than either Bill or I am."

"You don't mind?"

"No, I'm very proud of my heritage, but as they say, life goes on. I want to hold onto my ancestry but I realize in order to fit into society I had to make some concessions. My grandmother believes our son is special and it's her duty to teach him about the Hopi traditions and to prepare him for his future. Don't get me wrong, I think every grandmother and mother believes their children are special but my grandmother thinks Cody is an extraordinary child and has a special mission in life."

"What do you think she means?"

"Are you familiar with the term Indigo children? The generation of children who've come or are coming that will supposedly have a great and profoundly beneficial influence on our future society?"

"Yes, I think so. It seems to me I've read something about that."

"My grandmother used to talk about the Indigo children long before anyone else ever heard of them and years before any books about them came out. She said that selected from the thousands of Indigo children there will be twelve who will be very special and will have unique gifts and many unusual talents. She calls these twelve the Children of the Stars, or the Star Children. As they mature into adulthood, which will occur at the first or second decade of the next century, they are destined to be the leaders of those that have come to bring great changes into the world. Many Indigo children have already been born or will be coming soon. They are already connecting on a spiritual level and it will be their mission to help usher in a prolonged period of peace upon the world." Skylar allowed Annie a few moments to reflect on what she had described. She then continued, "Sounds a little preposterous, right? Well, grandmother believes Cody is one of the twelve."

"She told you all this?"

"No, well . . . not at first. Not until I found a very unique sand painting up in the hills. Magda is an artist in the old tradition. She creates original sand paintings and intricate medicine wheels. They're amazingly beautiful and many of the designs I use on my pottery I've learned from her. For grandmother it's a very spiritual thing and she learned this art form from her mother, who, I'm told, had mystical powers of some kind. Actually, Magda is considered by many of the people around here to be a healer. Getting back to the sand painting, it's not uncommon for me to get up very early when the sun is beginning to peak over the horizon, and wander about in the hills alone with my camera. It clears my head and I feel closer to God or the Great Spirit up there than I ever do in any church.

One morning, I was climbing in the foothills and I crawled down into a crevice. At the bottom there was this flat rock covered with fine white sand. On it was the most beautiful sand painting I've ever seen. It was different than any I had seen Magda do previously but I'm sure it was one of hers. It was a wheel about three feet across and the entire background color was a deep indigo blue. The main subject matter was twelve children holding hands in a circle. There were other symbols too such as birds and animals, suns and moons as well as planets and stars. Oddly, there was another child, a thirteenth child, who was not in the circle but off to the left side, facing away from the other children.

I was so excited I unbuckled the straps of my backpack to get my camera and as I turned to focus on it a sudden gust of wind completely destroyed the sand painting. I was so disappointed I almost cried. Intuitively I knew it must have special meaning. Later that morning when I asked Magda if it was one of hers she seemed very evasive. At first I was positive my grandmother had created the painting, but the fact that I had to climb down into such a difficult place to find it, makes me wonder. You can see for yourself, Magda is an old woman and at times it's very difficult for her to get around.

For weeks after that I kept questioning her and finally she told me about the Star Children. She said there are presently nine children but sometime in the near future there will be twelve to complete the circle. Eventually one child could turn to the dark side or could also be considered a leader, so there would still be a total of twelve children in the circle."

"That's amazing. Did she tell you any more about the children? Where they would come from or how she came to know that Cody was one of them?"

"No, I don't think so . . . Wait, it seems to me the circle was shaped more like a globe which might suggest the children could come from anywhere in the world. She also said each child would possess a gift for the world and would be appointed a guardian who would also possess a special gift. She also implied each child would have a particular animal or bird to protect them. Cody's protector is an eagle. The Hopi people call the eagle god Kwahu. I guess I was hoping when she said Cody had recognized something in you that you might have some knowledge about what she's talking about. When she told me this, I was excited and hopeful about getting more answers but now I think I was grasping at straws and I hope you won't feel that I'm crazy."

Annie studied Skylar's face and could see how deeply concerned she was about her son and grandmother. "I wish I could help but I know nothing about this. I must say, the whole idea is incredibly intriguing and I would like you to keep me posted when you learn more."

The young woman silently studied the pack of cigarettes in her hand and smiled at Annie, "I'm really glad Russell found out he had a son and such a nice family to be with him through his last years. His health hasn't been good and I think this will make a difference. When Molly called and told him about Harry, my grandmother was worried he might be someone who wanted to take advantage of Russell and then break his heart. You can see he's an extremely sensitive man and she's very protective of him, I think she sees him more as a brother than a friend.

Magda often walks out into the hills and smokes her little pipe that she says brings the power from the spirits into her vision. It's shaped like an old peace pipe or calumet. She got it as a gift from her mother. It's hand carved out of bone and is very beautiful. She was told to use it only when she needs spiritual advice. Taking another long drag from her cigarette she said "Not like these dirty things." She grinned and waved the pack of cigarettes in front of her. "Anyway, when she came back from her walk she was smiling happily and said she was told Russell's son would be pure of heart. I think she was right from what I can tell."

Annie smiled, "Harry is a very kind person. I saw that in him the first time I met him. You probably are aware that after his mother died he was raised by Molly's parents. They did a wonderful job, but there was always a deep, aching pain in his heart as to why his father hadn't come back for him and his mother. Now that he knows why, he seems to feel more complete and at peace. We have a very good life in Minnesota and as far as material things we have more than we can use, so you may want to assure your grandmother we don't expect anything from Russell other than his love. If he has made provisions for Magda they should stay the way it is."

"She said she already knows that. As I look back on my childhood I see that my grandmother has always been a remarkable person who has unlimited faith in the Great Spirit. Before I came to stay with her I was living with my parents in Alaska. I distinctly remember one occasion when I was only about five or six years old and became very ill. I had pneumonia and was so sick my mother called grandmother in desperation to come and get me because she was afraid I might die. I was in and out of consciousness with a very high fever and I think I remember my mother saying my grandmother was flying in to bring me back to New Mexico as soon as I was well enough to travel. Somehow, I got it into my head that Magda came to me in the shape of a raven and healed me. By the time she arrived I was already getting better and for years I was convinced she could shape shift herself into a raven and fly wherever she was needed. Grandmother taught me how imperative it is we live in harmony with the earth. She stressed that everything, including every rock, river, mountain, tree, fish, animal and person has the Great Spirit flowing through them and we must recognize that truth and treat each accordingly. Even now, when she kills a chicken she asks its permission and forgiveness before she chops its head off. Can you imagine the kind of world we could have if everyone believed and acted that way?"

"I know it would be a lot gentler than the one we have."

"In the Hopi tradition there's a legend that the first humans crawled through a hole in the earth from a sacred underground place called Sipapu. They wandered on the earth guided by the Great Spirit to find a land of peace and harmony. When they arrived the Great Spirit taught them to plant and harvest crops and before he left them appointed twin warrior gods by the name of Maseway and Sheoyeway to guard over them. Historians now say the Hopi are the descendants of the Anasazi people and they were forced to move about through various portions of these lands because of changes in the earth and its climate. Throughout many years they splintered into smaller tribes. They became the Rio Grande, Pueblo, Zuni, Pimi, Hopi and Papago. John Crow may tell you more about this tomorrow when he gives you the grand tour. He is a real history buff and often serves as a guide for the tourists that come here to visit."

Skylar stopped and looked directly into Annie's eyes and said, "Thank you for hearing me out. It isn't often our visitors show a genuine interest in our people and their ancient ways. I feel your spirit is pure and I can talk to you from my heart. I have a feeling we will remain close friends and that makes me very happy." Annie breathed deeply, smiled and placed her arm around the young woman's shoulder. "I'm so pleased to hear that, Skylar. It makes me very happy too."

The women walked for several minutes experiencing their connectedness without speaking. Finally, Skylar continued, "It's a shame but I think it's rather common for white people to base their opinions about Native Americans only on the stereotypes they've seen in the movies. You know, the stories about the savage red man who murdered the peaceful settlers and took their scalps as trophies. I don't think they've given much consideration to the suffering our people have had to endure. Assume for example if one day their villages, towns and cities were invaded by strangers with powerful weapons who would steal their land, homes and businesses, pollute their water supply, murder their men and rape their wives and children. How would they feel? And, after most of their friends and relatives were slaughtered like animals they would be forced to relocate onto the least desirable lands they called reservations to live in disgrace and poverty. It was really no different than what happened to the Jews."

Skylar peered into the darkness of the star filled universe and continued, "In many ways, our story is a sad one and I'm really sorry I seem to be going on and on but what so many white people don't seem to understand is that the value and significance of our lives was centered around our sacred traditions. We didn't need the white man's religion, our daily life and existence was based on our spiritual connectedness with the earth and all of creation. We didn't need new traditions as ours served us very well and I sincerely believe we would have evolved in our own way." She reached into her pocket and took out a small packet of breath mints and slipping one into her mouth, offered one to Annie and continued, "We'd better get back inside. It's getting chilly and I can see you're shivering. It's getting late too. I'm sorry, Annie. I'll bet you're exhausted and here I've been going on and on about something you probably already knew. I hope you won't think your newly found father-in-law's friends are totally strange. I think after you get to know us better you'll find we're actually rather nice."

"I think you are wonderful people to be so kind to us and I don't think you're strange at all. I have to tell you, I've had some rather unusual things happen in my life that I can't explain and maybe sometime you won't mind if I share them with you."

When they returned to the house Sky introduced Annie to her husband Bill and John's wife Isabella. Bill was not your traditional looking lawyer in a three-piece suit. He wore cowboy boots and casual western clothes. He had a boyish charm and laughed often and by the way he joked with Magda it was evident she thought the world of her granddaughter's husband. Cody stayed close to his dad's side and it seemed obvious he and his father shared a strong bond. Isabella was a tall, stately and extremely beautiful woman. She had dark olive skin, sparkling brown eyes and wore her long black hair pulled back with a silver and turquoise barrette. Her long, graceful neck was accented with slender silver earrings and her clothing reflected the finest expression of conservative southwestern culture. Molly was in awe of her natural beauty and appeared to be forming an immediate friendship with her. It was agreed Molly would stay with John and Isabella and Harry and Annie would sleep in Russell's spare bedroom. After everyone else had gone Harry and Russell remained by the fire talking. Annie quietly excused herself stating she was too tired to visit, but awoke later and realized it was after two when Harry finally came to bed.

Chapter 31

Early the next morning before Annie and Harry were up, Magda arrived to help with Russell's morning care. They could hear her bustling about as they lay in bed talking about the previous day. Harry shared some of the topics he and his father discussed and thanked Annie for helping to make their soulful reunion become a reality. Soon they could smell the delicious aroma coming from the kitchen and they joined Russell for a large breakfast that consisted of lightly fried corn tortillas sprinkled with longhorn cheese, onions and chili sauce and topped with a fried egg.

Magda's coffee was black and strong and as Russell concluded was "Guaranteed to put a spring into any weary traveler's step." He had added jokingly, "That is, if you are still lucky enough to have legs." Russell declined John's offer of a day of sightseeing saying all the excitement had worn him out and he planned to nap and maybe finish his painting later if he felt like it. They agreed to arrive back at seven to dine on one of Magda's special celebration feasts.

John Crow proved to be a wonderful guide showing them as much of the natural and cultural beauty he could fit into the day. The first stop was a visit to the Albuquerque Indian Pueblo Cultural Center that opened in August of 1976. He explained how it had dedicated itself to correcting misinformation about the Pueblo culture as well as protecting their history. Later, they toured the countryside and viewed sites of historical importance. John pointed out a Kiva with its ladder leading downward into its smoke hole, explaining the underground room was used for ceremonial functions and was considered the middle ground between the living and the spirits of their ancestors. He also explained how women in the Pueblo tradition held positions of power and authority giving them ownership of the cornfields, houses and the land. At the time of marriage it was also customary for the husband to join his wife's family rather than the other way around.

By the time they arrived at Isabella's gallery Annie wondered how she would be able to retain even a portion of all the fascinating historical information John had shared. Isabella welcomed her guests and pointed out paintings, jewelry, sculpture and pottery that reflected their rich southwestern culture. It was the first time they had an opportunity to see a collection of Russell's paintings and were immediately in awe of his talent. Several of his paintings depicted women warriors suggesting they were members of a small band of southern Apaches known as the Chiricahua who encouraged this role for women. Isabella explained in these tribes it was customary that the closest female relative of a slain warrior was expected to revenge his death. She was also expected to marry, bear children, keep camp and carry out the duties of traditional women's work. As they studied the faces of the proud women in each of the paintings they marveled at Russell's ability to capture their depth of courage and commitment of spirit.

Harry found himself feeling extremely proud of his father but had difficulty in expressing his feelings when Annie inquired about his impression of the paintings. Throughout all the years he wondered what kind of man his father might have been and of all the imaginary ones he invented none of them had even come close to the remarkable person Russell was.

When they arrived back at the adobe house it was again filled with the wonderful aroma of Magda's dinner. Russell sat in the living room looking rested and happy. His painting in progress sat untouched and John Crow teased him that a lot more napping must have occurred than painting. Magda had created a feast of roast turkey with chicken sausage stuffing, sweet potatoes and a huge salad. For dessert she served the traditional bread pudding known as capirotada and by the time they left the table no one could have eaten another bite. As they sat by the fireplace sipping coffee, Russell asked John Crow to bring out his painting of Mariah. As before, Harry found himself unable to speak as his childhood memories came flooding over him. He wiped the moisture from his eyes and after regaining control of his emotions, gratefully accepted Russell's offer of the painting of his mother as a gift but only after being assured his father would create another for himself.

A little before ten o'clock the conversation slowed and after praising and thanking Magda's for her delicious feast the visitors and hosts said good night. Earlier in the evening Annie called home to check on Jessie.

Martina answered and after assuring her all was well handed the phone to Jessie who spent the next ten minutes telling Annie about Thomas the cat, the tea party with Janet, Teenie and her dolls, how Teenie and Janet had bought her a new dress, and finally how Teenie had yelled at some man and called him a 'dum-imma-sol'. At that point Martina took back the phone and apologized for calling someone an imbecile and then explained while they were shopping a man had run a red light and almost hit their car. It was at that point those choice words accidentally slipped out. Annie giggled and told Martina not to worry that she was glad they were safe. Jessie took back the phone and Annie helped her say her night prayers and sent kisses and hugs over the phone before hanging up

Annie awoke early and quietly dressed without waking anyone and slipped out of the house. The phone call home had been comforting initially but now she realized how homesick she was for Jessie and their friends. Her thoughts turned to David and she wondered if his new medication was helping to reduce his headaches. She heard sounds from behind the house and following the fieldstone path found Sky working in the potter's shed Russell designed and built for her while she was still in high school. Since her grandmother spent much of her time helping Russell and Sophie, they felt it would be easier to have the shed where Magda could keep a watchful eye on her granddaughter. Russell agreed it was one way to have her near them and not running wild with her friends.

Sky waved a greeting as she continued to load the kiln located by the side of the shed and protected by a tile roof. "Good morning, Annie. You're up early after such a long day of sightseeing yesterday."

"Good morning, Skylar. How nice to see you out here. Yes, I'm surprised too. Last night when I went to bed I was so tired I thought I'd have to sleep until noon. I guess I'm used to waking early and this morning even with the time difference, my mind started working and I couldn't get back to sleep."

Sky closed the kiln door and checked the dials before turning it on and setting the timer. "I'm sure you miss your daughter"

"I can't believe how homesick I am for her. I miss her so much! It's the first time we've been apart since she came to live with us."

"I know what you mean. Whenever I have to leave Cody for any length of time I feel as if a part of myself is missing. Do you want to come into my laboratory and take a look at my new creations? Russell usually calls it my laboratory because I'm always experimenting with new techniques and glazes."

Annie was surprised to find the shed was larger on the inside than it appeared from its exterior. Lining the walls of the entrance area were rows of wood shelves displaying finished pots of various sizes and colors. Annie was awestruck by their beauty and craftsmanship.

"These are some of my better works. As we move back into the potting area you'll see some of my not so wonderful creations. The kiln-fired pottery was made using the techniques I learned in college. However, the work I'm most proud of are displayed separately over against that wall." She pointed to a row of wooden shelves that held several dozen pieces of extraordinarily beautiful pottery. Annie noted they were of a unique style with more delicate patterns and blends of wonderful colors.

"These are magnificent! I don't think I've ever seen anything quite so beautiful."

"Thank you. Your saying that means a lot to me. I hope other people will feel the same way. What makes this collection different is these were made using the traditional native pottery making techniques handed down through many generations. One of Russell's native artist friends has been helping me get back to my roots, as they frequently encourage our younger generations to do. He has taught me the knowledge and skill of how our ancestors created our traditional pottery. Since our people have been making pottery for over two thousand years it's logical that advanced and master potters would want to try to preserve and faithfully follow that tradition.

For these pots I dig my own clay that I find in certain fields and hillsides in the area. I gather the clay in the spring when it's moist and soft enough for me to harvest enough for the whole season. I grind small hard chunks into powder and add water and then knead it carefully with my hands to remove the small stones and other impurities. Then I add small pieces of ground up broken pots and mix it into the mud, forming the pot as I go. These are called shards and they help prevent the mold from cracking during the firing phase. They aren't fired and finished in a regular kiln. Instead, I use an outdoor fire fueled by manure. I use broken pots and corrugated tin in the fire to help focus the heat. In spite of all the care and precautions I use, the breakage rate is much greater than with the newer techniques and my loss rate is pretty high. Let me tell you, this is a labor of love."

They moved into the mudroom where a potter's wheel and stool sat along with counters and mixing areas. In all areas of the work shed Annie noticed how the natural light from the large ceiling and wall windows was used to the best advantage of the artist.

Sky continued, "Traditional Indian pottery is unique in that it's not usually formed on a wheel. We shape a base and then make the walls with coils of clay laid on very carefully by hand. The pot must be smooth and polished with stones and finally painted, etched or carved before it can be fired. For these I make my own paints from local plants and mineral powders and apply the paint with brushes made by chewing the end of a Yucca leaf until it forms a flexible fringe. Pretty cool, huh?" Sky grinned with pride and satisfaction and Annie reflected her approval, observing how deserving of praise she was for her accomplishments.

"They are truly remarkable! Do you enjoy the traditional way more than using the modern techniques you learned in college?"

"Oh, yes, much more, but finding a good teacher to apprentice under wasn't easy. It took Russell to make that happen. It shows again what kind of a remarkable man he is. Ready for a little history?"

Annie nodded affirmatively.

Native historians believe the first of the pioneering potters was a Hopi woman called Nampeyo and she is credited with reviving and adapting the patterns and shapes from ancient times. Some of the other famous potters that followed her inspiration were Maria Martinez of San Ildefonso and her husband Julian. In 1919 this couple developed what is now known as black-on-black pottery. They did this by smothering the fire with powdered manure during the firing process. This turned part of the pot shiny black and leaving other sections with a dull matte finish. Some other famous recent potters that use the native methods are SaraFina Tafoya, Rose Gonzales, Lucy Lewis and Marie Chino.

One of the artists who is also teaching me is Grace Sanchez. I absolutely adore her, but she's getting older and her health hasn't been the best. Right now, she's recovering from a slight heart attack but is expected to be back to teaching soon. I hope so because from the pile of broken pots over there you can see I'm still in need of a lot of instruction. At this time people who know the art world are saying Native American pottery is becoming an excellent investment. I'm not surprised, as after all, pottery is one of our oldest and most prized links to our past. I consider the pots on these shelves to be my best works so far and I would like you and Harry to have one. I hope you'll accept my offer to take a pot back with you as a gift from all of us." She smiled and for a moment Annie sensed she seemed a little unsure whether her offer would be accepted.

"That's very kind of you but you've put so much work into these, are you sure you really want to part with one of them?"

"I really do . . . that is, if you think they are good enough. I suppose you already have other marvelous works of art in your home?"

"Trust me, nothing as beautiful as your pottery."

"Thanks Annie, I don't think you're saying that just to make me feel good and I really appreciate it. Which one do you think you and your family might like?"

Annie took a couple of steps closer to the shelves and began examining a pot especially appealing to her.

Sky seemed a little embarrassed, so she continued, "Basically, there are three major designs. There are pots with figurines in white, buff, black, browns, red and orange design's, or polychromes like these on the top shelf. These styles are often produced by potters in the Acoma, Zuni, Cochiti, Santo Domingo, Jemez, Laguna, Zia or Hopi pueblos. Highly polished red or black pots with many etched or carved designs like the pots on the second row, are made by artists in the Santa Clara, San Ildefonso and San Juan pueblos. Then you'll see on the middle shelf examples of Micaceous pottery that contain tiny flecks of mica giving the pieces a faint sparkle. These are made by the potters in the Taos and Picuris pueblos. Sometimes artists in other areas decorate with mica as well. Of course, I'm still struggling to learn all of the various techniques."

Sky then pointed to a pot sitting on a ledge by itself, saying, "This is a rather good example of the Micaceous pottery. I think it's one of my favorites."

"That is absolutely gorgeous and if it would be alright with you maybe we'll pick that one, but I'd like Harry to see these first. He may prefer one of the more traditional Hopi pots and I'd like him to choose."

Magda rang the bell on the back porch indicating breakfast was being served and Annie and Sky headed toward the house.

The rest of the day passed quickly. Russell, Sky, Cody and Magna all reflected regret that the newest members of their family would be leaving early the next morning. John and Isabella Crow stopped by for a short visit and presented Molly with a silver Kokopelli Dancer pin, and Harry and Annie with a native quilt with a large mandela sewn into it. John promised to crate and ship the painting of Mariah, the quilt, and the pottery.

The following morning after tearful embraces and promises of another visit soon, they said their goodbyes. Cody stood slightly behind Skylar, shyly clutching her arm. His eyes then met Annie's and he slowly stepped toward her. He placed his small hand in hers and said, "Thank you for coming Natashka."

As the plane ascended into the clear blue southwestern sky everyone knew their lives would never be the same.

Chapter 32

Annie was back at work less than a week when she felt a need to ask David's advice about something that was troubling her. She tapped softly on his office door not wanting to disturb him in the event he was resting as she knew his headaches were becoming more severe. He immediately responded, and she was grateful to find him sitting at his desk going through a stack of mail. She was also relieved he appeared more rested and relaxed than when they first returned from their trip.

"Hi, David. Have you got a minute?"

"Yes, come in. I was just about to buzz you. I guess we still have that special connection."

He smiled and she felt less guilty about her reason for being there so she continued, "I think we'll always be connected, it seems no matter what happens we usually tend to be on the same wave length. Did you want to ask me about something in particular?"

"No, but by the look on your face I have the feeling there is something you want to ask me about."

"There is but it could take more than a few minutes. Are you sure you have the time? It could wait until later."

"No, go ahead." David reached over his desk and buzzed Janet, "Hold my calls for a bit." He sat back and folded his hands as was his habit when he was giving someone his full attention.

"This is a little difficult to explain. As you know, I've always had these vivid dreams, different than what I guess most people have, and I believe we decided it may have something to do with my ability to read people."

She paused as if searching for the most appropriate way to continue. "I'm not sure what to make of this but I've been having this reoccurring dream. I've had it almost every night since we arrived at Harry's dad's home in New Mexico. The theme is almost always the same with only a slight variation, until last night. I dream I'm walking on a path in a flower garden and it's a beautiful day. The sky is clear and blue and it's a very pleasant sensation. Each night the dream becomes a little more vivid to the point where I can actually feel the warmth of the sun and smell the flowers. As I walk farther on the path I see a gate on the edge of the garden until I'm standing in front of it and I stop to study it. It's obviously very old and it's covered with vines and flowers. The gate is charming and beautiful and yet I always awaken feeling I should have opened it and gone through, but I don't.

In last night's dream I'm standing in front of the gate as before, but all of a sudden it swings open by itself and I'm in front of a building with a door that has a very ornate brass door knocker in the shape of a human face. As I approach the door and I reach up to grasp the knocker I'm filled with a foreboding feeling, but I still rap and wait to enter even though I'm becoming extremely frightened. I begin thinking I should run away or else waken myself. Then, suddenly the door opens toward me and it's coming at me very quickly. I panic and raise my hand to stop it and instantly feel a terrible pain in my hand that burns so much it causes me to awaken."

Annie sat with her brow wrinkled and a pensive look on her face but didn't continue.

David leaned forward . . . "And?"

She looked at him and he could see the confusion in her face. "And this . . ." She held up her right hand and David could see several small blisters that had arisen on the inside of her distinctly reddened palm.

He took both of her hands into his and carefully studied the palm and fingers of her right hand, "You're quite sure you didn't have this when you went to bed?"

"No, not a trace. I'm absolutely sure of it."

He let out a low whistle. "Does it hurt?"

"A little, but it seems to be fading rather quickly. I think it scared me more than doing any real harm."

"What did Harry say?"

"I didn't tell him yet. He's still so high after meeting his dad I didn't want to spoil the memories for him by worrying about me."

Annie explained how Magda had looked into her hands and made a remark about seeing something unusual, but was unable to understand what was being said because the woman had spoken in her native language. "Do you think I made this up in my mind because of her comment? Kind of a psychosomatic wounding of myself"

"I don't know how to answer that because I've not heard anything like this happening to anyone."

"Leave it to me to come up with some weird thing like this."

David thought for a moment and continued to reflect on Annie's dream. "What do you think is beyond that door? Have you thought about that?"

"Yes, I have." Her normally pale complexion was even lighter than usual and as he studied her expression David knew she had already made up her mind.

"I'm quite sure the dream will not go away on it's own. I know I must inevitably have the courage to open that door and go inside. I guess I'm here because I wanted your opinion regarding how to prepare for it. What must I do to protect myself?"

When Annie emerged from David's office she seemed more relaxed and informed Janet she was going home to spend the rest of the day with her daughter. She invited Martina to join them for an afternoon of playing in the park. After dinner and a bedtime story Martina and Jessie went off to bed exhausted from their active day. Annie read for awhile, and after she was sure her family was asleep took a long cleansing soak in their whirlpool tub to which she added a cup of apple cider vinegar and a cup of sea salt. She rechecked Harry and found him to be sleeping soundly before she went downstairs and into the living room.

Lighting three candles she placed them at equidistant points creating a circle where she burned a small amount of sage to cleanse the area. She sprinkled the area she would be sitting in with holy water and placed a large upholstered pillow from the davenport in the center of the circle she had created with the candles. When she felt satisfied that all the preparations were in order she sat on the pillow in the lotus posture. Taking a series of deep, cleansing breaths she called upon the Holy Spirit to protect her from harm.

She began to visualize her seven chakras starting with the root chakra at the base of her spine, picturing a clear red color coming upward from the earth into her being and connecting her with the earth energy and all its inhabitants. She visualized the small wheel of the chakra whirling and swirling as it opened. From there she saw the red energy turn to orange as it entered the sacral plexus chakra. She visualized it moving up her body and the orange turning into a bright, clear yellow color as it entered her solar plexus, then green as it moved and stayed for several minutes in her heart area surrounding a pink rose. Slowly it transformed to blue as it gradually entered her throat chakra and became indigo as it entered her third eye area in the middle of her forehead. She allowed the indigo color to linger at the third eye for several minutes before gently visualizing the color melting into to a lavender hue as it entered the crown chakra at the top of her head. This allowed her to visualize herself opening herself to the power of the Holy Spirit and the universe as she silently asked for protection. In her mind the colors blended and all became a beautiful white light that gently flowed through her crown chakra and then downward to surround her aura, enveloping her with the energy of pure love.

Slowly she became aware of her surroundings as she heard the clock strike eleven. Thanking the divine creator of the universe for His protection she allowed herself a bit of time to reorient to her surroundings before attempting to move. As she rose to stand and began extinguishing the candles she realized her body was becoming older and how the stiffness of her joints was serving as a reminder.

She went up to bed and snuggled next to Harry feeling a sense of comfort and security she hadn't experienced for a long time. She slept soundly and dreamlessly through the entire night and as the following days and nights passed uneventfully she wondered if the entire episode had been the result of her overactive imagination. On several occasions during the week David inquired about the dream and she admitted it seemed to have gone away on its own. He smiled and cautioned her to continue surrounding herself with the protective healing light.

The following week Jessie complained of a sore throat and earache which seemed to worsen by morning. She had also developed a fever and was finding it difficult to swallow and speak. Because of her past history and hearing loss as a baby Annie decided to take her into the clinic for an evaluation. In spite of the antibiotics that were prescribed Jessie spiked an even higher temperature and the next day Diane Mandel decided she needed to be hospitalized as she was now on the verge of pneumonia and was becoming dehydrated.

Harry and Annie took turns staying with their daughter at the hospital. After the second day and night they learned David was not feeling well and Annie took over Jessie's hospital vigil so Harry could be at the office during the day. On the fourth day Jessie's temperature dropped back to normal and she was taking fluids and her appetite had returned. Dr. Mandel advised them if all remained well they could plan to take Jessie home the next day after lunch. That night Annie and Harry had their first undisturbed night of sleep in over a week. The next morning Harry arose early and whispered to Annie that he would check on Jessie from the office and she should sleep a while longer.

Shortly after Harry left the house Annie drifted back to sleep. In what seemed like only seconds she found herself standing before the open garden gate from her previous dreams. As she entered she saw the heavy door with the ornate brass knocker. She immediately felt the urge to waken herself but resisted the temptation remembering her commitment to find the meaning of her persistent dream. She reached up and took a firm hold on the brass handle and was surprised and relieved to find it was cool to her touch. For a brief moment she studied its unique design which was in the shape of a man's grinning face. The figure had horns and a pointy beard and it reminded her of Pan from her mythology studies.

Annie stepped back to allow the door to swing open and peered inside trying to get a clearer idea of what was in the room before she entered. To her surprise it was paneled with lovely dark wood and occupied by an older gentleman who was seated behind a large wooden desk. He didn't look up but made a gesture with his hand motioning to her to come in and sit down almost as if he'd been expecting her. Although she hadn't initially seen a chair in front of his desk she now noticed one and sat down. The man was writing intently in what appeared to be a ledger and ignored her presence, giving her an opportunity to study him as she waited for him to speak. He was old and wore a pair of wire rimmed glasses that rested on the end of his nose and in some ways reminded her of her mother's father, Adair Stattler, whom she had met only twice as a child.

Even to a child grandpa Adair seemed cold and arrogant. He was a distant, emotionless man who made it clear he wasn't fond of children, which still left an indelible and disdainful impression on her. The last time she saw him he was in his coffin at his funeral. She remembered that no one cried or appeared to miss him, not even her mother. Her thoughts of Adair were abruptly interrupted by a sarcastic voice.

"You certainly took your time getting here."

Annie was caught off guard by the tone of his voice and as he looked up she realized he was younger than her first impression and now seemed to remind her of her own father.

"Excuse me, sir . . . Where am I and who are you?"

The man stared at her through what now appeared to be horn rimmed glasses very much like the one's her father had worn when she was a teenager. He smiled and said in an amused voice, "Who would you like me to be?"

His remark confused Annie and she answered, "I'm not sure what you mean."

"Come now. You can't be that slow as to not grasp this situation." He sat back in his chair and touched the tips of his fingers together. "I can be anyone you want me to be. Who do you want me to be? I believe at first you thought I resembled your esteemed grandfather and then your own estranged father. Am I correct?"

"Yes, but . . ."

He cut her off, "But. But . . . Do you have any concept of how addle headed you sound? Perhaps you'd prefer someone else, say for instance . . ." He now resembled a much older man with long, flowing white hair and beard, very biblical in appearance. "You were expecting God, perhaps?"

His voice had taken on a mocking guttural tone and he spoke the word God as if it was spelled with a "w" in it.

She knew he was toying with her and she replied quietly, "No, not God. I wasn't expecting God."

He sighed audibly, "Well then, that's a relief. God is far too busy with wars and insurrections to be bothered with the likes of you." His features shifted back to that of a younger man with a more angular almost cruel appearance. "So we've come to an understanding then, have we not?" He didn't wait for an answer but continued, "You wish to know why you've been summoned here? I say to you, why not? Actually I find you quite dreary. Not at all my first choice but one doesn't always get his way in matters like this does one? 'Tis a dismal world you live in, is it not? Although you do have more backbone than I had initially thought, especially when I recall that unfortunate little episode back in high school. You haven't forgotten that have you? No, I thought not. You have a few hints of strengths but they're usually maudlin and befuddled. This feature, I might add, is not at all becoming to you."

The man looked up several feet above Annie's head and spoke in a tedious voice, "Yes, I'll be there in a moment. This is one of those untidy loose ends, hardly worth my time. Give me a few minutes."

Annie looked around to see who he was addressing but saw only empty space, for now even the structure of the room seemed to have disappeared.

"Now, let's see, where were we?" He began drumming his fingers on the desk and the sound grew louder and louder. Annie could feel the sound echoing in her head and she wished he would stop. The man peered at her intently, "Not unlike when you were a child, is it? Do you remember how your mother drummed her fingertips on the table while you ate your dinner? It was always when she was disappointed with you." He leaned forward and smugly confided, "You do know you were a terrible disappointment to your mother and father, don't you?"

"I suppose I was."

"You suppose you were? Now, that's a gross understatement! The truth is you were a disappointment to everyone. IS THIS NOT TRUE?" His last words were damning, biting and direct.

"I don't consider myself . . ."

"The truth is you don't consider anyone but yourself. You took the life of your unborn baby and now you have the audacity to feel you are qualified to raise someone else's brat! How selfishly presumptuous of you!"

Annie felt is if she was going to be sick so she took a deep breath. She remembered her previous discussion with David and with every ounce of strength she could muster she called upon the Holy Spirit to protect her. At that moment she was sure she saw the figure in front of her flinch. She spoke directly to him in a clear, strong voice, "Why am I here? Why did you bring me here?"

"Excuse me. Let me be perfectly clear about this. I didn't summon you. You came of your own volition because you were curious to see into the beyond. You felt you needed to see life on a grander scale. So now you don't like what you see? What a pity." He glared at her and turned his head slightly to the side with a look of total disgust on his face. "You mean nothing to me. Nothing! To me you are like vermin!"

Annie's spirit had been renewed and it was now her turn to peer at him. She was surprised to hear herself say, "Oh really? You say I'm nothing to you . . . and yet . . . Here I am taking up your precious time. I THINK NOT!" Her tone mimicked his earlier sarcasm.

The figure sat back in his chair and again pressed his fingertips together as he said in an amused voice, "Oh, my! What have we here? A mouse that roars? How typical of you humans, arrogant little rodents flexing your pathetic little egos."

Annie interrupted his caustic tirade. "If you despise humans as much as you say you do and find us so unimportant, why even bother with us? Why aren't you off conquering some other more advanced civilization? There must be other higher planes in this vast universe more worthy of your attention."

"Why indeed?" His voice was now even more sarcastic and his whole demeanor had taken on a slippery, whining quality like a snake about to encircle his victim before crushing it. "Why indeed? Do you know how many times I've asked myself that very question? You and all of humankind are pitifully stupid."

"You despise our stupidity?"

"No dear, you've missed the point completely." He stared at her over his glasses in a condescending manner and continued, "The two qualities I like best about humans are, number one, their stupidity or more aptly their gullibility . . . and number two, their excessive greed.

It's so . . ." He extended his hand out in front of himself as if examining a precious jewel . . . predictable. Humans are so completely predictable. It's almost boring. Of course, it's these two qualities we rely upon to accomplish our finest work. Have you not noticed how throughout history mankind consistently repeats its mistakes? Humans never learn from their past indiscretions."

He sneered and continued, "Oh, it's true that every hundred years or so we have to put a new spin on evil to keep things interesting, but regardless of what we do, you never learn. Take for example, how you chose to resolve your disagreements. Now that's where your predictability is like watching naughty children at play. In fact, this is one of your, and our, favorite pastimes. One on one, you figure out how to get even and you hurt, maim, or kill each other. Spread out the same behavior among countries and wars continue to be fought. You'll have to agree, every one of those little pitiful spats is a class act. Think back in history when pirates of yesteryear sailed the seven seas looting and plundering. Now we have modern day pirates but we call them CEO's and corporate raiders. Heroes and role models are no longer admired for how valiant they are but rather the size of their bank account or the size of their . . . ah . . . should we say their physical assets, or I might add, how creative their public relations firm is . . . Point of fact . . ." He snapped his fingers and a piece of paper with a familiar logo appeared. Do you recognize this? Of course you do, it's known all around the world. At first I assumed it was a big mistake. I thought the lemming might be more appropriate, but no, you humans have grown to love this symbol. The lowly leporid, and yet," he paused dramatically, "it succeeded in creating something titillating and risque for the masses to identify with. Something tangible, to allow them to feel virulent. An imaginary statement about their sexuality . . . or lack of it." He snorted in a most unbecoming manner. "It makes people feel they belong to some exclusive forbidden society and it gives them a feeling of power. Throw in a few hundred million dollars and willing celebrities, plenty of drugs, and a generous dose of silicone and you've created a legend.

Of course the timing was right and having a manifesto of human rights written by . . . Well, it doesn't matter who the charismatic fool was who wrote it, the main thrust is it gave everyone permission to live out their carnal desires and do what they want without those dreary burdensome moral concerns. And the part I really love best is, the hedonistic idea that as long as it doesn't hurt anyone else, it's all fine and good. I absolutely savor it! The inane idea that a human can stand alone with no sense of connection with others so they can pursue his or her darkest, most perverse behaviors and believe they aren't hurting anyone else. From my lips to his pen. I cannot wait to thank him personally.

Of course if a country is oppressed and the people are starving I then send them a revolutionary. Wasn't it Karl Marx who said in order to create a revolution you must have young people without morals? Well, it doesn't really matter who said it. In war, you can count on the fact that money is exchanged, power is shifted, hundreds, thousands or even millions are killed and new crop of temporary heroes have been created. It happens day after day, year after year, century after century. Do you see how predictably boring this has all become? Now, if a country is prosperous and times are good and people don't have to struggle, then we revert back to the Prince or Princess of hedonism. Give them plenty of money and glamour and let's not forget, the right public relations person, and we can sit back and let them rot from the inside like over ripened pomegranates. Oh, and that Prince or Princess of hedonism, be sure to give them feet of clay so they can be toppled more easily when society becomes bored with them.

Do you remember the old story, The Emperor's New Clothes? Everyone was perfectly happy in their fantasy world and the sly old master seamstress could have pulled off his scam if it hadn't been for that damnable child. Damn the children, you can count on them to tell the truth when everyone else is content to wallow in their mindless apathy."

Annie shifted uncomfortably in her chair and her adversary jumped up and pointed his finger directly in her face as he demanded, "Do I bore you, little girl?"

"No!" She found herself pushing backward into hardwood spindles of the chair as she stared into his piercing eyes.

"You humans say sin is the cause of all of mankind's ills. How convenient it is to pass the buck outside yourselves. You seem to forget that sin is a conscious choice, and greed, perversion, absence of love and all the rest are all conscious choices. So here we are talking about the honey filled trap of free will. We all want the right to choose our destiny yet all too often we fail to fully appreciate the natural consequences of our choices. That is until it is too late. So we blame others and whine that God has forsaken us.

He tapped his temple with his forefinger. "To put it as simply as I can, in the end it all comes down to gravity and balance. Gravity, because it's much easier to fall down than climb back up. Humans are basically lazy and self indulgent and even under the slightest stress they tend to fall down. Or better yet, they choose to lie down on purpose, to give up. Even someone as simple as you can surely understand that."

The figure moved around his desk and came even closer to Annie. She could smell his foul breath. "And, concerning balance, I must say it's comical to observe you humans try to stay in equilibrium. Watching you struggle to stay poised and not leaning too far in either direction . . . In here, I mean." He pointed to the middle of his chest. "You have no idea how discouraged we become when one of you has a temporary spark of courage to show some passion for goodness and attempts to stand up for your beliefs. Convictions. Now that's another story. Actually, it may surprise you to learn some of our finest moments have occurred through your religious zealots. Take for example, the inquisitions, the witch hunts, and the greatest irony of all, war and the belief that fighting eventually will create peace. We've seen dozens of absurd but highly entertaining battles where both sides rode off singing and praising God because they are equally convinced he's on their side. Now, those little comedies are like a Saturday afternoon matinee.

Most humans have taken the bait and deluded themselves by believing goodness is boring and evil has a forbidden sweetness that can delight and titillate the senses. That misconception is one of our most effective deceptions that have been so irresistibly and universally appealing. What you have yet to learn is only with great work does goodness bring sweetness, and our delightful and alluring games of evil can and will only bring you pain."

He smiled sweetly at Annie and made a benevolent gesture almost as if he was going to embrace her. Instead, he suddenly raised his arms menacingly showing his teeth as a predatory animal does when its about to attack. He made a hissing sound and for a second she thought she saw him stick out his forked tongue, wagging it mockingly with a jeering laugh. Annie shuddered and felt her body give an involuntary jerk as he turned his back on her and returned to his chair.

In the next instant his expression turned into a sinister sneer. "Do you understand, little mouse? You asked me why I bother with you. Can't you see? The diabolical thrill of it all, the unrelenting comedy of human errors sends chills up and down my spine. Humankind is undeniably skilled at turning something that was created to be good into something that's self-destructive. And, the biggest irony of all, they appear to delight in continuing to delude themselves."

Annie interrupted, "Why am I here?"

"You don't care for my dissertation on ethics and the reality of human nature? Well excuse me, I'm sorry I disappoint you." He appeared to pout.

"It's not that."

He slammed the ledger on the desk with such force that Annie was certain she saw sparks fly. "I told you, I did not summon you. Did you forget you came here of your own volition? I do not hold you against your selfish will. Get up and go!"

Annie looked down at her hands and closed her eyes.

"What . . . the . . . are you doing?" His voice was acrid and he spaced each word.

"I'm praying for guidance"

"Oh, for Chr . . ." He stood up and glared at Annie who quietly sat with her head bowed. Slowly she looked up at him and gently touched her forehead. With a sigh of relief she could feel her third eye had opened.

"This isn't about me at all is it? It's all about Jessie."

303

He continued to glare at her and his eyes glowed with piercing anger and contempt. "Give the child up! You will see she will bring you nothing but pain. Damn that child!"

"I love her and will never give her up." Her voice was strong and determined.

"Give her up!" His voice thundered and his ominous and threatening presence seemed to swell in size and ugliness. The air around them now seemed hot and stifling.

"No! I love her and you'll never get her from me. So help me God, I will protect her no matter what. Even if it means giving up my own life."

He glared at her and was about to pound on his desk again when Annie heard a familiar voice behind her. "She has accepted guardianship of the child. Give her what she came for." The voice was calm and clear and Annie turned to see her childhood friend who had appeared often in her previous dreams. The woman smiled and repeated in a firm voice, "You have no choice, give her what she came for." There was a swirling tension in the atmosphere that grew quickly as if all hell was about to break loose and in the next instant dead silence, as if they had entered the eye of a great storm. The male entity was gone and Annie found herself holding a small ivory box with a carving of a large cat on the top. Her friend smiled and beckoned to her as if the box was hers.

"The carving is a lynx which is symbolic of Jessie's animal spirit guide. She is already aware of him and calls him big Cha Cha. Go ahead and open it."

Annie carefully turned the tiny golden clasp and gently lifted the lid not knowing what to expect. The box appeared to contain only a small light that slowly lifted up and moved off into space as a butterfly would, freed of its captivity.

"There are eleven children in the circle now."

"I don't understand what happened. What was the light?"

"Jessie came from an ancient and noble lineage but because of a deadly rift in the family a great evil entered. Her mother was not prepared for her daughter's mission and because of painful circumstances in her life she became frightened and turned to drugs. She tried to be strong but gave into her fears. Because of the drugs her mother abused, Jessie suffered emotional trauma and a small part of her soul was snatched away leaving her vulnerable to the lower influences of the world. Part of your mission was to retrieve it back for her. She is now whole again." Her friend took the box from Annie's hand. "You may have trouble comprehending what I have told you, but I assure you it is all true. There are many like Jessie who need help retrieving a part of their soul that was lost by trauma or pain. This will be your new mission as well as protecting your daughter from the likes of him you just encountered. You need not worry, as you will receive guidance when you need it. I must go, may God be with you."

Annie was speechless as she watched her friend's image gradually fade from view. There was a feeling of aloneness and her body began to shudder gently in response to the emotional gravity of the situation. She glanced around making sure the menacing figure was gone. Slowly she felt herself being surrounded by a glowing white light that enveloped her entire being with unconditional love, a feeling she could only later describe as ecstasy.

She felt herself floating and come to a gentle stop. As she opened her eyes she gradually became aware she was in her own bed. The morning sunlight streamed in through the window and the clock on the bedside table said five minutes after nine. She yawned and lay quietly, remaining in a state of reflection about her strange dream. The phone rang breaking her reverie and as she picked up the receiver she heard Diane Mandel's voice. "Good morning, Annie. I hope you slept well. I have someone here who wants to talk to you."

"Hi, mama."

"Hello, sweetheart."

"I'm all good now, so can you come and get me?"

"Yes, I'll be there in a little while."

"Good."

She heard the phone clatter on the counter followed by Diane Mandel's voice.

"She's good to go, and wow, is she ever recovered. You can pick her up anytime after lunch. She's been burning up the halls and being Miss sociable with all the other kids."

"Thank you, Diane. We're so grateful. I'll be there shortly before noon."

Annie hung up the phone and looked at the palm of her right hand. It was completely healed except for one small star-shaped scar.

Chapter 33

David continued to feel ill but Annie and Harry had been so encouraged by his negative CT scan they didn't feel any immediate reason for alarm. On Wednesday morning when they arrived for work Janet waited until Harry left the building for a meeting at one of the plants. She caught Annie by the arm and told her David wanted to speak with her privately in his office. Janet then added in a very concerned voice, "Annie, he isn't looking well this morning. I think he might be sick. Really sick."

Annie knocked gently and when David didn't respond she entered his office and was alarmed that the room was dark and the blinds closed to keep out the sunlight. She tried to appear light hearted but as she proceeded into the room she felt her concerns growing. "Hi, David. Janet said you wanted to see me and now I find you sitting here in the dark. Is this a good time?"

"Yes, thank you for coming by. Please don't turn on the overhead light. The little one in the corner is fine. I need you to do something for me."

"Of course I will. Anything, just tell me what. Should I call Marty Rassmusson?"

"No, he can't help me. I need your expertise. This morning when I woke up I had the most terrible headache I've ever had and also realized my vision was blurred but I really don't believe it's the side effects of all the drugs I've been taking. There has to be something more. My vision seems some better but I feel sick all over."

"What can I do?"

"I want you to put your hands on my head and tell me what you see."

Annie was caught off guard by his request. "I don't think I could find anything because I've never done anything like that before. I'm not sure something like that is even possible. Marty said your CT scan was negative and a zillion dollar machine like that can do a much better job than I ever could."

"Annie . . ."

"That's dumb and I'd feel foolish. I can't do it."

"Annie." David's voice was firm, "I've never really asked you to do anything like this before but I need you to do this now. Please . . . it would mean a great deal to me. Worst case scenario is nothing will happen and I'd still get to feel your sweet hands on my head."

"This is insane. I admit, I can see some things about people but I'm not a doctor and I have no idea what I'd be looking for."

"So, that means you can be completely objective. You have no preconceived ideas about what you might find. Annie, I'm desperate. Please humor me."

"What if someone walks in on us? They'll think we've both gone over the edge."

"I've already told Janet we're not to be disturbed and I made sure Harry would be out of the office for most of the day, so you have nothing to worry about."

Annie took a deep breath and rubbed her palms together. At the same time she softly whispered a brief prayer remembering her dream friend's assurance that she would receive guidance when it was needed. As she put her hands on David's head she could feel the warmth of his scalp on the palms of her hands.

"That's not so bad, right?" David tried to keep his voice light.

"Shush, let me concentrate, I'm trying to center myself and I can't if you keep talking." Annie focused on clearing her mind and concentrated her thoughts on the inside of David's head as she stood silently with her hands lightly touching his forehead and back of his head. Slowly she moved her hands to the sides and he heard her sigh and whisper, "Okay . . . that seems okay . . . let's see . . . hmmm . . . that seems good . . . okay . . ." As she continued to move her hands slowly around his head she suddenly stopped and remained completely quiet as if focusing her concentration. David then heard her inhale quickly as her hands jerked slightly as if something unexpected had caught her off guard.

"Oh God, David! There is something. It's like a shadow, but it's behind something else so I can hardly see it. It's more like I can feel it and it's growing. It has small tendrils coming out of it and appears to be encroaching into the surrounding tissue."

She didn't move or speak and finally David said, "Are you alright? Answer me."

Annie's hands jerked again and fell away from his head. He turned to her and in the dim light he could see the color had drained from her face and she looked as if she was about to faint."

What is it?"

Annie shook her head as if coming out of a trance and as she dropped to her knees in front of David said in a quiet voice, "They need to repeat the CT scan or do an MRI as soon as possible. Something is not right in there."

By late afternoon Annie and David were sitting in Marty Rassmusson's office. He listened politely while Annie explained why she felt the scan needed to be repeated. He sighed and when he tried to dismiss her anxieties with his most scientific medical explanation she didn't back down. After seeing how earnest and insistent she was he finally gave in and ordered an MRI. David thanked him but interjected if he had refused they would have had no choice but to find another doctor who would perform the procedure. The MRI was scheduled for Friday afternoon at four o'clock.

Harry and Annie watched pensively through the glass observation window as David's body was gently being glided into the gantry of the huge machine. After what seemed like a very long time the technician announced the imaging had been completed.

David dressed and after what seemed like a long wait they sat looking through another observation window over the shoulders of Marty and a radiological oncologist plus two other men dressed in hospital scrubs. The overhead lights were out and they were peering intently at the MRI images that were mounted in sequence on the rows of glaring view boxes. They examined and reexamined the complicated trackings of the scan. After several minutes the radiologist removed a small hand lens from a drawer and placed it in front of his eye to further magnify a selected series of images he had placed directly in front of himself. After a moment of concentration he nodded to Marty and murmured, "It looks like she was right." The group of doctor's studied the findings as the radiologist pointed to a specific location on two of the images. The pensive group behind the glass partition watched as the overhead lights were turned back on and the view boxes went dark.

When Marty finally came out of the viewing room it was evident he was visibly shaken as he ushered them into a private office. He sat quietly at first and finally said, "I don't really know the best way to put this, but there is now evidence of a tumor growing deeply within the interior of David's brain. It's hidden so well we weren't able to see it on the CT scan even now when we go back and compare it to the MRI."

"Does it have little tendrils that are encroaching into the surrounding tissue?" Annie's voice sounded hollow.

Marty stared at her and said, "Yes, it does. You were right about that too." He went on to describe the exact location and type of tumor they suspected it to be and explained that because of its location the oncologists and radiologists agreed, surgery was not a viable option.

David sat silently, as did Annie and Harry. They glanced at each other and Harry held Annie's hand as Marty explained about the remaining options of radiation and chemotherapy. He pointed out while these interventions may be of some help in prolonging David's life by possibly two or three months, there was no real hope of a cure. He concluded by saying, "In other words, our best guess is you have maybe six to eight months left. I'm so sorry. I wish I could have a better prognosis for you. You may wish to consider going for a second opinion and I would understand that, but all of us who viewed your scan concur with the findings. This one is going to be pretty aggressive."

David stood up and shook hands with Marty. "Thank you. I want you to know I appreciate all you've done for me. I am quite satisfied you did your very best to help me."

Marty handed David a prescription and said, "It won't be easy for you as the tumor grows. I'll call you in a few days to talk about what additional symptoms you may experience in the coming months. This might not be the best time. You'll need some time to process all of this information. You may feel like you're in shock for a while, but slowly as the reality begins to sink in, I may be able to be of more help to you. I feel honored but humbled to have worked with you. You've been very understanding. Feel free to call me any time day or night."

Annie and Harry stood up to follow David as he prepared to leave. As Annie passed by Marty he asked her in a quiet voice, "How did you know . . . ?"

Annie smiled sadly and said, "It's kind of a long story and you probably wouldn't believe me anyway. Let's just say I made a lucky, unlucky guess."

Harry and Annie agreed with David it would be best to keep his illness confidential until he felt the appropriate time to tell his employees and friends. This would give him time to come to terms with the devastating news they had just received.

Chapter 34

Veronica and Michael continued to keep in touch but both were slowly coming to the conclusion they were not making any significant progress in their effort to unearth more information on Louis. Louis's office had been quiet except for routine business activities and in Veronica's estimation she had hit a blank wall. As she was about to hang up she added that Louis did have one call from the lawyer J.T. Blessing from his law firm on the west coast. "We haven't really heard from him since his little girl was kidnapped and murdered. I can't imagine how much pain he and his wife must be going through after losing their only child. The last news report said the young man responsible for her murder will probably plead insanity which would mean he would be sent back to a private hospital."

"I understand that's not exactly what Blessing is looking for is it?"

"No, not at all. He's pushing for the death penalty."

"Do you know what the call was about?"

"Nothing special. He was wondering if Louis had sent him a package and Louis said it had gone out and should arrive at his office this afternoon. He laughed and reminded him to be sure to send it back when he was finished with it. We send files and documents to him quite often so it sounded pretty normal. I'm sorry I couldn't come up with something more important and I hope you haven't given up on my case?"

"Don't worry about that. After my visit with Louis's aunt and grandmother in Phoenix I think you have every right to be concerned. As you know, David and I still want to know about his renewed interest in Mary Rose. I promise I'll keep looking."

David opened the morning newspaper as he ate his breakfast. During recent months his headaches had prevented him from doing much reading and now he only scanned the headlines and read things he felt might be important to him. He was about to lay the paper aside when an article caught his eye. There was a picture of a man standing by a small gravestone and the bold headline caption over the photo and story read: BLESSING SEEKS DEATH PENALTY FOR DAUGHTER'S KILLER.

David thought back as he remembered how several years ago the media had followed a different case of kidnapping and murder that ultimately had catapulted J.T. Blessing into the league of the big boy lawyers on the west coast. Despite the gory details and sensationalism he had successfully defended Lance Bennington, the twenty-year old son of famous movie director Gunner Grant. Grant was a Hollywood director known for his R and X rated movies filled with violence, nudity, explicit language and questionable ethics that invariably made him a huge amount of money at the box office. His son from a previous relationship had been accused of kidnapping and raping a six year-old girl. He killed the girl by cutting her throat and hanging her mutilated body from a tree in the Big Sur area.

Blessing's defense had been considered brilliant by many, playing on the sympathies of the jury by showing a young man who had been victimized throughout his life and who was much deserving of understanding and leniency. His mother was the former movie star, Lacey L'Amour, whose real name was Norma Bennington. He showed evidence that while she was raising him she had been a severe alcoholic and drug user and also provided testimony she had used mind altering substances at the time Lance was conceived, and during the entire time she had carried him. He argued while there was no denying his client had taken the little girl's life, he was the undeniable product of fetal alcohol syndrome.

He explained to the jury that by all standards his client had grown up in the lap of luxury, surrounded by all the extravagant trappings of his famous parents but because they were too busy with their careers he had been seriously neglected. He pointed out the child's parents had never married and his mother hadn't been sober enough to successfully guide him through his formative years. Blessing often referred to his client as a 'throw away child' who had become a 'seriously disturbed victim of circumstances'. When Lance was twelve his mother committed suicide and because he was unable to fit in with Gunner's new family he'd been sent to a private military school against his wishes. His behavior was such that no one could deal with his angry outbursts and he was quickly expelled. From there he'd been placed in various other schools and disciplinary programs for troubled youths.

After he was under suspicion for activities that involved cruelty to animals he was finally placed into a private psychiatric hospital. After a battery of tests and interviews he was released under state social services supervision even though his wide assortment of learned doctors couldn't establish a definitive diagnosis. In desperation Gunner tried to help his son by providing him with a variety of private psychotherapy sessions, but all efforts to help appeared to be more short term rather than the elusive long-term progress they had hoped for.

At age eighteen, Lance abandoned all formal education and became a serious student of the wicked ways of the world that included drugs, alcohol and endless parties. When the police arrested Lance and found the blood soaked clothing of the murdered child in the trunk of his car, Gunnar immediately consulted J.T. Blessing who was believed to be one of the finest defense lawyers in the San Francisco Bay area. At twenty years of age, the tall, lanky and ruggedly handsome Lance Bennington had placed his fate in the hands of Blessing to save himself from a life of imprisonment.

Attorney Blessing pointed out that at the time of the murder Lance was under the care of several prominent doctors and had recently been prescribed the drug Haldol. He also pointed out that Lance had been visiting his father's family at their home on the Big Sur when he ran out of his medication. Being unaware of the consequences of discontinuing the drug so abruptly he had apparently suffered a severe psychotic episode and committed the kidnapping and murder. Lance denied any recollection of committing the crime and therefore this was the reason he showed no apparent remorse. Blessing's defense was so convincing to the jury they deliberated for only five hours and forty-five minutes before reaching a verdict. To the horror of the six-year-old victim's parents Lance was found not guilty by reason of insanity and committed to a private psychiatric hospital rather than being sentenced to life imprisonment at a state penitentiary.

David remembered how the more liberal segment of the media hailed the outcome of the case as a victory for the mentally ill and J.T. Blessing became an overnight celebrity for his successful defense of an unfortunate psychotic who was a victim of his negative childhood experiences and the result of a deadly drug reaction. Many mental health professionals celebrated the case of an example of exemplary justice.

The publicity resulted in Blessing being interviewed on national television, and several afternoon talk shows depicted him as a hero courageously defending the interests of the emotionally disturbed and

313

mentally ill. He was lauded as a champion of the rights of misunderstood victims of child neglect who were accused of crimes they shouldn't be held responsible for. Almost immediately he was unable to accommodate all the prospective clients that now clamored for his services.

David scanned the rest of the article for more background on Lance Bennington. A little more than two years after Lance was committed to the private psychiatric hospital, through the influence of his wealthy father, the presiding judge authorized his transfer to a private clinic under the personal care of a prominent Austrian doctor by the name of Hava Hidelman. Dr. Hidelman was an internationally recognized authority on mental illnesses resulting from childhood emotional trauma and had a growing reputation for having claimed major breakthroughs in the clinical management of such disorders.

Two and a half years from the time Lance was put under Dr. Hidelman's care he was declared completely cured and was quietly released from the clinic. Somehow only the psychiatric world seemed aware of his release and in a small journal article they quoted Dr. Hidelman as assuring all concerned that Lance had been a model patient and was now well in every sense of the word and no longer posed a threat to society or himself. She had carefully documented his remarkable progress and planned to publish her findings in an upcoming book.

Less than three months after his release from Dr. Hidelman's clinic Lance Bennington was arrested for the kidnapping and murder of Blessing's four-year old daughter, Ashley.

Upon questioning, Lance freely admitted committing the crime expressing in a vindictive manner to reporters it was payback time and that J.T. Blessing had it coming for the shameful way he had treated him during his trial. He accused Blessing of convincing the press and the jury that he was nothing more than garbage, that he was insane and a throw away child, so he could gain fame and fortune while Lance rotted away in some stinking hospital.

From that time on J.T. Blessing was often quoted that he would not rest until Lance Bennington was put on death row and executed. The article continued with a statement made by the mother of the six-year old girl who had been Lance's first victim. "My heart goes out to the Blessing family for the loss of their daughter Ashley, as I understand the pain of losing a child to Lance Bennington. At the same time I cannot begin to comprehend the guilt Mr. Blessing must be feeling knowing it was he who was instrumental in releasing this evil young man and inadvertently allowing him to take revenge by killing his own daughter. May God have mercy on all of their souls." The article concluded stating Dr. Hava Hidelmen was unavailable for comment having returned to Austria due to poor health.

David laid the paper on his kitchen table and recalled a conversation he'd had with his father-in-law. The topic had been the responsibilities a person has in life and how each of us must ultimately accept the covenant of becoming our brother's keeper. Les believed each soul is so interlinked with every other soul, that no man stands alone in his behavior. He described passive participation as the concept that if you witness an act of violence such as a murder or a beating, and refuse to come to the aid of the victim, you become a passive participant. If you committed an act such as molesting a child and the child went on to become a molester, you passively participate in and share guilt of the harm done to each of his victims. This concept would also hold true if you were to project an idea such as racism or lewd behavior, or incited others to acts of violence. He described it as grossly irresponsible behavior, and even though society seems to somehow ignore the obvious responsibilities involved in assuming that role, the universe did not.

They had continued their conversation with a lively discussion as to how free will entered in, with David pointing out that every child who had been abused or molested still possessed the gift and responsibility of free will, and it would ultimately be their choice to continue or abandon the cycle. His father-in-law concluded by saying that even though from a contemporary legal perspective one couldn't be held accountable for every act of passive or irresponsible participation, karmically, no one could escape the infinite laws of a just universe. At the time David hadn't fully agreed with his father-in-law, especially regarding his views on the concept of karma, but now he was finally beginning to understand the significance.

Later that afternoon two young women sat in the library on the University of Minnesota campus. Stacks of law books covered the table as they researched information on a hypothetical legal case they had been assigned earlier in the day. The younger of the two got up from the table saying she needed a break. Her friend didn't speak but nodded acknowledgement she had heard her. Upon her return the girl held a copy of the Minneapolis Star and Tribune and scanned the paper as she nibbled on a breakfast bar. Suddenly, she sat up and pushed her long, dark hair out of her eyes. "Holy crap! Talk about creepy . . . You have to read this story, Zoey."

She slid the newspaper on top of the book that her friend Zoey Parker was extracting information from. "Not now, MiMi, maybe later. I don't have time to read it now. I've got to get this paper done before I go to work."

"No, really. Trust me. You have to read this story." She pointed to the photo with the headline caption BLESSING SEEKS DEATH PENALTY FOR DAUGHTER'S KILLER.

Zoey clutched the paper as she felt the blood drain from her face. "Oh my gosh!" She read the article in great detail and when she finished quietly said, "There is a God . . ."

The other girl looked intently at her friend, "What did you say?" Her voice had an incredulous tone.

Zoey reacted instantly as if she'd been caught saying something she didn't want anyone to know about. Her pale face colored and she stuttered in attempt to cover her embarrassment. "I said, "This is so very odd."

"I heard what you said the first time. You said there is a God, like you thought this Blessing guy had it coming. Zoey, the man lost his four-year old daughter for God's sake! He's a prominent lawyer and the creep psycho he defended took revenge on him by killing his daughter because the jerk off took offense at something his lawyer said in court to save him from going to prison. Think about it, that same thing could happen to either of us. We're going to be lawyers and you make it sound like you think . . ." She paused mid-sentence as she saw her friend burst into tears. Realizing her friend had been deeply affected by her critical remarks, she attempted to apologize. "I'm sorry, Zoey. I didn't mean to make you cry. Please don't. You don't even need to explain. Here, take my Kleenex. I'm so sorry for what I said. Why can't I ever keep my big mouth shut?" Now both girls were distressed, one for reasons she didn't wish to discuss and the other because she believed she may have hurt the feelings of the one true friend she admired more than anyone she had ever met.

Zoey pushed the newspaper away and gathered up her books saying, "I've got to go to work." As she looked into the confused eyes of her friend she said, "It's okay, MiMi, you didn't do anything. I just can't deal with this right now. I'll see you tomorrow."

Zoey Parker threw her books on the passenger side of the front seat of her beat up old Honda. She got into the car and sat quietly staring out the front window but her thoughts were racing back to her life five years before when she was a freshman at the University of California at Berkeley.

Young and impressionable, full of enthusiasm for life, she had come to sunny California straight off the farm from a little town in Iowa, looking for a good time. Those were the words J.T. Blessing used to describe her as she sat next to her lawyer. Her lawyer's name was Karen Dawes and they were in a meeting with Blessing discussing the fact that Zoey had been the victim of a date rape. She and two other young women had attended a party at one of the fraternity houses several days earlier. Dancing and partying was something Zoey had rarely done in high school because she had been too busy studying so she could earn a college scholarship.

She and her friends had been seated at a table having a beer when three guys came over and joined them. One of the young men asked Zoey to dance and when they returned to the table her friends were no longer there. She thought they may be dancing in another room or had gone to the rest room so she excused herself and went to the bathroom but didn't find either of them there. She came back to the table and visited with Ray, the young man she had danced with. The next thing she remembered was waking up in a dark corner behind one of the frat houses with her clothes torn and the distinct taste of blood in her mouth. It was then she became aware of the extreme pain she was feeling between her legs. She covered herself the best way she could and walked back to her dorm room where she showered and tried to clean herself up, and finally cried herself to sleep.

The next morning she skipped classes and went to a small nearby clinic she found listed in the student handbook. The doctor was kind and confirmed what she already knew, that she had been raped. He recommended she report the incident to the police and gave her a business card of a lawyer by the name of Karen Dawes who he felt might be able to help her.

Before she went to see the lawyer Zoey found Ray and confronted him. At first he denied knowing anything about the rape but finally admitted it had happened. He was adamant that he had no knowledge of the other two men's intentions and they had planned and executed the assault themselves. Just as he was admitting their involvement the other two men came over and began to question why she and Ray were together. One of them grabbed Zoey and pushed her roughly against the wall and threatened if she said anything to anyone she would seriously regret it.

Zoey sat sobbing alone for over an hour on a small grassy knoll behind her dormitory before she finally made up her mind to make an appointment with Karen Dawes. Karen explained that after the rape Zoey should have been examined immediately and reported the incident to the police but because Ray had admitted the rape they may have a chance to get him to confess again.

This was when Zoey met the illustrious J.T. Blessing for the first and only time. When he entered the conference room where she and Karen Dawes were waiting Zoey was impressed with his professional manner. He seemed kind and concerned and was very handsome. Blessing introduced himself and stated he was representing all three of the young men who were being wrongfully accused of rape. At first he was polite as he said, "You seem like a lovely young lady, away from home for the first time and without the watchful eye of your parents. I believe their names are George and Eve, and if my notes are correct they raised you in a good, strict, Lutheran family. Here you are in sunny California, young and impressionable, fresh off the farm in Iowa, and looking for a good time. It is important you understand there's no real evidence that anything happened to you as they seem to have misplaced the records at the clinic you went to, and the doctor said all he could really testify to was that you probably had relations with someone, but that it was inconclusive because you had showered and destroyed any clear evidence that might have remained.

The bottom line is, there is no real evidence of any kind that anything happened to you other than you had a good time. Maybe you drank a little too much, went outside with some guy or guys who got a little rougher with you than those Iowa farm boys do. The next morning when your Lutheran conscience started to kick in, you had second thoughts about what you had done and decided someone had to pay for your humiliation. I'm sorry, young lady, but it will not be my clients. These fine, upstanding young men are totally innocent of any wrong doing."

He paused and waited for her reaction and when she didn't speak, concluded with, "If you decide to press charges and go to trial, I promise you it will get very ugly. Think about George and Eve and their humiliation, and how your friends will shun you when they find out you've been making a false accusation. Is that what you really want?"

Karen responded with the fact that Ray, one of the three boys admitted to Zoey the rape had occurred. On hearing this, J.T. smiled, and informed them it was Zoey's word against the three of them. He reminded Karen, "With no records, no evidence and no witnesses you have nothing. Nada, zip, buttkiss. There are however, several young men on this campus who are willing to swear this young woman is known to be rather free with her body when she's been drinking. I assure you, to pursue this would not only be futile, but a very big mistake, and as you are aware Karen, I never lose a case."

J.T. paused and then smiled magnanimously before he continued, "However, I am prepared to offer you a generous compensation for your pain. You do understand this admits no guilt on the part of my clients, only that they wish to avoid an unpleasantness. There will however be a stipulation. You will never speak of this incident to anyone again. Please think about it."

Karen Dawes frowned as she listened to Blessing but Zoey remembered she found it difficult to comprehend what had just transpired. A pretty blonde woman knocked on the door and said, "Excuse me, I need to speak with you J.T."

Blessing excused himself politely and as he exited added, "Please think this over. My clients will need an answer when I get back. I'm due in court soon."

Karen Dawes took off her glasses and said, "That slippery son of a bitch! I heard he was slimy but this takes the cake. Did you catch his statement that the records at the clinic are gone? When I called for them two days ago they said there was a mix up but they would find them and get them to me that same day. Well, I'm still waiting. Now he tells me they don't exist. That bastard! I'd like to knock those arrogant white teeth down his lying throat" She placed her hand on Zoey's shoulder, "I hate to say this hon', but with J.T. Blessing running the show I don't think we really have a chance We're little and he's big in the legal world."

Zoey remembered how a wave of nausea had risen in her throat and she got up saying, "I think I have to vomit."

Karen led her down a winding hallway to a small private bathroom as she fought to keep from vomiting. She declined Karen's offer to come in with her as she already felt humiliated enough and didn't want to make it worse by having Karen see her hanging over the toilet. She remembered as she knelt before the toilet she realized how filthy it was and how awful it smelled, as if it hadn't been cleaned for a very long time. It struck her as ironic that educated and powerful people would even consider using such a filthy restroom but after meeting J.T. Blessing she concluded it was people like him who obviously made it that way. She lost the tiny breakfast she'd been able to force down and as she sat rocking back and forth on the cold marble floor she pounded on her leg shouting, "God damn it! God damn him!" In all her life she had never said anything like that before, but at that moment her rage was so great she honestly wished he would die. When she was sure she was over her nausea she got up and splashed her face with cold water. Drying her face with a paper towel she started walking back toward the room where Karen was waiting. Looking down the hall she momentarily became confused and realized she must have turned the wrong way and didn't know which room they had been in. She finally selected one, and looking in knew it wasn't the right one. She studied the hallway wishing she had paid more attention on her way to the bathroom. Selecting another she was about to let herself in when she heard the blonde woman's voice and then Blessing's. She froze with her hand still on the doorknob.

"Please see these are mailed ASAP. I believe I've signed everything I needed to. Thank you, dear."

"Don't you ever sign anything without reading it first? You don't trust me?"

"No, my dear, not even you. I make a practice of reading everything first, but I do thank you for bringing these over. I'm not sure how long I'll be tied up in court and these letters need to be sent out this morning. You have our plane tickets? Excellent! Tomorrow evening Celia and I will be sitting on the deck of a cruise ship sipping Margaritas and looking at the sunset over the beautiful blue Caribbean."

"I thought that was something you once told me you wanted to do with me instead of your wife."

"Don't be that way. I promised Celia first and anyway, she thinks it's time we have a baby, so we plan to be working on that assignment."

"Baby? Get real. Do you really want to have a kid?"

"Celia does. It will give her something to occupy her time, and she won't be so demanding of mine. To answer your question though, yes, I think it might be nice to have at least one child. As long as I don't have to take care of it. I've already got a full schedule."

"Then why don't you let me help you more? I can do a lot more than run a computer." She had emphasized the words 'a lot more', and Zoey couldn't help but notice her voice had taken on a more intimate tone.

"Maybe I'll take that under advisement when I get back. Right now I've got to get back to Karen Dawes and her sad little client."

Zoey was about to leave when she heard the woman ask, "So how is the ridiculous rape case going? I still can't believe you took that one on."

"I know, nothing more then a nuisance case, but it will pay for the cruise and anyway, I owed two of the kid's dads a favor. Karen Dawes is good but she has about as much chance of winning this as a snowball in hell. One of the boys foolishly admitted guilt to her client and he'd probably piss his pants if he had to be questioned in a courtroom. I have some of their friends who are willing to testify she sleeps around. There's no way these boys' daddies will let this go to court and ruin their precious namesakes' futures. As you know I can be malicious if I have to, and if Karen tries to press the issue the girl will lose and end up with her head spinning around faster than Linda Blair's in *The Exorcist*."

"Whatever J.T. Blessing wants, J.T. Blessing gets."

"That's right. Here, let me help you with those files and then I need to find a rest room."

By the time J.T. Blessing came back into the room Zoey and Karen agreed to accept the settlement. Three days later Zoey Parker was on a plane heading for Des Moines with a money order for twenty-five thousand dollars in her purse. It took almost two months for her to come out from her darkened bedroom and announce to her bewildered parents she was going to attend the University of Minnesota and become a lawyer who would work for women's rights and anyone else who was unable to fight the system.

As she started her car Zoey decided she would pray for the soul of Blessing's murdered daughter and his grieving wife, but he was definitely on his own.

Chapter 35

Michael arrived home about five in the afternoon. He expected to see Danny and Corey playing outside on such a nice day but they were nowhere around. Martha was standing by the stove putting the final touches on supper and Dixie lay by her feet. Michael kissed his wife on the cheek as she was checking the pork chops and stuffing in the oven and he couldn't help but notice an apple pie cooling on the counter. He lifted the lid on a large pot and saw his favorite vegetable dish, cauliflower and cheese as well as a small pan of baked yellow onions. He sampled one of her freshly baked chocolate cookies and said, "My goodness it smells wonderful in here. It looks like you've spent most of the afternoon in the kitchen. To what do we owe a delectable feast like this?"

Martha smiled, "We've all had a rough time these past few days and I thought we deserved some comfort food."

"Where are the boys? The house seems unusually quiet tonight." He accepted the cold beer Martha offered him.

"Danny's at a birthday party and Corey's due home soon. Why don't you go in the living room and sit down. There's something I need to talk to you about."

Michael paused in the doorway of the living room and noticed the old rust colored shag carpet had been vacuumed and spot cleaned. Everything was polished and dusted and there were fresh flowers on the center of the coffee table. "Just what is this something you're wanting to discuss with me? It must be pretty important for you to have gone through all this trouble. It's not Doreen again is it?"

"No, it's not Doreen. It has to do with the remodeling we've talked about." Noticing that Dixie was planning to plant herself in Michael's favorite chair, Martha caught her by the collar and continued, "Sit down, you must be exhausted. Anyway, I've been thinking now that Cory and Danny are living with us, it might be best if we postpone it."

"There's no reason to do that. We've been saving for a long time and there's more than enough money in the bank. I know you have your heart set on that dark green carpet with the pink roses, and you said yourself it's exactly what you've been looking for. If we wait too long you may not be able to find it again." He looked persuasively at his wife but he could see she had already made up her mind. He studied her hands as she sat wringing the kitchen towel and he continued, "It does seem a shame to let that money sit in the bank."

She smiled and said, "That's exactly what I was thinking, so I . . ."

The banging of the screen door interrupted their conversation, and Corey called out, "Hey, grandma and grandpa, I'm home. Boy, does it ever smell good in here." He entered the living room and when he saw the two of them said, "Is everything alright? You both look pretty serious. It's not about my ma is it? Now what's she done?"

Michael studied his grandson and smiled, "No, it's not about your mother. Come in here a minute, what's that silver I see in your mouth?"

"Yeah, isn't it cool? Grandma made an appointment for me to get my braces. I didn't think I'd ever be able to get them. Ma always found some excuse to put it off. Dr. Stock said if I'm patient and real careful it might be less than two years and I'll have a real Hollywood smile. Thanks, grandpa and grandma. You've made me very happy." Corey hugged Michael and then Martha. "Let's eat, I'm starving."

Martha looked over at her husband and gave him the look that still melted his heart after all the years he had known her. As he got up and followed his wife into the kitchen Michael said, "You don't know what a relief it is knowing we won't have to deal with the remodeling mess for awhile. On the other hand, I can't wait to sink my teeth into those pork chops and apple pie."

Later that evening Corey sat on the couch with Martha as she helped him with his math assignment and Danny and Dixie lay on the floor by Michael's feet. Corey looked up and said softly, "Thanks again, grandma. You'll never know how much I appreciate everything you have been doing for me and Danny. I wish we could live with you and grandpa forever."

"Well, Corey, I want you to know we love having you here with us too." Martha affectionately stroked her grandson's hair and marveled at the remarkable change in his attitude. The angry, belligerent young man who had just recently been taken out of his mother's home by the police was gone and she had her sweet, mild mannered grandson back.

The phone rang and Danny jumped up to answer it. His voice was soft but Martha could hear what he was saying. His answers were in monosyllables. "No. No. Yeah . . . and finally he said, "I gotta' go. Yeah, I'll get him." He held out the phone to Corey, "It's her. She says she needs to talk to you." Corey got up and took the phone from his brother. "What?" He listened for several minutes without speaking and finally said, "No. I gotta' go. Grandma is helping me with my math" He listened again and then said loudly, "Because, I don't want to!" He slammed the phone down hard and returned to the couch.

"Was that your mom?" Martha felt the need to get him to talk.

"Yeah."

"Is she okay?"

He looked up at her and said, "My mom is always okay. You know that. She just likes to bug everybody else and make them feel bad."

Martha sat quietly and after a moment said, "You didn't tell her about your braces?"

"I'm sorry, grandma. I don't want to be this way. No, I thought about it but I knew she would have said something to ruin it for me. She likes to do that . . . hurt other people and take all the good stuff and happiness out of their lives."

Martha felt her heart go out to Corey but she knew he was right. Doreen would have made some sarcastic comment to spoil his joy. She probably would have lashed out and accused her and Michael of trying to buy Corey and Danny's love so they could take them away from her. Then she would have started to cry and plead with Corey asking him how he could do this to her . . . as it was always about her. Corey needed braces for years but Doreen had always put it off. She needed a new couch, or a short vacation, or the drapes had to be replaced. There would be all hell to pay when she found out about the braces but Martha didn't care. They were on and they would stay on no matter how much Doreen protested. Martha hugged Corey and said, "Your mom will have to get used to your braces. I don't think she really means to be the way she is. Her doctor says she's sick." Martha's voice faltered.

"Don't feel bad, grandma, I know you did your best with her. You and grandpa are the two nicest people in the whole world. Maybe God gave her to you and grandpa because He knew you wouldn't give up on her no matter how terrible she was. Look at how good aunt Kathleen and

Thomas Michael turned out." He grinned, "two out of three ain't bad. Right?"

"No, I guess that's right. Two out of three isn't bad. You and Danny had better be getting to bed." She kissed them both and got up to turn down their beds.

After the boys were settled for the night, Michael helped himself to a second piece of apple pie. Martha sat on the arm of his old recliner, "You really don't mind that I used the decorating money without asking, do you?

"Martha, the look on that boy's face tonight was better than all the flowered carpeting in the world. Anyway, I'm making good money working on this investigation and with a little luck we should have enough to do the redecorating sooner than you might imagine."

Martha rubbed her foot over the rust colored shag carpet. "I kind of like this carpet. Thomas Michael helped me pick it out. Anyway, tomorrow there may be a vet bill for Dixie or new tennis shoes for our growing boys. We'll have to wait and see."

The following evening as Michael was about to turn on the news the phone rang. He heard Martha answer and then she appeared in the doorway, "Michael it's for you. It's Veronica and she seems pretty upset. She wants you to turn on Channel four."

"Yes, Veronica, what is it?"

"Do you have your television on?"

"No, I'm doing that now . . . Why?"

"Click on Channel four quick. It looks as if someone has granted J.T. Blessing his wish. Somebody assassinated Lance Bennington as they led him out of the courthouse. They said it was a single shot to the forehead. Probably a sniper."

"Holy Mother of God." Michael watched with a horrified fascination as the breaking news images on the screen showed people huddled around the lifeless body of Lance Bennington.

"I'd say that's pretty interesting wouldn't you?" Veronica's voice was tense. "Obviously from the way they're scrambling around they have no idea who might have done it."

"No, not a clue. It looks like the person who did the dirty deed was a true marksman. Did anything unusual happen at Louis's office today?"

"Not that I could tell. Business as usual."

"Veronica, I'm going to hang up so I can watch this. I think it could be important. I'll get back to you."

"Bye, Michael, call me if anything new happens."

As Michael watched the newscast unfold he became aware of a strange but disturbingly familiar sensation deep in his gut.

Chapter 36

The following morning David called Michael asking if he could stop at his office around nine as he had something important he needed to talk about. Michael brought up the subject of Lance Bennington's murder and David agreed it was a strange thing to have happened. Michael also mentioned how Veronica felt the fact that Lance had been shot by a sniper seemed a weird coincidence.

"What are you saying? Do you honestly believe there could be a connection between the two deaths?

"I don't know what I'm saying. Things just seem to be getting weirder and more tangled." After briefly discussing it more they agreed at this time it was too much of a stretch of the imagination that this murder would have any connection with Louis.

When Michael arrived at Sullivan Glass Janet brought him a cup of coffee and said there would be a short wait as David was in the middle of a call to his father-in-law but she felt it wouldn't be much longer. He commented on the engagement ring on her finger and congratulated her. It was obvious how much happier she seemed and his thoughts went immediately to Martha and the good life they shared. The possibility he might be putting their lives in danger bothered him. Later as he sat across from David he wondered if what they were doing would be worth their efforts.

David commented that Michael seemed to have a special knack for getting people to confide in him and probably that gift contributed to why he was such a good detective.

"You know the old saying, that you can catch more flies with honey than vinegar has some truth in it. I try to be as non-threatening and harmless as possible. People seem to respond to kindness better than a hard line approach. Only on rare occasions have I felt that threatening someone or using force has really helped."

"I'm glad to hear you say that because I have a job for you and it could become a little sensitive."

"Does it concern Louis?"

"No, this is personal and I know I can trust you to keep it in confidence at least for the time being. It's better too, if Janet, and Mary Rose and even Martha knows nothing about it. Harry and Annie are already aware of the situation but other than that no one here at the office knows. David paused for a moment and said, "I think it's probably become quite obvious that I've been having some health problems, mostly headaches. I really wasn't very concerned because I've always felt well and have tried to live a healthy lifestyle. I guess there's no easy way to say this so I'll cut right to the chase. I have a brain tumor. I'm dying, and I probably have less then a year to live, maybe closer to a half a year."

Michael was so stunned he didn't know how to respond. Finally, he leaned forward in the chair with his elbows resting on his knees and put his hands over his face. David could hear him taking a deep breath and then exhaling loudly before he spoke. "How could this have happened? You've always been the picture of health. I really can't believe it."

"I guess I felt the same way. I didn't see it coming. This is why I need your help."

Michael sat back in his chair and looked compassionately at his friend, "You name it and I'll do anything in my power to help in any earthly way possible."

"Good. I knew I could count on you. I'm reasonably positive I now know how this happened. I just got off the phone with my father-in-law and he agrees with me." David slowly explained about his MRI findings and how his father-in-law who is both a medical doctor and a homeopathic physician had suggested he go ahead and have a diagnostic procedure called Electro Acupuncture by Voll, or sometimes referred to as Electrodermal Screening. "He gave me the name of a doctor here in Minneapolis and I had my evaluation on Wednesday. Without getting too much into the technical aspects of this test, what they did was checked me for toxins or other factors that might have had a bearing on causing the tumor. The findings were pretty dramatic to say the least. Somehow it seems I have ingested or at least come in contact with herbicides, pesticides and a lot of other really toxic substances. Mercury being one of the more toxic ones."

Michael frowned and looked surprised but didn't speak.

"It had to have been something I had exposure to a relatively long time and I suspect it has to do with the little farm I own down by Faribault. Maybe you've heard Annie and Harry call it my Ponderosa. My suspicion is it's probably from the well water."

"Really? Did you have the water tested before you bought the place?"

"Technically, yes I did. In fact, I knew you'd be asking so I have the report of the water analysis from the public health department right here. See for yourself. You'll notice on the bottom where it concludes the water was safe for human consumption. To answer your next question, no, at that time I didn't personally have the water tested. I relied on the realtor who sold me the farm to have it done. That may have been my fatal mistake and that's where you come into the picture. The realtor's name is Delmar Fack and he works with Diamond Realty here in town. I need you to find him and figure out how this happened. The original owner of the property was Sven Ingvaldson."

As Michael got up to leave, David handed him another report, "You'll also be interested in seeing what I got in the mail yesterday. It's the new report on the analysis of the well water from the farm I sent in a week ago. Michael glanced at the document and only replied with a soft whistle.

As Michael drove back to his house he found himself becoming very angry with a man he had never met by the name of Delmar Fack.

Delmar Fack slammed his telephone receiver down so hard it bounced off the holder and flew across his desk and onto the floor. "God damn it! God damn it all to hell!" He threw the manila file he had been holding on the desk and saw the contents splay across it. Sitting back in his chair he brooded angrily. It should have been pretty damn clear to him that his whole day would be in the toilet when the friggin' highway patrolman pulled him over on his way into work and gave him a speeding ticket. He should have turned around and gone home and climbed back into bed, but no, he came into work hoping for the best, and now the whole day was going to be one big, rotten, super colossal disaster.

Dee Dee, a young blonde woman that occupied the desk next to Delmar's at Diamond Realty smiled her pseudo sweet smile and said, "What's the matter Fack? Women problems? Or did some shady little deal come back to bite you in the ass? It better not be business related or your hopelessly inept ass will be out of here so fast you'll have permanent skid marks on it. As you know, we don't tolerate screw ups in this office."

"Mind your own goddamn business," he growled.

"My guess, from the way the conversation was going, it had to do with business. Which by the way, I couldn't help but hearing since we are so very close." He knew she was talking about the proximity of their desks but she had paused at the right moment emphasizing the words we are, to make a joke about their intimacy or obvious lack thereof. She continued, "And, for your personal information sweetie, everything that goes on in this office is my business since, I don't need to remind you, I am the top salesperson." She turned to walk away but glanced back just in time to catch Delmar's obscene gesture directed at her.

"Why, Delmar, how unconscionably predictable of you. Well, fack you too, sugar. Didn't your mama ever tell you that little boys who do that to girls . . . When they die, their finger keeps sticking out of their grave and all the stray dogs and cats come by and pee on it?"

He could feel his neck redden as everyone else in the office was snickering and laughing as Dee Dee leaned over and added in a quieter voice but still loud enough for everyone to hear, "But then, according to your ex-wife, that finger is probably the biggest thing you've got to waggle at a woman."

Delmar ignored her sarcasm and opened the manila folder labeled Ingvaldson Property. He tried to gather up the contents, which were now strewn in every direction across his desk when he had slammed the folder down earlier.

He quickly glanced at the first several pages of copies of legal documents contained in the folder and announced abruptly, "I'll be back at two." His statement wasn't intended for anyone in particular as he pushed his chair back so hard it hit Ed Wick's desk behind him. The chair spun a half turn and tipped over as he went to exit the room. When he jerked the doorknob to open the door the knob came off in his hand. In his exasperation he was forced to endure the added humiliation of trying to fit the doorknob back onto its shaft and replace the screw that had fallen and rolled under a table. He got up from his hands and knees and gritted his teeth as he very slowly turned the screw with his fingernail. He then gingerly opened the door but not quite soon enough as Dee Dee added sweetly, "Hey Fack . . . You do know the bar next door doesn't open until noon? So, I guess we can reach you at home if some big financial emergency comes up, hmmm?"

Delmar was tempted to turn around and walk back to Dee Dee and slap her face but knew he was already on thin ice at work and couldn't risk any more trouble, especially after the phone call he'd just received. He bitterly remembered how, not long after Dee Dee had come to work at Diamond Realty, she referred to him as the Willie Loman of the real estate world. At first he thought she was paying him a compliment but his quick little burst of testosterone disappeared when Ed Wick explained who Willie Loman was, and he realized she was poking fun of him. Since then she insisted on making him the butt of her snotty little jokes and he wasn't sure how much longer he could take it.

He jumped into his rusted out red Pontiac convertible and tromped the accelerator so hard he felt gravel shooting out from under the tires and heard it splatter against the front of the building. His car fishtailed several times on his way out of the parking lot. Somehow, this show of power made him feel he'd made a statement to his co-workers. Once out on the freeway he kept glancing in the rearview mirror to be sure the highway patrol wasn't on his tail waiting to give him another ticket.

As he pulled into his driveway he failed to notice the unkempt yard and the bags of garbage sitting on the sagging porch of the small house he rented. He let himself in to face the total disarray that seemed to exemplify the state of his life and immediately poured himself a very large glass of bourbon. After greedily gulping it down he refilled his glass and sat on a sagging, orange and gold couch that was the only piece of furniture in the living room besides a large, ancient black and white television set. Only then did he allow himself to think about the phone call he had received from a man who had identified himself as Michael O'Grady.

At first the guy sounded friendly with his happy Irish brogue. He inquired about the availability of hobby farms, especially in the Faribault and Northfield areas. When Delmar mentioned two specific properties the caller expressed interest in learning more about them. At this point Delmar was becoming excited about a potential new lead, which he desperately needed to keep his job. Mr. O'Grady mentioned he had a friend, David Sullivan who owned a small hobby farm close to Faribault near a beautiful little lake.

Sitting on his couch in reflection Delmar realized at that point he had taken the bait like a hungry dog being offered a juicy bone. He had stepped right into it with both feet as he said, "You don't mean the old Ingvaldson farm do you?"

The man replied, "Why, yes, that name sounds familiar."

Delmar answered, "Well, what a coincidence. You're not going to believe this but I sold that place to your friend."

That's when the phone call had taken a slight turn to the left. Delmar knew then the man had hooked him and started to reel him in as he said, "Well, then I believe you're the man I need to talk to. My friend is thinking of putting the property up for sale and he did mention you might be the right person to handle the transaction since you're already familiar with the property."

Delmar began to reconsider his initial feelings of uneasiness and thought possibly lady luck had smiled on him and dropped a sale right into his lap. After all, he'd made a handsome commission on it before, more than enough money to pay off his ex-wife when she was threatening to take him to court. It was the next statement the caller made that caused him to have second thoughts. The man said, "I'm particularly interested in learning about the drinking water. I believe the property has its own well?"

Delmar hesitated before he answered, "Yes, I believe it does." It was at this time Delmar felt the need to point out the person who owns the adjacent property is an organic farmer who never uses any herbicides or harmful chemicals.

The caller said it was his understanding it was he, Delmar that had personally provided his friend with the results of the water analysis showing it was pure and safe for human consumption.

Delmar replied uneasily, "I could have. Hmmm. Let me think." There was a long pause while Delmar considered his options. "I believe I did send a sample in to the state to be tested myself. I sure did."

The man replied only that it all sounded very interesting and would he be able to meet with him at about two this afternoon? Somewhere in Del's disheveled brain a little alarm had gone off and he said, "That might be fine . . . Let me see . . ." as he pretended to check a non-existent appointment book. "Oh, no. I'm sorry. That's not going to work. I seem to be booked solid for the rest of the day . . . and for that matter it looks like my week is pretty much filled as well."

Delmar drained the glass as he muttered under his breath, "It was then the god damn worm had turned or . . . more appropriately the shit had hit the fan."

Upon learning his unavailability for the afternoon, the caller's voice changed and he said, "Well, then, Mr. Fack, I suggest if you know what's good for you, you'll un-book your afternoon. You'll cancel whatever it is you have scheduled for two o'clock and make yourself completely available to me." He paused and added ominously "Or you will really wish you had."

Del tried to protest but the man interrupted and said, "Don't even think about skipping out or I will hunt you down like a criminal because that's what I do best."

Delmar was now feeling the effect of the whisky as he sat in a slumped posture on his lumpy couch. He realized his career as a realtor had been less than notable. It was the last in a string of jobs that hadn't worked out. He'd been sober for over a month when he started at Diamond Realty and in the beginning he'd been moderately successful selling some smaller houses and commercial buildings that had been sitting vacant. His boss, George Diamond had provided encouragement and understanding confiding in Del that he too had a rough period in his life where he struggled to stay sober. He added with great pride in his voice that he had been in AA for over twenty years and would be happy to sponsor Del if he was interested. Delmar thanked him but politely declined his offer assuring Mr. Diamond he felt totally in control and there would be no need for AA. Throughout his life, as early as his teenage years, he couldn't imagine a life that didn't include alcohol. Hoping his estranged wife Melveena would see the change in him he'd worked hard to abstain and make his new job a success. That was until he met Melveena's new boyfriend Dennis, and they had sic'ed her lawyer on him for non-support and eventually threatened him with jail. After that, he had again taken refuge in the steady company of John Barley Corn.

About the time he was ready to admit defeat and leave town, an opportunity to sell the old Ingvaldson properly had unexpectedly landed in his lap. It was the last forty acres of the picturesque farmland that was left of Karl and Ida Ingvaldson's huge farm. It had been in the Ingvaldson family since Karl's father Sven, had immigrated from Sweden in 1901. In 1952, after Karl Sr.'s death the ownership was eventually passed to their sons Karl Jr. and John. John had already left the farm in 1953 leaving his older brother Karl to run it. Even though Karl Jr. was always considered to be a bit odd, he seemed to do fairly well on the farm without the supervision of his parents. As time passed, however, it became obvious to everyone in the area that he was rapidly deteriorating, both mentally and physically. As the story went, Karl Jr. had developed a running feud with his next door neighbor Emil Larson, who was a well-known and respected organic farmer. Karl learned he could get by with much less cultivation and crop rotation by using large amounts of herbicides, pesticides and commercial fertilizers. By the time Karl Jr. passed away from a heart attack at age sixty-seven, most of the buildings had fallen into such disrepair they were no longer useful for anything but kindling wood to fuel his wood stoves. Most of the farmland had been sold off earlier in various parcels to neighboring farmers wanting to expand their acreage. The forty acres that had been part of the original homestead had been retained by the remaining son, John Ingvaldson. In 1992 he had given Diamond Realty permission to sell the property but for many months no one had shown much interest in purchasing it.

About six months later George Diamond asked Delmar to clean up the property and to do whatever was necessary to make it presentable and hopefully more saleable. Delmar obtained permits to burn the main buildings which he did on a windless day in November when the weeds had frozen and a light dusting of snow had begun to cover the ground. He had puzzled over a building near the machine shed filled with rusty pails and fifty-five gallon drums of various substances and liquids. Thinking some of them might explode in a fire and not knowing what to do with them he decided the simplest solution would be to hire a friend with a front loader to dig a very large hole. Within an afternoon the tumbled down remains of the building and its contents were buried deeply out of sight. When the next snow came and with the ground frozen solid there was no evidence of a building ever having been there. Proud of his work he'd forgotten all about it until a few months later when he had the opportunity to sell the property.

The prospective owner asked him to check the well water on the property and he briefly thought about the rusting barrels he had buried the previous November. Afraid the sale might fall through and fearful he would lose his commission or worse get into trouble, he decided to send a sample of the neighbor's well water instead of water from the Ingvaldson farm. His reasoning at the time was it all came from the same general area didn't it?

At two o'clock sharp Michael O'Grady arrived at the Diamond Realty office and he and Delmar Fack were ushered into the private office of George Diamond. In less than twenty minutes with some skillful prodding, Michael had all the answers he needed. The story confirmed exactly what he'd learned from Emil Larson earlier in the day. Emil had talked about the shed containing Karl Jr.'s chemicals, some of which had been in storage there for more than a twenty years when pesticides and herbicides were much more potent and proportionately more dangerous. When Emil had questioned Delmar about how the chemicals had been disposed of he had been assured everything had been taken care of properly.

In truth, the contents of the shed had been buried in a location near the well that supplied the water for David's new little farmhouse. By the time Michael left the realty office Delmar had cried like a baby and promised he would not leave town under any circumstances. He also confirmed that no one in the realty office had been aware of his actions.

When Michael relayed the information to David he seemed relieved. For a few moments his friend seemed lost in thought and then turning his attention back to him had said, "Thank you, Michael. I guess now all we have to do is to get someone to clean up the area properly and see if we can get some help for our sad and misguided Mr. Delmar Fack. After all, he is one of God's children too." Michael puzzled over his friend's calm reaction and later that evening as he sat alone in his living room he found himself still feeling very angry and unsettled about the circumstances surrounding his day. Delmar might be one of God's children but Michael knew part of him wanted to take Delmar's scrawny little body and kick him into oblivion for what he had done. There was also another part of him that wanted to pity him for being such a pathetic, selfish loser. He wished he could have talked the whole situation over with Martha as she always had an amazing way of soothing him and putting things into their proper perspective, but he kept his promise to David and said nothing.

Sleep didn't come easy that night and at five o'clock the next morning Michael sat alone at their kitchen table thinking of David while nursing a cup of coffee and feeling very sad and lonely.

Chapter 37

David's phone rang at about six A.M. but he'd been awake for over an hour. Thoughts of what the next few months would bring into his life often invaded both his sleeping and waking hours. He answered the phone and was surprised to hear Sister Mary Rose's voice but instead of her usual cheery greeting she sounded upset as if she'd been crying. "Oh David, I'm so sorry to call at this hour but I need you to come and get me and drive me somewhere. I'm so upset I don't dare drive myself and I don't want to be alone. I just need someone with me."

David sat on the edge of the bed. "Mary Rose . . . what is it?"

"It's Jezzie. Oh dear lord, she's dead! She's been murdered!"

"Jezzie? Our Jezebel? That's incredible. Do you know what happened?"

"The police called. Someone killed her sometime last night. A jogger found her body about an hour ago by the little stream in the back of the park only a few blocks from here. The police are saying someone strangled her. That's all they would tell me so far. They want me to come down to the morgue and identify her body. I can't face this alone. Will you come? I don't know who else to turn to."

"I'll be there in about fifteen minutes."

David hung up the phone and tried to get his conversation with Mary Rose to sink in. Jezzie Smith . . . Jennifer Smith has been murdered. Who in the world would want to take her life, or more importantly, why? For a moment he felt the strange, almost surreal feeling when your mind doesn't want to accept something so foreign, that for a time it seems to detach and leave you in limbo. David remembered his tumor. Was he starting to get mixed signals? His thoughts ran through the conversation again and he came to the same awful conclusion. Jezzie Smith was dead. Perhaps there had been a terrible mistake. Mary Rose said they still needed her to identify the body and confirm it was really Jezzie. For now he wanted to believe the police were wrong.

Grabbing his jacket David left the house and was grateful the traffic was still light. By the time he reached Seaton House Mary Rose was standing outside on the porch. He could see she'd been crying and was holding a rosary in her hand. Her lips were moving as she prayed for Jezzie Smith's soul. She got into the car without speaking, still clutching her rosary tightly against her heart.

After she regained her composure she said, "Thank you, David. I didn't know who else to call. You've always been so good to us." Mary Rose pulled a slip of paper out of her purse. "Here's the address of the morgue where they are holding her body. I can't even start to imagine what this news will do to the rest of my girls. Jezzie had her faults but she was such a vibrant person and they all loved her. I'm not even sure I know how to contact her family."

"It will be alright, Mary Rose. I know how to find them. After Jezzie left here the first time she would call or drop me a note from time to time. She asked if I would call her if her mother or sister ever needed to reach her. For some reason, she always found it necessary to be on the move so it was hard to keep track of her. After a few years her calls and notes became less frequent and about a year ago I lost contact with her. That's why it was such a surprise to see her at Seaton House with you. Don't be concerned about contacting her family. I'll take care of it, if it's really her."

"I keep praying this is a mistake but they described her, and they also found her purse with her name in it. There was a note with the Seaton House phone number on it and a sizeable amount of money so they don't think it was a robbery. The police don't think she was raped either as she was fully clothed and there were no obvious signs of her being violated, but they said they will need to wait for the results of the coroner's examination before they can be sure. Ruling out the two most common reasons they can't seem to come up with another motive. The officer I spoke with said it seemed like a random killing. He asked if she might have been wearing any expensive jewelry and I told him I didn't think so. They believe it may have happened after dark, maybe around ten o'clock. This is probably the worst thing that could have happened to all of us and I wish I had paid more attention to when she came home at night. I guess I felt she was an adult so I didn't need to check on her. She had her own key and came and went as she pleased. Oh, dear God, who could have done this to

Jezzie?" Mary Rose broke down and started to cry again. When she finally regained control of herself she resumed praying the rosary and David was actually relieved because he had no answers for his friend.

As they viewed Jennifer Smith's lifeless body David felt a great heaviness and a painful ache that came from deep within his chest. It took all his strength not to break down. He knew this was about a young girl who had come into their lives at a time when she was a troubled teenager. For all practical purposes she seemed to have gotten her life back on track and now someone had abruptly and brutally taken it away. He stared at her blue tinged face, so young and pretty and at that instant he realized soon it would be his body lying on a similar cold table. He nodded affirmation of Jezzie's identity to the pathologist and turned away leaving the room without speaking a word.

After spending some additional time with Mary Rose he suggested she try to get some rest. He decided to take the day off and make the trip to Fergus Falls to bring the news of Jennifer's death to her mother and sister. The time alone allowed David to reflect on the many blessings he had experienced throughout his life and by the time he found the Smith's home he felt a strange sense of peace.

Jennifer's mother, Paula warmly welcomed David into her home. He was relieved to observe that she took the news quite calmly. He hugged her briefly and after she wiped the tears from her eyes admitted that in recent years she'd had a feeling Jennifer's life might end this way because of the way she had chosen to live it.

"It wasn't all her fault. As a youngster she was a good girl, but somewhere along the way things went wrong. After my husband Bill came back from the Viet Nam War he was so changed we didn't even know him. Before he left he and Jennifer were very close but when he returned we found the war had done terrible things to his mind. He had become paranoid, and for some reason we never understood, he seemed to focus his anger on Jennifer. Finally she couldn't take it any more and one morning we found she had run away. After we had Bill hospitalized at the Vet's hospital I tried to get her to come home but it was too late. After she tasted the excitement of the world outside of Fergus Falls had to offer she wasn't about to come back.

For a while I blamed the government for what happened to Bill, but of course they said it wasn't anyone's fault. After all, other men fought in the same war and they came home and lived normal lives. When Bill finally died I knew it was for the best because in some ways he was dead inside long before his body gave up. Now I feel at least indirectly, Jennifer is another victim of all of that foolishness. That's what most wars are about, just a bunch of foolishness to manipulate the economy. I'm sorry I sound so cynical. Thank you, for all you did for our daughter and for coming here today to tell us. The fact that you came in person means a lot to me. When my husband died we only got a phone call from some person we had never met and that was very hard to accept. It was so cold and impersonal. Bill gave all he had to his country by fighting in the war and yet when it resulted in him becoming mentally ill, it didn't really seem to mean that much to anyone but his immediate family."

David told her he would see that Jennifer's body would be brought back to Fergus Falls as soon as the police released it and before he left she gave him the name of the local funeral home he could contact. When he returned home he phoned the funeral home and made arrangements for the family to choose the casket and spray of flowers of their choice. He also requested they order two large bouquets of roses. On the roses one card was to read, 'In Loving Memory, from Sister Mary Rose and all of Jennifer's friends at Seaton House' and the other from him with the words, 'You are now at peace in God's hands.' Then David insisted and Paula finally agreed that all the bills would be sent to him.

During the next few days the police questioned everyone they felt may have had a connection to Jezzie but came up with nothing of significance. An examination of the body showed she had died of strangulation but otherwise had not been molested. All the police could provide regarding the identity of the killer was whoever committed this act of violence was physically very strong and Jezzie had died quickly before having a chance to offer resistance.

Two weeks after Jezzie's death Sister Mary Rose received a call from Officer Trevor MacElroy who told her they thought they had uncovered some information that could have a bearing on a motive for Jezzie Smith's murder. After checking with her previous employer in Las Vegas it was found she had done some creative bookkeeping shortly before she left town. Her employer wouldn't say how creative she had been but after extensive questioning they felt relatively assured he did not have any connection with her death in Minnesota. On further checking however, it was found that Jezzie's boyfriend who worked at the same casino had suffered a rather serious accident and was now in the hospital recovering from extensive injuries. When he was interviewed he denied anyone was responsible for his accident, swearing only that he had fallen asleep at the wheel of his car after working a late shift at the casino's blackjack tables. The officer went on to explain the Las Vegas detective who interviewed the boyfriend didn't completely believe his story and planned to check it out further. He concluded by saying, "We are considering the possibility someone may have followed Jezzie from Las Vegas to teach her a lesson. Who, we are not sure. It may have gotten out of hand resulting in her death, or as we stated before, it may have been a random murder that may never be explained. She may have been in the wrong place at the wrong time."

"Did you come up with anything from any of the people who use the park on a regular basis?"

"No, ma'am. There are some regular joggers, tennis and basketball players but none of them seem to be even remote possibilities. Like I said, maybe she was in the wrong place at the wrong time. You said she used to go out after dark to have a smoke. She may have strolled over to the park because it was such a nice evening and who knows, maybe she stumbled onto something she wasn't supposed to see."

"Officer, my girls here say there was a young man she used to flirt with . . ."

"Yes, we know. We've already checked him out. He was at work until midnight. We have about a dozen people who can vouch for him. Anyway, we don't think he's the type. We understand your concern and we won't give up until we find her killer."

"Thank you. You will call me if you hear anything, won't you?"

"Yes, Sister, I will. Good bye."

Michael called David to check in even though he had nothing new to report. The whole episode of Jezzie Smith's death had taken its emotional toll on everyone and Michael worried about his friend's already heavy burden. "Hi David. How are you taking all of this? It seems you've been given another extra load on top of an already devastating one."

"I'm alright. I try to keep busy by getting everything at work and in my personal life in order without arousing suspicions about what I'm facing. Harry and Annie have been a great help. I couldn't have better friends and I thank God for them. You too, Michael, and I mean that from the bottom of my heart."

"You still haven't told anyone at work then . . . or Mary Rose either?"

"No, I need more time to work with our attorneys on the creation of the Sullivan Charitable Foundation that I am planning that involves the disposition of some of the shares of our company. I think Mary Rose has all she can handle for now. Jezzie's death shocked her deeply and has affected her almost as if she had lost her own daughter. I guess some of the girls are having a really hard time too. Jezzie was a little flighty but she had a way of charming her way into people's lives and hearts. Mary Rose called to tell me that Ellen, the girl Jezzie shared a room with, is having an especially difficult time and asked if I would come by and try to talk to her. After the police interviewed her she was so upset they were afraid for her and her unborn baby."

"Martha said the same thing. She got to know Ellen quite well from the time she spends there and she said the girl hardly eats anything and just lies in bed crying. Personally, I still don't buy this random murder idea and maybe someone from Las Vegas did come to teach Jezzie a lesson. It's too early to talk about but maybe there's something else going on. Something everyone is probably overlooking. Just between you and me, I plan to do some poking around on my own. Good luck talking with Ellen."

"Thanks. I'll be sure to let you know if I learn anything."

Michael hung up the phone and sat quietly mulling over the events of the past few months. The question that continued to nag at him was why were all of these seemingly unconnected incidents happening at almost the same time?

Chapter 38

Martha waved goodbye to the boys as they left for school and picked up her purse and the pan of warm cinnamon rolls she had baked earlier that morning. Michael lowered his newspaper and raised his left eyebrow. "Am I to believe those wonderfully delicious looking concoctions are not going to be for us?

Martha patted her husband's shoulder, "Sorry dear, these are on their way to Seaton House. The girls are still terribly upset about Jezzie's murder and I thought this might help."

Michael smiled as he knew Martha often equated love and concern with gastric satisfaction. "How is Ellen doing?"

"She's still having a difficult time. She stays in bed crying and that certainly can't be good for her baby. She still has about a month to go before she delivers but hardly eats anything and if she isn't careful she could go into premature labor. Mary Rose had David try to talk to her but I'm not sure if it actually helped. Maybe it did for awhile but yesterday the police stopped by to ask her a few more questions and when they left she started crying again. They've tried to be kind when they question her, but I don't think they realize how fragile she is at this time."

Michael pushed his chair back and said, "How about if I give it a try? I'll be careful not to upset her more than she already is. I think there may be a possibility the reason she continues to be so upset is that she knows something but is afraid to come forward. Don't you think it's possible Jezzie may have shared something with her that may have a bearing on her murder? You know how close roommates can become."

Martha studied her husband and was struck by how his mind worked. His years of police work had honed his sense of logic but had not damaged his compassion for others. She held him in a special place in her heart and because he was her husband she knew she had an emotional bias. In spite of that she earnestly believed him to be the finest man she had ever known and the only man she had ever loved. "To anyone else I would say no, but I'm sure you'll be gentle with her. I'm starting to think you could be right about the fact that she knows more about this whole thing than she's willing to tell the police."

"Run it by Mary Rose, but leave out the part that she could possibly know more than she's saying. It's only a hunch and I think it would only make Mary Rose anxious for the girl's safety. In the meantime I'll give David a call and get his thoughts on Ellen. If Sister and you agree it's all right I'll be over in about an hour. You can give me a call with a yea or a nay."

A little over an hour later Michael tapped on the half opened door to Ellen's room. He could see her lying on the bed with her face to the wall and her body covered with a pale blue bedspread. One of Martha's cinnamon rolls and a glass of milk sat untouched on her bedside table. With Jezzie gone the single bed next to hers was made up and ready for the next young woman who would occupy it.

Michael gently tapped on the door again and stepped halfway inside the room. "Ellen, may I come in?" There was no response from the girl so he paused thinking she may be asleep. In a slightly louder voice he continued, "I'm sorry to bother you . . . it's me, Michael O'Grady. I'm Martha's husband. He saw her head move slightly in acknowledgement that she'd heard. "May I speak with you for a few minutes? I know this is a really difficult time for you, losing someone you had become so fond of. We all cared about Jezzie. She was a remarkable young woman." When she didn't respond Michael continued, "You're probably aware of the fact we are all very concerned about you and your baby. Trust me when I tell you I've seen a lot of grief in this mean old world and regardless of how tough it can be, somehow by the grace of God, eventually it always gets better. I know at this time you probably believe you'll never get over Jezzie's death but the pain will lessen and soon you'll remember all the good times you shared with her. I don't know if Martha ever told you but our son Thomas Michael was murdered. At the time I felt like I wanted to die but slowly came to realize he would have wanted us to go on with our lives. It took a while but gradually, when we would think of him we were able to focus on the good times we'd shared together. Looking back now we realize one of the things that seemed to help the most was when the man who killed our son was caught and punished. I think it was very important for our family to know that he would never hurt anyone else's child. Have you thought about how important it is that the person who did this to your friend must be stopped from doing this to anyone else? The other girls at Seaton House and anyone else who might come in contact with this person deserve to be protected from him. Please, Ellen, may I come in?"

The girl nodded slightly and then struggled to sit up pulling the bedspread tightly around her swollen body. "Yes, it's okay." Her voice was weak and she was congested from crying. Michael entered the room as the girl tried to blow her nose. Her bed and the floor around her were littered with used tissues. After she blew her nose and wiped her puffy eyes she wrapped her arms around herself in an unconscious attempt to protect herself and her unborn baby from what might be coming. Michael sat on the chair next to her bed but made no effort to provide a reassuring touch as her body language indicated she wanted to be left alone.

"I'm wondering if I could ask you a few questions about the night Jezzie died. I know you've already told the police everything you remember but there are a couple things I was hoping you could help me clarify. I would be grateful for your doing this so I can better understand what might have happened to our friend that night."

"Okay . . ." Ellen's voice indicated her reluctance as she paused, and then looked directly into Michael's eyes. Feeling his concern she slowly began to share her story. "The night before Jezzie was killed, Sister had gone to a meeting and was going to be late so Jezzie was looking after everyone."

"You and Jezzie went to pick up pizza at about eight-thirty from Pa Pa's Pizza?"

"Yes . . ."

"You got back here about nine-thirty or so."

"Yes, that's right."

"PaPa's Pizza isn't that far from here so I find myself wondering why it took so long to get back?"

The girl looked away and finally said, "I told the police there was a mix up on the order so we had to wait for it, and also the traffic was bad."

"Okay, but one of the girls, I think her name is Sally, said the pizza was cold and Jezzie had to reheat it."

The girl continued to look away, "The traffic was bad and uh . . . it just took a long time." Her voice trailed off.

"Ellen, the young man at the pizza place that waited on you said you and Jezzie picked up the pizza at exactly eight-thirty. According to his recall there was no mix up in the order. He said he remembered Jezzie because she seemed to be flirting with him and had talked him into giving you a free order of bread sticks. I have two questions and then I'll leave you alone. One is why did it take you over an hour to get back here and the other is what happened to the order of bread sticks? None of the girls remember having bread sticks."

Ellen looked up at Michael and then hung her head.

"Please talk to me Ellen. These may seem like little things but maybe they could help find the person who murdered Jezzie."

Ellen looked pleadingly at Michael and finally said, "She made me promise not to tell."

Michael tried not to show his impatience, but was encouraged by his progress. "Let's start with the bread sticks. What happened to them?"

"I ate them."

"On the way back?"

"No, while I sat in the car waiting for her to come back."

"Come back from where?"

"I'm not really sure. It was very dark and I don't know my way around here at all, not even in the daytime. I'm from Minot, North Dakota and I haven't the slightest idea where we were."

"That's alright Ellen. Take your time. You're doing fine. Let's go back to the time you left Pa Pa's Pizza. When you left the parking lot which way did you go?"

"As Jezzie started to pull out into the street she spotted Philip Johnson's car drive by. He's the guy who plays tennis and jogs in the park where she was killed. The park is down the street from here and that's where she met him. He's real cute and Jezzie was always flirting with him. He's polite and nice to us but I don't think he was interested in Jezzie. That didn't stop her from trying to get him to pay attention to her."

Ellen shifted her weight and sat more upright against the headboard of the bed. She lightly blew her nose again, keeping the tissue in her hand. "Anyway, as she pulled out she decided to follow him. I told her not to but she said it would be fine and she wanted to talk to him. It had something to do with one day when we were visiting with him in the park. I remember she asked him if he had been in Las Vegas earlier in the year. He told her no, he had never been in Vegas. She told me she was sure she saw him at the casino where she worked, and now she was really curious about him because he didn't seem like the type of guy that would be lying about something like that. We followed him to a place outside of town. All I remember was there were a lot of big trucks parked everywhere. She stopped far enough away so Philip wouldn't see her car and she told me to stay put while she got out to spy on him. That's when I ate the bread sticks. I was really hungry and I had no idea what she was doing. Besides, I was scared"

"How long was Jezzie gone?"

"I don't know, maybe five or ten minutes. I can't really remember but when she came back she was very excited. At first she didn't say very much only that she remembered more about when she'd seen Philip in Las Vegas and made me promise not to tell anyone we had followed him. That's when she said to say there was a mix-up in the orders and the traffic was bad if anyone asked what took us so long. I feel terrible. She made me promise and now I feel guilty I'm not keeping my word to her. I know she really cared about me and we had become close friends so I didn't want to betray her. After we got back we ate the pizza and then came up here to our room. That's when she gave me this." Ellen reached into the small drawer of her bedside table and took out a small packet of wrapping tissue. She carefully unfolded it and held up a gold locket and chain. She opened it and held it out for Michael to see. "She told me to keep a picture of my baby in it. I'm giving it up for adoption and this way I'll always have a picture of my baby close to my heart. Did you know Jezzie had a baby here a few years ago? It was a little boy. She had a locket with his picture in that she wore all the time. Her little boy is the reason she recently came back to Seaton House. She wanted to look through the records and find out who adopted him. She was able to find the couple's name and as it turned out, they're living right here in Minneapolis. I don't know how she figured out how to recognize him but one day she got to see him after his mother dropped him off at daycare. That was another secret we had. Jezzie had a lot of secrets. Her plan was to come here and find her son and when her boyfriend came with all this money he was going to have, they were going to take the little boy and move to Paris. I know that would be against the law but she wanted him so much. It's the main reason I haven't told anyone, especially the police.

When Jezzie found out her boyfriend had been beaten up and was in the hospital because some guys found out they had taken money from the casino where they worked, she said she needed to get her hands on some quick cash so she could take her little boy and leave the country. And, there's something else . . . Sister doesn't know this but she had another small room somewhere else. I think it's at some little motel and this is where she kept her luggage and other stuff. Everything she didn't want Sister to know about. I think it was like the Haven Inn or Leisure Inn. I don't remember for sure. All I know is it's not far from here, maybe a mile and a half."

"Can you tell me about what she found when she spied on Philip Johnson?"

Ellen held out the locket. "Here, you take this and send it to her mother or her sister. I don't feel I should keep it after breaking my promises to her." Michael took the locket from her.

"Jezzie said when she peeked into the window of the building he was talking to an older guy behind a desk. She saw the man had a thick wad of money and he showed it to Philip and then put it into an envelope. He handed the envelope to Philip and they exchanged a few words before he started heading for the door. When she saw him leaving she ran back to our car and we drove away before either of them could see us. She was excited because she was positive she knew where she had seen him before. One night when she was at work at the casino she saw her boss with another man she didn't know, and Philip with them in her boss's office. She couldn't hear what they were saying because at the time she was talking on the phone in an office across the hall, but saw the man she didn't know give Philip an envelope full of money, just like this man did. She didn't know why they gave him all that money back then, or what was going on now, but she was pretty sure Philip would be willing to share some of it with her just to keep her quiet."

"Blackmail?"

"I don't think that was what she meant but now looking back I guess it might be considered that."

"Did Jezzie tell you who the man was that Philip met with that night?"

Ellen hesitated and said, "Oh, Mr. O'Grady, I'm so afraid this is going to get me in trouble. This is all so very confusing."

Michael smiled slightly and assured Ellen she had nothing to fear and promised to look after her.

She reached back into the drawer of her bedside table and pulled out a picture and handed it to him. Jezzie swiped this from Sister's office when she was supposed to be doing bookkeeping."

Michael held it up to the light and studied it closely. It was a picture of Sister Mary Rose, Louis, David, and two other people Michael didn't recognize.

Ellen pointed to the picture. "It was this guy." Her finger rested on Louis's face. "You know, the one who has been helping Sister get a new car and fix the heating and other stuff. At first I didn't believe Jezzie when she told me but she insisted it was him. She kept saying that people who put on a good show of being all proper and good aren't always what they seem on the surface. I tried to get her to forget about it but the next day she found Philip's telephone number and called him and asked him to meet with her."

"What time did she call him?"

"I know it was around noon because I was watching *Days of Our Lives.*"

"And you're sure she called his apartment and not his place of work?"

"I'm positive. Jezzie said she was going to meet him at about nine thirty that evening in the far end of the park. That's all I know. She never came back."

"You didn't tell any of this to the police?"

"No, I was too afraid, and besides, I promised her I wouldn't. Anyway, the police said Philip was at work from ten that morning until midnight. The electronics store he worked at had some kind of a Midnight Madness sale promotion going on. There were tons of people who said he was there all day . . . so who would believe my story? All I knew was what Jezzie told me."

What color car did Philip drive the night you and Jezzie saw him?"

"That was another strange thing I was confused about because even though it was dark I was pretty sure his car was black but later I found out his car is dark blue." Ellen's baby kicked and she turned to sit on the edge of the bed. "I'm sorry, but you'll have to excuse me. I'm afraid I have to go to the bathroom."

"Thank you, Ellen. You've been very helpful. Perhaps even more than you know. I'm not sure what all this means but I want you to know none of it was your fault so you must not blame yourself. I think you'll be greatly relieved to have shared this information with me. For now, what you've shared is between you and me. You've given me some important leads to follow up on and I promise you I will. It's important for you to be at peace about this and concentrate on having a healthy baby. Relax, enjoy your food, get some sleep and leave the rest up to me." Michael handed the locket back to Ellen, "I know Jezzie would want you to keep this." As she awkwardly lowered her feet to the floor to go to the bathroom Michael was pleased to see Ellen eyeing the cinnamon roll with renewed interest.

As Michael left Seaton House he tried to make sense of what Ellen had told him. There was no doubt in his mind she really believed she was telling the truth but he wondered if she could be mistaken. He knew it was common for witnesses to be wrong and be susceptible to believing what they imagined they had seen or heard. In the end he concluded she would have no reason whatsoever to intentionally mislead him.

Michael had seen Philip Johnson and met his parents and had to agree with the police's conclusion that he didn't appear to be the type of person that would lie or be involved in criminal activity, and certainly not commit a murder. But then from what he'd read neither did Ted Bundy and a whole lot of other creeps who had once been altar boys.

Philip was tall, blonde, athletic, and appeared extremely sincere when questioned by the police. According to the homicide detective he answered every question completely and without hesitation, all the time looking directly at him. He didn't hesitate in the slightest when asked if it became necessary, would he be willing to take a lie detector test. There were at least ten co-workers willing to testify that because of their big promotional sale, he had never left the electronics store from ten in the morning until after midnight. Michael pondered over all the information and reflected that if the sale was successful and the store always crowded, he could have gone into the bathroom and perhaps slipped out the back and not be missed for a half hour or more. Phillip seemed so likable it would be realistic to consider his buddies at work would probably cover for him. He also had very strong hands, the hands of a tennis player, hands that could have easily strangled the life out of Jezzie Smith.

Philip's parents, Ralph and Cordelia Johnson were also cooperative when Michael visited with them while waiting for their son to be questioned at the police station. Ralph did most of the talking while Cordelia stood quietly crying into her handkerchief giving herself a bedraggled mouse-like appearance. When addressed directly however, she seemed nervous and high-strung, but still came off as a warm and caring person.

The part of Ellen's story that intrigued Michael the most was Philip had supposedly met with Louis and seemed to be doing some kind of business transaction that caused Louis to give him a sizable amount of cash. There was also the incident in Las Vegas where Jezzie claimed to have seen someone give Philip cash. Michael couldn't help wonder what kind of work Philip Johnson was doing for individuals away from his regular work that involved large sums of money.

Michael entered David's office and found him sitting at his desk but facing the window staring out at the skyline. He turned and greeted him and Michael never ceased to marvel how his friend always seemed serene even in the face of what was happening in his life.

Michael shared with David about his visit with Ellen and his feelings about Philip Johnson and his parents. He intentionally saved the most interesting part he learned from Ellen concerning Louis's transaction with Phillip for the last. After Michael mentioned that Ellen pointed out Louis's picture in the photo, David leaned back in his chair and said in a low voice, "Bingo. Maybe there is a connection."

After the initial flow of adrenaline and shared amazement, they both came to the same conclusion . . . Ellen's story, as remarkable as it seemed, simply would not stand up to what the police were saying. They both hoped her emotional state might take a positive turn since her visit with Michael realizing that this alone was as important as anything else, at least for the time being. For now they agreed to remain silent about what she'd said.

David thanked his visitor and as Michael got up to leave their eyes met and he sat back down. Michael realized he couldn't leave it alone and he back-pedaled by saying, "Why on earth would Ellen pick Louis out of a photo and why in God's name would he be meeting in some out of the way place with Philip Johnson? When you think of it though, Ellen said the place had a lot of big trucks parked around . . . and there's no way she could have known about his Tru Star Trucking Company. So that part at least sounds feasible."

Michael paused and reflected further, gradually reviewing and sorting through the pieces of the puzzle. "Did I tell you I went over to the neighborhood where Philip lives? His apartment is maybe three blocks from where they found Jezzie's body. I talked to some of the neighbors and a neat old lady that lives in the same building. All of them said the same thing, that he's a very nice young man and never would any of them believe he could have been involved with the murder. An old lady, Essie Applegate, who lives in the same apartment building as him is a real character but she's pretty sharp. Her son owns the building and she has appointed herself as the official crime stopper for the neighborhood. She has this huge dog that's almost bigger than she is. She calls him Baby and together they patrol the whole area. The dog might be a mastiff or some other huge breed but she claims he's not dangerous. He's gentle as a lamb, or so she insists." Michael chuckled, "Of course, I don't think anybody is likely to put that claim to the test because there's absolutely no doubt in my mind who would come out the loser. I decided to join her as she walked 'patrol' as she calls it, and she told me about the neighborhood and all the tenants in the building. When we were in the backyard Philip came casually walking through with a couple bags of groceries and briefly stopped to visit with us. Earlier Essie had informed me how much Baby liked Philip, but now as I think about it more, it seems kind of strange the dog just sat there looking at him. Not even a tail wag. As we visited a little while longer, Baby laid her ears back on her head and that's when Philip said something like, sorry, Baby . . . no treats for you today, maybe tomorrow. Essie started fussing with the dog telling it not to be so cranky just because Philly didn't have a treat for him. Now, I don't know a lot about dogs but I thought Baby could have shown a little more enthusiasm for Philip, seeing how, according to the old dame, they were such good buds. As Philip went to enter his apartment Essie scolded him for leaving his patio door open. She said anyone could get in and it wasn't safe. I guess that's something to think about . . . but maybe not."

David frowned, "So, actually all we really have to go on is Ellen's story."

Michael folded his arms across his chest. "It looks like that's about all we have so far." He leaned forward, "Unless . . . no that's probably too far fetched."

"What are you thinking, Michael? Tell me since we don't seem to have anything else to go on."

"Essie Applegate kept singing Philip's praises and one of the things she mentioned, a couple of times actually, was that he doesn't drink or smoke. He's like Mister Clean Gene Athlete."

"So?"

"So, this is a real long shot I know, but how come he would have a scars that look an awful lot like old cigarette burns on his forearm?"

"I don't know. Are you sure about that?"

"It sure looked like it to me. His parents said he excelled in sports in high school and he's never given them any problems, even while he was growing up. They are very strict Baptists and my guess is that smoking wouldn't have been real acceptable. This is probably nothing but since I need to look into getting my grandson a birthday gift maybe I'll try the store where Philip works. The only way I can think of that someone could be in two places at the same time is if they have the ability to bi-locate or if there are two people who really resemble each other. Philip told Jezzie he had never been in Las Vegas but she told Ellen she was positive she'd seen him there earlier this year. Ellen also said Jezzie called him at his apartment the day of the murder but we know he was at work. So who then, did she speak to? I know it sounds like I've taken leave of my senses Michael, so I'll be going now, but if any of this should start to make sense I'll get back to you.

Michael entered the store where Philip Johnson was employed and was pleased to see him helping a customer picking out some new electronic equipment. As Michael sorted through the video games a clerk came over and asked him if he needed help. He visited briefly with her, making small talk as he watched Philip ring up the customer's order. As Philip began replacing some of the items he'd taken down to show his last customer Michael moved in a bit closer. Philip was wearing a long sleeved pullover sweater so Michael was unable to see his forearms. Michael picked up a walkman that was laying on the counter, and attempted to engage Philip in a friendly conversation. "Excuse me, I'm looking for a birthday gift for my grandson. What can you tell me about this particular model?"

Philip smiled but showed no sign that he recognized Michael from their earlier meeting with Essie Applegate. He explained the various features on the walkman and handing it back to Michael, while reaching for other models in the same price range from the display on the shelf behind him. Michael watched carefully but at no time were Phillip's forearms visible for inspection. Michael finally chose a moderately priced walkman deciding it would make an excellent gift for Corey. He pretended to browse through some video games and Philip took the walkman to the check out counter. Michael was about to give up when a customer came in and asked about returning the computer he had wheeled in on a shopping cart. As Philip reached to lift the bulky computer monitor out of the cart he unconsciously pushed up his sleeves and Michael had a good view of both of his forearms. At that moment, as he would later tell David, "He made my day."

As Michael slid into his car he reached for the trusty phone book he always carried under his car seat and looked up the address of Ralph and Cordelia Johnson. Etiquette may have suggested it would be better to call first but in this case he was hoping to find Cordelia home alone without Ralph to do her talking for her.

The Johnson home was a well cared for modest two-story, brick structure in a quiet neighborhood. When Michael rang the doorbell he saw Cordelia peek out from behind the curtain. When she didn't come to the door he continued to ring the bell. Finally, a stressed, frightened looking Cordelia came to the door explaining that her husband wasn't home and she really would prefer not to talk with Michael until Ralph returned from his errands, which should be very soon. He replied he understood completely but wondered if he might come in and wait since he'd come from across town and the traffic was heavy. Reluctantly she agreed and after sitting together in an awkward silence for several minutes, she offered him a cup of coffee. Michael accepted and slowly he could feel her relaxing and becoming less nervous. He generously expressed his admiration for their home and complimented her decorating. Spotting a photograph of Philip on an end table next to a well-worn recliner, he commented on how lucky she and Ralph were to have such a fine young man for a son. He mentioned that his only son, Thomas Michael had died and how he wished he could have lived to carry on his family name but unfortunately, that would never be possible.

Cordelia sat looking very sad as Michael spoke of Thomas Michael, her eyes taking on a glassy, wet look and her hands were tightly clasped around a soggy looking handkerchief in her lap. It was evident to Michael that her emotions were very close to the surface and this he knew from past experience could be used to his advantage. Michael noticed another picture of Philip taken when he was a toddler and as Cordelia spoke of her baby boy he could hear the emotion creeping into her voice. She told Michael that he had been an easy child to raise and how she wished she could have had more children but wasn't able to. At this point she stopped abruptly and Michael suspected she knew she had divulged more information than she should have. Her posture stiffened and she twisted the handkerchief she'd been holding. Michael moved quickly. "You only have the one son?" Cordelia anxiously looked at the door in anticipation as if hoping Ralph would come bursting in and save her, but there was no reprieve.

353

Michael realized she was now wrestling with some kind of moral dilemma, so carefully timing his next question he took a chance, "What happened to Philip's brother? The look of shock and surprise on Cordelia's face was nothing less than if Michael would have slapped her.

She stood up and said, "You'll have to leave now. I should have never let you in."

Michael looked at her and he knew she was very frightened but he persisted, "I can leave now but if I do I'll go straight to the police. I don't think that's what you want me to do, so my suggestion is that you tell me about it and we can keep it between you and me."

Cordelia returned to her chair and placed both hands over her face as she began to cry. It reminded Michael that her pose made her look even more like a pathetic little mouse caught in a trap.

"You don't know what you're asking. Ralph told me not to let anyone in the house until this horrible thing was over and now I've ruined everything. I don't know what to do." She rocked back and forth, "What should I do? What can I do?"

"Like I said, I'll go if you want me to but the police will be coming back to talk to you, is that what you would prefer?"

"No! No, please! You can't tell the police. He said he would kill us."

"Who said?"

"The other one, Jimmy. We thought he was dead, that he had died in the fire with my sister many years ago, but obviously he didn't."

"You're talking about Philip's twin?" Michael could feel his excitement growing. "You gave your sister one of your babies and he has come back here to Minneapolis now?" She didn't answer but continued rocking back and forth.

Cordelia was very close to becoming hysterical so Michael spoke quietly, "Cordelia, try to get hold of yourself. As difficult as this is for you, it's probably not as bad as you think. I know Philip didn't strangle that poor girl, but it is very important to know about Jimmy so he can't hurt you or your family."

Michael handed her a clean, white handkerchief from his pocket as she had dropped the one she'd been holding and softly repeated, "Tell me about Jimmy and I promise you I will not involve the police. You gave one of your twins to your sister to raise?"

"No, you don't understand. My sister gave me one of her babies. I couldn't have children but my younger sister had twins. She was living on a farm near International Falls and before she had the twins her husband left her. As she came closer to delivering her babies I went to help her because she was living in the middle of nowhere and so poor she hardly had enough to eat. I took care of her for three months before the babies were born because she was so sickly. We didn't know she was expecting twins because she only saw a doctor once in the beginning of her pregnancy. When two babies came out it was like God meant for me to have one of them.

We gave her ten thousand dollars for Philip and through the years I would send her a little money every once in awhile, so she would have enough for her and Jimmy to live on. Since she had the babies at home no one in the area knew there were two, and when I came back I pretended Philip was mine. Ralph tried to warn me all of this could come back on us but once he held Philip in his arms I was able to change his mind. He's a very good man and we don't want to have to face this now. I hope you'll understand. Anyway, my sister was never very well and Jimmy ended up looking after her as soon as he was old enough. I only saw Jimmy once when he was about ten and he and Philip were so identical if they had been standing together I wouldn't have been able to tell them apart. I don't think either of the boys knew they had a twin brother.

When Jimmy was about fourteen we got word that he and my sister had burned up in a house fire. It was real cold that week, way below zero and the fire department figured the old furnace had overheated and exploded. None of the authorities ever doubted it was anything but a very sad accident. I went to the memorial service but Ralph didn't go. He said the less we had to do with all of it the better it would be for Philip. As I mentioned, Philip didn't know about his twin brother until a couple weeks ago and he still doesn't know that Jimmy has threatened Ralph and me. Jimmy showed up one evening and asked us all not to tell anyone about him for personal reasons. We had no choice but to finally tell Philip how because of my sister's poor health we had helped her out by raising one of the twins. As you can imagine, Phillip was both excited and confused. We told him we knew we should have told him the truth sooner but we didn't know when the right time would have been. So far, Philip thinks it's just great that he has a brother and especially a twin. We're sure he doesn't have any idea that he may be posing a threat to our safety. He thinks Jimmy works for the government as some kind of a special agent and that's why he was willing to keep his identity a secret from the police."

"What is Jimmy's last name?"

"Jimmy Becker . . . or I should say I think he goes by Jimmy Becker."

"So, Jimmy Becker attended the public schools in International Falls. Do you know of anyone up there that may have been a close friend of your sister, or maybe the name of his father?"

"No, as far as I know both my sister and Jimmy kept to themselves. I don't have any idea where Jimmy's father might be. Hardly anyone came to the memorial service. It was real sad to see how few people seemed to care about them. The only one who seemed to show any concern was one of Jimmy's teachers. I remember her because she was the only person willing to speak at the memorial service. She was such a lovely woman and said Jimmy was very smart and even though he had a short life, she would never forget him."

"Cordelia, this could be very important. Please concentrate really hard. Do you think you can remember the teacher's name?"

"No, I don't think so. That was such a long time ago. I only remember she had a sweet sounding name. Let me see . . . Yes, I do remember, her last name was Robin. Yes, I'm sure now . . . She told me her name was Libbie Robin."

"Thank you, Cordelia, I know this has been painful for you to talk about but this could be the most important information we have that will help protect you and your family. You go ahead and wash your face and don't talk about this with anyone else. You don't even have to tell Ralph if you don't want to. I'll leave that up to you. The important thing is not to let Jimmy know that I know about him."

"He's living with him now. You know that don't you?"

"Jimmy is staying with Philip in his apartment?"

She nodded solemnly. "He stayed with him for the first few days and then left for about a week. Now he's back but he usually only goes out at night. As I said, he told Philip he's working for the government on some case that has to do with national security and he showed him papers that supposedly say he's with the FBI. He made us swear we wouldn't go to the police or let anyone know of his whereabouts. Of course, Philip thinks Jimmy's for real and is going along with this as his brother can be very charming, but of course I don't believe him. Not after he threatened us and said that if we say anything to anyone, the Bureau would hunt us down and eliminate Ralph and me. What kind of an FBI agent would threaten to have his own aunt and uncle killed?"

Michael thanked Cordelia with the promise that if necessary they would be provided every protection possible and he wouldn't involve the police, at least not until he was absolutely sure they had solid evidence.

Michael drove directly home where he could shut himself into his office for privacy. Martha was baking cookies to take to Cub Scouts, and Danny sat by the kitchen table sampling them as they came out of the oven. Michael stopped only long enough to say hello and take a few of the warm cookies with him into his office. He smiled as he heard Danny confiding to Martha that his ma makes dumb cookies because she puts stupid things in them like sauerkraut and junk like that. He added his ma's cookies make him want to puke and the kids laughed at him for bringing them to school. As he closed his office door behind him Michael concluded Danny was not exaggerating because he'd sampled Doreen's cookies and it was a pretty accurate assessment.

Michael dialed the number for information, but was told there was no listing for Libbie Robin in International Falls. He then asked the operator for the number for the administrative offices of the International Falls public school system and waited as the phone rang. He knew it was a long shot that Mrs. Robin might still be working but felt it was the next logical place to start. The woman who answered the phone was friendly but when he asked if Libbie Robin still worked in the school system he was put on hold and shortly after the line went dead. Michael dialed back and the same woman answered and apologized saying it was her first day on the job and she must have pushed the wrong button. After what seemed a very long time another woman came on the line and informed him Libbie Robin had retired from teaching and wondered why was he trying to reach her. Michael explained he wanted to talk with her about one of her former students he was writing an article about, and someone suggested she might be able to reflect on his childhood. He was again put on hold and when she returned she stated that school policy would not allow her to give Michael the number directly, but that she would be happy to give Libbie the message and let her decide if she wished to speak with him. Michael gave her his name and number and hung up the phone. When the phone rang and he picked it up on the first ring. "Hello, Mrs. Robin?"

After a brief pause a very sweet voice replied, "It's Miss Robin, and I believe I have the pleasure of speaking with Michael O'Grady?"

"Yes, this is Michael and I want to thank you for returning my call. I really appreciate your time and I was wondering if you would be willing to tell me about one of your former students?"

"Well, it depends. Exactly who are you interested in learning more about and what is the reason for your inquiry?

"I'm trying to find out about James Becker. I believe he died in a house fire about ten or fifteen years ago. I was curious because I think he could be a relative of mine." Michael hated not being honest with such a sweet lady but it was the best response he could come up with on the spur of the moment.

"Whom do you think he would be related to?"

"My mother may have been a second cousin to his mother. At least I think that may be the case. I've just begun researching my family tree so I don't have a lot of information."

"Mr. O'Grady, you may not know this, but I was a teacher for a very long time and one thing I became quite adept at was knowing when someone was not being completely truthful with me. Now then, would you like another go at it before I hang up the phone?"

"Michael chuckled as he said, "Sorry, Miss Robin, let me start over. I'm a private investigator and I'm doing some work for Cordelia Johnson who really is a sister of Jimmy's deceased mother. For reasons that are confidential I need to find out about Jimmy's life before he died."

"That's much better Mr. O'Grady and I can't see it would do any harm, seeing how James has been gone for such a long time. What would you like to know?"

"Anything you can tell me about his life. If he had any close friends or how he spent his time."

"James was a very intelligent boy, good looking but always rather quiet. His mother wasn't well either physically or emotionally. I believe James ended up taking care of her much more than she looked after him. As he got older James seemed to keep to himself. I think it may have been that he was embarrassed about how he and his mother had to live. The farmhouse they lived in was in terrible condition and I don't think they had enough food some of the time because most of the little money they had was mainly used for doctor bills and medicine for his mother."

"Were you ever aware of any abuse James may have suffered by his mother?"

"No, not really, I wouldn't say actual abuse . . . it was more neglect. I think his mother was good to him but she was sick all the time and the poverty they lived in was very evident. His clothes were very shabby until he got old enough to take care of himself and I believe he became rather aloof to compensate for his embarrassment."

"You never noticed any scars or anything unusual on James?"

"Not that I remember. You see, when he was younger the older boys would pick on him but as he got older he learned to defend himself. He was a slender boy but very strong. He used to go hunting a lot and earned extra money by trapping beaver and mink and shooting ducks and geese to sell to some of the people around here. Yes, I remember he was a very good hunter and trapper."

"But you don't remember if he had any obvious scars?"

"Not that I can think of."

Michael was about to give up when he added, "Miss Robin, did James smoke?"

"I don't think so, he was only about fourteen when he died. Why do you ask?"

"I'm not sure. It's just that someone mentioned he had cigarette burns on his arm."

There was a long pause and Miss Robin said, "Now that you mention it, you may be right. I believe I do remember an incident where an older boy and James got into an altercation at school. The older boy was accused of putting out several cigarettes on James's arm. The other children who witnessed the incident said James never even flinched but just stood there looking the older boy in the eyes as if nothing was happening. Then he suddenly punched and kicked the older boy knocking out both of his front teeth. It was so strange now that I think back. It wasn't long after that incident he and his mother burned to death in that terrible house fire. It was so sad . . . I always thought James had great potential but he really never had a chance did he?"

"I guess not. It was a real tragedy. Thank you for talking with me Miss Robin, you've been very helpful. Oh, and one more thing . . . I would appreciate it if you wouldn't mention my call to anyone."

"I'm happy you feel I was able to help, Mr. O'Grady. It was nice to think of James and his mother again. Please remember in the future, it's really quite useless to try to fool a former schoolteacher."

"Thank you, ma'am. I'll try to remember your words. That's excellent advice."

Michael immediately called David and asked if it would be convenient for him to stop by his house around seven-thirty that evening. He found it difficult not to blurt out everything he'd learned from Libbie Robin. He found himself again experiencing that familiar rush of adrenaline and was chomping at the bit to find more about how Jimmy Becker could be linked to Louis Welheim.

That evening, as he and David sat visiting in his living room, they came to the same conclusion. They were quite sure it was probably Jimmy Becker who had killed Jezzie to keep her quiet about whatever she saw, but they were still unclear why Louis would want Jimmy to come to Minneapolis. Another assignment, but what? Regardless how it was configured, it looked like Jezzie must have been an unfortunate victim in their strange agenda. Neither David nor Michael saw her as being any more involved than what Ellen had shared about her blackmail attempt. Jezzie had naively assumed that Jimmy was Philip making it a simple case of mistaken identity. No surprise either, considering how remarkably they resembled each other.

Both agreed they didn't yet have enough evidence to involve the police. The safety of Ellen and her baby and the Johnson family, was still a high priority and linking Jimmy with Louis in any crime or other unlawful activity was not yet possible.

Michael sat back and rubbed his chin, "I've spent a lot of time trying to learn more about Louis without it getting back to him but that man runs a very tight ship. There has to be someone who knows more about him but I haven't had any luck finding out who that may be. I used to work with a really clever cop over on the north side by the name of Harley Hansen and I think I could use a little of his help now. Maybe tomorrow I'll try to track him down. Part of the problem is, so many of these guys have retired and are either dead or living somewhere else where the weather is seventy-five degrees all year around."

"Has Veronica come up with anything new at his office?"

"No, she said Louis's personal assistant, this Geesela gal, is very protective of his privacy and questions even the slightest thing Veronica has tried to find out about him. So far, Veronica has been able to come up with reasonable stories to cover her inquiries but feels if she pushes too hard, or in any way is being considered too curious about Louis's private matters, she could lose her job."

"I'm very pleased with the progress you've made today and knowing you as I do, I'm confident you'll find that one person who can tell us about the real Louis Welheim."

They visited for another half hour and as Michael got up to leave he asked David if he'd heard anything more about Delmar Fack.

"Actually, yes, I did. It's coincidental you asked. My father-in-law called before you got here and Del is finally doing a little better. The first week was pretty rough but now he seems to be settling in. I had Dick Jackson accompany Del on the plane trip to Vermont because he'd spent some time out there about ten years ago and wanted to go back for a few weeks himself. I told Dick that Del could have a couple of drinks on the plane to get him to Vermont but once he set foot on the resort he had to start drying out. As you know, that can be a real tough time for someone like Delmar who's been a heavy drinker for most of his life. On the third day they caught Del walking down the road, suitcase in hand saying he had decided this whole thing wasn't for him. That's when they had to sit him down and finally got it to sink in that his stay at Waldon's Resort wasn't just a social call. The arrangement is, if he wants to avoid being prosecuted he has to stay at the resort for a full year, with the hope that when he's ready to leave he'll have a different outlook on life. For most of his life Delmar has been like a man caught in quicksand and the more he struggles the faster he sinks. At Waldon Resort they'll offer him a helping hand but whether he accepts it or not will be up to him."

"That sounds all good and noble and I really admire your doing it for the poor sap, but after all my years on the police force it seems a bit risky. There are always those people that take advantage of the situation and when the hand-out is gone they go right back to their old abusive behavior patterns."

"True, and that's why old Delmar will be there for a full year instead of a month. He kept saying they had no right to keep him against his will and even threatened that they shouldn't be surprised if they found themselves fighting a lawsuit for false imprisonment. That's when they once again explained I could have had him prosecuted for what he had done and if he would rather be locked up in prison that could be arranged. My father-in-law said it took Del about three seconds to change his mind."

"So, tell me a little bit about this Waldon Resort and what makes it so different from other rehab facilities?" His mind had started replaying images of his daughter Doreen's last visit to the emergency room and her current stay up in the shrink ward.

"Waldon Resort was originally started in 1943 by a wealthy man named Klemmet Erickson who lived in New York City with his wife and two children. He was the owner of a major publishing empire consisting of a daily paper and a couple other popular magazines. The story goes when Klemmet was on his way to work on his forty-ninth birthday he stopped at a newsstand to pick up the morning paper to check out how the war was going. From there he drove to the nearest drugstore to stock up on enough antacid to get him through the day. He passed a shelf of books and a copy of Walt Whitman's Leaves of Grass caught his attention. I believe his exact words were, 'the book took on a luminous quality . . . as if it was a message meant just for me.' That very week he made arrangements to sell his publishing company and a month later purchased the land in Vermont, which he turned into a resort where people could go to get away from the stresses of the world.

Believing Klemmet had gone crazy, his wife refused to follow him. It was only after he built a comfortable house on the property for her and their two girls, that she relented and joined him. She eventually became personally involved and learned to love and share his dream. My wife's family joined him in 1945. You may remember my telling you my father-in-law is both a medical doctor and a homeopath. He had been recruited by Klemmet to set up the healthcare component of the resort. One of Angela's favorite uncles is a minister who made wonderful contributions to the program. Later a chiropractic doctor friend of the family joined them bringing chiropractic services into the facility as well. That's how Waldon Resort began many years ago.

It's reputation soon spread and people coming there now have access to all kinds of holistic care including nutrition, acupressure and acupuncture as well as aromatherapy. Visitors can learn meditation, Yoga, Tai Chi, Qi Gong or whatever else the staff feels may help their guests.

I met Angela's grandfather here in Minneapolis in 1968 as I was finishing my last year of college at the University. At the time I was disillusioned with the way the world seemed to be going and I also had the mistaken idea that all my father cared about was making money. To me his business was always more important than anything or anyone and there was no way I was going to become someone like him. To me, Waldon's Resort and Angela's family seemed like a little bit of heaven on earth. I went there to help with the business part of the resort and I met and fell in love with Angela and we were married. We were extremely happy and I felt as soon as our baby was born I would have everything a man could ever want in this world.

It was at that time my life took a very interesting and painful turn. I guess you've heard some of this before, how Angela died suddenly of a brain aneurysm. It was so unreal because when I came home and found her, she was still sitting in the rocking chair where she'd been sorting through baby clothes. When I went over to her she looked as if she was sleeping. The baby, a little boy, had died shortly after she had, but they removed him from her so we could all see him. It was strange for me because of their family's philosophy and belief system, Angela's parents view death differently than most people do. Of course it was a great shock to everyone and they grieved for a while, but within a few hours of her death they began celebrating her life instead. While we had only talked about it philosophically, I knew that she had wanted to be cremated, which is what was decided. At the memorial service everyone was laughing and joking because they were celebrating the fact that she and our baby were now in perfect happiness with God. They gave thanks for the gift of having had her and our tiny son in their lives even if it was for such a brief time.

As you can imagine, this was a very difficult time for me because the concept was easy to grasp when it was someone else's family, but because it hit the very core of my soul I didn't want to accept it. I think on the surface those first weeks I appeared to accept her death but part of me still wanted to blame someone for my having lost her. For some unconscious reason I'll never understand, I picked my father to blame because I believed he had never accepted my wife and what her family's values were. Because of this I missed being with him the last few days of his life when we could have talked openly and shared our feelings. It was only hours before he died that I was able to tell him I loved him. Angela's father and mother and some of the other people that provide counseling at Waldon Resort were the reason I was able to get my life back on track. By tapping into their wisdom and concern I hope I will be able to help Delmar in this same way, but only time will tell."

"You wouldn't happen to have a business card or a phone number for the resort? I'd like to talk to someone about my daughter and explore whether they feel they could be of help to her."

"I do and I think that would be an excellent idea. How long do you think it will be before they release Doreen from the hospital?"

"Very soon, and I've been thinking it might be good for her and her boys to go there for a month or so. Is it expensive?"

"For your family, I'm quite sure something very reasonable could be worked out." Call this number and ask to talk with Les." David handed him a card and added, "Good luck with your family. I know how much they mean to you. And good luck in finding someone who can tell us more about Louis."

Michael paused as he began to leave, "I really have to ask, is there a really a Walden's Pond at the resort?"

"I guess you might say so . . . but technically it's really more of a Walden's Lake.

Chapter 39

The next few days Michael called and visited every place he thought he might pick up additional information about Louis but without any luck. He spoke briefly with Veronica but she had nothing new to share. She did mention, however, that Louis's wife Estelle had been discharged from the hospital and was now at home under Ethel Danner's watchful care.

Across town, as Dr. Suzen Shepherd made her rounds on the psychiatric floor a cleaning lady stopped her and handed her a sealed envelope. She explained it was found in Estelle's bathroom after she had checked out and since it was addressed to Dr. Shepherd, the woman had taken it upon herself to deliver it in person. Thinking it may be a thank you note Suzen slit the envelope and took out a piece of notebook paper. She recognized Estelle's handwriting.

> *I live in a world of gray illusion because I allowed my spirit to slip away like an insignificant wisp of smoke in the morning sunlight. I fantasize about a world that is black and white, where good and evil, sacred and profane can be easily recognized, but now realize only I have the power to create this world. I used to measure good and evil by the amount of pain I experienced and often wondered if I was too proud or too weak to look into my soul for the answers to my questions. I've put my trust in people who gave me empty guarantees because I didn't know what else to do. For years I existed with the inevitable pain but now realize that pain has revealed that I am one of the chosen ones and I alone possess the power to change this evil world. E. W.*

Suzen re-read the note and went to the desk where she located Dr. Priester's home phone number and dialed it. He answered it on the fifth ring and she identified herself and explained the purpose of her call.

"Dr. Priester, this is Suzen Shepherd. Thank you for taking the time to talk with me. I was wondering if I might speak to you about your patient Estelle Welheim?"

His reply was short and terse, "Estelle is doing splendidly at home and there is no reason for you to have any more concern about her. Thank you for your assistance with her care. I trust you received Mr. Welheim's check for the time you spent with his wife?"

"Yes, I did. Thank you, but I . . ."

"Then I believe our business is concluded. Good bye."

After he hung up on her so abruptly she dialed his number again but this time her call went unanswered. She tried several more times during the day but was never able to reach him.

Shortly after three o'clock that afternoon Michael stopped at The Office Bar, in North Minneapolis. He knew several of his ex-colleagues still hung out there and hoped he might be lucky and bump into somebody he knew. Back when he started on the force The Office had been a regular hangout but now was considered to be one of the seedier watering holes in this end of town. As he entered he was hit with the stench of stale beer, cigarette smoke and rancid cooking grease. While the smell was all too familiar and no surprise, he wondered why anyone would choose to be in such a place if they didn't have to. The bar was dimly lit and at first it was difficult for him to make out the faces of the few customers who sat nursing their drinks.

He looked around hoping to see if Harley Hansen might be at the bar but didn't recognize anyone. During his years on the force Michael considered Harley to be as honest and discreet as anyone he'd worked with and he had only the highest regard for him. A heavyset, middle aged man and an emaciated looking woman were bickering loudly by the juke box and the bartender told them to pipe down without looking up from the newspaper in front of him.

As Michael turned to leave, a man sitting closest to where he stood spoke, "Long time no see, stranger."

Michael turned back and carefully studied the face of the man who had addressed him but couldn't identify him.

Michael spoke cautiously, "Hi. How's it going?"

Taking another sip of his beer, the man forced a smile and finally said, "You really don't know who I am do you?"

Michael searched his memory as he stared at the bloated face in front of him. He thought about the sound of his voice and was about to concede when his mind jumped into gear, "Al? Al Quantera? Is that you?"

Al placed his beer on the bar and thrust his hand out for Michael to shake. "Hey, pretty damn good, Mikey. You were always good with names and faces. You look good so I guess life must be treating you well. How's it shaking?"

Michael took a seat on the stool next to Al and said, "Not too bad. I'm pretty much retired now but I do a little investigative work once in a while just to keep from getting bored."

"And the family? How's Martha and the kids?"

"Good, Doreen's a teacher and has a couple boys and Kathleen's on the police force out in California. You probably recall my son Thomas Michael was killed in the line of duty here in Minneapolis."

"Yeah, I do remember. Some slimebag drug dealer got him. Jesus, I'm sorry that had to happen. God knows, that should never have happened . . . Damn shame!" He drank deeply from his glass.

"How about you? It's been a long time." Michael couldn't help but notice how tough his old friend looked. He remembered that he and his wife Leona had been a fairy tale couple everyone envied. They were one of the perfect Ken and Barbie couples in the old days.

Al finished his beer and motioned to the bartender to bring him another. "Well, Michael, to be perfectly honest, my life pretty much sucks. You want a beer?" Michael declined as he noted how red and glazed Al's eyes were even though it was still early in the afternoon.

"I spend most of my days right here at The Office. I had to take an early retirement. The year before I retired Leona got sick and was diagnosed with Parkinson's. Vickie, our daughter was still pretty young, so I took over caring for both of them. We were lucky though, Leona had been working for an insurance company at the time they diagnosed her so we had real good coverage. She's been in the nursing home almost five years now and doesn't really know us any more. They have to tie her in a chair because she shakes so much. Vicky's a nurse and works at the same nursing home Leona's at so she gets the best of care. It was a real Godsend having good insurance because it would have ruined us financially."

"I'm sorry to hear that about Leona.

The bartender brought the beer and Al again drank deeply. "Life's a bitch, ain't it? So, Mikey, what brings you down to this shit hole?"

"I was looking for Harley Hansen. Do you have any idea where I might find him?"

"Oh yeah, he's down in Texas. Said he never liked these Minnesota winters 'cause the cold bothers his arthritis. I guess I don't blame him. Hell, if it wasn't for Leona and Vicky, I'd be down there with him sucking up the booze in the sun."

Michael hesitated and then decided to take a chance with Al. "I'm trying to dig up information on a guy but I want to keep it on the Q.T. It's nothing serious really. He's a friend of a friend of mine and I need to get some more personal background on him."

"Oh yeah? So what's this guy's name? Maybe I can help you out."

"The guy's a big wheel in real estate. His name is Louis Welheim." Michael tried to keep his voice casual but was sure even in the dimly lit room he saw Al flinch just before he quickly looked down at his beer. As Al reached for his glass his hand was shaking and he almost spilled it on himself. Michael heard him curse under his breath. He quickly drank half of the contents and looked around as if he was checking to see if anyone might be listening to their exchange. "God damn it, Michael. Leave that bastard alone! I tell ya, you have no idea who you're dealing with."

Michael was caught off guard never expecting such a strong response from Al. "So, you do know something about him? Talk to me Al. You're starting to worry me."

Al lowered his voice and looked straight into Michael's eyes saying, "God damn, son of a bitch!" Al finished his beer and set the empty glass back on the bar. "I should've known this day would come. Trust me on this one Michael, or you could end up with your life in the crapper just like mine . . . or even worse."

Al got up from his stool and headed for the back of the bar. "I gotta' take a leak, and if you're as smart as I think you are, you won't be here when I get back."

Michael watched Al as he walked away grabbing the bar to steady himself as he threaded his way back to the men's room. It occurred to Michael that Al might not come back and instead exit out a back entrance but something inside told him to wait and not follow him. He was relieved when he saw him returning and stopping to drop a quarter in the jukebox and punch some of the buttons. A record dropped into place and a voice crooned to his lover to put her head on his shoulder. Al nodded his head to the bartender and said something and as he sat down the bartender brought two more beers and placed one in front of Michael. As a gesture of acceptance Michael placed his hand on the glass. Al waited until the bartender went back to his newspaper.

"Hear that song? Leona and I used to dance to that all night long." Al looked at Michael and for a brief moment appeared to study his face and then quickly looked back down at his beer. "I knew you'd still be here when I got back. It was never your style to give up just because things got tough. But don't say I didn't try to warn you. That's one mean old bastard you're investigating. People have a way of dying when they get in his way. As for this friend of yours, he'd better be aware of the fact that Louis has no friends."

"Go on."

"Damn it! I should've kept my mouth shut but this whole thing is slowly eating my guts out. I hope to God I'm not putting you and your family in danger. Do you remember my old partner Joe Caruso?"

"Yes, I remember. He was killed in a drug bust that went bad. I think you ended up in the hospital. They said Caruso was probably to blame for what happened because he was trying to be a hero."

"Yeah, I know that's how it got written up but it's not what really happened. You see Joe had been meeting with this young intern who was working in the delivery room the night Welheim's kid was born. He claimed the nurse on duty had failed to call him until Louis's wife was already going into shock. Because of it, both mother and baby were in pretty serious danger. They were able to save them, but after that both the nurse's and the intern's careers fell apart. A few days after this incident the intern was falsely accused of taking drugs from some of his patients and was fired from the hospital. Then he was arrested for possession of drugs that were found in his apartment and some bimbo testified against him saying he had sold her cocaine on several occasions. After that, he couldn't set foot outside his apartment without getting hassled by the police. Finally, he told Joe he was leaving the good old United States and moving to Canada because he couldn't take it any more. He never made it. Somebody mugged him so it looked like robbery and he died. The case was never solved. Before he died he swore to Joe he had never used or sold drugs and asked him if he could look into it for him, because he was sure

Welheim was behind it. Of course Joe kept his word but I honestly believe it cost him his life."

The couple that was bickering earlier started arguing loudly again. Michael and Al looked in their direction as the woman was now shouting accusations at the man that he was flirting with the guy sitting next to them. She stood up and threw a drink in his face and stomped out of the bar yelling obscenities as she exited.

Al looked at Michael and said, "Damn friggin' drunks, they should lock 'um all up and throw away the keys. Getting back to the story, Joe started checking on what the young man told him, and quietly began gathering information on Welheim. Joe was the best partner I ever had. He was honest as the day was long and I don't think he ever killed anyone in all the years he worked on the police force. For the next six months or so, he had this little notebook he wrote in and kept in his breast pocket. About a month before he died he told me he was onto something big. A week later he told me he'd learned something so incriminating he felt his family could be in danger. Two days later his house was ransacked and it scared the shit out of him. That's when he told me that if anything ever happened to him I had to be sure the notebook would be given to the FBI and not the police at our precinct because the biggest drug supplier to this area had moles inside all the precincts."

"Did he mention any of the mole's names to you?"

"He figured in our precinct it was Gordy Fresner, but he wasn't sure. You remember him? That little needle nosed, son-of-a-bitch who always was trying to stick his pecker in everyone else's business. He also thought maybe Bennie Jordan. He suspected Bennie because he always seemed to have more money then any cop could have earned honestly. About that time Joe's car and locker were being gone through daily and I started to notice that was happening to mine too. The day before Joe died I got the message loud and clear to back away."

"How so?"

Al looked around the bar again. "I got a present in my locker. It was a little box containing a pair of my daughter Vickie's underpants. The reason I knew they were hers was because with Leona being sick I always did the laundry so I was sure they were our daughter's. Someone had made a deposit on them if you get my drift. As I stood there looking at them that asshole Bennie came over and told me I had a phone call. When I picked up the phone some dirt bag told me what he had planned for my daughter and my wife if I didn't back away from what Joe was sticking his nose into. God, it shook me up so bad I almost puked on my shoes.

The next night Joe and I got a call about a drug bust. The call came in about nine o'clock and Joe was so nervous he acted almost paranoid. He was driving the squad car and hardly talked at all except to tell me he was sure we were being followed. He said he was going to the FBI in the morning to give them his notebook, but if something happened to him I should remember the angel. He was about to explain further but when we pulled into the alley we saw four young punks exchanging money for bags of what looked like drugs. They split as soon as they saw us, and Joe took off running but I stooped down to pick up one of the bags they dropped. I heard a shot and saw Joe fall to his knees and by the time I got to him I could see blood pouring from the wound in his forehead and he was stone dead. The next thing I knew I woke up in the hospital because somebody tried to bash my skull in. I'm sure the only reason I survived was because the assholes thought I was dead."

Michael frowned, "He said what? Remember the angel?"

"I was two weeks in the hospital and when I got out I'd almost forgotten what he'd said to me. When I did remember it didn't mean a thing to me, but as I sat at home trying to recover I had a whole lot of time to think about it. Joe was a holy man . . . well at least compared to me. His family grew up in the same neighborhood he and his wife still lived in. One block from the same church he was baptized and married in called Our Lady of Hope. I'm sure you know which one I mean."

"I do, I have a friend who served as the priest there for many years. I sometimes go to mass there myself."

"Joe used to tell me when he was growing up his mother would go there to help with the cleaning because it was a way for the parish to save money. She would take him and his brother with her and while she did the cleaning they'd explore all the nooks and crannies in the church."

Al looked behind him nervously as two men entered the bar and took a seat in a nearby booth. He moved a little closer to Michael and continued. "He told me there's a little bathroom back by the entrance to the choir loft that seldom gets used anymore since they made a new handicapped accessible one somewhere else in the church. He told me that he and his brother would sneak in there and smoke sometimes when they were waitin' for their old lady. As you go up the stairs to the choir loft, half way up there's a statue of an angel that sits in an indented cove in the wall. He said the angel is standing on one foot while the other foot is slightly back, but sorta raised up. If you reached up behind that raised foot there is a space big enough to put your hand in. Joe and his brother used to hide cigarettes and other shit in that space. He said it was the perfect hiding place."

"What makes you so sure he hid the notebook there? Did you ever go and check?"

"Hell no! Are you crazy? I've never been in that church and I don't plan to go anywhere near it. I thought long and hard about it but then I look at my daughter Vickie and I know I can't do it. My house has been broken in to at least a half a dozen times since Joe died. The last time was only about six months ago. The bastards never take anything but everything is gone through as if whoever is doing it is looking for something specific. I can honestly tell you, it's killing me living this way."

"Did Joe ever tell you who the big supplier was he had a lead on? It sounds as if he had a pretty good idea who was bringing the stuff into Minnesota." A loud burst of laughter from a table near the bar made Al flinch nervously and he licked his dry lips. He said something but another loud burst of laughter drowned out his words forcing Michael to lean into Al.

"What did you say?"

"It's him. The black hearted friend of the friend of yours. He owns the truck line that brings the shit from across the border into Arizona and then in to Minnesota. Joe estimated it was at least a couple million dollars worth of drugs a year. Somehow he smuggles the stuff over the border from Mexico to Arizona but Joe never told me how he does it. I think that may be in the notebook. Welheim likes to punish people and anyone who poses a serious threat dies like Joe did. I'm telling you the truth, that's one cold-hearted, son-of-a-bitch. I still have nightmares where I see the blood gushing out of that hole in Joe's forehead. In the dream I'm crying for someone to help but no one seems to care." Al paused for a moment and once again looked directly into Michael's eyes and said, "God damn it! I don't know if it was a good idea for me to tell you all this. You gotta' be really careful Mike. This time you're dealing with the devil himself."

Michael thanked Al and left the bar feeling shaken. As he stepped out into daylight he unconsciously sucked in the fresh air as if to clear the putrid atmosphere of the bar from his lungs. The adrenaline rush he was experiencing so vividly during the conversation was completely gone and he felt old and weighted down. He sat quietly in his car reflecting that sometime during his conversation with Al, unbeknownst to either of them, the invisible albatross that had been hanging around his old friend's neck had split in two and silently slipped itself around his own. Now there were two of them . . . and later, when he would tell David what he had found out, it would silently split again like some mutant gene, and there would be three. The weight would continue pulling them down until they could figure out the best way to deal with Louis or likely die trying. Part of him wanted to go to the church to confirm the notebook was behind the statue but another more sensible part of him resisted. Getting out of his car he used a pay phone to call David at his office. They decided to meet at David's house at eight-thirty after his appointment with Dr. Marty Rassmusson to discuss some of the difficulties David might expect in the coming months. He and Marty were planning to grab a bite of food later but David assured him he would be home a little after eight.

Chapter 40

When Michael arrived home he found a note saying Doreen had called and invited the boys and Martha to come and have dinner with her at the hospital restaurant. He was not at all surprised he hadn't been included because Doreen had continued to exclude him or Martha just to let them know she was still in control. He found the sandwich Martha had fixed for him in the refrigerator. He poured a cup of cold coffee and retired to his office. After eating half of his sandwich he turned his attention to the piranha in the aquarium beside his chair. The fish appeared to pause and defiantly return his stare. It then turned abruptly, churning the water and causing one of the aquarium plants to break loose and float to the top. Michael was amazed how quickly the fish had grown from the size of a silver dollar to a hard, muscular predator almost the size of his hand. The piranha threaded its way majestically through the remaining plants but now seemed unconcerned with a world that did not fit into the radius of his glass confines. Michael had recently begun to think of it as 'Little Louis'. He reached into the plastic bag of feeder gold fish he'd purchased earlier and dropped one of them into the tank while watching Little Louis do his dance Macabre. Its powerful body wove back and forth with an almost hypnotic rhythm as it slowly courted the unsuspecting prey. In an instant the goldfish disappeared and Little Louis turned and casually swam away.

Michael dropped two more feeder goldfish into the tank. He leaned over to study the fish as it swam seductively across the front of the tank as if trying encourage him to continue dropping in the rest of his dinner. As it wove back and forth it's silver body glistened giving it a deceptively strange beauty but Michael was acutely aware that it's sharp little teeth could tear the dip net to shreds if it felt so inclined. Normally, the underbelly was a pale orange but at feeding time it appeared to take on a deeper, more aggressive reddish hue. When he mentioned this to Martha she had laughed and reluctantly he conceded it might simply be the reflection of the shell chips on the bottom. Little Louis turned impatiently, flipping his tail and again churned the water. Michael dropped the last four gold fish into the tank and watched them glide gratefully into the tank of water, naively relieved to have escaped the confines of the small plastic bag.

Checking the clock and seeing he had some time before his appointment with David, he revisited his conversation with Al. The information he had supplied could be the missing pieces of the puzzle and clarify the enormity of the situation with Louis. There was no question the man they were dealing with was dangerous. Michael thought about his family and the possibility he was putting them in danger frightened him. Mary Rose was also vulnerable but there was no way of knowing at this point how much of a concern this should be. Al speculated that Louis was bringing millions of dollars worth of drugs into Minnesota so the stakes were very high.

Michael leaned over and took the picture of Thomas Michael and his best friend Thomas Patrick Rourk from his desk. The picture was taken when both boys were about eight and each had huge gaping holes where their front teeth had been. T.M. and T.P., Frick and Frack, Pete and Re-Pete. They had been inseparable. They both loved to fish and the day Thomas Michael died they had made plans to leave on a fishing trip on Little McDonald Lake near Perham. Thomas Michael stopped on his way to work to tell Martha and Michael where he could be reached if there should be a need, and in return they told him to have a wonderful fishing trip and a good day. He had countered with his usual response that every day was a good day when he could be fishing with his best friend.

The next time Michael saw their son he was lying in the street in a pool of blood, shot point blank with a sawed off shotgun. He remembered almost going into shock when the EMT pulled back the blanket covering him. Later, when his body had been transferred to the morgue Martha said she wanted to see her son's face one more time. He remembered how he had broken down having to tell her there was no face to see. When Al said he still had nightmares about seeing his partner's face covered with blood Michael knew first hand what he was talking about.

Before leaving home he called his daughter Kathleen. He felt it best not to provide her with any of the details of what he was working on but only asked her for the name of a contact on the Minnesota Drug Task Force she felt would be trustworthy and dependable.

Later as Michael relayed Al's story to David he knew without any reservations that he had to do this for his son and all the other young people who might lose their lives to drugs . He made a special point to confirm the fact that Al had completely convinced him that Louis was an extremely dangerous man and not to be underestimated. It was at that time both men were forced to acknowledge the incredible danger they were placing themselves in.

David also voiced his concern for the safety of Sister Mary Rose. "Do you think Louis intends to hurt her?"

"I don't think so. I've been giving that a lot of thought and I could be wrong, but I don't believe that's his style. Al and Veronica both implied that Louis enjoys toying with people and making their lives miserable. From the little I have been able to learn about his personal life, his wife is virtually a prisoner in their home. It would seem he added to her isolation by sending their son away to school in Switzerland. When I talked to the tennis pro at the country club where Estelle used to play tennis I learned the young man that gave her lessons had an unexplainable accident and broke his arm shortly before he was fired from his job. The intern who Louis believed screwed up the birth of his son also had all kinds of nasty stuff happen before he died, so we know Louis can be malicious when he feels he has been wronged, but I still can't see him hurting a nun. Especially when the nun is Sister Mary Rose, a woman he may still feel a strong attraction for. Even guys like him must have some kind of moral code. Veronica is positive the whole scenario about closing down Seaton House was engineered by Louis. By making Mary Rose believe she would be losing Seaton House he was able to come to her rescue and use the situation as a ruse to get close to her again."

"That's probably accurate. The critical question that still remains is what Jimmy Becker is doing here and what his next assignment might be."

"I suppose there could be a couple of other options we aren't looking at. Maybe there's someone in Louis's less than respectable operation here in Minnesota who has been giving him trouble and he feels he needs the person out of the way. Al said if anyone gets in Louis's way he eliminates them."

"Possibly."

"Or, I just thought of something else. Apparently, Louis has plans to build a new group of upscale townhouses but the word is he's having problems getting the required variances. What started out to be a routine project for him is now getting sticky and expensive and maybe he just wants to eliminate a key player among the opposition. Who knows? Maybe this whole thing with Jimmy has nothing to do with Mary Rose."

"I hope you're right but you need to promise me that for the time being you'll not go near the statue at the church. Don't even think of touching that notebook until we're sure what we're going to do with it. You don't want to put your family in danger and we don't want Louis and his minions to know we know anything about it."

"I agree. That's one promise I can give you easily."

"Also, at this point it's important we leave Veronica out of this as well. She's to know nothing about what we've learned about Louis."

"Again, I agree. I guess for now we need to sit tight and see how this all plays out." He gave David the information he'd gotten from his daughter about a reliable contact on the local drug task force and thought about leaving but reconsidered as he was curious to find out what David had learned from his doctor. "How was your dinner with Marty Rassmussen?"

"Food was good, but I have a feeling that's not exactly what you were asking about."

Michael didn't respond so David continued, "The meeting with Marty went about the way I expected. He was kind and very professional, but not at all optimistic. I could sense it was difficult for him to talk about it. I've done some reading on my own regarding what I can probably expect in the coming months and it isn't real encouraging. The pattern of deterioration in this type of brain tumor isn't good and the thought of what I might experience isn't even remotely pleasant."

"Are you afraid to die?" Michael knew the question wasn't being fair to David but as a friend he felt the need to ask it.

"That's a fair question. I guess the thought of how I may have to live during the next few months may be a lot scarier than the dying. The time I spent at Walden Resort has changed my attitude about dying. I remember when Angela's grandfather was nearing death he was still such a remarkable man and enjoyable to be around. He used to tease me that he'd hand picked me from all the young men at the University to come to Walden Resort. He claimed all the time I thought he was feeding the squirrels he was really waiting for me to come to him.

That man could sing so beautifully it would bring tears to everyone's eyes. He'd sing the old hymns and make them come alive. I'll never forget, his favorite hymn was *How Can I Keep From Singing?* The words went something like, *No storm can shake my inmost calm, as to this rock I'm clinging. For Jesus Christ is Lord above, how can I keep from singing?* Shortly before he died he suffered a major stroke that took away most of his ability to speak. Angela and I were by his side during his last moments and we could tell he was trying to say something. She bent over close to him and said he was trying to sing the words from that old song. He had no fear of death and he died in peace.

I don't know, throughout my life I've tried to be the best person I could. According to Ghandi, the seven capital sins are: wealth without work; pleasure without conscience; knowledge without character; commerce without morality; science without humanity; worship without sacrifice; and politics without principle. I've tried to keep those thoughts foremost in mind as I've lived my life. I'm not sure I've always succeeded but I've tried."

"Do you think about the hereafter and how it may really be? Like our familiar perceptions of heaven and hell, God and the devil?"

David smiled, "I think almost everyone when faced with their mortality gives that some serious thought, I know I certainly have. Angela said her grandfather taught her at the initial time of death each soul will judge themselves. She didn't know for sure about the final judgment, when supposedly every soul will stand before the throne of their Creator but initially as we stand stripped of our humanness we will be our own harshest judge. She felt Heaven is being in the presence of a loving God force, or having the ability to rejoin the awesome creative energy we came from. Hell will be of our own creation, a reflection of the way we lived our life and the knowledge we have chosen to be separate from this force because of our pride and ego. Each soul will create their own hell and will possibly endure a different torment and suffer pain in proportion to their need for cleansing. If we were stingy our hell could be to live in the torment of never having enough. If we had lived a life of cruelty we will be forced to live with the constant fear and hatred of others. Pretty much in keeping with the philosophy that what you have sown you will reap, and always present will be the excruciating pain of not knowing the sense of love and being separate from our Creator.

As for God and the devil, I happen to believe there is really no comparison there . . . even though many people, even entire religions seem to believe there are these two equal and opposite forces. God and the Devil, represented as Good and Evil. It is my view that God is eternal and omnipresent and the devil or Satan came later. He or it became a reality only when humans acknowledged their ego and expressed their fatal, sinful desire for separation and complete control, which in essence was the choice to be separate from their Creator. God gave all his subjects free will and the force we refer to as Satan is the human expression of using free will in a selfish way, therefore, as a negative choice, but in no way should it ever be compared with God, not in power and certainly not in splendor. I believe evil or the devil exists only because the Creator allows it to exist as a means of helping souls to come to gradually learn the laws and effects of natural consequences."

Michael shifted in his chair and studied his friend who spoke in such matter-of-fact tones about his beliefs.

"It's an ego thing, the idea of pride cometh before the fall. Earlier I was thinking about Louis and others like him and I was wondering how they justify what they are doing. Each of us should have that inner voice that brings us into existence and tells us what to believe and who we are. The little voice that admonishes us when we feel we've screwed up and tells us how wonderful we are when we succeed. But as we know, history has repeatedly shown us even kings and prophets have deluded themselves and others with the misguided belief that only they were in control of their destiny. In the end they find themselves nothing more than cosmic dust like everyone else.

To me, arrogance and self-absorption are the first signs of operating out of fear rather than faith. A person who denies some kind of divine power may be an example or end product of extreme deprivation of human love. Since they have never experienced the awesome majesty of a loving protector, it's easier to deny the possibility that anything so magnificent could exist for them or someone else. Eventually they become unable to experience any form of real love and ultimately believe only they can control their destiny.

I'm quite sure there is much we were never intended to know. To answer your original question, am I afraid of dying? I suppose I really won't know for sure until that moment arrives. I hope by that time I'll have come to terms with it. We all have to decide how we feel about dying because it's something we must do by ourselves. We can pray and have faith or not acknowledge a divine existence at all, but in the end we'll all face death alone with only our beliefs to comfort us. We'll face our creator unadorned of earthly accolades, and at that point, nothing will matter except our relationship with the force we believe in."

David smiled and his voice took on a reflective tone as if he was talking to himself rather than to his friend. "Facing our imminent demise I think it's common for us to try to bargain with God. Like a man who finds himself drowning a mile out at sea. He pleads with God to spare him and promises to give his entire fortune to the poor if he is saved. He believes God hears his prayer and with a new burst of strength he swims onward. As he makes it to within a half mile of the shore he amends his plea by pledging if he's spared he'll give away most of his fortune to the poor. When he starts to see land near approaching he amends his pleading again promising he will give a respectable portion of his fortune to the poor, and as he reaches the shore he says, 'Well God, I guess I made it. We'll have to see about that fortune later. I think I'll still need it." The point being, in the end, when our time comes to die we will die no matter what we've said or promised or how many times we prayed in church."

He looked up at Michael as if suddenly realizing his friend was still listening. "Don't get me wrong, I believe religion or some type of organized spiritual belief is still the backbone of civilization and was originally meant to lead and comfort its followers. I think we'd have to agree though that history confirms that far too many atrocities have occurred because of the misguided fervor of some of it's most zealous advocates. I also believe contrary to many true believers that the Bible was written in an ambiguous format so that it's readers would have to search their hearts to know the true meaning. And yes, I think it's possible that some theologians may have interpreted scripture to support their own prejudices but I suppose at times we've all been guilty of that. I don't know if we really have all the knowledge we need to live a good life, but the one thing that really concerns me is not so much what I've done in this life, but rather what more I could have done?"

David finally paused and looked directly at Michael and said, "Well, speaking of what more could we have done, it would appear we may have it in our power to stop Louis from killing more people and putting his drugs out onto the streets. Our job now is to decide the best way to do this so he can't slip through the cracks in the legal system."

Chapter 41

David called Sullivan Glass and asked Janet if there was anything he urgently needed to attend to at work. She assured him everything was being taken care of under the watchful eyes of Harry and Baxter. He loaded his car with the boxes he'd packed earlier in the week and headed for the hotel where Molly was staying. He found it easier to take entire days off now since he knew the transfer of the company his father had founded and entrusted to him was functioning smoothly with continuous growth and prosperity. Most of David's free time was now being spent inconspicuously ridding himself of his earthly possessions and completing all the legalities involved in disembarking from his life. Janet, Baxter and several of the other key personnel had recently been told about his prognosis but many of his employees and friends still didn't know. Dr. Rassmusson suggested that because of the precarious location and aggressive nature of the tumor it would be realistic to be aware that as it grew David's capabilities would likely diminish abruptly and now would be the time to complete all of the important things he needed to do.

When he arrived at the hotel a young bellman helped David unload his boxes onto a cart and deposit them outside Molly's door. The bellman offered to assist transferring the boxes into her suite but David thanked him and sent him on his way with a generous tip. Before departing the young man grinned and told David he felt Sara Brown was one of the prettiest and nicest ladies staying at the hotel. David knocked lightly and announced himself. Molly had been expecting David and invited him in and as she did so poked her head out and thanked the bellman who was standing halfway down the hall trying to get a departing glimpse of his favorite occasional resident.

David slid the boxes into the room and couldn't resist teasing Molly. "Harry said you seem to be irresistible to the younger men and now I see what he meant."

Molly laughed as she closed the door and leaned against it. "I think they see me as a combination of the desirable but unattainable woman, and a mother figure. All I know is when they look at me with those adoring eyes and call me ma'am, I feel really old and end up picturing myself as the scandalous Mrs. Robinson from *The Graduate*." David was amused that for a moment she appeared embarrassed and attempted to hide her emotions by picking up a book and examining it.

"My goodness, when you said you had a few books I could borrow I had no idea you were talking about a traveling library. It could be several years before I can return them all."

David placed the last box near a small table in front of a love seat. Even though he had gotten to know Molly over the past few months he still couldn't bring himself to tell her how serious his health problems were. "You may consider them to be on semi-permanent loan and if I don't need them in the next ten years they are yours forever . . . No argument."

"Thank you. That's very sweet of you! I've been reading a lot since I moved back to Glenwood. I don't seem to find much on television that's of interest and I've relearned to appreciate my solitude so I know I'll make good use of them. Would you like a cup of tea? I ordered a pot of Chamomile and would love to share it with you." David smiled at Molly and her cheeks reddened slightly as she quickly added, "Unless you're in a hurry?"

"No, there's no hurry. I have the day off. It's one of the perks of owning your own company. Kind of like being a freelance author of children's books."

David grinned and as their eyes met she couldn't help but notice again how very handsome he was. For some unexplainable reason she felt herself becoming self-conscious for a second time which she tried to hide by pouring the tea and handing him a cup.

"Harry mentioned you've recently finished a new book and your publisher likes it so much she is considering having you write a series."

Molly smiled as she handed David his cup of tea, "Yes, I can't believe they feel I'm capable of doing that and yet I must admit, I'm excited about it." She moved her hand in front of her as if pointing to an imaginary banner. "Sara Brown, defender of small children's minds and general all around good story teller. Who would have thought the tiny terror of Lowry and Glenwood would someday climb the lofty literary molehill of respectability?"

"Harry has told me about some of the more colorful escapades you and he embarked on. It sounds as if you had a wonderful childhood."

Molly sat down on the opposite end of the loveseat and took a sip of her tea. "We really did. I think growing up in Lowry and Glenwood was very special. Of course I couldn't wait to get away from the small town mentality and move to the big city. Looking back, I don't know how I could have survived without Harry. All the years we were growing up I wanted to believe I was in charge of everything and the brave heart. After all, I was older, and, as you know, when you're a kid that's always a big deal. Now, as I've matured and have hopefully become a little wiser, I realize he was the brave one, and I was the strong willed brat of a kid who used my big mouth to make people believe I was important."

"That's not what he said. According to Harry, you were always the champion of the underdog and never afraid to speak your mind, no matter what the consequences were."

"That's so like Harry to say something like that. I think my mom was the one who taught us to look out for people who weren't as fortunate as we were. She told us it was important to always tell the truth and defend our principles. Somehow though, when I believed I was too old to be under her influence, her values became less important to me. For quite awhile I took the easier way, or what I thought was the easier way. Actually, as you might expect, it often turned out to be the more painful way."

"I think I know what you mean as I grew up in a home where both my parents were kind and honest but I didn't really recognize these qualities in my father until after he died. I know I've told you about my life and how Angela's family was remarkable in so many ways and I still consider her family as my mentors and main source of inspiration. It was they who helped me realize the different ways people show their love not only for the people they are closest to but universal, unconditional love for everyone. No one was ever excluded from their love and acceptance, and at no time did they seem to question God's love for them, no matter what came into their life. Even when Angela and our baby were taken away so unexpectedly, they didn't question why it happened, but gratefully rejoiced for the joy she had brought into their lives. As you might expect, at first I had a very difficult time accepting her death. It seemed so cruel and unfair for God to take someone so loving and vibrant with the incredible potential she had. She was young and beautiful and about to bring our son into the world and then suddenly both were gone. I felt there was no justice in this world. As time went on with the continued help of her family I came to realize it was my good fortune to have loved her and that it was her time to withdraw because all of us had lessons to learn without her help."

"You miss her don't you?"

"Every day . . . every minute of every day." He looked into Molly's face and she saw the pain in his eyes. She had noticed a change in him over the past few months that she didn't quite understand. He smiled sadly and continued, "From what Harry has told me you feel the same way about your husband Steven."

"Yes, like you, I miss him all the time. I still find myself getting stuck in the mire of why did it have to happen. After I got over the initial shock of his death and my miscarriage, I went into a deep depression and tried to withdraw from the world. I floundered in self-pity and instead of allowing myself to heal I became more and more angry with God for taking him away. That may sound a little strange because at that time God was still a rather intangible concept in my life, but who else was there to blame? At times my anger was even directed at Steven for leaving me but since he was gone I began taking it out on everyone around me who seemed to have more than I did. I must admit, I think I went a little crazy. I tried all the usual band-aids people use, antidepressants, sleeping pills and alcohol but they only made things worse. It reminded me of when I was little and I had a temper tantrum. I would hold my breath and kick and scream and go after anyone who I believed was standing in my way of getting what I wanted. I was a crazy woman. I hurt people because I couldn't get even with God for what he'd done to me. It took some pretty hard knocks on the side of my head before I came to my senses. The best thing I did was to move back to Glenwood away from all the noise and confusion so I could get myself centered again. I have two favorite sayings now. I have no idea who said them but whoever it was they were very smart. One of them is if you want to make God smile, tell him your plans for the week. So you learn to live in the now and accept the unexpected. The other is, when you're up to your ass in alligators, it's difficult to remember your initial objective was to drain the swamp. The idea that you often start out with good intentions but before you know it, things have run amuck and you find yourself in more trouble than you could have ever imagined. Both of these sayings have given me a lot to reflect on." Molly took a sip of her tea and grinned as she said, "David, in some ways you remind me of my cousin Clayton. You both have a serenity that I can almost feel."

"I would like to meet him. He sounds like a wise old soul who has come back to help the world even though he could have moved onto a higher plane."

"I think so. He helped me realize I was a good person even if some of the things I'd done were not so good. Through his influence I was finally able to ask forgiveness of most of the people I'd hurt which was very comforting but, as you might expect, I still have trouble forgiving myself. I feel I'm making progress and slowly healing but it took him to point out that healing is an ongoing process. We all need to work at healing all the time. You've probably noticed, I still tend to be the queen of instant gratification. You can imagine how that goes . . . I want it all now, instant healing, instant happiness, instant wisdom and, of course, instant patience."

David set his cup down and leaned back giving himself the chance to study the charming woman in front of him. For a moment he truly regretted his lack of time in this world, and wished he could have another year to continue their friendship. "I think all of us have that trait in us. We often pray only when we want something and become disillusioned when our prayers aren't immediately answered. We resist pain of any kind believing it's always bad, and we want to blame someone else when things go wrong even when the results were the expression of our exercising our free will. We regret the time we have wasted only when it's too late to realize what we might have accomplished. It seems difficult for humans to learn the simple but powerful principle of natural consequences. So, you're not alone Molly, it's a part of the human condition."

"Exactly . . . more tea?"

"Yes, please." He held out his cup and she poured carefully as a big smile crossed his face. "I believe you are progressing very well"

"I admit I still have a problem with how we impart a greater worth to certain people, like celebrities and look the other way when they screw up but are so quick to criticize some of the less fortunate. I remember reading this little poem somewhere but again, the source escapes me:

I am the King, I wear the ring. I make the rules, I rule the fools.
I sing and dance and drop my pants, yet all the while, the people smile,
They do not care that it's not fair. You see I am the King, I wear the ring!

385

Somehow the silly poem seems to sum up our need to always have popular friends and associate only with the right people. We pay homage to the elite and need to believe some people are superior to others. Kings and Queens and fighting machines." Molly stopped talking and narrowed her eyes as she peered at David, "Am I talking to much? I am! I'm talking way too much. Lately Harry scolds me for thinking and talking only about myself, and what's important to me. He even suggested he almost liked me better when I wasn't always obsessing about my spiritual growth. He said I was a lot more fun."

David studied Molly to the point where she felt herself becoming slightly uncomfortable.

"What? Do I have dirt on my nose or something caught in my teeth? Why are you looking at me like that?"

"I was thinking how intelligent and charming you are and what a excellent job you've done in making yourself into an extremely beautiful woman."

Molly was clearly caught off guard and for one of the few times in her life was totally speechless. The color rose in her neck and she could feel her cheeks burn. She placed her cup down and then picked it up again. Finally, she looked at David and said, "Why, Mr. Sullivan, I do believe you're flirting with me."

David grinned, "Why, Ms. Brown, I do believe you're correct." He leaned forward and kissed her gently on her mouth.

Molly felt her lips tingle and a faint numbing sensation that moved into her cheeks and down her body. A sensation she hadn't felt for a long time and had missed and still longed for.

He leaned back, smiled and said, "Sara Brown . . . I hope you'll never forget what a lovely and desirable woman you are. I know for a fact there are a lot of men who would be very pleased to share their time and their love with you."

Molly studied David's expression. She saw a man who was totally charming and sincere and she knew in her heart that he was not like most of the other men she had known except for one or two. It was apparent he was telling her something he felt was true with no expectation of receiving anything in return. She realized he was intrinsically very much like Steven and for a brief moment she again felt the stabbing pain deep inside that she knew was still connected to the loss of her husband. "Thank you for saying that. It means a great deal coming from someone like you. I still have times when I feel like I might not be loveable and if I were to be completely honest, I'd have to say I'm almost afraid to let myself love again."

She looked down at her teacup and continued, "I remember back when the book and movie *Love Story* came out and that catchy phrase 'Love means never having to say you're sorry' was bantered about. One of the men I had an affair with used that phrase as a way of justifying his numerous lovers, like all is fair in love and war . . . no apologies, no explanations, no commitments necessary. He also used Robert Herrick's poem that advised young virgins to make much of their time. Do you remember it? *Gather ye rose buds while ye may, old time is still a flying, and this same flower that still smiles today, tomorrow will be dying.*

For him love was just a word that helped him use sex to bolster his sagging ego. Actually, I thought the phrase 'Love means never having to say you're sorry' meant you could love someone but never had to feel sorry for having loved them. I guess it was that way with my first husband. I've never been sorry I loved him and that he had loved me. Unfortunately, at that time I didn't really understand what true love was but what we shared remains important to us. We're still good friends and even though he's remarried, we continue to share the kind of love good friends do. It wasn't until I met Steven I finally knew that love was much more than that pale statement of not having to say you're sorry. I think with Steven I finally realized what true love could be. It was like a glimpse into eternity and so profound it seemed to transcend the boundaries of the human experience. We were so immersed in each other we felt our souls had become one and felt such joy we'd end up crying in each other's arms. Ours was to experience the gift of such exquisite pain and ecstasy we believed we would burst with emotion. The person you share this depth of love with is so profoundly important they become primary in your every thought and yet somehow there's still space for both of you to keep your separate identities and grow. Does that make sense to you?"

"Yes, completely. I think you and I have walked that same path." David leaned back against the loveseat and a great sadness seemed to engulf him. "Unfortunately, I don't think many people experience what you're talking about. Maybe it's because they've never met the right person . . . or maybe because they fear the risks involved in letting someone come that close to their soul. I think both of us were very blessed, even if what we had with our spouses didn't last nearly long enough. We both experienced that glimpse of eternity. The feeling of completely immersing ourselves with another person and yet remaining separate and complete." He glanced at his watch, "I'd better be going now Sara, but promise me you'll at least think about allowing yourself to find love again."

"I assure you I will when I'm ready. Thank you again David. Actually, I can't thank you enough, not only for the books but for caring enough to say what you did."

David got up and turned to leave and Molly followed him to the door. She felt she had to ask, "You've chosen not to love again haven't you?"

He stood silently as if weighing his thoughts and then said, "Probably not in this lifetime, but who knows, maybe we'll meet again?"

Molly felt tears springing to her eyes. She smiled and replied, "Maybe, indeed . . . until then."

"Good bye, Sara Brown. I feel blessed to have known you."

Months later, Molly found herself reflecting on the conversation she had shared with David. Slowly, she came to realize that his kiss had been like the books he had given her, subtle and treasured gifts. Just as her affair with Graham Stone had eroded her self-esteem, David's gentle kiss, in some small but large and wonderful way, had helped to restore it.

Chapter 42

The phone rang and as Harry reached to pick up the receiver he glanced at the clock on the bedside table. It read twelve-fifteen A.M. and his thoughts immediately jumped to his father. "Hello" . . . he dreaded phone calls at this hour.

"Hey, cuz. Did I wake you?"

Harry's heartbeat slowed slightly. "Molly, do you have any idea what time it is? I know you tend to be a night person but some of us are not. Some of us have real jobs."

He could hear Molly's evil little chuckle as she said, "Sounding a bit cranky aren't we?" Her voice was cheerful and she continued, "Yes, dear cousin, I do know what time it is. It is exactly twelve-sixteen but this is mucho important."

"All right, tell me so I can be mortally shocked and then go back to sleep. After all, I just saw you this morning."

"I" . . . big emphasis on the I, "got a speeding ticket on my way home from the cities, outside of Glenwood."

"Whoopy ding! So how could that possibly be of interest to me at this time of the morning except for me to feel glad you probably got what was coming to you for having such a lead foot?"

"Cranky, cranky, cranky. Well, to go back to the beginning, after I saw you, David dropped off some books for me at the hotel. Anyway we had this nice talk that really affected me. He is such a remarkable man, as you already know. Anyway, as I was driving along I was thinking about some of the things we talked about and I also started to think about how people always say there are no accidents. That everything is meant to happen exactly when it's supposed to be happening."

"Yes, go on."

"So I'm driving along, very deep in philosophical thought and all of a sudden I see these flashing blue and red lights behind me and a highway cop pulls me over. He comes over to the car looking all stern and pissy-antie, wearing a pair of those big official sunglasses, and says, ma'am, do you have any idea how fast you were traveling?" Molly dropped her voice for the highway patrolman's part in her narrative to Harry. "I smiled real innocently and say, no, not really, officer. Which was a big lie because as soon as I saw the flashing lights I glanced at the speedometer, and of course, no one in their right mind is about to admit it."

Harry could feel his humor returning and he said, "So how fast were you going?"

"Let's just say you really don't want to know but if I'd been going any faster I should have had a pilot's license. Anyway, he decides to enlighten me and he had me dead, right on the nose. I guess he had a radar gun or whatever they call those things. So, I say, oh my, that's not good is it?? All the while trying to play sweet and innocent. Of course, the guy never even cracked a smile and said, no ma'am that most certainly is not good. May I see your driver's license?' About this time I'm thinking, oh crap, I'm really screwed now, so as I'm digging my driver's license out of my purse I decide to try a different approach. I smile real apologetically and nonchalantly say, my brother is a highway patrolman, Daniel Brown. Do you know him? I figure at this point I have nothing to lose so maybe I should let him know I have an important blood relative on the force. Well, he doesn't respond in the way I'd hoped but instead says, ma'am, this is my first day on the job, so it's all new to me. He goes back to his patrol car where he checks out my past driving record, which isn't all that stellar, and proceeds to write me a ticket. He doesn't say another word and I know I'm really, really in deep shit now. I can hear Daniel's voice the next time I see him because he still likes to play the all-knowing big brother when it comes to anything pertaining to the law. Anyway, I take the ticket and try real hard not to show him how pissed I am and in my most polite voice say, 'Thank you, Officer . . . ?" Excuse me . . . I can't seem to read your name on the ticket . . . My not so subtle way of telling him he has shitty handwriting. He looks at me and says, Officer Pecar. so, I say, Pecar? Do you by any chance know Peter Pecar? When I say that, he laughs and pulls off his sunglasses and says, Yeah . . . Pecker boy . . . Hi, Sara. Oh my God! Harry, I thought I would die right then and there. He has wonderful silver grey hair now and he's big, not the tall, skinny kid he was in high school. His body is all filled out and well I have to tell you, he's in great shape for the shape he's in. Once he smiled that sweet, shy smile of his I felt my heart jump like I was back in high school."

"Molly, this is all very enlightening but don't you think this titillating bit of news could have waited until morning?"

"No! Now don't be that way. Just listen because there's more. About eight o'clock this evening my phone rang and it was him. We talked until just before I called you, and . . ."

"And?" He knew she wanted him to drag it out of her.

"And, he asked me to go out with him and I accepted. We're going out to eat at The Minnewaska House and maybe go to a movie. He was married but now he's divorced. He said he and his wife just drifted apart and after their kids were grown they mutually decided to part. He said at first the kids didn't think the divorce was such a good idea but after they talked it over everyone agreed it was for the best. He moved back to Glenwood because the stress of the big city was getting to him and he loves to fish, but his wife stayed in Minneapolis so she could go back to college. After we talked for a while he admitted he had a crush on me in our senior year of high school but he was too shy to ask me out. Oh, Harry, this is so fantastic!"

"Interesting . . . just think, you could become Molly Pecker. I like it. It has a certain ring to it. Sara Cornelia Pecker, even better. Too bad you're not a little younger . . . You could have had a whole pack of little peckers . . ."

"You ass! Actually, there are already three little peckers and four-and-a-half grand-peckers."

"Instant family! How convenient, no muss no fuss, just apply and watch it dry."

Molly ignored his sarcasm. "Peter said one of his daughters told him it was time to pull his head out of his tackle box and find a female friend. I simply can't believe I have a date with Peter Pecar. I guess that's all I have to tell you, so say hi to Annie and kiss the babe. How's the little angel?"

"Both are fine, but I still have a question. After all the hearts and arrows did Romeo still give you the speeding ticket?"

"Of course. Peter is a very honorable man. He said, Sara, if you aren't willing to do the time, don't do the crime. Isn't that just adorable?"

"Positively retro Beretta. One more question. Did his kids get picked on and called Pecker like he did?"

"I asked him that and he said as soon as his kids were old enough he enrolled them in karate classes and after that it never became an issue."

"Smart guy. Goodnight, Molly." He waited for her to say the last words she always had to have.

"Harry?"

"Yes, Molly?"

"That speeding ticket could have been the best money I ever spent. Cross your fingers, I think I could be in like."

Harry hung up the phone and turned over to put his arms around Annie who he knew had been listening to their conversation. "Molly thinks she's in like."

"In like?"

"That's what she used to call it when it was too early to call it love."

Two days after Molly's phone call Harry called upstairs to Annie asking where she'd put the box of cat food but couldn't hear her answer over Jessie's singing and pounding her spoon on the table. He fixed her a bowl of cereal and told Thomas and Bentley to be patient until Annie came downstairs. He repeated his question when she entered the kitchen and she responded saying, "I told you there isn't any left, you'll have to open a can of tuna and Jessie, please keep the noise down."

"I brought a box home yesterday morning. I know it wasn't a very big box but they couldn't possibly have eaten it all already."

Annie gave Harry an exasperated look and then over at Jessie, "Jess, tell daddy where the cat food is."

Jessie put her spoon down and in a very serious voice said, "I slushed it."

Harry repeated her words, "You slushed it?"

"I didn't say slushed it, I said fl . . . slushed it."

"You flushed it? Like down the toilet flushed it?"

"Yes."

Annie interjected, "So Jessie, tell daddy why you flushed the cat food."

"I already told you why." Jessie gave her mother an exasperated look.

"I know you've already told me, but now tell daddy."

Jessie sighed loudly as if the whole topic now bored her. "Cause Thomas said he didn't like that kind."

Harry looked at his daughter and said "Thomas the cat told you that?"

"Yeah."

Again Annie interjected, "Now tell daddy what else you flushed down the toilet."

Jessie put her hands over her eyes and sat not saying a word.

Annie looked at Harry and said, "You know the new hearing aides we just had Jessie fitted for? The ones we haven't even gotten the bill for yet?"

"Slushed?"

"Slushed! She took them apart and what didn't slush was ruined."

"Don't tell me, Thomas told her to?"

"No, her little friend Onna, you know, the one no one else can see did it. Anyway, we have an appointment tomorrow to get her re-fitted. For some reason she didn't seem to like the new ones but is perfectly happy to have her old ones back. I thought I'd stay a little later at work tonight to catch up on the paperwork, but Martina will fix supper for you and Jessie. She has to go home tonight but will pick up Jess and me about twelve-thirty tomorrow and that will still give us enough time to get Jessie's picture taken after her fitting. She's offered to stay the night if we should decide to go out and eat. Think about it, it's been a long time since we've gone out on a date."

Chapter 43

The following morning David awoke early as his head was pounding and he felt the room spinning around. He also had recurrent bouts of nausea and blurred vision. None of the new prescription pain relievers were able to give him relief and seemed only to cloud his thinking. For the past two days he had chosen not to use them and they remained in their containers next to the kitchen sink. He drank a glass of orange juice and by the time he finished his shower he was feeling some better. While he was dressing the phone rang and as he picked up the receiver his thoughts returned to the morning Mary Rose called to tell him about Jezzie's murder.

"Hi. David . . . it's me, Mary Rose."

"Good morning, Sister. Is everything all right?"

"Oh yes, everything is fine. I wanted to tell you Ellen had her baby early this morning and she's doing very well. She had a little boy and even though he weighs not quite five pounds, all parts are accounted for and everything seems to be working fine. Ellen is relieved her baby is healthy and I cannot praise Dr. Roy's bedside manner enough. He was so good with her and considering the fact she was a basket case near the end of her pregnancy, it's amazing, she had no problems during the delivery."

"That's a relief! Thank you for letting me know. Are you still at the hospital?"

"No, I'm back at Seaton House getting ready to leave for St. Cloud. My cousin Cathy Matthews had coronary bypass surgery and I told her last week I'd come and spend a few hours with her. Since there were no complications during Ellen's delivery, Dr. Roy assured me she and the baby would be fine and Martha promised she would come by to sit with her. They've gotten to be good friends and I think Ellen sees her as a substitute mother figure. David, I realize you're very busy, but if you have a few minutes I know Ellen would love to see you."

"I'll try to stop. After all of the emotional trauma she's had to go through, I'm very thankful she's okay. I'll bet you're enjoying your new car. Isn't it nice to finally have a more reliable one?"

"It's a coincidence you should ask. It was running just fine until last night. I was going to take a spin over to the drug store, and for some reason, it wouldn't start. Louis told me if I ever had any problems with it I should let him know immediately, and when I called him he said he'd send a man over later this morning to take a look at it. As it turns out, it's my lucky day because he has to be in St. Cloud also, so he offered to let me ride with him. He'll drop me off so I can be with my cousin, and pick me up after he finishes his business. Sometimes he can be such an old fuddy-duddy. He said it would be better if I didn't tell anyone he was giving me a ride because people might misinterpret. Isn't that dumb? Like nowadays anyone would even care."

"Don't worry, I promise your secret is safe with me. Have a wonderful time with your cousin and thanks again for calling to tell me about Ellen. Is she planning to keep her baby?"

"No, but the family that's adopting him told her they want her to be a part of her son's life. It's what they call an open adoption, so she's thrilled about that. Bye, David, have a wonderful day."

He hung up the phone and realized with Ellen out of danger he and Michael could move ahead with their investigation of Louis and Jimmy Becker. Time was running out. He wondered about the breakdown of Mary Rose's new car thinking perhaps it was a bit too convenient for white knight Louis to come riding in. He pondered the matter and in spite of the uncomfortable feeling he had about her being with Louis for the whole day, he had to push it aside, acknowledging that Mary Rose had an uncanny ability to take care of herself. With God's help, of course.

When David arrived at work, Janet was on the phone and as he passed her desk she handed him several notes. He entered his office and sat down at his desk, sorting through the messages;

 'Call Michael today. Nothing urgent but he does need to talk to you.'

 'Annie said to remind you she won't be in today. She's getting Jessie re-fitted for her new hearing aides, but will be home until twelve-thirty if you need to reach her'

> *'Mary Rose called and asked if you could meet her at four o'clock today at her favorite park bench.'*

David stared at the note and re-read it realizing that it didn't make sense. He buzzed Janet. "Janet, the note from Mary Rose, was that from today?"

"Yes, her secretary called about a half-hour ago."

"Not Mary Rose?"

"No, it was the new secretary, you know, the one that replaced Jezzie. I think her name is Nona, or Nola. She was a little hard to understand on the phone but said it was private and that you'd understand. She said you didn't need to call back, but to please be sure to be there. I think it could be one of those emergency fund requests Mary Rose makes of you every so often. Don't you think so?"

"You're probably right. Thanks, Janet, I'll take care of it." David puzzled over the note, and finally came to the conclusion it clearly didn't make sense. He immediately revisited his earlier conversation with Mary Rose and the fact that her new car wouldn't start and Louis's convenient need to go to St. Cloud on business that same day. It also seemed strange he had told her not to tell anyone she would be riding with him. He remembered the conversation Michael had with Louis's grandmother and aunt and how they said Louis never forgot nor forgave any previous wrongs he had to endure. He also recalled Mary Rose describing how angry Louis became when he found out she had chosen to forsake him to love a God he didn't believe in.

David felt himself shudder involuntarily as he wondered if Mary Rose was in danger at this very moment from someone she trusted. He re-read the note for a third time and remembered Michael saying the retired policeman he had spoken to at the bar said Louis was certainly capable of murder if someone was an immediate threat, but he usually preferred to play with his victims and watch them suffer. It was possible Louis was plotting some kind of revenge on Mary Rose for rejecting him and wanted to see her suffer as he felt he had suffered years back. As far as David could tell she wasn't in immediate danger, unless he was suspicious that possibly Jezzie had shared something with Mary Rose that could link him to her killer? To kill a nun would not be an honorable thing, not even to someone as ruthless as Louis. So how else could he hurt her? He had already toyed with her by making her believe she could lose Seaton House and then deceived her into believing he had restored it to her.

David reviewed all the confusing facts again. As he pondered the details of Louis's personality suddenly an unthinkable thought came to mind. Louis could hurt Mary Rose by taking away someone she cared a great deal about. Had it been Jezzie, or could it be someone else Louis might view as competition for Mary Rose's affections. Not God, Louis had already learned that God was her first love but after all these years that had probably become a moot issue. So who would Louis believe was next in line for Mary Rose's affection? David thought about the many times Mary Rose had teased him about how she loved him like her brother. David felt sure she had expressed these feelings about him during her visits with Louis. As he reflected on the possibilities, the whole notion sounded too bizarre to even consider, and David wondered if the tumor in his brain, and the heavy medications he had been taking to tame his pain were creating strange thoughts in his mind? Unthinkable thoughts of paranoia and impending doom that sounded too crazy to share even with his closest friends. He sat for another moment with a growing tightness in his chest and thought quietly to himself, "Oh God, please help me. Give me strength to think through this clearly."

For the fourth time David read the note. The phone call, with its purported message from Mary Rose, would get him to the park bench overlooking Minnehaha Falls. This was the place where she would often go to meditate and pray, especially when she needed to sort through what God's will was for her, or when an important decision had to be made. On numerous occasions she had invited David to join her so they could discuss the best courses of action for Seaton House and her beloved girls.

Another bizarre thought crossed David's mind that this could also be a place where he would be a prime target for someone like Jimmy Becker and his rifle. There were trees on both sides and on the bluff across the creek where a sniper could hide undetected from anyone who might happen to be in the area. It could be Louis's ultimate revenge. Not only would Mary Rose lose someone she loved and admired, but also her other benefactor. It would also explain the meeting between Louis and Jimmy Becker and the money he had given him. In a warped way it all started to make sense, especially if Louis had even the slightest inkling that David was becoming suspicious of his personal and business motives. He felt a sudden chill run down his spine as he put the note in his pocket and took an envelope from his desk drawer that had Harry's name on it. He added a few more paragraphs to the letter inside and sealed it and put it in his breast pocket. As he stood up to leave he had to steady himself from the vertigo he was now routinely experiencing. Passing Janet's desk he said, "See if you can get Harry to handle the two meetings I have scheduled for today. I'm going out for a while. Tell him something unexpected came up. He'll understand." He paused and laughed, "I guess I have a date with an angel about an urgent matter."

Janet smiled and acknowledged it was as good as done. Then she added, "An angel? That's sounds like it could be interesting."

David's first stop was at Our Lady of Hope Church. He let himself in the side door that he knew would be open. He thought it was sad that now many churches had to be kept locked if they were unattended, to prevent them from being robbed and vandalized by people who had no intentions of praying. He was relieved to find the church empty and the only sign of life being the ever-burning red sanctuary lamp that signified the presence of the Blessed Sacrament. He walked to the church entry and followed the curved choir loft staircase to the cove where the white marble statue of the angel stood artfully poised on one bare foot. He glanced up the staircase to be sure he was alone and carefully reached behind the angel's raised foot. Just as Michael had described to him, his fingers felt a small cache. His hand was slightly larger than the tiny hiding place but by fully extending his forefinger and thumb was able to wiggle in and with great relief felt them touching the small notebook he was seeking. He held his breath as he struggled to get the pages between his fingers solidly enough so he could extract the precious evidence from its angelic protector. By bending it slightly, he was able to slip it out fully intact. Holding the notebook firmly, David took a deep breath and was overcome with a great sense of relief. He quickly glanced through the handwritten pages and saw it was indeed what he'd been hoping for. This was the link that would tie Louis to the drug trafficking he and Michael suspected him of.

He descended the staircase and walked briskly to the church's downstairs office where throughout the years he had spent many hours visiting with Father Sean. He paused to listen and when he was sure he was alone turned on the copier and made a copy of the entire contents of the notebook. He clicked the machine off and returned to the choir loft stairs and replaced the original notebook into its well-protected hiding place.

Once outside he drove about a mile from the church and found a public telephone where he dialed the number of the policeman Michael's daughter Kathleen had assured them was a trustworthy person on the local drug task force. About twenty minutes later an unmarked police car pulled up and the driver introduced himself as Casey Baylor of the Minneapolis Police Department. He provided his identification and invited David to get into his car. The two men talked for about a half hour and concluded their discussion by David giving him the copy of the notebook pages. It was agreed that Casey and his most trusted men would be stationed outside Philip Johnson's apartment around four that afternoon to intercept Jimmy Becker. The notebook, along with Becker should lead them back to Louis Welheim. If all went as planned the original notebook would be delivered to Casey, but only after Jimmy was in custody. David stood and watched as Casey Baylor drove away knowing the ball was now in his court. He had no choice but to believe his new acquaintance was not one of the officers who had sold out and was indeed a servant of the people who would live up to Kathleen's high recommendation.

David checked his watch and realizing it was already almost eleven o'clock returned to his car and drove to Harry and Annie's house. He rang the doorbell and Jessie opened the door.

"Hi, Daybid."

"Hi sweetie, is your mama at home?"

"Yeah, she's in the bafroom." Jessie looked at him with a very serious expression on her face.

"May I please come in?"

"Yeah, I'll get mama."

Jessie walked to the bottom of the steps and called out, "Mama, Daybid's here."

Annie came to the top of the stairway. "I'll be right down David. It seems I'm having a bit of a bad hair day." He could barely hear her as she added, "Oh, Jessie, how could you?"

Annie finally came downstairs zipping the back of her skirt and David noticed her hair seemed quite different from the way she usually wore it.

She stopped when she saw him looking intently at her hair. "It looks bad doesn't it? Oh shoot! Dang it!"

David tried to keep from smiling but couldn't help himself. "So, what did you do to it?"

"Jessie was playing in my bathroom and unbeknownst to me rearranged the stuff on the counter. As you know, I don't see well, so I rely on all the stuff on my counter being in a certain order. Well, I reached for what I though was the hair spray and sprayed my hair with deodorant. Thank God I didn't spray my underarms with hair spray or I'd be walking around with my arms stuck to my sides. Do you think it would help if I wore a scarf?"

David grinned, "I think I'll take the fifth on that one. You do whatever you think is best and I'm pretty sure you'll be fine. Anyway I'm glad I found you at home. I have a couple things I wanted to drop off for you and Jessie." He handed her a small box. "I found these the other day when I was going through some of my mother's things."

Annie opened the box and carefully lifted out a antique marcasite cross on a silver chain. "It's beautiful, I love it. Thank you. Help me put it on, will you? Maybe if I'm lucky everyone will be so busy admiring my beautiful cross they might not even notice my hair."

David smiled at Annie's pleasure with her gift. "This is for Jessie." He took a box from the dining room table where he had placed it when he came in. Jessie sat on the floor cross-legged and eagerly pulled the top off the box.

"Oh, mama, look! Oh Daybid . . . It's so pretty." She carefully touched the child sized tea set trimmed with violets and gold edging, her brown eyes growing larger and filling with awe.

"I'm glad you like it, Jessie. This set belonged to my mother when she was about your age and since she never had a daughter of her own, I know she would want you to have it. Now you and your little friend can have tea together."

Annie knelt down by her daughter's side and said, "David, it's gorgeous. It scares me to think it might get broken."

"Don't worry, mama. Onna and I will be very careful."

David studied Jessie, "So, how's Onna doing?"

"She's fine. But sometimes she makes me do things and I get in trouble."

"Really?"

Annie stood up. "Its true. She told Jess to flush her new hearing aides down the toilet. David, I forgot to put my watch on, will you visit with Jessie while I run upstairs to get it?"

When Annie returned David and Jessie were sipping water out of the tiny lavender and gold cups and Annie thought she'd never seen anything quite so sweet. They visited a short while longer and David excused himself as Martina arrived. Jessie went to David and hugged him. "Bye, Daybid, I love you."

"I love you too, sweetie. Be a good girl and take good care of your mommy."

Annie smiled and said, "Tell David what Aunt Molly always says. "See you later alligator. After awhile crocodile."

Jessie stood looking at David with a very solemn expression on her little face and finally said in a very quiet voice, "No."

Annie rolled her eyes, "Sometimes I don't understand you child. Thanks David. I guess I don't have to tell you how much I love you." She hugged him and was a little surprised at how long he held her before letting go. No further words were spoken as he moved toward the door and left.

Checking his watch David noticed it was lunchtime but since he wasn't hungry, drove directly to the assisted living facility Father Sean and several other retired priests now called home. He spent the next hour in the privacy of Father Sean's room and when he left felt a sense of inner peace he hadn't known since he'd learned he was ill. He drove to the cemetery where his mother and father were buried and stood briefly looking at their graves. He placed his hand to his lips and moved his fingers across their headstone. He walked back to his car and drove back to his office.

As he passed by the open door to Harry's office he tapped gently on the frame. They visited briefly making small talk about David's visit with Jessie and Annie's hair. Harry smiled with pride and wished his friend a nice day. David stopped at Janet's desk and he informed her he would be in his office making personal phone calls and didn't want to be disturbed. She nodded she understood and asked if he'd called Michael. David answered he hadn't but he was on his list.

At three-thirty David left his office and closed the door. He thanked Janet for all her help and gave her a hug. Initially she thought his gesture to be a bit strange but knew with his illness he had become more sentimental so she didn't give it another thought.

David drove directly to the parking lot near the spot above Minnehaha Falls that Mary Rose called her prayer and divine inspiration station. At exactly seven minutes before four he seated himself on their familiar wooden park bench above the falls. The afternoon was bright and warm and he glanced around and was grateful to see there were no children in the area. As he watched the sun's sparkle off the water spray of the falls he found himself quietly thinking the words of the old hymn Angela's grandfather had sung so often.

> *No storm can shake my inmost calm, as to this rock I'm clinging.*
> *For Jesus Christ is Lord above, how can I keep from singing?*

David thought how everything in the universe is always changing and how we have no choice but to change with it, and then about his parents. At last he whispered his final words, "Forgive me Father . . ."

Chapter 44

Michael spent most of Friday waiting for the phone to ring. After all these years of living on the edge while serving on the police force he still had difficulty dealing with patience and now found himself pacing the floor. Martha had left to spend the day with Ellen as soon as the boys headed for school, but not before explaining to the couple who were adopting Ellen's son were coming to the hospital around eleven. She said she wanted to talk privately with Ellen before they arrived and took leave of Michael with a quick kiss and a sweet look of maternal concern on her face. As she was going out the door she stopped and told him she felt honored that Mary Rose had asked her to do this since they all knew this was an especially emotional time for the young mother who wouldn't be able to take her baby home. A baby she'd carried inside her body all those months. Michael had listened but his mind wasn't really on the conversation. Once he learned Ellen and the baby were fine he knew it was time to act on the information he and David had collected about Louis.

He'd left a message with Janet to have David call him when he got to the office but that had been several hours ago. Earlier in the day Veronica called asking if there were any new developments since the last time they had spoken. He felt a twinge of guilt when he told her there were none, however, felt justified thinking it was for her own good. As much as he admired her, he realized that with her working with Louis every day she could inadvertently let something slip that might jeopardize their investigation. She seemed discouraged and ended the conversation by saying she'd probably been wrong about the whole idea of Louis being involved with her half-brother's death. He tried his best to encourage her to hang in there by saying sometimes the darkest hour always comes before the dawn, but he knew it probably sounded like so many other lame platitudes people used to make others feel better when they probably had no idea about the outcome of the situation.

Michael tried to busy himself with little projects that kept him indoors and near the phone. He secretly wished he could be outside on such a beautiful day and around eleven let his impatience get the best of him and called Janet again. She assured him she'd given David the message but he had left to do a few errands and would probably call him as soon as he came back. A little after one Michael sat down at his desk in his office to eat the tasteless grilled cheese sandwich he'd made that left him wondering what Martha did differently to get hers to be so tasty. After all, who could screw up a grilled cheese sandwich? His final conclusion was obvious. He could.

As he finished his lunch his attention shifted to the aquarium and Little Louis. As he studied the water he noticed it seemed cloudier than usual and realized there was none of the usual movement Little Louis made as he wove his way among the plants, tearing off leaves and sending pieces floating to the top. He felt a little shock as he saw his beloved fish lying at the bottom of the tank. His lifeless body slightly tilted and resting on its side like a ship that had sunk to the ocean's bottom after being a casualty of an unexpected storm. Little Louis was indeed dead, his rapacious eyes now clouded with a white film. Michael took the dip net and gently fished the lifeless body from the bottom of the tank and carried it into the kitchen where he placed it into a zip lock bag. He marveled at how the strong and muscular hand-sized fish that had greedily eaten all the feeder goldfish yesterday morning now lay limp and dead. He put the zip lock bag into the freezer compartment of the refrigerator thinking he would bury Louis somewhere in the yard after he heard from David. A goldfish you might choose to flush down the toilet but a fish the size of Little Louis deserved a decent burial.

At a little after three the phone rang and it was Veronica saying she'd been left alone at Louis's office and decided to call Michael again even though she didn't have anything new to report. She laughed and said she had a feeling she was supposed to call him but obviously had been wrong. Michael asked how she happened to have the office all to herself and she relayed that Louis had gone out of town on a business trip and Geesela had gone home early with a migraine. "Michael, I've been giving serious thought to finding another job. I feel like I've hit a solid brick wall here and maybe it's God's way of telling me to look somewhere else." She sounded so depressed that against his better judgment Michael told her not to give up, as he was almost sure he may have a new, viable lead. Veronica tried to press him for more details but he held his tongue. He hoped he hadn't said too much already.

"Darn it! I know in my heart that Louis is involved."

"Are you at Louis's office?"

"No, don't worry. I would never use an office phone for a personal call like this. I'm on my break and at a pay phone down the street. We have an automatic pick up at the office if both Geesela and I are not there. If she asks where I was I'll tell her I ran down to the drug store two doors down to get some aspirin. I'll make her think there's some bug going around that's giving us all headaches."

Michael felt a little more relieved. "Good thinking."

"I was thinking that Louis has this saying in German, 'Lass sich die schwachen selbst zerstoren'. I asked a German lady who is in my book club what it means. At first I didn't say it right but she was able to understand it enough to translate it into English. She said it means 'Let the weak destroy themselves'. She also said she remembered as a child in Germany hearing some of the Nazi officers joke about that. The idea that they could count on the weak to eventually destroy themselves anyway, so they were doing them a favor by helping them along. She was kind of shocked I would know about that saying, so I told her I read it in a book."

"Not a very nice philosophy is it?"

"No. I've also heard Louis comment to one of his closest lawyers something about Der Wolf. He'll say, maybe its time for Mr. so and so to meet Der Wolf. He says it when he thinks no one can hear him and like it's their own private little joke, but I have no idea what he means by it."

"You've actually heard him say that?"

"Yes. Several times, but like I said, it's always when he thinks no one else is within hearing distance. Does Der Wolf mean anything to you?"

"Maybe . . ." Michael could feel an uneasiness growing inside. "Where did you say Louis was going today?"

"I believe he had a meeting in St. Cloud."

"Is he alone or did someone go with him?"

"Gosh Michael, I don't know, he was already gone by the time I got to the office, and old Geesela, who probably got her early training with the SS during the war, makes it a point of honor not to let me know too much of Louis's personal business."

"Thanks for calling, Veronica, I need to hang up now to make a phone call, but I'll get back to you if I learn anything new."

Michael tried David's office number but got a busy signal. Next he dialed Janet's reception desk and got another busy signal. He hadn't heard Martha's car drive into the driveway and was surprised when the kitchen door slammed. He got up and went into the kitchen. She smiled brightly and asked, "What on earth are you doing in the house on such a beautiful day? I thought you'd be outside all day long."

"I've been waiting for David to call. He didn't stop at the hospital to see Ellen and her baby did he?"

"No, he didn't. I was there the whole time with Ellen and I'm sure I would have seen him. Oh, Michael, you should see that little boy. He has a full head of black hair and the bluest eyes. The couple that are adopting him are very nice and they already seem to adore him. They live here in Minneapolis and are completely open to having Ellen remaining a part of the baby's life."

"Did you say Mary Rose was going out of town today?" Michael tried to keep his voice sounding casual even though his heart rate seemed to be growing at an alarming rate.

"Yes, I told you that. Don't you remember? That's why I spent the day with Ellen, because Mary Rose couldn't be there. She went to spend the day with her cousin who had bypass surgery."

"And where is that?"

"Michael, what's this in the freezer?" Martha held out the zip lock bag that contained his fish.

"Little Louis."

"Who?"

"You know, my piranha. As you can see, he's very dead." He could feel himself becoming impatient.

"So, what in the world is he doing in my freezer?"

"Don't worry, I'll bury him later. I didn't want to miss David's call. Where did Mary Rose go?"

Martha was digging in the top of the freezer compartment so she didn't hear his last question. "I can't say I'll miss him. Now you can get some pretty fish. Maybe some angelfish or those big goldfish with long tails and bulgy eyes. Nice fish that eat fish food and not other fish. The boys want pizza tonight but I think you and I will have grilled chicken breasts, it's much healthier." She pulled out a frozen package. "What do you think?"

"Chicken is fine. Martha please . . . where did Mary Rose go and did she go by herself?"

Martha frowned at her husband, as it was not like him to sound so irritated. "I told you she went to St. Cloud to visit her cousin who is in the hospital. Her car wouldn't start so she got a ride with someone who was going there, but I don't know who it might be because she didn't tell me."

Michael left the kitchen abruptly and headed for his office.

"Is something wrong, Michael?"

"Now Martha, don't you go putting your worry machine into overdrive. I need to make a phone call." Michael dialed the number for David's office but no one answered. He quickly dialed Janet's number, which was still busy. He redialed David's number and it rang four times but no one answered so he hung up muttering to himself, "Come on, Janet dear get off the damn phone." On the second ring he was relieved to here Janet's cheerful voice, "Sullivan Glass, how may I help you?"

"Ah, Janet darlin', it's me Michael. Is David there?"

"Oh, Michael, I'm so sorry, you missed him."

"Did he seem all right to you? It seems a little strange he didn't return my calls."

"He seemed fine, considering what he's going through. Some of the pain medications bother him, and of course he seems a lot more emotional lately, but I think he's fine. Why?"

"Do you know where he was going now?"

"Yes." She hesitated and then added, "I believe he had an appointment to meet Mary Rose at four at the park bench overlooking Minnehaha Falls. The one she calls her inspiration station."

"Are you sure?" Suddenly Michael seemed to be having trouble breathing.

"Yes, I'm quite sure. I took the message myself this morning from Mary Rose's new secretary. I think her name is Nona or Nola. David and I figured it might have to do with Mary Rose's cash flow. She usually meets him there when she's having some financial emergency. Of course, I don't know that for a fact, but it could be the reason."

Michael interrupted her, "Do you have any idea what his errands were this morning? Think hard Janet, this may be very important." "No, I'm sorry Michael, he didn't really say. Wait . . . I remember now, he did say something that seemed a little strange. He joked that he had a date with an angel. Does that mean anything to you?"

"Holy Mother of God! I can't believe it. Thanks, Janet." He abruptly hung up the phone and after quickly filing through his billfold dialed the number his daughter Kathleen had given him for Casey Baylor, the cop she'd recommended on the Minnesota Drug Task Force. Michael had met him before and felt he could trust him to assist with the Welheim case.

"Baylor here."

"Casey, oh God, I'm glad you're in. This is Michael O'Grady. Did David Sullivan contact you this morning?"

There was a silence.

"God bless it man tell me, this could be a matter of life and death."

"Yes."

"Did he give you a notebook? Please, I have to know."

"Michael, I'd like to tell you but . . ."

"Jesus man, you have to tell me. I think David may be in serious danger. Did he give you a small notebook?"

"A copy. He said if we get Becker you'd give us the original. We're leaving now to stake out Philip Johnson's apartment. David said we could pick up Jimmy Becker there and he'd have evidence on him that would be instrumental in bringing down Welheim."

"Jesus, Mary and Joseph, this whole thing is going down right this minute! What in hell was he thinking? Oh God, I hope I'm not too late."

Michael tore out of the house so fast Martha didn't have time to ask where he was going. He squealed out of the driveway narrowly missing the neighbor's car that was parked across the street by the curb. He didn't even notice Martha standing in the driveway wondering what was happening to her husband. Michael used his experience as a policeman to find the fastest route to Minnehaha Falls in the shortest time possible. On several occasions he narrowly missed other vehicles as he darted in and out of traffic. He ignored traffic lights and twice drove over curbs when cars in front of him wouldn't respond to his horn and give him the right of way. It was the first time he ever yelled at a pedestrian to move it or lose it, and didn't even notice when they responded by giving him the finger.

Chapter 45

He had been thinking a lot about life and death lately, the exactness and the ambiguity of each. The eternal arguments about when life begins and when it ceases to exist, and the perpetually unanswered question of where *does* life go after it flees the bonds of our fragile shells?

He felt giddy and light-headed, as if he had taken too many pain pills, but he had been careful not to take any for twenty-four hours. One should meet death and eternity with dignity and an unclouded mind. If truth were to be known he was afraid to die, and yet deep down in the innermost chasms of his soul he instinctively knew he was more terrified of living. Pride, fear and justice had waged a relentless war in his mind but in the end, all had reconciled. His dark tumultuous emotions had finally melded with unshakable determination and given him strength. To equate his actions with courage would be a fallacy for even now, at this crucial point in time, he had been unable to completely justify his choice. Would the end justify the means? Should one die to save many? Even Jesus was said to have experienced a fleeting moment of mortal misgivings in the hours before his death.

There would most certainly be people who would beg to differ and question his mental capacity considering his circumstances, the omnipresent, gossiping newsmongers. He took a deep breath and concluded it no longer concerned him, for he had already come too far. Time was running out and there was no turning back. The die had been cast. He remembered a forgotten phrase from some yet unscathed recess of his brain and whispered it as if trying to reassure himself. "*Omnis mutantur, nos et nutamur in illis.*" All things are changing, and we are changing with them.

Once again he started to softly sing the words of that old familiar hymn as he surveyed the breathtaking panorama of the falls. It would be the last earthly view he would experience and he wanted to absorb it into his entire being. He stopped singing and began to whisper. His face was drawn and his words were hardly audible. David let out a deep sigh as tears flowed freely down his cheeks, "Forgive me Father, for what I am about to do . . . ." The afternoon sun warmed his face as if reassuring him all was well. He saw a glint of brilliant light reflect off something in the verdant foliage across the river followed by a piercing crack.

Later, his friends would express relief and take comfort in the thought that he had probably not suffered, but that was not completely true. For one brief, exquisite moment it was as though all the pain he had endured in his entire life had been gathered into one tiny point that penetrated the center of his forehead causing his world to explode into a shower of stars. He only vaguely remembered his body being thrown backwards and within the same second another body, also his but more ethereal, being projected forward like a missile with such great force that every cell in his being cried out with unforgiving pain. He spiraled into space engulfed in ecstasy, all his earthly burdens absolved.

Chapter 46

Harry left work an hour early and was looking forward to a quiet weekend with his family. He drove into his driveway and stopped as Thomas the cat sauntered across the garage floor. As he entered the house it seemed unusually quiet except for Martina talking in Spanish on the kitchen phone. He knew she was visiting with one of her relatives, probably one of her children, and was amazed at how fast she talked. She stopped for a moment and holding the phone between her head and her shoulder to free her hands said, "Hello, Harry. Annie's upstairs shampooing her hair and she asked me to give you this." Martina opened the refrigerator and handed Harry a glass of wine and the stack of mail that had been lying on the kitchen counter. She resumed her conversation without missing a beat.

He accepted the wine and the mail and headed into the dining room where he noticed a lovely little tea set sitting on the table. Moving on into the living room he saw Jessie laying on her back on the couch with her old baby blanket pulled up covering her face so she could suck her thumb undetected. He stood watching her, assuming she was sleeping but sensing his presence she pulled the blanket down and looked at him. Finally she said, "Hi, daddy."

"Hi, sweet pea, were you taking a nap?"

"No."

He placed the stack of mail and his wine glass on the end table and sat down on the edge of the couch next to his daughter. "Are you okay? You look like you might not be feeling well."

"I'm okay."

Annie came downstairs and at first Harry was surprised to see how dressed up she was but then remembered they had talked about going out to eat.

"I made a seven-o'clock reservation for us at the Century Room. I thought we'd splurge and go to someplace really elegant to celebrate your new duties at Sullivan Glass . . . that is, if you're not too tired? Janet said you had to take over two of David's meetings."

"Yes. I did, but that sounds great. You look beautiful in that dress. Kind of like Snow White." He couldn't resist teasing her.

"Thank you, Prince Charming. I even have a new necklace to wear. Well, not new . . . actually it's very old." She held up the marcasite cross for her husband to see. "David stopped to visit us before we left the house this morning and gave me this, and Jessie that delicate little Nippon tea set. They belonged to his mother and he said we are his family so he wanted us to have them. That's so sweet of him. I know all the medications he's had to take are hard on him but he seemed rather happy today. He said he felt better today than he has in a long time. I feel so sorry for him. He gets emotional when he talks about leaving us. Sometimes he almost starts to cry and it about breaks my heart."

"So, what's with our little munchkin here?" Harry turned back to Jessie who was laying quietly, listening intently to their conversation.

"I'm not sure. She's been moping around all afternoon. I took her temperature but it's normal. Maybe she's worn out from all the errands we did. Diane thought it was strange Jessie had destroyed the new hearing aides so she insisted they retest her hearing and it turned out the corrections they made on the new one weren't quite right for her. This one will be more accurate and she thinks Jessie will be much more receptive to wearing it. The retesting took a little longer than we'd planned but we still got her picture taken and stopped to see the bunny rabbits and puppies at the pet store. Martina said that she'll watch her closely and call us if there is a concern. I gave her the number for the restaurant. Are you sure you're not too tired to go out? We could postpone."

"No, honestly, I'm fine. It was a good day. I'll sip on my wine and read the mail before I go up and shower. We have almost three hours before we need to leave and by then I'll be refreshed and as good as new. I must say though, after a day like today I have a much clearer understanding of what running your own company can entail. Thank God for Baxter, Janet and you."

"I see you got a letter from your dad. The last time I talked to Sky she said he seems to have gotten his second wind and is painting more and sleeping less."

"I hope so. That man has more talent in his little finger than most of us have in our whole body." Harry picked up his wine glass and mail and headed for his recliner. He slipped the letter from his father to the back of the stack saving it for last. Molly would have teased him about that. She would have ripped it open first but Harry would save it until last so he could savor the anticipation.

"Here, daddy." Jessie stood beside his chair still holding her ragged baby blanket. She held out a white envelope for him.

"What's that, baby?"

"From Daybid."

"Did he leave this when he was here earlier?"

She shook her head up and down.

"I saw the pretty tea set."

She nodded again.

"Maybe you and I can write a note to him and tell him thank you and how much you like it."

Jessie stood silently looking at Harry for a while and quietly said, "No."

"Don't you want him to know how much you like it?"

She continued to stare at Harry as if he wasn't fully comprehending what she was trying to say, so she spoke again, "No. Daybid's gone." She took her blanket and crawled back on the couch covering her face with it once again.

Harry stared at his daughter and was puzzled by her lack of emotion. He wondered if he should try to talk to her but it was obvious she wanted to be alone with whatever was bothering her. He felt sure she was coming down with something. He opened the letter from David. It was typewritten which didn't surprise him as David's usual precise penmanship had changed noticeably in the last month.

Friday, September 11, 1998

Dear Harry,

I suppose I could write volumes on how much you, Annie and Jessie mean to me but I know that you already know that so I'll not belabor the point. I love you all and shall be eternally grateful to each of you. I'm so pleased that you have accepted my offer to take over the company my father founded and I know you will do an excellent job.

With Baxter and Annie's help I'm confident it will be in good hands. Baxter has agreed to be there for you anytime you need him but said he had no desire to take on full responsibility at his age. Besides, he said he's having too much fun traveling and playing with his grandchildren.

All of the legal paperwork has now been signed, and my lawyers will dispose of my remaining estate in the manner I've designated in my Will. Lee Ann, my housekeeper and her son will take over my home and Gretta, my faithful dog will be in their care. I have provided them with enough funds to maintain the house for a long time so it will never be a burden for her. I want you to be aware that if ever the company I have entrusted to you should become too heavy for your capable shoulders that would be the time for you to sell it.

Your friend and brother forever,

David Sullivan

At the bottom of the letter was a note David had scrawled in his own hand:

> *Our legacy is not how much we have gained, but what we have given.*
>
> *Not who has loved us, but who we have loved.*
>
> *Not who our fellow man says we are, but who God knows us to be.*
>
> *We must all be willing to die so we can find life.*

Chapter 47

As Michael pulled his car into the Minnehaha Falls parking lot and skidded to a stop, he could see the flashing lights in his rearview mirror from the two police cars that had been pursuing him for the last few miles. He'd ignored the warning bursts of their sirens and driven even faster. They must have called in his license plate numbers and realizing who he was, no longer tried to pull him over or stop him.

Feeling a chill of revulsion, Michael started blowing the horn the moment he was able to see the park bench with David sitting on it. The clock on his dashboard read one minute to four. His friend was sitting still as if completely unaware of the danger he may be in. Michael released his seat belt and opened the car door before the car had come to a complete stop. He bolted from the car yelling as the police cars pulled into the parking lot. One of the policemen had a bullhorn and called out a warning to get down, but the figure on the bench did not respond or appear to notice the commotion. As Michael bounded closer to David he saw a flash of light from the trees on the other side of the falls. Experiencing a pang of helpless grief he tripped and felt himself falling headlong forward onto the grass as he heard the distinct crack of a rifle shot. He pulled himself up just as he saw his friend's head jerk back violently and his body topple sideways.

Someone screamed as Michael struggled to pull himself to his feet. By the time he reached him blood was streaming out of David's forehead and the front of his jacket was already soaked in crimson. Michael felt David's neck to see if he could detect a pulse but there was none. It was all over. By the time the policemen reached them they found Michael cradling his friend in his arms and both were covered in blood.

Chapter 48

Harry was about to head upstairs to take a shower when the phone rang. Almost at the same time the front doorbell rang and Annie called out for him to answer the phone as she headed to the door. Harry picked up the phone and before he could say a word he heard Janet's tearful voice. "Harry, oh, my God! . . . Have you heard what has happened? David's dead! Someone shot him as he was waiting to meet Mary Rose by Minnehaha Falls." She started sobbing and at that same instant Harry heard Annie screaming. He dropped the phone and turned to see Michael standing by the front door. His face was ashen gray and blood stains covered the front of his jacket. Annie turned and ran to Harry, throwing herself into his arms, weeping hysterically. Michael stood with his arms hanging down at his sides looking completely grief stricken. Finally, he said, "That bastard killed him! He killed our David and now I'm going to get him. As God is my witness, I'm going to get him."

Casey Baylor and his task force intercepted Jimmy Becker as he was about to let himself into the patio door of his twin brother's apartment. He seemed totally surprised the police would suspect him of anything and willingly went with them to the precinct headquarters. He told the police he'd been out for a run and a thorough search of the apartment and his car resulted in no evidence whatsoever to suggest that he owned any kind of firearm, much less that he had assassinated David Sullivan.

In another part of town, Louis Welheim pulled his car into the front drive of Seaton House. He got out and escorted Sister Mary Rose toward the front door where they were met by Nola the new secretary. Between sobs she relayed the tragic news of the murder of David Sullivan. Louis expressed shock at the announcement and tried to console Mary Rose by extending both arms in a stilted effort to embrace her. She pulled back abruptly and taking several steps away from him she quickly entered Seaton House. As if reconsidering she turned to thank him for his kindness but stated she needed to be alone. With a cold sense of satisfaction, he noticed the pain in her eyes and the tears that were flowing freely down her face as she closed herself into the small room that served as the home's chapel.

Louis was more than mildly surprised to learn the police had apprehended a suspect in the shooting of the prominent businessman, but smiled to himself when it was announced a few hours later that the arresting authorities were facing the possibility of releasing him for lack of any definitive evidence.

Chapter 49

Sergeant Bennie Jordan left the police station at four-o'clock Saturday afternoon. He visited his usual hang out, drank two beers and then stopped at a pay phone a block away. He dialed Louis Welheim's private number at his home. Louis answered and Bennie assured him things were going well.

"That's one real cool dude you got there. Christ, he's got balls of steel. He didn't even break a sweat when they questioned him. Sits around reading GQ like he's at an airport waiting for his flight to go on vacation. His lawyer, I think his name is Crown, showed up already this morning and the word is, if he gets his way Towers should be out Monday morning, Tuesday at the very latest."

"Good. Any thoughts about how they picked him up?"

"Nothing. Even though homicide has the case they got a new guy by the name of Casey Baylor who seems to be poking his nose into the investigation. He's the top drug task force man, and comes to us by way of California. Word on the street is he's one tough son-of-a-bitch. Honest too, and as we know, that can be a deadly combination. He's got a few good men as they say, and no one gets close to any of 'em so we hear almost nothing of what prompted them to focus on Towers. Something kind of strange though, they keep calling him Becker.

I don't understand why Baylor is involved seeing how it's a homicide, but some of the guys are speculating they're trying to tie Towers, or Becker as they call him, to that girl that got strangled in the park. Their thinking seems to be there might have been some connection, like possibly a drug deal involved. Sounds like a stretch to me."

"Did they bring Philip Johnson in for questioning?"

"Yeah, but that preppie prick is as confused as everybody else. Even though Towers has a solid identity they keep calling him Jimmy Becker and that's confusing the hell out of everyone."

418

Louis smiled at Jordan's last remark. "Keep me posted if anything new develops."

"Will do."

Michael hadn't slept a wink since David's murder. He spent all of Saturday until dark combing the neighborhood for the car and gun Jimmy Becker had used. Some of the officers working homicide were now looking into the possibility there may have been another person involved. An accomplice, who may have driven the car and taken the gun with him after dropping Jimmy off a couple of blocks away. Michael didn't believe that was the case because Jimmy Becker's profile as a possible assassin was that of a loner. It was his show, and he needed to be completely in control.

Early Sunday morning Michael left the house before Martha and the boys were up and headed to the police station to see if there had been any new developments. He stopped at Casey Baylor's office not knowing if he would be there at this early hour but was not surprised to see him sitting at his desk with his head in his hands.

"Mind if I come in?"

"Michael, I'm glad you're here. Come in. First off, I want to tell you I'm terribly sorry about what happen to David Sullivan. I had no idea what was really happening. He told me he had a meeting with someone important to the case but failed to expand on who that person might be or that he was intentionally putting himself in that much danger. I guess I was so blown away by the contents of the notebook and what it could mean, I didn't get all the details. Damn it! Part of this was my fault. I jumped the gun."

"It doesn't really matter now. David was an extremely intelligent man and certainly knew what he was doing. I'm convinced he told you exactly what he wanted you to know. You may find this difficult to understand but the more I think about it I know he wanted it to end exactly the way it did. He was a dead man already and at most had only a couple months to live. He had a fast growing tumor that was rapidly destroying his brain."

"I'm sorry, I had no idea. He also failed to mention that fact when we spoke."

"He was the finest man I've ever met and to have all this happen to him . . ." Michael sank into the chair and he felt a great weariness envelop his body and his spirit.

"Can I get you some coffee?"

"No, I was wondering if there was anything new on our boy."

"Becker, or I should say, James Towers? A little, well, at least something that may prove helpful. I spent most of the day, and part of the night trying to find out more about him. It seems James Becker, the twin of Philip Johnson, is officially dead. James Towers on the other hand, is very much alive and is the adopted son of a woman whose name is Madeline Towers. Madeline was the only daughter of a man by the name of Tyrone Towers."

"Michael looked up, "The old movie star?"

"Close but no cigar. That was Tyrone Powers and this is Towers. Seems like he made a ton of money in construction and real estate like our friend Louis. He died in a construction accident and left all his money to his unattractive and slightly reclusive daughter. It seems she spent part of her time in California and the rest lazing around the south of France. On one of her visits to California she somehow acquired a teenage son. My guess is it was she who was responsible for creating the new identity for James Towers.

James didn't always live in poverty as we might have suspected, but learned very quickly to appreciate the good life. From what I can gather he took a special liking to racing and is a very skilled racecar driver. Shortly after he turned twenty-one, Madeline died in a house fire that was ruled accidental. Conveniently, her only son James was out of town at the time and when he learned the tragic news about his mother he broke down and spent a few weeks at a private clinic to help him recover from his grief. After a respectable time of mourning he collected her life insurance money, plus all the proceeds of his mother's estate and moved back to her chateau in France. I got most of this information from the police detective who was investigating the fire as a possible arson. He was convinced that Madeline's adopted son had something to do with her death but he couldn't prove it. It was he who reminded me that serial killers often start their careers with arson, were you aware of that?"

Michael shook his head no.

"Because of this, it was very interesting when David shared the fact that Jimmy Becker and his mother also died in an accidental house fire, or at least the authorities believed they did. Anyway, from that point on James Towers has not had so much as a parking ticket. He has been, according to the detective that got his information from the French authorities, often suspected of multiple scams that have netted him a lot of money but no one has ever caught him with his fingers in the cookie jar.

For the scams he sometimes worked with a woman by the name of Juliet Newberry, also known as the Countess of Newberry, Juliet Day, Latifa Kingsley, and Anastasia Towers, plus several more aliases, but her real name is Judy Goldman from Queens in New York. She and James sometimes traveled as husband and wife, or as brother and sister, or as two strangers who just happen to become introduced to each other, depending on whatever the scam required. Judy Goldman was an aspiring actress in New York who did fairly well because not only is she quite exotic and beautiful, but also a pretty talented actress. When she was twenty-two or so she moved to Paris using the name of Juliet Day where she met and married the Count of Newberry, who was in his late seventies. After a two-month honeymoon, and we might speculate, a few conjugal romps between the sheets, the good Count's heart gave out and she inherited not only his title, but also all of his money, much to the despair of his family. I think it was shortly after that she hooked up with Towers.

About a year and a half ago Juliet got into some kind of a situation with the French police but somehow slipped away before they could file charges. Since then, no one seemed to know where either of them were. This same detective tells me he's convinced James Towers is a serious hit man for hire but again, no one has ever been able to link him to anything. What we do know is on at least two separate occasions he's been spotted in a certain area just before a hit takes place. Bottom line is we have to find that gun before Monday morning or we are toast and Becker walks. With his track record if he walks out that door we'll have about as much of a chance of a snowball in hell of ever finding him again.

The required bail money won't slow him down for a minute and his lawyer Sylvester Crown, is called Sly Crown for a reason. He used to practice in the Seattle area but his wife is in the early stages of lung cancer. She has a sister who's married to a doc at the Mayo Clinic so last year they moved to Rochester so she could be under Mayo's care. Crown is considered one of the finest lawyers in the country and a formidable opponent, so without that gun Becker will probably be history. We're still a little confused how Crown got called in on the case since Becker never made a call to anyone much less a lawyer. Maybe this is where our friend Welheim fits in. He's probably covering his ass, and his assets."

"Are they completely sure about the make of the gun?"

"We're almost sure we have it nailed down. Homicide recovered a slug at the scene and are almost positive it's the one that that killed David. It was shot from an Italian 6.5 Carcano bolt-action rifle. Ironically it's the same kind Oswald used to kill Kennedy. Something Becker might do to add a little notoriety to his killing."

At that point Officer Bennie Jordan poked his head into Casey's office and said brightly, "Hi guys, how's it going? Come up with any new leads?"

Casey Baylor sat back in his chair and pushed it away from his desk looking directly at Bennie. Michael could almost feel the temperature drop in the room. "Hello, Bennie. Michael and I are catching up on the Vikings. Since I'm from California I'm going to need some tutoring."

Bennie frowned and it was obvious he wasn't welcome. "Yeah, sure, go Vikings go. Good to see you again, Michael."

Michael reflected on Casey's reaction to Bennie and his body language. His eyes and face held a bitter expression so Michael waited until Bennie turned a corner down the hallway. He reached over and closed Casey's office door. "I could be wrong and correct me if I am, but my guess is we were just talking to one of Louis's moles."

"And you would say that why?" Casey's face and expression remained unchanged.

"The cop who told us where to find the notebook said he was quite sure about that. He said Bennie always has way too much extra cash and toys for a cop's salary."

"Interesting, and I thought I disliked him because he's such a nosy bastard."

Michael couldn't help but chuckle, "The other name he mentioned was Gordy Fresner, so keep that in mind."

"Oh, yeah. That one surprised me too but he was also mentioned in the notebook as a possibility, but thanks, I'll take that into consideration. So, tell me, do I look as tired as you do?"

Michael pretended to scrutinize Casey's face, then using his best Irish brogue said, "To quote a dear friend of mine, you look as if you have a banshee ridin' on your coat tails. My daughter Kathleen says you're a good man and I know now you're the one I want to be handling this investigation. With a little luck and some good police work we'll nail Becker's ass and then go after Louis. I swear, my friend David will not have died in vain."

"Thanks, you have a wonderful daughter and now I see where she gets her determination. She . . . ." He hesitated as if he was having a hard time finding the proper words, "is a very special friend."

As Michael turned to leave he stopped and faced Casey, "You don't think there was another person involved in the actual hit do you?"

"Nope, not his style. He's too much of a loner. On a scam he might have a partner but to kill someone I think he would want that all for himself. You realize he enjoys killing don't you?"

"Then you suspect that the gun has to be somewhere in the neighborhood along with the car he drove."

"Yep. Becker claimed he was out jogging, but he was hardly breaking a sweat when we picked him up. Hell, it was still almost ninety degrees out there. The place he stashed them can't be too far from Philip's apartment. My guess, considering the time involved from when David was killed and when they picked him up, it has to be within no more than in a two or three block radius."

Michael left the police station and drove directly to Our Lady of Hope, which was still almost empty except for the few regular early risers who came to pray the rosary before the first of three scheduled Sunday masses. He went directly to the side altar and lit two candles, one for David, and one for the safety of the people who would help bring his killer to justice. He prayed to Saint Anthony to help them find the gun that had taken his friend's life.

By five-thirty Sunday afternoon Michael was so discouraged he didn't know where to turn next. He and another officer named Red Flynn had scoured the entire four block neighborhood for the second time. Homicide had already searched the homes and back yards and finally expanded their search to an additional five block perimeter. Most of the residents were helpful allowing them to look into their garages and trunks of their cars. Some grumbled about being called away from their dinner tables or their television programs. He and Red looked into doghouses, fish houses, utility sheds, under stacks of wood, into dumpsters and garbage cans. Red even climbed into a tree house but they hadn't found a trace of anything resembling what they were searching for. Their hopes rose briefly when one homeowner who had been out of town, told them his garage had been broken into but after a thorough search of the garage and the yard it was determined only a case of beer and a package of steaks from the freezer were missing.

Earlier in the afternoon Red had bought them each a couple cheeseburgers and fries, and now Michael was feeling indigestion and a gnawing pain where he knew his gall bladder was located. He and Red decided to split up to save precious time. Michael took the back end of the second block from Philip's apartment while Red took the front. At about six-thirty when they rejoined, Red said he was exhausted and decided he needed a break. Michael asked if he had any Tums or other antacid tablets and if he did, he would continue for a bit longer. Red produced a slightly wrinkled foil packet containing an Alka-Seltzer from his breast pocket and they parted company.

Michael approached a large, older home on the corner of the next block and spotted a middle-aged woman placing a bag of garbage into a container. She seemed moderately friendly so Michael asked her if he could bother her for a glass of water to take an Alka—Seltzer. She seemed to hesitate until Michael explained he was a detective helping to search for the weapon that may have been involved in a murder. He showed her his identification and she apologized for being suspicious, and asked him to come in.

As he stood waiting for the tablet to dissolve he watched her take a pan of brownies out of the oven and place them on the counter. She looked carefully at Michael and realized how tired and drawn he appeared. "My goodness, you look bushed, how long have you been searching the neighborhood?"

"Since about eight this morning."

"Have you eaten anything?"

"Only two cheeseburgers and some fries and I think they're the reason I need this." He drained the glass and placed it back on the counter. "Thank you, I needed that."

"I have a piece of chicken and some bread that's still warm from the oven. Could I make you a sandwich? I wouldn't mind at all and it would be my way of thanking you for trying to keep the neighborhood safe. My mother lives here alone and I only come over a couple times a week to check on her so I really appreciate what you're doing. Especially after that poor girl was strangled in the park and now with another shooting by the falls. Please sit down. It will only take me a minute to fix it and you really look like you need a rest."

The tantalizing smell of the food caused Michael to realize how hungry he was and the thought of chicken surrounded by warm bread was too tempting to refuse. The antacid had calmed his gut pain but his feet and legs were still protesting the unaccustomed walking.

"That's very kind of you, if you're sure it isn't too much of a bother."

"My name is Lois Tanner and my mother is Gertrude Webster. She'll enjoy meeting you because she's such a people person and the days get long for her living here alone. I've tried to get her to move where there are other people her age but she says she isn't ready to live with a bunch of old fogies. I always find that rather humorous because she's almost eighty herself." She stepped to an adjacent doorway and called out, "Mom, come into the kitchen and meet one of the detectives who's investigating the murder that happened Friday afternoon at the falls." She finished making the sandwich and placed it in front of Michael. "Would you rather have milk instead of coffee? It might be easier on your stomach."

"That would be fine."

"The lady who cleans for mother on Saturdays said there were two policemen here after lunch yesterday and they searched the garage and looked all through mother's car, but you're welcome to do it again if you want to.

Mom, this is . . . excuse me, I think I've already forgotten your name."

"Michael O' Grady. I'm pleased to meet you Mrs. Webster." He made an effort to stand.

The small woman who entered the kitchen seemed unusually spry for being almost eighty. "Don't you go standing up, just finish your sandwich and then Lois can cut you a couple of her prize winning brownies."

"Thank you ma'am, this is delicious. I had no idea how tired and hungry I was." Michael studied the little lady and found she reminded him a little of Essie Applegate. He thought it had something to do with the sparkle in her eyes. Even though she was elderly, life hadn't been able to rob her of that. She also had a daughter who seemed very close to her and exemplified that remarkable bond that existed between mothers and daughters, and fathers and sons. How different it could have been if Thomas Michael had lived and was here to help.

"Did you know the poor man who got shot?"

"Yes, I did. He was one of my best friends and that's part of the reason I feel I can't give up until I find the weapon that will link the man the police have in custody with the bullet that killed my friend."

"I sincerely hope you can find it. I simply cannot understand how someone could do something like that to another human being. To think he might have been living in this very neighborhood is enough to make you want to lock your doors and not trust anyone. We had another murder here not so very long ago, but I'm sure you're already aware of that." Gertrude folded the napkin sitting on the table in front of her and then picked it up and shook it out. "Some poor girl who was out for a walk in the park. I warned the neighbor kids not to be out alone after dark. You know, you can't tell what kind of creep might be hanging around in the shadows."

Lois set a generous piece of brownie in front of Michael and refilled his glass of milk. The older woman continued, "I see a difference already. They're aren't nearly as many people out running or going for walks since she was murdered."

"I suppose not. Mrs. Webster, do you often sit outside on your porch?"

"Oh my yes, all the time when the weather permits. I like to visit with the people who walk by."

"Do you remember if you might have been outside on Friday afternoon about four or four-thirty?"

She thought for a moment, "No, I don't think so, not at that time. I like to watch television about that time so I won't miss the news, and of course, *Wheel of Fortune*."

Michael finished his brownie, "That was excellent and I'll be eternally grateful." He put out his hand to express his gratitude to Lois and then reached out and gently placed his hand on Gertrude's forearm. He looked directly in her eyes and said, "Thank you, you're both very kind." On an impulse he reached into his breast pocket and took out the picture of Philip Johnson he had discreetly borrowed from his parents' house. "Mrs. Webster . . ."

"Please call me Gertrude. You do realize Mr. O'Grady, there really isn't that much difference in our ages." She smiled sweetly and fluttered her eyelashes and for a moment Michael had the definite feeling she was flirting with him. He could see Lois trying to suppress a smile as he continued, "Gertrude." He cleared his throat, "Do you think you've ever seen this man, maybe out for a walk or a run past your house?"

She took the photograph and held it up close to her face, "Why, yes, of course, that's Philip. He's such a dear young man . . . so polite and kind.

426

He runs by here almost every morning before he goes to work. He used to come by in the evenings just before dark but he doesn't anymore since that poor girl got murdered."

"Did he ever stop to visit with you?"

"Oh, yes, he did two or three times in the evening. In the morning he waves and I suppose that's because he's in a hurry to get to his job."

Michael looked at Lois and back at Gertrude. "Might I be so forward to ask what you talked about?"

She smiled sweetly and fluttered her eyelashes again, "Of course, I don't mind. We usually talk about the weather, and one time he asked me if I lived alone. He also asked me if I got out much and if I was still able to drive anywhere. He likes cars and seems to know a lot about them."

"Did he ever ask if he could borrow your car?"

"Oh my, no. I told him that someone had taken the distributor cap off and hid it so someone else couldn't drive." She smiled sweetly as she looked at her daughter.

Michael sat quietly wondering if he should pursue the topic any further. "Your daughter said the police looked through your car yesterday when they were searching the neighborhood?"

"Yes, the woman who cleans for me said they were out in the garage for about ten minutes. She said they were very polite and assured her they didn't find anything." Gertrude paused and appeared to be thinking and then offered, "You know, now that I think about it, I did tell Philip about Bob's car. The Trans Am. I told him how my son Bob had restored this fancy old car when he was in high school and had taken it out for one last ride this spring when he came for a visit. That was a few months before he died."

Michael looked at Lois as if he wanted her to explain.

"My mother is talking about my brother's car in the old carriage house at the far end of her lot. Most people don't even realize it's there because the windows are shuttered and the front doors are padlocked and covered with vines. Looking at it you'd suppose there's no longer a way to get in, but if you look really close you'd see there is a tarp hanging over a pair of sliding doors in the back. There used to be a dirt alley back there but the city decided to sod it over about twenty years ago when they installed the new underground utility lines. It's grown over now and nobody ever goes back there but Bob was able to get his car out onto the street by driving over what's left of a small cinder block retaining wall. A few years ago my

427

brother sprayed the tarp to look like the stucco on the back of the garage so no one would break in and vandalize his car. He took it out for a ride in April shortly before he died of cancer. His son lives in Denver and is supposed to pick it up but he hasn't had the time yet."

"Didn't the police ask about the carriage house when they were here?"

"I don't know. I suppose they saw it but must have noticed the padlocked door and vines covering the front, so it probably looked like it hadn't been opened for many years. The cleaning lady talked to them and she wouldn't have known about the car or the sliding back doors. She said mother was napping and that's why they didn't talk to her."

"Lois, do you or your mother have the keys to Bob's car?"

"Yes, they're hanging by the back door. You see, there's a hook the keys are hanging on. In fact, he had two sets of keys." She took a key ring off the hook and held it up for him to see.

Michael took it from her and he could feel his heart beating faster. "But there's only one set of keys on the ring. Can you think of an explanation for that?"

Lois looked inquisitively at her mother and Gertrude said in a mildly defensive tone, "Don't look at me. I've never touched the keys since Bob was here, and I don't have the slightest idea where the other set could be."

Michael withheld a slight smile and said, "Could I use your phone for a minute? I need to make a quick call and maybe later, could we take a stroll out to the carriage house?"

Michael dialed Casey Baylor's office number and was relieved when he picked up on the first ring. He briefly explained where he was and what he had learned. "This could be a wild goose chase but something tells me differently. I think you and the guy heading up the homicide investigation should be here when we take a look in the carriage house, so no one can say anything was obtained illegally. Like I said, it may be nothing. It's your call."

"Thanks Michael. Don't do anything until we get there. None of our teams have come up with squat. At this point what you're on to may be the only thing we have going for us."

Exactly fifteen minutes from the time Michael hung up the phone Casey and another officer from the homicide division pulled up in front of Gertrude Webster's house. In spite of how promptly they responded, it seemed like hours to Michael. He was having difficulty keeping his mind on his pleasant conversation with Gertrude without aggravating the worried look on her daughter's face.

As the two men came up the sidewalk, Michael, Lois and Gertrude went outside to meet them. After introductions were made and permission was again given to search the carriage house, they walked around the big old home, past a large perennial garden, and around to the back of the vine covered building. Casey and Michael pulled vines and the tarp to one side and found the carefully disguised release lever beneath the roof overhang. They glanced at each other and slowly slid one of the heavy wooden doors a couple feet to the side. Since the old structure had never been outfitted with electricity it took a few moments to adjust their eyes to the darkness. Sliding the doors all the way open, the late afternoon sunlight revealed the outline of a car covered with another tarp. Michael noticed the protective covering had almost no dust on its surface.

Dick Frammingham of homicide carefully pulled the tarp aside and revealed a fully restored mint condition 1968 dark blue Pontiac Trans AM. Michael found himself feeling the way he did before opening a door expecting to find someone on the other side with a gun pointed at his head. He handed Dick the set of keys and held his breath as he watched him carefully unlock the driver's side door. Dick was wearing rubber gloves as he slowly opened the door. He clicked on his flashlight and beamed it around the inside of the car. Finding nothing unusual he nodded his head toward the trunk. They moved around to the rear of the car and he slid the trunk key into the lock being careful not to touch the car. The trunk popped open and everyone strained to see what was inside. Casey Baylor was the first to speak, "Ladies and gentlemen, I believe we've hit the mother lode".

On the floor of the trunk of the Trans AM was not one, but what appeared to be two high power rifles. One was in a carrying case and the other was lying on top with the scope still attached. Casey pointed to the top rifle, "This looks like it could be the one Becker used to take out David Sullivan. He pulled out a handkerchief from his back pocket and carefully slid the zipper down just far enough to see the contents of the case. I think this one is a 223 semi-automatic breakdown and if we're in luck maybe it could be traced to other murders. Get Ted Blanchette down here to dust for fingerprints before we attempt to move anything." He bent down and appeared to study the weapons more intently. Taking out his ballpoint pen he slid the cased rifle to the side. "Let see . . . What have we here?" On the end of his pen hung a small gold chain with an attached locket.

Michael stepped forward and studied the locket as it dangled from Casey's pen. "If that locket has a picture of a baby boy in it my guess is we could call that the frosting on the cake of justice. It looks almost identical to the one Jezzie gave her roommate Ellen to keep her baby's picture in. Mary Rose or Ellen should be able to tell us if this one belonged to Jezzie. Why is it these sick bastards can't resist taking a trophy?"

Chapter 50

At exactly seven-o'clock Louis Welheim pushed his chair back from the dinner table and thanked Ethel Danner for the excellent meal she had prepared. This was the third day in a row he'd eaten alone because Estelle had complained of being too ill to join him. Ethel assured Louis she would bring Estelle a small snack around eight, before she gave her the new sleeping pill Dr. Priester had prescribed.

Louis excused himself and instructed Ethel he was expecting several important calls and did not wish to be disturbed under any circumstances. He entered his office and closing the door behind him, selected his favorite music. Normally he would have started working on a project immediately, but tonight he sat staring at his desk, feeling melancholy. It wasn't that he was unhappy with the proceedings of the past few days. Yes, there were a few issues, however he felt secure about the eventual outcome. He finally realized he was brooding because he felt he completely lacked the insight for understanding women. He had never understood nor respected his mother, and although he had loved his grandmother and aunt, he found their misguided meddling in his life totally unacceptable. Back in Germany he'd been willing to give his heart to Ivy and when he finally shared his feelings with her, she had turned her back on him and gave her love to some non-existent God. He married Estelle believing her to be the perfect partner and she turned into a neurotic alcoholic who had given him a homosexual son.

Reaching down he opened his desk drawer and released the catch that allowed him access to its secret compartment. He removed the small gold ring and slipped it on the end of his little finger to have a better look at it. Slowly turning his hand, he studied the small band of ivy that was engraved on the ring as he thought about his Ivy who now went by the name of Mary Rose. With a twinge of self-disgust he replayed in his mind how upon learning of the death of her beloved friend David Sullivan, she had not fallen into his arms for comforting as he had expected . . . but as before had turned her back on him to be with her damnable invisible God.

He pulled the ring off his finger and placed it back into the envelope and then into the drawer. He clicked the hidden compartment lid shut as the phone rang. He picked up the receiver knowing who it was before he spoke.

"Good evening Louis. How are you? J. T. Blessing here."

"Yes, J.T. I'm fine. Thank you for having Sylvester Crown step in and take over so quickly. I think it was wise not to have you or any of my regular lawyers handle this little glitch with James. I know if you recommended Crown, he'll do a good job."

"Let's put it this way, I consider myself to be among one of the best lawyers available, but going up against old Sly would make even me nervous. He should have Towers, or Becker as they're calling him, sprung by tomorrow morning and within a few hours not even God will be able to find him. I also want to thank you for allowing him to handle my problem. It ended something quickly that could have dragged on in the court system for years. "

"I'm still puzzled how the police were able to apprehend him. James has always been so careful and I consider him to be one of the finest in his field."

Louis swiveled around on his heavy leather chair and looked upward at the huge painting of the two great wolves of Woden. His initial focus was on Geri, the black wolf, the one trained to carry out the wishes of the king and destroy his enemies. He smiled to himself as he thought of Der Wolf, or James Towers. "Good, it's wise to get him out of the country as soon as possible and keep him out of sight until this little inconvenience blows over."

Louis suddenly became aware that the door to his office had opened and without turning around said sternly, "Ethel, I told you, I do not wish to be disturbed."

There was no answer so he turned his chair around to find himself surprised to be facing not his faithful housekeeper, but his wife Estelle. "Go back to bed Estelle, I'm too busy to speak with you now."

Estelle pushed the door shut behind her and locked it. She turned back to her husband and raised her hand, which he was shocked to see clutched one of his German Lugers. "Did I surprise you Louis? Are you dismissing me so soon? Go to bed, Estelle, I'm too busy. Take your pills, Estelle. Don't bother me, Estelle. Well Louis, I believe I have your full attention now, don't I?" She staggered slightly but caught her balance and put her other hand up to steady the gun.

Estelle was dressed in a pink satin bathrobe and feather trimmed slippers. She seemed calm and determined and she gave no indication that she had been drinking.

Louis sat up straight in his chair and carefully laid the phone on the desk as he spoke in a quiet but firm voice. "Put the gun down, Estelle. You do realize you're acting like a complete fool."

"Shut up, Louis. This time you will listen to me. Everything is clear to me now. You took my life away and I let you. Then you took my son away and I let you do that to protect him from you. You've kept me prisoner in my own home and I allowed you do that because I'm weak and I don't know how to stand up for myself. But Louis, when you killed my Fluffy, you crossed over the line."

"Estelle, you don't know what you're talking about . . ."

"Louis, I said shut up! Yes, I do know what I'm talking about." She reached into the pocket of her robe and pulled out part of a rhinestone studded dog collar with its metal tag still attached and tossed it on the desk in front of Louis.

"The plumber found this out by the fountain when he repaired a leak in the pipe on Friday." She repeated her earlier statement, "Everything is clear to me now." She widened her stance and used both hands to steady the gun.

"Estelle, no! Don't . . . You can't be serious. Oh my God . . ."

"There is no God. Remember Louis? That's what you always tell me. It's just you and me now and I've decided to take back my life." She fired the gun and it recoiled in her shaking hands. The first shot hit him in the shoulder. Louis tried to stand as Estelle continued pulling the trigger until the gun was empty.

Estelle walked closer and picked up the phone Louis had placed on the desk when she entered the room. Before she hung up she spoke calmly to the caller, "My husband won't be needing your services any longer." She unlocked the door and opened it and stood facing a white faced Ethel Danner. "I believe it would be prudent for you to phone the police now." She smiled at her housekeeper and calmly returned to one of the side chairs, placing the gun on her lap.

The 911 dispatcher that picked up the receiver couldn't understand a word the hysterical caller on the line was trying to tell her. In desperation she finally raised her voice warning the woman that if she expected to get help she would have to calm down and stop screaming. After what seemed to be a very long pause mixed with muffled sobs Ethel was finally able to gather her senses long enough to give the address and a few sketchy details that allowed the dispatcher to continue her job. As she relayed the information all the she could say for sure was there had been a shooting that sounded like a domestic confrontation.

Two policemen that were patrolling in the neighborhood arrived at the Welheim estate within minutes and were met at the front steps by a semi-hysterical woman who pointed the way to her employer's office. With guns drawn they entered the paneled room and found a late to middle-aged, white male sprawled over the back of a leather chair. His head was thrown grotesquely backward as if he were having one last look at the huge painting on the wall behind him. He appeared to have been shot at close range in his shoulder, chest, and neck at least five or six times. Next to him sat a silent but smiling, attractive women in a pink satin bathrobe with a gun resting on her lap. One of the policemen held his fingers to the man's throat checking for a pulse while the other officer carefully extracted the gun from the woman's lap.

The policeman examining the victim spoke first. "He's gone."

His partner knelt by the woman and asked, "Can you tell me what happened? We have to know."

The woman looked at him, smiled and calmly replied, "Sprechen Sie Deutsch?"

"Shit, I don't think she speaks English. Now what do we do?" The other officer replied, "Try again. Tell her again that we have to know what happened. Maybe she's in shock. And Mirandize her. We don't know for sure she can't understand English."

The younger officer did as he was told and all the while she continued to smile at him. When he was finished he asked again, "Can you tell us what happened? We can try to help you."

Es macht nichts. Es ist mir egal."

"Ma'am, this is really important. You could end up going to prison."

"Na ja, es waere kein grosser Verlust!"

"Damn it! She didn't understand a word I said."

The woman continued to smile and then spoke in a very calm voice, "On the contrary young man, I understood every word you said. I simply asked you if you spoke German. Then you read me my Miranda Rights and told me you could help me. I answered by stating it doesn't matter. I don't care. Then you said it was important, that I could end up in prison, and I replied, so what, it wouldn't be much of a loss. Am I correct?"

The young policeman stared at her, "Yes, ma'am that's just about it in a nut shell."

"To answer your question, I shot my husband because he killed my dog Fluffy. Now, that wasn't so difficult was it?" She held out both of her wrists. "So, handcuff me and take me in. It's time I leave this house anyway. One prison shouldn't be much different from another."

As they were leaving the room she paused, "Do you like the music? This was one of my husband's favorites. It is from Wagner's opera Tristan and Isolde. This particular piece is called the Liebestod, or Love-Death where Isolde sings over Tristan's body. She imagines him alive, smiling and transfigured. In the end she sinks softly with the music into the golden peace of death that will reunite her with her lover. It's only an opera. Pure fiction. I, on the other hand, live in the real world. I am extremely pleased my husband is dead. It's a shame it took me so long to realize it."

By ten-o'clock on Sunday night the news of Louis Welheim's death was the featured story on every television and radio station. Not only in Minnesota but all across the country. The heady feeling Michael and Casey had experienced a few hours before was now replaced by shock and disbelief. Reporters swarmed over the grounds of Louis's estate trying to learn the details that might help to explain the bizarre murder of the wealthy businessman. Estelle Welheim was taken to headquarters and booked for her husband's murder. On the advice of her psychiatrist Doctor Roland Priester, she was immediately transferred to an undisclosed private psychiatric lock-up facility.

Michael left Casey Baylor's office a little after one A.M. Tossing and turning until after four, he finally fell into a troubled sleep and didn't awaken until almost two-thirty the following afternoon. As he ate the brunch Martha prepared he began explaining all that had happened since he'd left the house on Sunday morning. Martha listened intently and brushed tears from her eyes with a dinner napkin as Michael reviewed the details surrounding David's death, his assassin, and finally the unexpected demise of Louis. After they finished gathering up the dishes, Michael gently put his arm around Martha's shoulder and they went into the living room settling close together on the couch. They sat silently for some time and finally Martha leaned over and kissed Michael on the cheek and said she needed to call Kathleen to let her know what had happened.

Leaving Martha to grieve with their daughter Michael quietly left the house and drove to Harry and Annie's home to see how they were doing. He found Harry and Jessie in the backyard putting up a new swing and helped Harry secure the ropes on the lower branch of an old oak tree near the garden. As soon as it was judged safe for use, Jessie tried it out and declared it to be "per feck!" She played on the swing for about fifteen minutes as Michael and Harry talked quietly between the calls for "Push me daddy" and "Higher, daddy, higher." Harry let her coast to a stop as they heard Annie call out announcing lemonade and cookies for everyone. As they entered the house Annie and Michael's eyes met and she broke into tears. His heart went out to his friend as he realized she was still having a very difficult time. As they visited she showed him the letter David had left at the house for Harry and cried when she read the last few hand written lines aloud.

"In my heart I know why he did what he felt he had to do, but the horror of how and why it happened still has me in shock. When you came here after finding David with his blood still on your jacket and told me about the strange obsession Louis had with Mary Rose, and how you suspected this was his way of hurting her I couldn't believe it. I'd always felt in my heart that Louis wasn't a nice man but I never dreamed he would have any reason to hurt David."

"None of us did. I guess both David and I were more worried that Louis might hurt Mary Rose. How's she doing, by the way?"

"You know Mary Rose, she has that deep and undying faith that always gets her through every crisis. Harry and I decided not to tell her all of what you shared with us about Louis out of respect for her, and for his family. At least we can keep the reporters from having a field day with all the juicy tidbits."

"That was partly why I came over. I can't see that it would help anyone to know those details, so as soon as things settle down I plan to check with Casey Baylor to learn if he's found anything more that might connect Louis's motives to Mary Rose."

Annie leaned over and touched Michael's arm, "Thank you for all you've done."

Harry put his hand on Michael's shoulder. "I know David appreciated all the work you did for him, and he made a stipulation in his will to pay for your daughter's hospitalization. No matter how long it takes, and also to make visits to the Walden Resort available to your family anytime you'd like. That includes round-trip plane tickets and any other expenses involved."

Michael put his head down, "God bless him. Martha and I have had more than a few sleepless nights wondering how we were going to pay Doreen's hospital bills."

Jessie came over and whispered in Annie's ear and she smiled at her daughter. "Of course I'll make mac and cheese." She looked up at Harry and then Michael. "Jessie's hungry and I was about to fix dinner. How would you like to eat with us?"

"No, thanks Annie, I haven't seen my grandkids for two days so I'll be heading home. I'll let you know if there are any new developments."

Michael arrived home and found the boys had been invited to eat at a friend's house so he and Martha ate by themselves. When he told her about David's gift to their family she started to cry. "I was so worried and I didn't want to tell you about the call from Doreen's doctor with everything else that was going on. Saturday morning Dr. Shepard called and she wants to keep Doreen at least another month, it seems she slapped one of the other patients and when a nurse tried to stop her she hit her too."

Michael told his wife about Walden's Resort and showed her the brochures. "David said they're very good with family counseling and if Suzen Shepherd agrees, I'd like to send Doreen and the boys out there for their Christmas vacation. Now Martha, I can see that look is asking if we can afford it? Yes, we can because it's all compliments of our dear friend David, even the plane tickets. It's a wonderful opportunity. They have skiing, horseback riding and a lot of other fun things for the boys to do. And remember, their clinic is based on the holistic approach to healing so they do testing for toxins and other nasty chemicals Doreen may have put into her body. Who knows, maybe they'll find some physical explanation for her being the way she is."

"I think it sounds wonderful."

When they finished eating Michael offered to help with the dishes but Martha told him to turn on the news and see if there had been any new developments. As he watched he wasn't surprised that the unnamed suspect the police had in custody for David's murder was now also under suspicion for the murder of Jennifer Smith. At eight-o'clock he could no longer keep his eyes open so he kissed Martha on the back of her neck and trudged his way to their bedroom.

Michael got up early and went to the eight o-clock Mass at Our Lady of Hope. He arrived a half hour early and sat quietly thinking about all the things that had changed in his life during the last six months. Father Aston took a few minutes during his short homily to acknowledge the passing of David Sullivan. He described David as a dear personal friend as well as one of the benefactors who's generosity had made the new roof on the church possible, even though he was not Catholic or a member of their parish.

After Mass, Michael went to the side altar and lit two more candles, one for David and one for the continued success of bringing down Louis's drug empire. When the church was almost empty he walked back to the choir loft and followed the winding stairway to the recess that housed the marble angel. He stood before the statue studying the face of the eternally youthful being who stood so joyfully on her one small marble foot. He said quietly, "Well darlin', I've come to relieve you of the secret you've been guarding so carefully over the past years and to say thank you." He sat down on the steps and slid his hand up behind her raised foot and was relieved to feel the corner of the notebook. He carefully pulled it out, and hesitated before he opened it, trying to decide if he really wanted to know what was inside. Finally he flipped through the pages reading small snatches of what the deceased officer had written. When he was satisfied that Al Quantera had not been exaggerating, he put the notebook in his breast pocket and headed directly for Casey Baylor's office.

Michael felt a sense of immense relief as he entered Casey's office and found him sitting at his desk sorting through the stack of papers in front of him.

"Don't you ever go home?"

Casey looked up and smiled, "Hey, Michael, my wife is asking the same question. I've been expecting you. Come in and close the door behind you."

"So, how's it going?" Michael sat down on the chair across from Casey.

"As far as I can tell, pretty damn good. They've already taken Fritz Mueller and several of his men into custody and are in the process of taking the trucking company apart piece by piece. One thing about old

Fritz and Louis is that they kept very precise records. We had a little trouble getting past Louis's lawyers at his office, but once they realized a judge had provided us with the necessary search warrants they backed down. The copies from the notebook David gave us was more than enough to get our foot in the door with the judge, and the stuff that came out of Louis's office was like a map to his whole empire."

"I'm glad to hear that." He reached into his breast pocket and produced the original notebook. "I think you've earned this." He handed the notebook to Casey.

"Thank you, I knew you would bring it in but its still a relief to have it in my possession. I'll be sure to get it in the safe and be sure I'm the only one who knows it's there. Old Fritz had quite a set-up down in Douglas, Arizona. Douglas is southeast of Phoenix on the Mexican border next to a town called Agua Prieta."

"Isn't that the general area they refer to as cocaine alley?"

Casey nodded, "They had a similar set-up to one that was busted several years ago under the front of a concrete business. Fritzs and Louis's company had a couple of huge warehouses on their property. The bigger of the two buildings was used to repair and maintain all their rigs. It housed a series of hydraulic lifts that were used to work under the trucks. As it turned out, it also had a hydraulic lift mechanism under one of the workbenches that covered the entrance to a two hundred foot concrete tunnel that led into another storage building in Auga Prieta. Our man down there didn't give me too many of the details but he did say the diameter of the shaft was about five and a half feet and that it was thirty feet underground. The cocaine from Mexico was brought into Fritz's warehouse from the tunnel under the work bench, placed into some cleverly designed retrofit compartments under the driver's seats of the trucks they were working on and then sent out on their regular runs. A lot of the stuff made it here to Minnesota but it has also been shipped to other parts of the United States. I mean, we're talking hundreds of millions of dollars worth of cocaine. This is one big motherfucker of an operation. I sincerely want to thank you Michael, I know we could never have pulled this off without you and David helping us find that notebook."

"I'm glad it's all working out. I needed to do this for David and for my son Thomas Michael. Who knows? It's possible it was Fritz and Louis who supplied the drugs to the dealer who murdered my son."

"Kathleen told me about him and how painful it was to your entire family. Have you had a chance to talk to Kathleen yet to give her an update?"

"No, Martha has though. You know, the mother-daughter thing. This whole thing has been really hard on Martha. She's a mighty strong woman but what with our other daughter and all, she was about ready to cave. It's a good thing they could have some time between themselves first."

Then Michael winked at Bayler and said with a guarded smile, "I was such a wreck I likely would have spoiled Kathleen's image of me. I thought I'd give her a call tonight."

"She'll be very proud. Like she wasn't already. Quite frankly, I was a little disappointed the first time I met you." Casey pushed his chair back from his desk, a slight grin forming as he played with a pencil.

Michael looked at Casey as if he didn't quite understand what his point was.

"From what Kathleen told me I expected you to be at least two feet taller, with a white hat and a big old hero badge pinned on your shirt. He laughed, "She adores you and said Thomas Michael did too."

"Well, bless her big, little heart. I still have another daughter who doesn't quite share her view, but like my grandson said, two out of three ain't bad."

"Kathleen told me about her sister. Is she still in the hospital?"

"For now, I guess we'll need to take that one day at a time."

"That reminds me. I got a call from a Dr. Suzen Shepherd. She was wondering who would be defending Estelle. It seems she took care of her for a very short while when Estelle was in the hospital, and she's willing to testify in her defense. She quite sure she can provide documentation about how Louis was able to keep her over medicated and a prisoner in her own home."

"I know Suzen and she's a good woman. She's the doc who's working with my daughter. I'm glad she's willing to help Estelle. How about the housekeeper, Ethel Danner . . . can she add anything to the investigation?"

"Now, that woman is a real piece of work. It took us almost twenty minutes to get her to stop blubbering long enough so we could ask her a few questions. She finally admitted having made the phone call to David's office to lure him to the falls so Becker could kill him. I'm convinced she had no idea why Louis wanted him up there. She also believed she was helping Estelle by keeping her under control for Louis. According to her, Louis was a wonderful man who didn't deserve to die. I guess the fact that he put her daughter through college, and gave both of them places to live and cars to drive made her believe that justified whatever he asked her to do for him without asking questions. She kept saying it wasn't his fault. She'll probably walk away with only community service. Estelle's son Eric is flying in tomorrow from Switzerland and he was quite adamant that he doesn't want Ethel to suffer in any way. Sounds like a fine young man."

"So, how did Jimmy Becker take the news of Louis's death?

"I think he's finally starting to sweat. Even when he realized we had the guns and the locket he believed Louis was powerful enough to get him off. The minute he heard about Louis's death it finally started to sink in that he was in serious trouble. Two or more murders will mean life in prison or possibly even death row and that will dictate a major change in his lifestyle. "

"I was meaning to ask you, did you ever find a small book, like something a child may have written among Louis's personal belongings?"

"No, we went through that house with a fine tooth comb and I never saw anything like that. Is it important to the case?"

"Maybe, at least it might help us to understand why Louis acted the way he did. Would you mind if I stopped at his house and asked Ethel about it?"

"Be my guest. We have all the forensic evidence we need and I'll tell the boys to expect you. We still have a man outside the house to keep the reporters and the other nosy people away. I must admit, I still have a problem understanding how Estelle could have killed Louis over some overgrown dustmop called Fluffy. I suppose it was the straw that broke the camel's back or an accumulation of things she endured over the years that she was married to him. She's quite fragile emotionally."

"That would be my guess also. Well, I'd better be getting home and try to get hold of Kathleen."

Casey stood up and shook Michael's hand. "Tell Kathleen hi from me. I really owe her a lot. Shortly before I left California my marriage wasn't going so well. We had another baby on the way and my wife wasn't sure we needed to bring another child into the world if we were on the verge of breaking up. Kathleen sat me down and told me to get my act together and save my marriage. I'll never forget her little pep talk. My wife and I took her advice and after Josh was born we came here to live. I love my wife and to think I almost walked away from her and our family really scared me. You have a wonderful daughter."

"Thanks."

"Oh Michael, there's one more thing. Gertrude Webster said to greet you. She thinks you're the cat's meow." He grinned, "I'm quite sure those were her exact words."

Michael ran some errands and stopped to see Father Sean who invited him to have coffee. He explained about David's final visit and assured Michael that he had been fully prepared for his death. When Michael pressed him on the fact that David wasn't Catholic, and how he have been given the last rights of the church, Father Sean assured him it was as God would have wanted it. He then added that in God's eyes we all belong to the same church.

Michael arrived home as the boys were coming home from school and helped them work on a skateboard ramp they were building in the back yard. Martha informed them they wouldn't be eating for another hour so Michael read the paper and Corey and Danny parked themselves on the floor doing their homework. As Michael sifted through the newspaper he felt a gentle tug on his sleeve.

"Grandpa?"

He looked up, "Yes, Danny?"

"Do you miss your fish?"

"I guess so. He was a good fish."

"I miss him too. Grandma wants you to get some goldfish, but they're kind of wussy, don't you think?"

"Yeah, kind of wussy. What kind do you think we should get?"

"A kid at school has two Siamese fighting fish and they're kinda cool. But I don't think we'd want fish that fight, do you?"

"No, I don't think so."

"How about angelfish? They're pretty."

"I think that's a grand idea. The angels have been pretty good to us lately."

"Grandpa?"

"Yes, Danny."

"Did you know she can't come home yet?"

"You mean your mom?"

"Yeah, I overheard grandma telling someone she tried to slug another patient and then hauled off and slugged the nurse."

Corey rolled over and started to laugh, "Now, that's a big surprise isn't it! Oops . . . sorry grandpa."

"No, it's okay Corey," Michael thought about the times he'd seen welts on his grandson's face and neck.

"Grandpa?"

"Yes, Danny."

"Grandma's worried about how much money it's costing to keep ma in the hospital, isn't she?"

Michael laid his paper aside and studied his grandson's worried little face. "She was before, but the man who died on Friday was a good friend of ours and he left enough money to pay for all of your mom's hospital bills for as long as she needs to be there. So, we don't have to worry about those bills anymore."

"So, maybe we should just leave her there forever."

Corey started to laugh again, "Now there's a great idea! Sorry . . . it just slipped out."

Michael didn't comment on Corey's last statement because he knew it would take time to heal the pain Doreen had inflicted on her boys. "Come here, I'd like to show you something. That same man suggested when your mom is well enough to travel you can go with her to spend some time at this resort. I'm thinking maybe Christmas vacation." He showed them the information on Walden Resort. "They have skiing and horseback riding and all sorts of cool things to do. They also have a special program to help families to work out their problems."

Corey initially seemed excited but then said, "I don't know grandpa, it looks pretty expensive."

"Not a problem, it's all paid for, even the plane tickets."

Danny seemed to not share his brother's enthusiasm, "Are you going to come too? I don't want to go if you can't come."

"Well, I hadn't thought about it much but that does sound like a good idea. We'll all go together, grandma too."

Corey sat on the footstool by Michael's feet. "He was really a special friend wasn't he?"

"Yes, he was. Probably the best friend I ever had."

"How come God lets people like him die and really awful people like the man who killed him live?"

"I used to wonder about that too, especially after your uncle Thomas died. It seemed unfair but then I got to thinking that the people who are really good have probably learned all the lessons they came to earth to learn, so God takes them back to be with Him. The rest of us that are left here are maybe good people too, but probably still haven't learned all the lessons we need to know. So for that reason, we have to stay here for awhile longer and try to learn more of the things our souls still need to learn."

Michael could see Danny was trying hard to understand the conversation. "But then God should leave more good people here to help us."

"Sometimes he does, but we don't always listen to them anyway. Kind of like how kids don't always listen to their parents. Sometimes to make us understand we have to make the mistake before we realize it's for our own good."

Corey grinned, "Like when you told me not to jump my bike off the neighbor's ramp when they weren't home and I did it anyway and broke my arm."

"Yep, kind of like that."

Chapter 51

An hour later the phone rang and Martha answered it in the kitchen. Michael could only hear small parts of her conversation and it sounded like she was having trouble understanding the person on the end of the line.

"Michael, it's a lady by the name of Ethel Danner and she seems pretty upset. She says she needs to talk to you." Michael went into the kitchen and Martha handed him the phone.

"Misder O'Grady? I'mb nod sure you remebber me. Excuse mbe, I have to blow mby dose." He could hear her blowing her nose loudly. "I'm back, please excuse me but I've been crying all day. I hope you remember me. We met the day you came to my employer's house looking for your grandson's dog. I recognized your name from the paper this morning where it said you had helped to find the person they think murdered that poor girl in the park. The day you stopped here you gave me your phone number so if I saw your grandson's dog I could call you . . . but now I know you're a private investigator and that's alright because you were so nice and now I'm wondering if I could talk to you in private because I have no one else to talk to and . . ."

"Hold on Ethel, you're talking so fast I can hardly understand what you're saying."

"Yes, I'm sorry. I really have no one else to turn to and I must talk to someone. I don't dare talk to anyone else, especially the police until I ask someone else's opinion. I need someone I can trust who won't misinterpret what I saying. You seemed very kind and wise. Could you come over to talk?"

Michael quickly explained the situation to Martha and left for the Welheim's residence. Red Flynn stopped him at the driveway entrance and waved him on after giving him the thumbs up sign and congratulating him on his excellent detective work. As he walked up the sidewalk Ethel opened the door and almost pulled him inside. He decided she couldn't have looked any worse if she had tried. Her eyes and nose were red from crying and her face was swollen and blotchy.

"Please come into the living room. I need to ask your advice on something and I have no one else I can trust. I suppose I should have told the police but they don't always understand things. They just want the facts and they don't understand that everything isn't always black or white. I know now that some of the things I did over the years were probably not always the right things to do, but at the time I felt I had no choice. Mr. Welheim was always so good to me and my daughter, at a time when no one else cared and I felt I owed him my loyalty. Now he's dead and Estelle is locked up for his murder. How could things have gone so horribly bad so quickly?"

"I realize it's been a terrible shock to you."

"Tomorrow Estelle and Louis's son Eric is coming in from Switzerland. He is bringing his friend with him and this is where I'm having a real problem."

"How so?"

Ethel started to cry again. "I . . . I j-j-just don't know what to . . . t-t-tell Eric."

"Ethel, I'm sure the police have already explained the whole situation to him."

"But they don't know the whole story. I mean what really happened."

"Now, Ethel, please don't tell me you lied to the police."

"Oh my, no, I would never do that. I just didn't tell them all of what really happened. You see, I only answered the questions they asked. Mr. Welheim always told me not to volunteer too much information and to only answer questions giving the least amount of information possible, so that's what I did."

"Why don't you tell me what you didn't tell the police, and then we can decide how, or if, to tell Eric."

Ethel was sniffing between sentences so Michael offered her his handkerchief.

"Last Friday morning I made the phone call asking Mr. Sullivan to meet Sister Mary Rose at a park bench by the Minnehaha Falls. Louis asked me to do this and I did. I never questioned why Louis wanted me to make the call as he wouldn't have liked it if I had. I told his secretary I was the new secretary at Seaton House and that my name was Nola because that's what Louis asked me to do. Later that morning, when Estelle and I were in the backyard, she noticed the fountain had water all around it like there was a pipe leaking so I called the gardener who in turn called a plumber. Mr. Welheim was in St. Cloud so I took care of it like I am expected to do when something comes up out of the ordinary. The plumber came right away and we sat and watched him work. Just before lunch I came inside to fix Estelle a sandwich and left her watching the plumber but where I could keep an eye on her through the window. I saw them visiting but didn't think anything of it until all of a sudden Estelle came in and said she had a headache and wanted to lay down. I sat down to watch *Days of Our Lives* and after it was over I saw the plumber had left. Estelle wouldn't come out for supper Friday night and all day Saturday she stayed in her room. Mr. Welheim didn't seem to mind so I didn't worry either. She didn't come out all day Sunday until I heard her lock herself into his office and then I heard the gunshots. I called 911 and when the police came she told them she killed him because Louis had killed her dog Fluffy. The police found a piece of the dog's collar on the desk in front of Mr. Welheim's body."

"Okay, so somehow she found out Louis had killed her dog because why? Oh, I think I get it. Did the plumber find the dog's collar when he dug up the leaky pipe by the fountain?"

"Yes, but you see, Louis must have buried Fluffy there, but he didn't kill her. He didn't like the dog but he never would have killed her."

"So, how did Fluffy die?"

"Whenever Estelle had to go to the hospital I would take care of Fluffy. The morning Fluffy died I was out in the backyard with her and she was wandering around sniffing all the flowers and bushes like she always did. I turned my back to check if the few tomato plants we had in patio pots had any ripe tomatoes and all of a sudden Fluffy let out a terrible yelp. She had gone behind some hydrangea bushes and by the time I found her it was too late. This huge dog was standing over her and he had ripped her stomach out. All of her intestines were hanging out and the poor little thing was dead. She never had a chance to run away."

"That's strange! What kind of dog would do that?"

"He looked like a wild dog. Scruffy, like he wasn't anyone's pet. Big, like he might be part German Shepherd, but all gray. He bared his teeth and I could see they had Fluffy's blood on them and around his jaws. I didn't know if it was going to attack me so I started to scream and turned to run. When I looked back the dog was gone. I called Mr. Welheim at the office and he came right home and he sent me inside so I never knew where he buried Fluffy. He made me promise not to tell Estelle what happened and instructed me to tell her Fluffy had run away."

"So it was a stray dog?"

"I don't know that for sure. At first I thought it might have been a wolf but Mr. Welheim scolded me and said there aren't any wolves in this area. He seemed to get real upset that I would even suggest it. I guess because he really likes wolves. He has that big painting over his desk."

"Interesting. So, now you're wondering how Estelle will react if she finds out that Louis really didn't kill the dog?"

"Yes, I know she will feel terrible. She is so fragile already it just might send her permanently over the edge."

"Ethel, I don't think knowing this would benefit anyone, certainly not Estelle, and probably not Eric either. I think the best thing would be to try to forget it. It can be our secret . . . just between you and me."

"Oh, thank you, Mr. O'Grady. That's what I thought too but I wasn't completely sure. There's something else too, but I think I've already decided to tell the police."

"What's that?"

"Well, this is awkward for me to talk about but I think you'll agree it's probably important. All the years when I would accompany Estelle to visit Eric in Switzerland, Mr. Welheim would often have me wear certain things under my clothes. Usually it was a special corset or sometimes a pad I wore between my legs. If we flew commercial Louis always made sure we had the same young man who would check our bags and let us through the screening areas. I knew I was being used to carry things for Mr. Welheim."

"Things? What kind of things. Like drugs?"

"No, never drugs. Usually it was diamonds, but sometimes it was bundles of cash. As you can see I'm a large woman so I had no problem getting through security. We went so often they seemed to consider us regulars and it was never a problem. Mr. Welheim used to whisper to me before I left the house on those trips that this would be our little secret and he would always pat me on the back and slipped a hundred dollar bill into my hand when we said goodbye."

"I think it would be a good idea to tell the police about that."

"I will . . . I suppose they will want to know about his Swiss bank accounts too."

"That would be my guess." Michael sat quietly thinking. "Mrs. Danner?"

"Please call me Ethel."

"Yes, of course, Ethel . . . Perhaps you can help me now with something I've been wondering about. Did you ever notice if Louis had a small book that he probably kept somewhere private? It would have been handmade, like something a child might have created."

"No, I don't think so. But as you probably know, Mr. Welheim was a very private person. He really didn't share much of a personal nature with me. Of course when you live with a family as long as I have you often learn things inadvertently. Things that families keep hidden from the public eye."

"Do you mean like Eric being homosexual?"

"Yes, that and other things."

"Would you care to share any of that with me?"

"Not at this time. I feel I still owe this family so much and I don't want to risk hurting them any more then they already have been."

"I understand, but the reason I asked about this book is, I believe it contains something that could hurt Estelle and Eric if it should fall into the wrong hands. Like if a tabloid newspaper might come in possession of it. Louis's grandmother told me about it."

"The police searched his office and the whole house."

"I know, but I still think it must be here, possibly in his office because it was of a personal nature. He wouldn't have wanted anyone to see it so he probably hid it somewhere. Do you mind if I have a look?"

"His office is right in there. If you feel it could be hurtful to Estelle or Eric, I think it would be alright to look."

As Michael walked into Louis's office the huge painting of the wolves was the first thing to meet his gaze. He let out a low whistle, "The great wolves of Woden."

"Yes, but how did you know that?"

"His grandmother told me. The white wolf lying down is Freki. Her job was to kill the weak and the aged, those who were considered insignificant to the king. The black wolf was used to destroy the king's enemies. Probably the one Louis referred to as das wolf."

Michael looked through the massive desk beneath the painting but all the drawers were empty. The police had confiscated all his papers and files leaving only the furnishings. "It looks like the police took everything and they're quite sure the book wasn't with his papers."

"Mr. O'Grady, are you sure this book could hurt Estelle and Eric?"

"Well, I haven't seen it, but if it's at all like what his grandmother described, yes, I think it could."

"Take another look at the drawer on your right. Louis always kept that locked but one evening something came up with Estelle. She tried to cut her wrists and I admit I panicked and came bursting in here unexpectedly to ask for his help with her. That's when I saw him hide something in the drawer like he didn't want me to see it. Her wrists were bleeding even though we wrapped them so he had to take Estelle to the hospital in a hurry. A little later I came in to turn off the lights and out of curiosity I peeked into the drawer to see what he tried to hide from me. Louis hadn't taken the time to put the contents of the drawer back, but I know he shoved something into it even though when I looked it was still empty."

Michael studied the woman and tried to understand what she was getting at. He leaned forward and slid his hand slowly around the entire surface of the inside of the drawer. At the farthest point in the back his fingers felt a small lever and he heard a click as the bottom of the drawer popped up. Beneath it was another space that contained a small book and an envelope. The cover of the book was made of firm paper and tied with a thin leather thong that had been threaded through three holes in the edge that served as the binding. On the cover was a child's drawing of the two wolves of Woden. Michael looked at the pale pink envelope that was addressed to Gerhard Welheim in Berlin, Germany. The return address bore the name Ivy Stockel. As he opened the letter he found a small gold ring engraved with a delicate wreath of ivy and a black and white photograph he knew must be of Louis and Mary Rose back when she was still Ivy Stockel. Louis was handsome but very stern looking for such a young man. Mary Rose was beautiful with her long blonde hair and wearing a vibrant smile. Michael read the letter and the inscription on the back of the picture and put everything back into the envelope. He opened the book and was surprised to see how short it really was. Somehow he had expected it to be bigger. Page by page, he read Louis's youthful tale of the great King of Volkland. The book ended by proclaiming, the great king ruled his kingdom with his beautiful queen and his faithful protectors Friki and Geri by his side, and they all lived happily ever after.

Michael looked up at the painting of the great wolves and thought, maybe in that world you could protect your king but here in the real world almost nothing is black and white. There would always be the unexpected gray we have to deal with.

Ethel interrupted Michael's thoughts, "You can take it with you if you promise it will never be used against Estelle and Eric."

"Thank you, Ethel. I give you my word of honor."

As Michael drove home he thought about the strange ideas Louis learned as a child, probably at the knees of his Nazi parents. He thought of how Gerta and Marianna had told him about how Louis had been beaten and locked in a room all alone sometimes for days so his mother could go partying with the German officers. To protect himself he had created his own fantasy world. Louis had been the king and in a strange way, Ivy was to be his queen. He had created the black wolf in Jimmy Becker who destroyed his enemies. Michael pondered over the white wolf. Who was the white wolf? The protector of the king who's job it was to get rid of the weak and insignificant. Suddenly he remembered the phrase Veronica had translated and shared with him. Let the weak destroy themselves, and at that moment he knew . . . Louis's white wolf was cocaine.

Five days following David's murder a quiet memorial service was held in the same Lutheran church his parents had been buried from. He had been cremated as he had wished with most of his ashes to be placed beside the grave of his wife Angela and their baby son in Vermont. Harry, Annie, Mary Rose and Michael took a small vial of his ashes to the cemetery where David's parents were buried.

As Harry pulled back a small patch of grass Annie sifted the remainder of David's ashes onto the earth. Harry pressed the grass back into place and Mary Rose laid a single red rose on the spot. She spoke softly. "Red is the color that signifies a martyr and the blood that he shed to protect us from the evils of Louis and his kind. I believe God will judge David as such. His legacy to the world was not just his life but also his death. May his soul rest in peace."

451

Chapter 52

After everyone else was asleep Annie ran a hot, herbal scented bubble bath. The family evening together had been peaceful as she and Harry enjoyed occupying themselves with Jessie who had recently learned to play Chutes and Ladders and Candyland. Annie found herself pleasantly surprised at how quickly Jessie learned the concepts of each new challenge.

She reflected on the intense love she felt for Harry and Jessie and couldn't even start to imagine what that love might look like if it were converted to visual energy. She smiled at how she thought it would light up the whole room and be visible for miles around. She recalled that she had another experience that helped her understand what pain and suffering looked like, or at least felt like. After her senior year of high school she traveled to Europe with several of her friends. In the outskirts of Paris she had entered an old stone museum and suddenly became extremely ill. Pain and suffering seemed to surround her and threatened to suffocate her but as soon as she stepped out of the building her symptoms subsided. Later she learned the museum had once served as a facility for the criminally insane. It had frightened her so much she vowed never to let anything like that happen again. But now it had happened again and she knew it could continue.

Annie added more hot water and turned on the bubbler. The moving water caressed her body and she felt herself becoming more relaxed. As always, the unanswered question of her role as guardian of her precious little Jessie, one of the Star Children, was foremost in her mind. What would be expected of her unique gifts to help guide her daughter? How would Jessie interact with other star children and what were they expected to do for the world in the coming years? In her dream her friend had said the circle was almost complete and she found herself wondering if her words had been fulfilled. What would the coming years bring? She thought of her daughter and at how much progress she'd made in the past six months. Her speech had improved dramatically and yet when she was alone she would revert back to a strange little language only she seemed to understand. She had her own version of Ring Around The Rosie . . . Ringa ringa rosie, na da sir ka glo see, ah vill, ah vill, shul kom don.

She loved singing the rhyme whenever she played by herself and it was always in the strange sounding language she wouldn't share with Annie or Harry. Annie felt it may have happened because of Jessie's distorted hearing from the time she was a baby, but it seemed strange that her version of the rhyme persisted now when her hearing was nearly normal and her pronunciation of everyday words had improved dramatically. Harry had tried to explain it by telling her how he and Molly had developed their own version of Latin when Molly's brother Daniel had been studying to become an altar boy. Ad deum qui laetificat juventutem meam, had become, a day um day um quip e kwap, juicey to ta may ah. They were convinced they knew Latin and no one could tell them differently. She had reluctantly agreed it could be a possibility but she was not totally convinced.

As the warmth soothed her aching body Annie let Jessie's version of the song run through her mind. Ringa ringa rosie, was of course, Ring around the rosie. Na da sir ka glo see didn't seem to make sense . . . Ah vill ah vill . . . Annie thought how Jessie often got her vowels mixed up, like when she called her imaginary friend Onna instead of Anna. "Ah vill . . . o vill . . . e vill." Annie sat up with a start. "Evil, evil, shul kom don." She repeated the words to herself, "Evil, evil and she gasped out loud, "Evil, evil, shall come down." She repeated the poem again this time concentrating on the new version, "Ring around the rosie, na da sir ka glo see." Annie said the words over and over in her mind until they finally seemed to make sense. "Could it be, Ring around the rosie, now the circle closes. Evil, evil, shall come down?" Annie felt that in some childish way Jessie seemed to be grasping a glimmer of her future. At first she shuddered at the thought and then a deep sense of peace settled over her as she whispered to herself, "Through Divine intervention, she and the other Star Children have come into the world to take on the forces of the dark side."

Chapter 53

April 5, 1999

"Hi, Annie, it's me, Sky. Is this a good time to talk?"

"Hi Skylar, yes it is. Both Jessie and Harry have decided on an early bedtime since tomorrow is her 5th birthday. She's so excited and I think it's imperative she gets enough sleep tonight."

"I've sent two presents in the mail earlier this week, one from us and one from Russell, so she should have them by tomorrow."

"They arrived today, and I had all I could do to keep her from shaking them to pieces. I hope they're not too breakable."

"No, I packed them really carefully. How's Harry?"

"He's well, but he seems to get very tired by nighttime. By nine-o'clock he can hardly keep his eyes open. I think sometimes running his own company takes a heavy toll on him even if he loves every minute of it."

"Great! I was hoping to talk with just you. Russell's doctor isn't sure but he thinks he may have suffered a slight stroke. He's fine now but I'm really glad your family is coming for a visit this week. I'm sure he'll be fine but I wanted to let you know. Both he and Cody are excited to meet Jessie and possibly Russell allowed himself get overly excited. Cody and Uncle John have been working on a special fairy garden to surprise all of you. Uncle John says Cody is a natural gardener. He laughs about how Cody tells him which plants are happy and which ones are sad. Cody also decides which areas they would prefer and points out which ones are thinking about dying. I think he gets a lot of his sensitivity from my grandmother Magda. She's always telling him about how the Great Spirit lives in trees and mountains and in the wind. Yesterday, Cody's teacher sent a note home saying that even though he's an excellent student he tends to daydream in class. He told me he wasn't daydreaming he was listening to a tree outside the window that was crying. Later that afternoon the city sent some guys out to cut the tree down because it was diseased. Go figure that one. He might be my son but I don't always understand him. If I ask him about it he gets that look on his face like why even bother explaining it . . . you wouldn't understand anyway."

"Don't feel bad, Jessie does that with me more and more. Has Magda said anymore about the Star Children?

"Not really, only that the circle is now complete. According to her all the children have been chosen. That brings me to something else. Yesterday, when I was standing in the grocery check out line I was reading the headlines on those tabloids they sell, you know the ones. Alien baby living inside man's head, that kind of stuff? They had one called Beyond Astrological Press, or something like that. The headline said: Top ten astrologers predict the future for the new millennium. The article beneath contained subtitles that included terrorist attacks on U.S., unprecedented stock market losses, earth disasters, cloning of humans, alien contact, escalating wars, and children sent to heal the world. I bought a copy, and inside they quoted some woman from Vancouver, Canada who spoke about the Star Children having been sent to heal our ailing planet. I can tell you, I felt a chill run down my spine. She specifically mentioned a boy out east somewhere who can see and speak to dead people and a girl in India who can heal. I saved the copy for you."

"That's incredible."

"Has Jessie shown any unusual signs?"

"She still has her invisible friend Onna, and says she talks regularly with our friend David who was murdered last fall. Sometimes she knows things before they happen, and will answer questions before someone has a chance to ask them, but other than that she seems pretty normal. So far there have been no objects moving around the house by themselves."

From the time Annie shared her dream about taking guardianship of Jessie she and Sky often spoke of the Star Children. "Oh wait, she has this strange language she uses sometimes. I used to think it was because of her hearing loss but she pronounces all her other words just fine and she only uses it when she thinks no one is listening. I have an idea concerning it but I will save until we get to visit in person."

"Hmmmm. That's interesting. Cody does that too. I thought it was baby talk, but he too does it when he thinks no one else is around. He's shy with people but he loves animals and they respond to his affection. Sometimes he seems like a little Doctor Dolittle the way he talks to all the animals around here. Oh, Annie, I guess I'll have to hang up now.

My girlfriend and I are teaching a pottery class at the high school and I heard her honk. See you in a couple days. Uncle John will meet you at the airport. Give my love to Harry and Jess."

The next morning Annie called out to Harry as he was backing out of the driveway. "Don't forget to pick up a bottle of chilled Chardonnay and one of Merlot for the adults tonight. You know Molly and her chilled wine. Martina, Jessie and I are going to the grocery store to pick up a few items for the birthday party and I want to stop and put some flowers on David's and his parents' graves. I haven't been to the cemetery yet this spring and I feel like I want to do it. The last few days I've been thinking about David." She waved good-bye to Harry as she and Jessie climbed into Martina's car.

The grocery store wasn't busy so they were able to finish their shopping in less than a half hour. When they were ready to check out Annie selected two bunches of spring flowers and one long stemmed red rose from the floral department. After loading the groceries into the car, Martina drove them to the cemetery. Annie found the graves and placed the flowers in the urns and the red rose between the two graves. She walked to a nearby building to get water for the flowers. When she returned Jessie and Martina were walking down a narrow cinder path and she could hear her daughter counting the headstones. Her speech and pronunciation continued to improve since she'd gotten her new hearing aides and Annie was grateful to have enrolled her for preschool in the fall.

Annie poured the water into the urns and stood looking down at the graves. Tears began forming in her eyes as she spoke quietly to herself, "Dear David, I miss you so much. My heart and head understand why you did what you felt you had to do but it still hurts. I know it was better for you to go quickly but it was painful for the rest of us. I thought when you asked me if people could ever block me from getting into their thoughts it was because of the day I had teased you about stepping out of the shower, but now I know differently. Even so, I wonder if I hadn't been so preoccupied with my hair that morning whether I could have picked up on what was going on in your mind. Maybe I could have stopped you. Harry keeps telling me that in the bigger scheme of things it happened exactly as it should have. No coincidences, no accidents. Jessie never played in my bathroom until that morning. She moved things around and I picked up the wrong can and sprayed my hair with deodorant. That's where my thoughts were when you came by for your last visit. Harry calls it the dance of life and says we're all participants whether we're aware of it or not. He's gotten so philosophical during the past year. Surprisingly, I think Molly has helped him with that. In her own irreverent way, she's come to understand the way the world works better than most people. Michael assured me you died instantly but I still wish it hadn't been at the hands of Louis's assassin. I'm sure you already know Jimmy Becker got two life sentences, one for your death and one for Jezzie's. They also have reason to believe he killed Lance Bennington as a payback favor from Louis to J.T. Blessing. Fritz Muller and four of his men are in prison for drug trafficking and there could be more arrests. Interpol is looking into Louis's operations in Europe and Michael is convinced because of your bravery a lot of people will suffer a whole lot less. Estelle is dying of cancer so I guess she took back her life too late, but her son Eric is always at her bedside. Maybe in some ways her life is better now even though she has so little time left. Veronica works for us now and with her in the office I'm able to spend more time at home with Jessie. Michael recently assured Veronica that before long they will have solid evidence that Jimmy Becker killed her stepbrother. They're almost positive the bullet they retrieved from his truck was fired from the same rifle."

Annie bent down and moved the rose slightly even though she was unaware why. She stood up and continued, "I wish you could be here for Jessie's birthday party. According to her, you've already promised you'd be with us. She told me it was you who scared me the other night. That's pretty amazing because she mentioned it before I told anyone that during the night I felt someone sit on the edge of our bed. It seemed so real I even turned on the light to check. So, dear David, was that really you? It's strange but I seem to have redeveloped a fear of something I thought I had learned to accept. I'm afraid to look into people's hearts because of what I might see. I remember you told me the final war to end all wars and bring peace must take place not on some bloody battle field, but rather here, in our hearts. You used the Sanskrit word Anahata, for the heart chakra. You said life is but a passage to find the truths in our hearts that eventually will bring us to the Peaceful Kingdom." She paused as if searching for some form of validation, and then added, "Harry keeps reminding me that I have to view my abilities as a gift and I know he's right for Jessie's sake. She's so very different from most children."

She smiled sadly as she thought of her precious child. "I have no idea what the universe has in store for our little girl but I know I love her with all my heart. I've promised God that all of us will be there for her just as you were for me when you recognized I had certain special abilities. I know you already know all of this, but it's something I feel I have to speak out loud and hope you don't mind." She sniffed and wiped her nose. "You'd be very proud of Harry and the way he's taking care of your company. He and Jessie are my salvation. Thank you for bringing them into my life."

She stood another moment looking down at the spot where they had placed David's ashes now covered with her single rose.

"I guess that's all I have for now except I know September eleventh will always be a very sad day for me. I trust you're happy being with Angela and your son. Goodbye for now, David . . . I love you."

By noon Annie had most of the food ready for the party and Martina left for a few hours promising to be back by four. Annie frosted the cake with the purple frosting she and Jessie had created by mixing blue and red food coloring. Jessie sat drawing by the counter as Annie studied her.

"Did you know aunt Molly is bringing her new boyfriend tonight, and Robert Bartusek is coming with his girlfriend, Jane?" Annie made a point of staying in touch with Betty Bartusek's son who was now living in a group home. He was presently working as a bag boy at a small grocery store and doing very well, considering his circumstances. Over the past few years he had lost weight and had been seeing a girl who often came to the group home to visit her friend. Three months ago he had professed his love for her and asked her to marry him. Jane was delighted but now her parents were faced with the decision if they should allow her to marry Robert. Since the girl was also mentally challenged Annie understood how concerned her parents were about their daughter. It seemed strange to Annie that Betty, the one person who loved Robert the most, had to die before Robert had gotten his life in order.

"Trevor, Alison, Kitty and Brenton are also coming at about six o' clock. Brenton's mom is dropping them off." Jessie looked at Annie, smiled and nodded her head yes.

When Annie had finished decorating the cake she placed it on the center of the counter where she was fairly sure Thomas the cat wouldn't bother it. "Well, I think that does it for now." She walked to where Jessie was coloring and admired her drawings. "Those are very nice."

"I know. This is Barney." Jessie held up her picture.

"I really like that you made him yellow instead of purple. He looks a lot happier to me. And what's the other one?"

"That's ring a ring a rosie."

"So it is and it's very nice." Annie studied the picture intently. There was a circle of children that were all holding hands. Another child stood alone on the outside of the circle. Annie counted the children and was not surprised to find there were twelve in the circle. "How come this one isn't playing with the other children?" She pointed to the lone child.

Jessie took a deep breath as if she really didn't feel the need to explain her drawing. "Cause, they doesn't know the rules." She sounded quite exasperated.

"Jess, is that a boy or a girl?"

Jessie shrugged.

Annie continued to study the picture. "This one is missing a leg, do you think you should add it?"

"No."

"Okay, that's fine. Let's put the drawings up on the refrigerator so daddy can see them when he comes home." She found the scotch tape and taped them in place. "Maybe we can show your grandpa Russell and Cody what a good artist you are when we get to New Mexico. Would you like me to read to you?"

"Yes, from the book aunt Loll . . . no, Molly gave me." They sat together on the couch reading the nursery rhymes with Jessie picking her favorites. "Now this one."

Thirty days hath September, April, June and November;
All the rest have thirty one; February twenty eight alone,
Except in leap year, at which time February's days are twenty nine."

After awhile, Annie glanced up at the clock on the mantle. "Oh, Jess, I'd better stop now, it's getting late and I need to do some vacuuming."

"Just one more, please? The day one."

"Okay, one more."

Monday's child is fair of face. Tuesday's child is full of grace,
Wednesday's child is full of woe, Thursday's child has far to go,
Friday's child is loving and giving, Saturday's child works hard for its living,
And a child that's born on the Sabbath Day Is fair and wise and good and gay,"

"So, what day did I get borned on?"

"Well, I looked that up. You were a Thursday's child so you have far to go."

Jessie sat looking at her mother and Annie found herself marveling at her daughter's large brown eyes.

"Did you know my other mom?"

"No, honey, I didn't. All I know about her is she is Hispanic, which means she probably came from Mexico like Martina's relatives. She was very young when she brought you into Diane Mandel's clinic. You were very sick with ear infections and an elevated temperature. She loved you very much but realized she couldn't take proper care of you. The only information she gave the nurse was that your name was Jessie and you were born on April sixth, 1995."

Jessie sat quietly and as Annie got up she said, "Jess, why don't you put your head down for a little while and shut your eyes. You look a little sleepy."

Jessie slid her little body sideways and closed her eyes as Annie covered her with the throw that was lying on the back of the couch. As she started to walk away she heard Jessie say,

"Mama?"

"Yes, Jessie?"

"Member that baby that tried to come to you before? That was me . . . I couldn't come then, but I knew you'd find me."

Annie stood silently not believing what Jessie just told her. Later, when she told Harry about it he assured her of what she already knew. Of course he would never have said anything about her abortion to Jessie. She knew her daughter's statement was one of those things she would keep in her heart and often ponder but never fully understand.

Later that evening Harry and Annie were standing in the kitchen alone together. Everyone had left except Molly and Pete PeCar, who was putting the training wheels on Jessie's new birthday bike. Annie put the last plate in the dishwasher as Molly came into the kitchen.

"Well, loves, I think we're going to be leaving so you can put the birthday girl to bed. Great party! Excellent cake and I really appreciated that Harry has classed up and now serves the wine chilled, and not with his usual tacky ice cubes floating in it. Maybe with a little luck you'll get that boy trained after all. Oh . . . excuse me Harry, I didn't see you standing there."

She hugged Harry whose body remained passive with his arms folded across his chest. She ignored his obvious lack of response and went over to

Annie and gave her an affectionate hug. Annie smiled at Molly and said, "I really like Pete a lot. He seems like a wonderful person."

Harry stood watching his cousin but made no effort to move. "So just how serious are you and lover boy?"

Annie rolled her eyes and shook her head at her husband's blunt question.

Molly held up her hand, "No, no. That's a fair question and I don't mind answering it. Not to worry dear ones, I'm older and hopefully wiser now so I don't plan on jumping into this relationship without careful thought. On the one hand, Pete is kind and generous, good looking, intelligent, funny, and as honest as the day is long. I also adore his family. But, and this is a big but, on the other hand, one must also take into consideration this is a man who stores his fishing leeches in his fridge, refuses to bait my hook, makes me pull up the anchor, and allows his dog Pharaoh to sleep on the foot of his bed. This dog, I might add, weighs more than I do and eats like a Clydesdale horse. He also, the dog not Pete, gets his jollies by rolling in the dead carp he finds on the lakeshore. I obviously need more time to think this over. Tonight when we leave here, lover boy goes to his daughter's house and I go to my hotel room. Why risk ruining a great friendship?"

Molly turned to leave and then paused. She turned back, "Oh, by the way, did I tell you I leave for Africa in the morning? There are a few things I need to lay to rest before I can even think about starting a serious relationship. Say hello to everyone in Arizona for me. And Harry, please close your mouth. You look like a overgrown bird waiting for a worm."

Harry helped Jessie with her pajamas and into bed. He sang her another happy birthday song and listened as she recited her bedtime prayers. They visited a little longer and he kissed her goodnight. Annie smiled as she thought of Jessie's wide-eyed excitement as she unwrapped each of her birthday gifts. Something stirred inside her as she thought how proud Harry was when he rolled in their daughter's first two-wheeler bike and the little shriek of delight that escaped from Jessie. After finishing with the clean up she peeked into Jessie's room and found her still awake. She sat down on the edge of her bed. "I think it's going to storm tonight, will you be afraid of the thunder and lightning?"

"No, I'll be fine. I love you mama."

"I love you too, baby." She leaned over and kissed her daughter's forehead. As she stood up to leave she walked over to the window and watched the lightning streak across the black sky as it ushered in the first thunderstorm of the season. She looked into the troubled sky and felt a tear run down her cheek. She wiped it away as she thought about the condition of the world. What kind of world would it be in the coming years for Jessie and the other Star Children?

Deep down Annie knew the question that haunted her the most was the acceptance of these special children. What part would they play in the conversion of the world and who was the child who left the circle because they didn't know the rules? Was it as simple as Jessie said, they simply didn't know the rules or did they choose not to know them and were banished from helping to bring peace into the world? If so, how would their role change? Could this child assume the role of antagonist and oppose the efforts of the Star Children? The thought caused her to shudder as if an unseasonable chill had entered the room.

During most of her life Annie felt optimism about the human condition in spite of civilization's long history of conflict and violence. She reflected on the impending millennium and realized humanity may not be progressing after all as it was about to complete the bloodiest century in the history of mankind, with over one hundred million deaths resulting from acts of violence in the last one hundred years. I wonder, she thought, if God and all His angels don't sometimes get discouraged with us?

A flash of lightning lit up the room followed by a shattering clap of thunder. When silence returned Annie heard her daughter's soft little voice.

"Don't cry, mama, we'll all be fine. Our angels will watch over us."

Epilogue

September 11, 2001

Annie struggled to awaken from a terrible nightmare. In her dream she was surrounded by fire and the deafening sounds of the whole world exploding around her. Smoke and debris were pelting down and she felt she was about to die. Sirens were wailing and people were screaming for help but she was unable to see where they were. A large iron girder came crashing down directly in front of her blocking her path. As she fought her way through the smoke and falling debris she heard crying and stumbled over a small body wedged beneath a pile of rubble. Annie knelt to see if she could help the child but she realized she was too late. The little girl appeared to be slightly younger than her own daughter. The look in her eyes portrayed confused terror that would haunt Annie for the rest of her life. She tried to speak and Annie thought she heard the word 'mama' but the blood gurgling in her throat made it impossible. She whimpered and her body jerked as her short life ended. Annie reached down and felt for a pulse in the child's neck as a crimson stain flowed from the side of the child's mouth onto the white ashes surrounding her. Annie put her head down on the dead child's chest and wept inconsolably. "Why is this happening?" She felt herself engulfed by silence even though the destruction around her continued. As she looked up she saw her childhood friend standing serenely before as if she were unaffected by the devastation.

"The seventh seal has been opened and the seven angels with their trumpets are assembled as foretold in the Book of Apocalypse. The great war between good and evil wages on and as in every war, the innocent will die alongside the unbelievers. Their death is a gift to those left behind to remind them of their own mortality and their need to return to their creator. Mother Earth seeks retribution for her mistreatment. Crying and wailing will be heard all over the earth as people beg for mercy. The devastation will continue and will not cease until all who have not perished unite and hear His voice in the peaceful silence of love."

For a moment Annie felt disoriented, as if she had left her body but then returned with a terrible jolt. She lay in the blackness trembling and covered in cold sweat. As she struggled to sit up and shake off the terrible images, she remembered that today was the third anniversary of David's death, and she again acknowledged how much she dreaded this day.

Hours later, she sat dazed before the television watching the devastation along with all the other terrified Americans as the news played and replayed the tapes of the airplanes striking the World Trade Center. Later she couldn't help but wonder how a small circle of twelve children could possibly help a world so steeped in violence.

One's destination is never a place, but rather a new way of looking at things.

Henry Miller

CPSIA information can be obtained at www.ICGtesting.com
Printed in the USA
269146BV00003B/3/P